RELICS OF POWER BOOK

THE LOST
SENTINEL

EMMA L. ADAMS

To be notified when Emma L. Adams's next novel is released, sign up to her mailing list.

PROLOGUE

"Humans are so breakable, aren't they?" whispered the Relic.

Crimson streaks painted the courtyard of what had once been the grandest estate in the city of Tauvice, while Naxel Daimos stood in front of the twisted ruins of the front gates. The crumpled form of Volcan Astera lay at his feet, his sightless eyes reflecting the bright-red thorns curling around the staff Daimos held in his hand.

A smile stretched Daimos's mouth as he nudged his enemy's corpse with the edge of his staff.

Not so high and mighty after all, are you?

Inside his pocket, the Relic stirred, its whisper grating against his ear. "You owe me payment."

"Yes, yes, fine." He was aware that he'd created quite the ruckus in his attack on the Astera estate and that that decision may come back to bite him at some point. Maybe he should have pillaged a peasant's house or something before unleashing the Relic in such a conspicuous manner, but it'd all been so *easy*. He'd simply walked up to the gates and blasted them straight off their hinges, and Volcan Astera himself had come running to confront him at once. He couldn't have timed it more perfectly if he'd tried.

The grey-haired man at his feet appeared harmless now, unimpressive and frail—perhaps because Daimos had taken more than his life. The Relic had demanded blood, and he'd been more than happy to deliver. Now, he pressed the oval-shaped stone to the red-streaked flagstone and whispered the correct words in the old tongue, one few people spoke these days. Volcan Astera had known the language inside out, but his vast stores of knowledge hadn't helped him in the end.

Before his eyes, the bloodstains began to evaporate, one drop at a time. He watched, mesmerised, his own blood racing in his veins, as the force inside the Relic eagerly sucked at the crimson stains until they vanished beyond the surface of the stone, imbuing it with a ruby-red glow of satisfaction.

"Payment complete." He pocketed the stone once again and took up the thorn-covered staff in both hands. The crimson vines intertwining along its length matched the tall, thorny plants curling around the edges of the gate. One could not fault old Astera's sense of style, despite his many other shortcomings.

"Thanks," hissed the Relic. "Now move out of the way before someone alerts the authorities."

Daimos swallowed down an irritable retort—he now held the most powerful force in the nation in his own hands and it was absurd to allow himself to be given orders by a mere *rock*—but the Relic was right. He needed to move. He'd done what he'd intended to do.

All the same, he'd expected to feel a little more triumphant. After those long weeks of trawling mountain passes and forgotten roads had ended in his discovery of a Relic long believed to be lost, he'd imagined this moment a thousand times. Now, that very same Relic hummed contentedly in his pocket, and its power was his to wield. Why, then, did the gaping hole inside his chest persist, as though the spectre of the man who'd seen to his family's banishment haunted him still, when that very same man lay dead at his feet?

He raised the staff. "You serve me now, Astiva, son of Gaiva. The Astera family is no more, and you belong to me, Naxel Daimos."

A breeze stirred. *Yes,* he thought. *You obey me now, Astiva. Show me your power.*

The breeze became a strong wind, lifting the hairs on his head. The ends of his embroidered coat—stolen, of course— lifted off the ground, and he braced the staff against the flag- stones to keep himself from losing his balance. That would hardly be a dignified way to start his partnership with Astiva.

"Stop that!" the Relic in his pocket hissed. "You're behaving like a child. Wait until you're out of the city before you start playing with your new toy."

"Quiet," he muttered irritably.

Fine, maybe he needed a little more practise, but he had more than enough time to learn. He glanced down at the staff and startled at the crimson glow that now emanated from his left hand. Unbeknownst to him, the staff's thorns had snaked across the back of his hand, though he felt no pain where they pierced his skin. As he watched, the colour solidified until he appeared to wear a glove of pure crimson, his knuckles spiked with thorns.

"Thorn-hand." An unexpected laugh escaped when the truth dawned on him that this must be where old Astera's nickname had come from. Still chuckling to himself, he bent over the dead body of the staff's former owner, confirming that old Astera's left hand bore the same crimson stain as his own, although the thorns had shrivelled and died along with their owner.

As he rose to his feet, the Relic made a low noise of warning. He hadn't taken a single step when a blast of wind struck him in the back, too sharp and swift for him to keep himself from sprawling onto the flagstones. Pain speared his hip where it struck the stone, and he scrambled upright as a figure stepped over the ruined gates. A tall, broad man, dressed in a red cloak identical to the one worn by the man who lay dead at Daimos's feet—and carrying an identical thorn-covered staff.

Oh, Powers, he thought. Another Astera had survived? The Astera family must have split Astiva's magic among its members, but he thought he'd already killed all of them. Worse, the Relic had gone awfully quiet in his pocket, and his grip on the staff felt uncertain compared to the strong, confident way the newcomer held its twin.

Crimson thorns pierced its owner's left hand, forming a mirror image of his own, but the newcomer didn't so much as stumble as he sent a roar of wind sweeping towards Daimos. This time he was prepared enough to grip the staff with both hands, but it wasn't enough to keep from being tossed aside like a ship in a storm. The Relic jarred against his side when his back hit the flagstones again.

No. He refused to die when he'd come this close to his goals, least of all at the hands of this *child*. This must be Volcan's son, who was barely into his twenties, yet he wielded the staff without voicing a single command. As Daimos scrambled backwards, the fierce grey eyes of the younger Astera looked down upon him without mercy.

Sliding his free hand into his pocket, Daimos whispered the Relic's name. "Orzen. I need your help."

"What do you promise me this time?" the Relic whispered back. "Destroying this one will take more than the blood of an old man. I need more."

"The lifeblood of the youngest Astera," he murmured. "When we kill him, I'll give you every last drop."

At once, the stone lit up in a crimson flare. The young Astera's angry grey eyes widened as a blast of ruby-red light slammed into him, and it was his turn to struggle to keep his feet. Seizing his chance, Daimos advanced on the boy, raising his own staff.

"Astiva," he intoned, loud and clear. "You answer to me now."

The thorns on his hands glowed, bloodred and vibrant, and a gust of wind swept up as the Power answered his call. Weakened from the Relic's strike, the young Astera faltered as Daimos turned the magic of his own deity against him. Flagstones cracked, walls crumbled, and Daimos stepped back to avoid being hit by the debris.

"You fool!" yelled the Relic. "Unless you're trying to escape our agreement by burying us both under a nobleman's house, I'd suggest you exercise a little restraint."

Daimos opened his mouth to shout a retort, but the

ground cracked beneath his own feet. He leapt clear of the gap in the flagstone, and his gaze found the young Astera lying sprawled amid a pile of shattered stone. Daimos approached him carefully, but the boy was barely conscious. Blood streamed from his mouth, and his fingers curled limply around his staff.

"I'll take that." Daimos swayed on his feet as he bent to take the boy's staff for himself. Evidently, the magic he'd used had taken more out of him than he'd expected, but Astera was in a worse state. Yet his lips moved when Daimos lifted the staff from his grip, though the words were inaudible.

"What did you say?" he growled.

"You can't wield that staff," whispered the young man. "It will destroy you..."

A jolt of sudden anger shot through Daimos. What right did this child have to look at him with such defiance even at his moment of death?

"You're mistaken," Daimos told him. "Tell me, are there any more of you that I need to kill, or are you the last one?"

Astera simply gave him a hard stare in response, but Daimos was certain that this man was the last Astera he needed to worry about. If any others survived, he'd easily be able to find their hiding places. The mark of Astiva was difficult to hide, and with two deities on his side, the mere idea of anyone denying him anything he asked for was laughable.

All the same, the notion of stripping away the youngest Astera's confidence before dealing the final blow was tantalising enough that Daimos allowed a smile to creep onto his mouth as he pointed the end of the staff at its owner. "I think I'll take your deity away from you, before I kill you."

The boy raised his head. The deep tan of his face had faded to grey, and his fingers twitched as if to grasp the staff that was no longer there. Even if by some miracle he survived his wounds, the shock of losing his Power would surely kill him in the end.

The same fate had befallen Daimos's own father.

Yet despite himself, he found himself feeling some measure of pity for the boy. The youngest Astera hadn't been part of the contingent who'd banished Daimos's family; he'd have been an infant at the time, if he'd even been born yet. On the other hand, the Invoker families had been a pestilence upon the nation for countless generations, and in the long term, Daimos was doing everyone a favour by bringing an end to their tyranny.

More to the point, if he survived, the boy would hunt him for the rest of his days. It was far better to finish him off beforehand. Kinder, even.

Daimos spoke the deity's name again. "Astiva."

As he raised the twin staffs, the boy's hand twitched again, grasping a piece of shattered stone. Even wounded as he was, he insisted on putting up a fight.

"I don't think so." Daimos brought the left staff down upon the boy's hand. Bone cracked; the stone slipped from his grasp. To his credit, the young Astera didn't utter so much as a cry of pain. His eyes had glazed over, his breathing shallow.

"You'll... never be worthy of Astiva..." The boy's voice faltered on the last word.

A new burst of rage took hold of Daimos. "I *am*

worthy," he said as he brought the twin staffs down for the killing blow.

———

The city of Tauvice was ablaze. A trail of fire moved like a serpent through the streets, and the two deities tracked its process through the window separating them from the world below, watching the flames leap across the street to the wooden roof of a temple to the lesser gods.

"Not the offerings!" cried Xeale. "There are so few humans who remember our names, much less have the kindness to pray to us."

"Oh, but they won't forget this in a hurry." Kyren cackled, eagerly leaning through the window to see the chaos unfold in the city below. A row of houses ignited along the seafront, while ant-like figures fled the roaring flames. "Look at them run!"

"Orzen is having the time of his life down there," remarked Xeale, who currently resembled a large grey dove. The deities' forms were fluid, but most tended to mimic creatures or beings from the mortals' realm, an old habit from a time the humans had long forgotten. "I do hope he knows what he's doing. Humans are not known for their reliability."

"Oh, this one will be different." Kyren, who currently wore the form of a towering black raven, spoke with a barely restrained laugh. "He's giving Orzen free rein, the fool."

"Yes, and what if he manages to get himself killed in the process?" responded Xeale. "If his Relic ends up buried at sea, then he might have to wait another few thousand years for it to be recovered."

"One of us might as well get to have a little fun," said Kyren. "Has it truly been that long?"

Xeale's feathery wing brushed the edge of the window, his beak not quite touching the realm on the other side. None of the humans below could see either of them; even if they hadn't been too occupied fleeing for their lives, the realm of the Powers remained as inaccessible to mortals as the human realm was to the pair of them, including the wastelands that lay south of the lands the humans called Aestin, cut off by an impassable range of mountains. Yet one human had ventured south and had been rewarded handsomely. Might others follow suit? If they did, then perhaps one would finally bring what the deities needed.

Of course, then the fires igniting the coastal city would be the least of humanity's problems, but the fault was entirely their own.

"Who knows," said Xeale. "Maybe one of them will unearth *my* Relic next."

"Mother help them all if they do." Kyren smirked. "They're not ready for this. None of them are."

1

Zelle Carnelian was on her way to the Sentinels' outpost when she ran into her first tourists of the day.

The man and woman both wore long travelling cloaks that must be newly purchased, as they bore no stains or markings from the road. If Zelle had to guess, they'd taken a carriage until the roads had come to an end close to the village of Randel, nestled between patches of dense forest. Catching sight of Zelle, they hurried in her direction.

"Is this the outpost?" The woman, whose deeply tanned complexion indicated she'd travelled from the eastern spear of the continent, held a crumpled, hand-drawn map in her hand. "The Sentinels' outpost, near the location of the lost Relic?"

Zelle stared at her for a moment, baffled that anyone would think the outpost would be situated close enough to human habitation for hapless tourists to wander into.

"No, the outpost is up in the mountains. You won't reach it before sunset."

Not unless they knew the shortcuts, that was, and Zelle had no intention of enlightening them on the matter —nor anyone else who was willing to risk being eaten alive by a wyrm or dashing their brains out on the harsh cliffs in their quest to find the supposed lost Relics of the gods. Would-be adventurers came here in droves during the summer months and either returned home empty-handed or not at all, yet the stories persisted. The mist-wreathed expanse of Zeuten's famed Range certainly looked alluring from the ground, but Zelle had spent years traipsing all over the mountain paths and had found nothing in the way of mythical Relics.

Besides, Zelle didn't trust anyone who aspired to hero-ics. They never met a pleasant end.

The two tourists exchanged dispirited glances.

"In the mountains?" echoed the man. "Are you sure?"

Of course I'm sure. The Sentinel is my grandmother. Not that she'd ever tell that to these two strangers. From outward appearances, Zelle looked like any other villager from the Range, with neither the classic black hair nor the tanned complexion of her mother's family. Her freckled face and the reddish tint to her brown hair she owed to her father, along with the pale complexion of someone who'd spent most of her childhood with her nose in a book rather than embarking on the wild travels of her ancestors. She could blame some of that on her dear departed Aunt Adaine's habit of remarking that adven-tures belonged between the pages of a book and nowhere else. These days, there was no need for heroes in the country of Zeuten.

"We're all better off without them," Aunt Adaine had often added. "We don't bother the gods, and they don't bother us in return."

Easy enough, since no living person recalled the times when the deities had ever been anything more than a word uttered in anger or prayer, or a silent recipient of an offering left on the doorstep. As for their Relics, most people had more important things to concern themselves with than the mysteries of the Range and the inhospitable lands to the north.

"We can always wait until the morning," suggested the woman. "Explore the trails instead."

"Do that," Zelle encouraged. "You've come such a long way that it would be a pity to waste your trip. Try the Randel Inn. They offer reasonable rates on rooms, and the owner is very knowledgeable about the walking routes in the forest."

If they asked the advice of a local, they were less likely to fall victim to one of the mountain's pitfalls. The forest might be dense, but the villagers were familiar with its trails and paths, and the newcomers ought to be able to avoid any wild predators if they returned before nightfall.

"Thank you." The woman turned to her companion. "We'll explore the forest. There are rumours of abandoned settlements, so we might get lucky anyway…"

As the tourists departed, Zelle watched them leave, their cloaks trailing behind them. Then she turned back to the stretch of pine trees clothing the mountain's base, contemplating the dark mass of clouds blooming on the horizon. Typical of Grandma Carnelian to neglect to check the skies before leaving for the outpost. While her visits were primarily for the purpose of scrounging up any old junk that her grandmother could spare to sell in the shop she'd inherited from her aunt, Zelle suspected that if she didn't make the occasional journey here to check on the old Sentinel, she'd probably have got herself killed long ago.

Once she was certain the tourists had gone, Zelle sought out a shortcut that sliced through the forest directly to the base of the mountain. Silence wreathed the thick pines, the faint hum of the villagers' chatter fading with each step and shadows stretching across the leaf-strewn paths. When the rain began, it would turn the paths into puddles and render even the smoothest trail into a treacherous bog. The return trip would not be pleasant, but an isolated outpost in the mountains was no place for a ninety-five-year-old woman to spend the night.

As Zelle walked, a faint rustling sounded from amid the trees to her left. Her shoulders stiffened, her gaze skimming her surroundings, and she caught sight of a pale shape sticking out of the bushes. Her heart leapt into her throat. That was a hand... a *human* hand.

Zelle walked closer, spying the hand's owner. The man wore the garb of a messenger, with his sack of letters lying nearby, but it was the arrow piercing his throat that caught Zelle's attention. No wild animal had killed him. Travellers undoubtedly had a habit of dying in strange and unpleasant manners in Zeuten's wilder regions, but this was different. A human had committed this murder—but who would lurk in the foothills of the Range, shooting down messengers? Her family were the only people who willingly ventured into the woods, aside from the occasional hapless tourists, and she knew nobody in the village with that level of skill with a bow. Much less a desire to fire upon oblivious messengers.

A quiver of alarm snaked through her. Grandma Carnelian was armed at all times with her Sentinel's staff, so whoever had fired the arrow was likely to come off worse from a confrontation with her, but Zelle herself had no weapons but the cheap knife she typically carried on the road. She gripped it tightly as she left the body behind and returned to her route to the mountains, the first rumble of thunder echoing in the background.

The path wove between thick pine trees, closing the distance between the woodland and the foot of the mountain in a matter of moments, and yet Grandma still did not appear. Nor did whoever had shot the arrow. Instead, she found herself facing the sheer cliffs of the Range, shrouded by bruise-coloured clouds.

Stifling a shiver, Zelle pulled her thick wool coat more tightly around herself and continued on until she came to the narrow slash in the cliffside which led into a cave containing a set of stone stairs hewn into the very mountain itself. No tourists would easily stumble upon this particular spot, yet Zelle remained tense as she hurried up the stairs. The echo of her footsteps pursued her, punctuated by the occasional rumble of thunder. When she neared the top, a faint whistling reached her ears from outside. The wind had picked up, the storm moving faster than she'd anticipated.

The stairs came to an end in a small cave, whose narrow opening led out onto the mountain itself. Zelle approached the exit and was greeted by the sight of a torrent of snow racing downwards at the mountain path. A fierce wind propelled the swirl of flakes into the cave entrance, and Zelle had no choice but to brace herself for the onslaught as she walked outside. Her steps slowed as she pressed a hand on the nearest cliff to keep her balance, the other shielding her eyes as she looked for any signs of her grandmother.

A short distance away stood the first outpost of the Sentinels, a crooked towerlike construction whose slanted walls made it appear to be leaning against the cliffside. As a child, Zelle had once remarked that it looked like it'd travelled halfway across the mountain and had to stop for a rest. Right now, she sincerely hoped her grandmother had had the sense to get indoors before the storm had struck, because the snow had already formed a thick crust around the tower's base and clung to Zelle's feet as she covered the short distance to the tower.

To her intense relief, the door was unlocked, so she wrenched it open and slammed inside.

"That's one big storm," she murmured, brushing snowflakes from the sleeve of her coat and running her fingers through damp tendrils of reddish-brown hair. "Grandma?"

No response came from within the Sentinel's quarters, which appeared untouched since her last visit. Inside the main room, a fire lay guttered and empty. The shelves to either side were packed with books, the air replete with the scent of old pages. She'd spent many a happy childhood hour nestled in the window seat, thumbing through old storybooks while Grandma and her sister Aurel discussed Sentinel matters. Today, though, a sense of neglect permeated the tower, and most of the valuables had been stripped away over the years.

At one time, their family had held enough wealth to

rival the Crown Prince, but their fortune had dwindled away with each passing generation, and so had their numbers. Zelle's own father had met a tragic end in a boating accident, while her mother had died of a sickness when she was eight. As a result, Zelle had begun to help her aunt in the shop from a young age and had quickly learned that her family's history held little value in the modern world. Many Zeutenians prided themselves on having nothing to do with the scheming magicians in Aestin, and the Sentinels were the sole reminder that those ties had ever existed.

Of course, there were always the few who were keen to probe her for knowledge of the lost Relic of legend, but with the way her family's luck usually went, the legend probably referred to some mundane object a settler had lost on the trek through the Range rather than anything of worth.

Oh, Powers. I'm starting to sound just like Aunt Adaine. And just where is Grandma?

Zelle strode through the quarters, peered into both the main bedroom and the guest room, and was readying herself to climb the stairs into the Sanctum when her gaze fell on a long stick of dark wood, half concealed beneath an armchair. Her grandmother's staff. The Sentinel never let it leave her sight if she could help it, and she muttered to her staff more than she talked to her own grandchildren. If she'd left it lying on the floor, then something must be horribly wrong.

Zelle's fingers closed around the end of the staff. A sudden voice rang out, sharp and demanding: *Put me down!*

Her hand opened of its own accord, sending the staff

clattering to the floor. Her heart thudded against her rib cage, and her mind recoiled from the knowledge that the staff had *spoken* to her. Only the Sentinel was supposed to be able to hear its voice.

"Where's Grandma?" She scrambled to pick up the staff again, but it tumbled from her grip as though it would sooner lie neglected than allow her to hold it. Gritting her teeth, Zelle crouched down beside the prone wooden stick. "I'm not an intruder. I'm Zelle, the Sentinel's granddaughter. Where is she?"

This time, when her hand coiled around the staff's length, a jolt of awareness shot through Zelle's nerves to her fingertips. *Zelle,* the voice said. *Ah yes, the talentless one. Still alive, are you?*

"Excuse me?" She pushed to her feet, keeping a firm grip on the long wooden staff. "Where is Grandma? This place looks deserted."

She went through a door.

Zelle stared at the carved stick for a moment, wondering if the staff might be lying to her. Why, she couldn't say, but she shouldn't be able to hear its voice at all. "What is that supposed to mean?"

Are you simple?

"Not in the slightest." She narrowed her eyes in a glare in response to the insult, though the Powers only knew if the staff could see her face when it didn't have eyes. "Tell me where my grandmother is, or I'll chop you up and use you as firewood."

You would never.

How had her grandmother endured the staff's stubbornness for so many years without tossing it away in frustration? She muttered to it a lot, Zelle knew, but she'd never heard it talk back. Not until now. A sentient staff wasn't too unusual here at the outpost, where the Sanctum was full of ancient tomes teeming with secrets and rattler-imps lurked in the shadows, but she hadn't expected the Sentinel's staff to be this... temperamental.

I can tell you're going to be a difficult one, the staff remarked.

"Speak for yourself." Her gaze snagged on the window, from which she could usually see all the way down to the forests surrounding the village below. Instead, snowflakes swirled in thick dervishes, and the wind rattled the window in its frame. If Grandma wasn't inside the outpost, then Zelle had no chance whatsoever of finding her until the storm abated. There were worse places to be stranded in a snowstorm, given that the Sanctum contained books which weren't available anywhere else in the nation, but for once, the notion of losing herself between the pages of a story was far from Zelle's thoughts.

What could possibly have dragged her grandmother away from her staff, and why had she even come here in the first place?

Zelle suppressed a flinch when the wind struck the tower like a heavy blow and the staff in her grip grew cold. *Someone's coming.*

———

The storm began when the young man was halfway across the Range. One moment, the sky was clear; the next, clouds rushed in, bringing a sweep of snow which numbed his hands and froze his skin to the bone. His battered leather travelling boots skidded at every other step, threatening to send him into a fatal tumble. But he kept on, because the alternative was death. He felt its cold presence lurking inside him, like the jaws of some beast waiting below a sheer and inevitable fall. Yet a single image remained etched in the front of his mind: a red leather-bound book. Once opened, they said the book would give its discoverer what they most wanted in the world. For that reason alone, he had to survive.

The mountain had other plans, however, and the path grew more treacherous with each step. On either side of him, the ground dropped away, with nothing to grab onto if he were to slide too close to the edge. If he hadn't spent the last few weeks existing in a place far beyond fear, he might have returned to steady ground to take a ship home, to live out his last days in the land of his ancestors. Then again, in his current state, he might not survive another voyage across the ocean. And so he stumbled on, both hands gripping his staff tightly. He'd bought it with the last of his coin, and while it was nothing more than an ordinary walking stick, he could still imagine that he sensed the ghostly presence of his deity under the surface.

He kept going uphill while his hands grew red with cold and his feet numbed in their boots. Gritting his teeth against the bitter wind, he kept his gaze fixed on the peak of the mountain visible beyond the sweeping snow. Occasionally, he wondered what kind of people lived up here in the most desolate part of the world. Who in their right mind would trade safety, security, and human company to guard the secrets of the Powers? If rumour was to be believed, the rest of Zeuten had turned its back on magic altogether, but there was little information on the

Sentinels save for tall tales carried across the sea. He'd paid them little notice in the past, and if he closed his eyes, he could imagine his father berating him for putting his faith in a mere rumour—but his father was gone, and tall tales were all he had left.

Then he came to a halt. Ahead of him lay a bridge of dark wood lashed to the cliffs by ropes. It did not look sturdy in the least, judging by the creaking and groaning that came with every gust of wind. Mist swirled around its edges, and when he risked a glance down into the valley, he saw nothing but a black mass that might have been trees. It was a very long, grim fall.

"The Powers grant me safe passage," he murmured, the wind snatching the words from his mouth. Turning back at this point would be as fatal as the alternative. Nothing to do but walk and hope whatever deity dwelt within this mountain was on his side.

He took one step then another. The bridge bucked and swayed with every movement, each step dragging for an eternity. His heart hammered frantically, as though to remind him he had a limit on his life whether he made it to his destination or not. Then he lifted his head, and a rush of rejuvenating energy bolstered him.

There it is. The crooked stone tower appeared like something out of a dream, forming a splash of shadow against the bitter whiteness. The outpost of the Sentinels of Zeuten… and his last chance.

The bridge rocked again, and his heart gave a lurch. He had never feared heights, but he wondered why the bridge hadn't been built with safety in mind when the Sentinels were so vital to their nation. Unless it somehow judged him unworthy and was trying to throw him off the mountain, that was. He kept onward, step by step, suppressing a gasp of relief when he found solid ground beneath his feet. A rocky path led the rest of the way up to the tower, the stones buried in piles of snow.

The mountain, however, wasn't finished with him yet. As soon as he began to climb, the smooth rocks had him scrambling and slipping. His path slowed to a steady crawl, and when he slid too close to the cliffside, only luck stopped him tumbling over the edge. He kept on, wedging his numb fingers into cracks in the rocks and trying not to look down. He wondered if he'd left his courage somewhere back home, though admittedly, no one in their right mind would attempt to climb this bare rock and be anything short of terrified.

Waving farewell to his last vestiges of dignity, he remained flat on his front, hauling himself up the stone path by sheer force of will. The tower wavered before his eyes, appearing no closer than before, and when he pulled himself upright in the hopes that using his feet might quicken his pace, he slipped. Arms wheeling, he sought to regain his footing, but a blast of wind caught him at the edge. He found himself clinging to the cliff by his fingertips, the icy shadow of death looming closer than ever.

"Curse you, Powers, you temperamental bastards," he snarled, losing his head completely. Even in his current state of panic, he was vaguely aware that cursing the names of the Powers upon one of their sacred mountains was probably the worst thing he could have done. Yet the echoes of his own shouts gave him something to focus on that wasn't the sheer drop, and he managed to heave himself up to safety.

Breathless, he lay facedown on the path, and several

moments passed before he was able to focus on his surroundings. When he pushed to his knees, a sudden booming voice spoke in his ear: *WHAT DID YOU CALL ME?*

The breath froze in his lungs, and try as he might, he couldn't lift his head to look upon the speaker. His whole body felt weighted down by an invisible force.

The image of a leather-bound book wavered in front of his vision before darkness filtered in.

2

After the staff's ominous warning, Zelle expected to find the shadow of some mountain beast lurking on the doorstep, but when she peered out into the storm, she saw nothing but snow. Not one to sit around and wait for her oncoming doom, Zelle got a fire going and left the staff propped against the armchair while she went to search for her missing relative. She doubted her grandmother would have ventured into the Sanctum without her staff, but she was at a loss to think of any other possible hiding places.

On the other hand, it wouldn't do to leave the staff unattended if its warning of intruders proved true. She searched every corner of the lower floor for clues as to her grandmother's whereabouts, clouds of dust making her cough when she moved the furniture to look underneath the chairs or behind the bookshelves. The rooms seemed smaller than she remembered, though she'd stopped coming up here each winter after she'd begun working full time in Aunt Adaine's shop. Sometimes she missed the days of roaming the Sanctum as a child, but even rooms of ancient texts lost their attraction after a while, not least because she couldn't read half of them.

Upon returning to the main room, Zelle's gaze fell on the window again. A single book lay on the table beneath, and as far as Zelle was aware, it hadn't been there the last time she'd been in the room.

When she picked up the leather-bound volume, a sharp sting in her left hand made her drop it on the floor. "Damn rattler."

Rattler-imps were one of the more peculiar inhabitants of the Sanctum. Made entirely of shaping-magic, presumably left behind from the days when the deities alone had inhabited the mountains, they were inclined to take the form of whatever object the unlucky target was likely to pick up. In this case, a book. Crouching, Zelle examined the embossed cover, which was a fairly good likeness of a handbound volume. Except most books didn't have pointy ears. Careful to avoid getting bitten again, she flicked the end of its ear with her finger.

The book jumped into the air, transforming into a winged humanoid figure the length of her palm. The imp opened a mouth that looked too large for its elongated head and let out a rattling screech. With an eye roll, Zelle snatched the imp by a feather-like wing and carried it over to one of the cabinets at the back of the room. Inside, amongst other odds and ends, was a collection of empty glass jars. Picking one out, she lifted the lid and shoved the struggling imp inside. The creature leapt up with a screech, but Zelle had already slammed down the lid and twisted it tight.

"That's one pest taken care of," she said, not sure

whether she was addressing the imp or the staff. "If you ask me, Grandma ought to have paid me for ridding the place of these things every winter when I was a child."

She'd done her level best to keep them out of the tower during her visits, but neglect seemed to breed the blasted things and her grandmother had never been inclined to keep the place clean.

The original Sentinels didn't get paid, the staff told her.

"The original Sentinels had the blessing of the Powers," Zelle retaliated. Gaiva Herself had supposedly led the first Sentinels to the outpost, though it was the nameless Shaper whose magic had allegedly created this very tower. Personally, Zelle was more inclined to believe the Sentinels had hewn the tower from the rock with their own hands; like the other two Great Powers, the Shaper had departed this world countless years before humans had ventured into the Range.

Zelle's gaze landed on the staff, belatedly aware that its voice had spoken in her mind despite her hands being nowhere near its wooden surface.

What are you looking at?

"You can talk to me when I'm not holding you." More to the point, it could apparently see her too. "I didn't know you could do that."

Your imagination is clearly limited.

"I'm starting to understand why Grandma likes to pretend to be deaf."

The imp would have to stay in the jar until the storm passed and she could let it outside, but frankly, the tower's pests were the least of her problems. Should she brave the Sanctum and hope the staff would keep her safe from any potential dangers lurking in its corners? If some magical interference had taken Grandma, there was no telling what she might find, but it was that or leave her to her fate.

By the way, said the staff, *there's someone outside.*

Zelle crossed to the window, hoping irrationally that it was her grandmother and that the staff had been lying to her all along. "I don't see anyone. Did you mean a person?"

Yes.

That was impossible. Zelle's family were the only people in the whole of Zeuten who knew the way to the outposts, and enough deterrents lurked amid the paths that nobody would stumble across it by accident. Facing the window, Zelle squinted at the mass of white outside. "There's nobody there."

Look closer, said the staff. *It's the man I sensed coming here earlier. Also, I think he's dead.*

"Well, that's inconvenient." Hoping those fools from the village hadn't somehow followed her, she climbed onto the chair beside the window to peer through the thick swirls of snow. Sure enough, she could make out a vaguely human shape slumped on the path leading up to the tower.

He's not magical, I don't think, added the staff. *The mountain would have thrown him off if he was.*

"What do you expect *me* to do about him, then?" she queried. "This isn't a place for casual visitors. And if he's a lost hiker, he's very, *very* lost."

What to do? She wasn't heartless enough to leave someone to freeze to death outside, and yet for all she knew, the stranger was the person responsible for Grandma's disappearance. He must surely know this was an outpost of the Sentinels, and if he had the faintest clue where her grandmother might be, Zelle needed to know.

"Powers have mercy," she muttered, retrieving her wool cloak from where she'd hung it on a hook near the door. She wrapped the cloak around herself tightly, fastening every clasp so as not to let the vicious wind cut through. She already wore thick wool stockings, but she added another pair before pulling on her tough leather boots. On a whim, she also picked up the staff. It was the closest thing to a walking stick she had, and she'd have considerable trouble keeping her footing on the steep slope with that dreadful wind outside.

Drawing in a deep breath, she opened the door. The first blast of wind almost took her off her feet, and the door rattled in its frame so violently that it was a wonder the hinges didn't give.

"If I die, it's your fault," she told the staff, which made no response.

Closing the door behind her, she began to descend towards the snowdrift where the stranger lay half-submerged. Her feet sank into the whiteness, and each shuffling step made ice trickle down her ankles and into her boots. The stranger didn't move an inch. He'd made it close enough to the Sanctum for her to suspect that he'd held on for long enough to come within sight of the tower before collapsing.

"I'm coming to help," she called to him.

To her surprise, he stirred a little. So he was alive after all—and a real, solid human being, not some conjuration of the mountain's magic. When she moved closer, he lifted his head, and it surprised her how young he was. His dark hair pooled around his brown, angular face, and his grey eyes were wide as they took her in.

"What are you?" he asked, his lips blue with cold. "Are you a witch?"

"Am I a *what*?" She came to a halt with the staff wedged into the snowbank. "If you're looking for the Sentinel, you're out of luck. She's gone."

He dragged himself to his feet, as though by some miraculous act of will, and peered at her. "I'm not here for the Sentinel."

"Then what?" she challenged. "It's hardly the weather for a hike, you know."

Another gust of wind caused the stranger to fall forwards onto the snow once more. Despite the walking stick he held in both hands, he looked hardly capable of supporting himself on his own feet.

"There's something I need to find." His voice was muffled against the snow. "A book."

Zelle stared at his bowed head. "You climbed up the Range during a storm, in the most remote part of the continent, for a *book*? As opposed to certain death?"

No response came from the young man. He appeared to have passed out.

"Well, that's just bloody outstanding."

The howling wind struck, forcing her to brace herself against the staff for balance. *Powers. I have to get back inside.*

Her gaze drifted back to the slumped form of the man. He wasn't dead. At least, she hoped he wasn't. She crouched down, feeling for a pulse at his wrist, and the faintest flutter against her fingertips confirmed he lived. She dropped his hand, somehow both relieved and put out, because now she had another task on her hands.

Holding the staff awkwardly under her arm, she took hold of the man's shoulders and attempted to drag him through the snow. *A witch, am I?* His words had echoed the sentiments of a superstitious villager, yet his accent sounded foreign and his accusation had been odd enough for her to want to question him again. Assuming he ever woke up.

She wedged the end of the staff into the snow to free her hands. "A little help would be nice."

The staff, naturally, remained silent. Leaving it standing in the snowbank, she hauled the stranger the rest of the way uphill to the tower door. Her shoulders ached and her hands were numb under her gloves by the time she laid the young man's body down in the hallway. She then darted outside and grabbed the staff from its position in the snow, where, oddly, not a single flake had settled on the knotted wooden surface.

"You're welcome," she told it.

The door slammed shut behind her at another gust of wind, and it took all her willpower not to sink to the floor. Instead, she dragged the stranger closer to the fire burning in the grate, glad she'd had the sense to light it earlier. After she'd discarded her own sodden cloak and boots and laid them out near the fire to dry, she contemplated the newcomer. He'd dropped his walking stick outside in the snow, but he wore a thick travelling cloak which might conceal any number of lethal weapons. He might have asked for her help, but she'd be a fool to lock herself in the tower during a storm with an armed stranger.

Her shoulders protested as she wrestled the sodden cloak off the stranger, finding three knives in the pockets. Underneath, he wore a ragged tunic and some trousers that had clearly seen a lot of wear and were hardly suitable for the weather outside. He'd been on the road for a while, she guessed, judging by his unshaven jawline. But it was his colouring that caught her attention. Nobody in Zeuten had that deep a tan. His attire was odd too. The cloak was well-made, but his other clothes were cheap-looking and worn. Most travellers tended to have money, and there wasn't so much as a single coin in his pockets. She rummaged around in his cloak before giving up and stealthily checking his trouser pockets too.

I'm not stealing from him, she reasoned. *Just being cautious. And nosy, perhaps.*

None of his pockets yielded anything more, though. Strange. He didn't *look* like a petty thief or criminal, despite his ragged appearance, nor did he resemble the ill-prepared tourists she'd left down in the village. He'd also said he wasn't here for the Sentinel but for a *book.*

What kind of book would bring a man into the most desolate place in Zeuten? A rare one, she'd guessed, though he didn't look anything like a fanatic collector either. *Desperate* was the word she'd use, given that he'd somehow climbed all the way to the tower in a storm without using any of the Sentinels' shortcuts. A person more superstitious than she might have said he'd had the blessing of the Powers themselves, though in the stories, the Powers rarely singled someone out for benign reasons. Leaning over him, she caught sight of the glint of metal at his neckline. A closer look showed her a circular medallion around his neck. With careful fingers, she caught its string and tugged it upwards to touch the cool

31

metal, but she sensed no living presence like she did when she touched the staff.

A memory flickered into her mind of standing in her grandmother's living room as a child while her family met with a group of well-dressed travellers from across the ocean. They'd paid her no attention, but she'd silently admired the silver buttons on their coats, and the sheen of the medallion around the stranger's neck brought back that same image.

Aestin. Powers above, he must have come from the distant continent over the sea, which made him even more desperate or foolish than she'd imagined. Aestinians hadn't turned their backs on magic as most people in Zeuten had, but if he was an Aestinian magician, what use would he possibly have for anything the Sentinels might have to offer? Their own magic was paltry compared to their neighbours across the ocean.

Zelle rose to her feet and walked over to where she'd left the staff beside the wall. Despite having been buried in a snowdrift, the wood remained bone-dry. "Do you think he's the one who took Grandma?"

I have never seen him before in my life.

"You didn't answer the question." Blast the Powers, she hadn't counted on being trapped in her old childhood haunt with a stubborn artefact and a confused stranger. Especially with the storm showing no signs of abating even as the light outside dimmed with the sinking sun. "What am I supposed to do if he means me harm?"

You think he'll cut your throat while he's unconscious?

"I took his weapons," she murmured. "But he's still stronger than I am."

You're the one who brought him in here.

"What else was I supposed to do, leave him to die?" Zelle shook her head. "The Sanctum's magic protects us against anyone with ill intentions, doesn't it?"

I have no need of protection.

"Of course you don't." She scowled at the staff. "If he's not magical, then why would an Aestinian come here?"

And why did he have no coin and few weapons? He must have been on the road for a while, but venturing into the mountains armed with nothing but a couple of flimsy knives was asking to meet an unpleasant end. Admittedly, no knife or bow would help against the beasts that lurked among the highest peaks, but the staff claimed he held no magical gift of his own either. He'd thought *she* was a witch, in fact. She'd never met an Aestinian in the flesh aside from those brief glimpses during her childhood, and Zelle wondered if their ideas of Zeutenians were as fanciful as the villagers' tales of the people from across the sea who still lived in the magic-rich old country.

When the staff made no response, Zelle drew in a breath. "I'm going to shut him in the guest room until he wakes up."

That would be the easiest way to keep him out of her sight while she attempted to wrangle answers from the staff about her grandmother's whereabouts. While part of her wanted to search the Sanctum, leaving the stranger alone downstairs in an unlocked room didn't strike her as a good idea.

Whatever he was doing here, his appearance did not bode well.

The man's head throbbed when he came to wakefulness, with the vague memory of being dragged across a hard wooden floor. Yet when he dove into his other memories, he found nothing but a fuzzy haze. At least he lay on a soft surface. A mattress, and not of the itchy, straw-filled variety he'd grown accustomed to in recent days. At least, he thought he had.

He shifted, rubbing the back of his head as though it would dislodge the thoughts stuck in there. They lurked in the background, like a word on the tip of his tongue, just out of reach.

Right. Start with the basics. How did I get here? He thought back, but the only clear image he could grasp showed him a steep path up a mountainside. A sheer drop and him hanging on in the face of grim death... and then, like a miracle, the tower appearing before him.

That was it. Nothing more. The next logical question was *where am I?* He opened his eyes fully and found he was in a small bedroom with bare floorboards and no furniture save for a small wooden armoire next to the bed. A pillow cushioned his aching head, but the slightest movement reminded him of other small injuries he'd suffered during the climb up the treacherous pass. Injuries he frankly didn't remember sustaining.

Think. What happened before the mountain?

As he screwed up his forehead, more images flashed before his eyes. A ship, buffeted against waves. A whirlpool like the maw of a great beast opening to swallow the world. His hands clinging desperately to the ship's side, his hands and face numb, a horrible pain cutting through his core like something vital had been stripped away.

The echo of the pain made him recoil, but its absence was somehow more disconcerting. As was the knowledge that he could recall neither the name of the one who'd caused him such pain… or his *own* name.

Who did this to me?

He pushed upright and heard a distinct movement on the other side of the door.

Instinct had him on his feet in a blink, searching for his weapons. They were gone—the person who'd brought him here had removed his travelling cloak too. He'd been soaked through from his trek through the snow, true, but he couldn't guarantee that everyone who lived in this strange place was friendly.

He opened the armoire and found several moth-eaten outfits and little else. A carved wooden stick lay near the back, though, and he gripped it in his hand before facing the door, and whoever stood on the other side.

3

E vita Govind had never intended to be an
assassin.

Presumably, at least some of her fellow
novices had made this their life's goal, but she hadn't
spent her childhood dreaming of leaving her coastal
village to join the near-mythical Changers and hunt trai-
tors to the Crown. If such a thought had ever crossed her
mind, she certainly never would have pictured sitting in a
cave halfway up a mountain while the wind punctuated
Mastery Amery's speech with a melancholy howling.
Hardly ideal conditions for a mountain hike, let alone a
life-or-death trial, but the Changers took any kind of
adverse weather conditions as a personal challenge.

"Today," Master Amery said, his voice echoing around
the cave, "is your first test to prove you are worthy of
joining the ranks of the Changers."

Evita's heart skipped—with excitement, she told
herself. Not nerves. Changers were fearless, and she was
more than ready to prove herself as worthy amongst the

most elite assassins on the continent. So she'd never actually *killed* anything yet—that spider she'd squashed on her first day didn't really count. And to be truthful, the notion of killing people wasn't an appealing one either. Not humans, anyway.

She was here to learn how to kill a god.

Master Amery cast his gaze amid the novices, his silvery cloak catching the light streaming through the cave opening. "It is time for you to witness marvels that most of you will only know about through legend and tall tales. There is magic in these mountains which stems from a time before humans walked among these rocks, and this same magic will answer our call."

Magic. Finally. The wind howled again, whistling throughout the cave, unless it was some beast the Master had brought here with the intention of letting it feed on any unlucky recruits who failed the day's trial. Given the hints he'd dropped so far, it wouldn't surprise her. She'd barely survived the two weeks of preliminary training, and more than half the other recruits had crawled home after the first week, nursing broken bones and bruised egos. The twenty or so who remained wanted this as badly as she did.

"If you are chosen to be worthy," said Master Amery, "you will be renowned by the powerful and feared by the weak. You will be able to move like shadows and sneak up on your enemies before you take their lives. We are Changers, and it is our duty to serve the Crown."

I'm not sure about the duty part, but the rest, I can do. Every time she began to have second thoughts about pledging herself in service to the Crown, she reminded herself that she had no other life to go back to. The last traces of her village would be nothing but ashes by now, and her throat tightened at the memory of her childhood home silhouetted in orange light as she'd fled for the road north. The others might have come here for a shot at glory or the honour of serving the Crown of Zeuten, but for Evita, this was her only option left.

Master Amery's cold stare passed over his audience and lingered on Evita, who looked stonily back. He was the first obstacle between her and her goals, and she'd inadvertently crossed him on her very first day here, when she'd asked if it was true that he'd once been a merchant in Saudenne prior to joining the Changers. Inane questions, it seemed, were not tolerated, but she'd had trouble picturing the Master in anything other than the silvery cloak he wore. He might be as short and as rangy as the pet eagle he kept in his office, but his serious face gave the appearance of being hewn from rock, and he was rumoured to have been at the top of his own novice class many years ago.

"Can anyone name the Power whose magic is rumoured to dwell in these mountains?" he asked.

Silence answered. Evita fidgeted in the uncomfortable chill; her plain black cloak was made of a thin material which did little to keep the cold out. It wasn't until she attained a senior rank that she'd obtain a silvery cloak like Master Amery's—said to be woven from the magic of one of the Powers themselves—but that Power wasn't the one the Master had asked her to name. When nobody else spoke up, Evita said, "No, because the Shaper doesn't have a name."

"You might as well tell me that the rain is wet."

Laughter rippled through the other recruits, while

Evita suppressed the urge to return the Master's biting comment with one of her own. She hadn't come all this way to get herself kicked out of the trials at the last moment or to find out the hard way if the rumour that he was inclined to throw recruits off the mountainside if they annoyed him turned out to be true. Vekka shot a smirk in her direction from among the assembled novices as if to goad her into speaking, so Evita bit her tongue and prayed to whatever deity might be listening that their first test would not involve teamwork.

"We live in the shadow of the Range, believed to be the last creation of the nameless Shaper," Master Amery continued. "And we wield the strength of Gaiva Herself. It is She who will answer to our call."

She'd bloody well better answer to me, considering I've come all this way. Gaiva, mother of all the Powers, would be more than a match for the beast who'd burned her village, surely.

Master Amery snapped his fingers and vanished into thin air, silvery cloak and all. In his place stood a thick-furred snow leopard. Evita's mouth fell open, and she quickly closed it in case he mistook her shock for fear. Several gasps suggested most of the other recruits had never seen anything like his transformation before. No surprise there, because the Changers prided themselves on keeping their ways a secret, and none of the novices would reach that level of training for several years, assuming they lived that long.

You wouldn't call this superstitious nonsense if you saw it, Mother, she thought as the mottled snow leopard paced in front of them. Like many Zeutenians who lived on the coasts, Evita's parents hadn't put much stock in the tales that drifted over from the few merchants or travellers who ventured near the Range, but a part of Evita had always been certain that every tall tale held a sliver of truth.

There came a ripple of silver, like a curtain lifting in the air, and then Master Amery stood before them again.

"By the *Powers.*" The exclamation escaped her before she could think better of it, and her words echoed for several moments afterwards. Master Amery gave her a wilting look, but the other novices gaped at him with equal levels of awe.

"That is what awaits you, if you survive to see the end of your training." Master Amery knelt and then raised his hands, lifting the silver-tinted folds of a second coat, near-identical to his own. "You won't have access to your own cloak of Changing for some time, but for the purposes of this test, you'll share this one between you."

Every pair of eyes in the cave was riveted greedily on the silvery cloak, including Evita's, while Master Amery beckoned them outside through a cave opening.

"Come." With the silvery cloak draped over his arm, he indicated a narrow path snaking around the front of the mountain. "Follow me."

The novices obeyed, emerging from the cave one at a time. Evita's heart gave a skitter at the sight of the sheer drop, but she forced herself to watch the shaved head of the novice in front of her instead as they made their way around the curving path. Eagles wheeled in the sky above, some larger than a person, but none made a move to attack them. Perhaps even the predators in the mountains feared the Changers.

The path steepened, and Evita climbed after the

others, teeth chattering. Her coat's thin material let the wind bite at her exposed skin, while she'd lost sensation in several of her toes a long while ago. The numbness in her feet didn't make climbing the slippery path any easier, and she couldn't stop her mind from conjuring up images of her broken body lying on the rocks below. Thus far, she'd managed to mask her fear of heights, but any sensible person would have second thoughts about this treacherous route.

Ahead of her, Vekka turned back to shoot her a mocking look from beneath his thick brows, as if daring her to give in to her fear and run. He'd had it in for her from the moment they'd got into a scuffle on their first day and she'd come out of it the victor by the dirty tactic of throwing dirt into his eyes. It'd hardly been a fair fight given that Vekka was more than twice her size; at nineteen, Evita still hadn't outgrown the gawkiness of early adolescence and her arms were long and clumsy with little muscle. Still, once she gained access to her own Changer's cloak, she wouldn't have to worry about avoiding brutes like him.

While clouds gathered farther across the Range, promising a storm, the sky above was as pale as the snow on the mountain peaks as they reached a bluff leading to another cave opening.

There, Master Amery indicated to the recruits to spread themselves across the rocky ground. "The purpose of today's test is to demonstrate your skill at stealth. Failure will doubtless result in premature death."

Evita's shoulders tensed as he held up the silvery cloak for them all to see, then handed it to the nearest recruit —Vekka.

"Put on the coat," he ordered. "And enter the cave. You will go in one at a time and retrieve a token from within. If the Powers deem you worthy, you will make it to the end unscathed."

If the Powers deem you worthy? Is one of them *waiting back there in that cave?* She doubted that was the case, but she could never be certain which surprise the Master would have in store for them next.

"And if they don't?" Vekka asked. "What's in there, wild beasts? Will we be able to take any weapons, or—"

His mouth shut like a trap when Master Amery glared at him. "No. If you are truly stealthy enough to become a Changer, you will be able to pass through undetected. The cloak will render you entirely unseen."

So that was the nature of the first trial. Not a real surprise, because stealth was an essential skill for an assassin, and rendering someone invisible was the most basic function of the cloak of Changing. Only those with years of experience would be able to use the same magic to take on the form of an animal—or even fly—but invisibility was impressive enough on its own.

Shaking off his evident discomfort, Vekka pulled the cloak on and vanished. Heart in her throat, Evita averted her gaze from the sheer drop and watched the spot where he'd disappeared, but not so much as a footstep indicated his location. *Yes. That's exactly what I need.*

All the same, a trickle of doubt slipped into her mind. The Master had made it clear that despite the showy nature of their powers, the cooperation of their deity was dependent upon their goal to protect the Crown. Evita held no opinion on the Crown Prince of Zeuten, any more than she did on the royalty in general, and for the first time, she wondered if the deity would somehow be able to sense her lack of devotion. Yet the novices had come from all over Zeuten, from remote countryside villages to the capital of Saudenne, and not all of them would have strong feelings of loyalty to a Crown Prince they'd never met. Right?

To maximise the suspense, the Master fired random questions at the recruits while they stood shivering and nervous on the bluff, waiting for each novice to return from the cave. To Evita's surprise, they all did, some within a short while, some after such a long time that Evita thought they'd met an unfortunate end. When each returned, they gathered outside the cave entrance near Master Amery, with Vekka occupying a prominent position among them. When he caught her eye, a sneer appeared on his face as though he was calculating how he might reach out and trip her when she entered the cave.

"You!" snapped Master Amery. "Evita. You're up next."

Gaiva's tits. Vekka's smile grew wider as he sat on the rocky promontory, stretching his arms behind his back as though to demonstrate that it'd be easy for him to snag her by the ankles and yank her flat on her face. Worse, Vekka seemed incapable of going anywhere without the company of at least three brutish fellow assassins flanking him, and his current followers had all completed the trial. They watched Evita with eager eyes as though preparing to use their collective brute force to drive her back before she ever reached the cave.

Evita had no intention of giving them that chance.

"Are you sure?" She fought to keep her tone even. "Doesn't one person passing the test prove we're all worthy of the Powers, Master?"

"If you're looking to meet with the Powers face-to-face, then feel free to take five steps to the right." Master Amery snatched the cloak back off the novice who'd just stumbled from the cave, shaking like a tree in a gale, and held it out to her. "Alternatively, you can keep that trap of yours shut and prove your worth."

Evita's mouth had got her into trouble on a regular basis for as long as she could remember, but it seemed to her that a short dive off a cliff's edge might be in her future whether she kept quiet or not. To get past Vekka and his friends, she'd have to move fast. She highly doubted the Master would intervene if they decided to enact revenge on her at this precise moment—brawling wasn't permitted, but Vekka was sneaky enough to trip her and make it look like an accident. And one wrong step might send her plummeting to her doom.

Evita's heartbeat fluttered as her fingers brushed the cloak of Changing, as fine as spider-silk and almost as invisible to the naked eye. Curiosity momentarily pushed past her apprehension when she swung the cloak over her shoulders. The sensation was like slipping underwater or throwing on a shift made of nothing but air. At once, the others' gazes slid straight past her as if she didn't exist. Even Vekka's confident expression slipped when she disappeared.

Despite her predicament, a sense of triumph came over Evita as she imagined how differently her life might have turned out if she'd had access to this power when she'd lived in the village. She'd have been able to avoid the advances of the village blacksmith without having to resort to making excuses and then, in a fit of desperation, blurting out that he resembled a goat. She'd have been able to hide before he'd drawn her into the conversation which had splintered their friendship—

Don't think about that, Evita. It's done. They were dead, all of them, and Evita was the last survivor.

With one eye on Vekka, she approached the cave. He made a casual swipe at the air, missing entirely. Evita suppressed the urge to give him a firm kick, not wanting to push her luck. Instead, she entered the cave through the slash in the cliffside. If the cloak's magic deemed her unworthy or realised that protecting the Crown wasn't her primary goal, then it was too late for second-guessing. She was in. The trial had officially begun.

Darkness filled the space in front of her, while the only light came from faintly glowing moss on the cave walls that illuminated the stalagmites jutting from the ceiling like crooked teeth. She took a few quiet steps forwards, squinting through the gloom in search of a token... though she hadn't the faintest idea what one looked like. She might have asked beforehand, though she doubted Master Amery would have told her.

A breeze stirred her hair, and a low growling echoed within the cave. Her blood froze, and she halted in her tracks when she spotted the source of the noise. A large, scaly beast lay curled within a nest of twigs and leaves in the centre of the cave—which also contained several shiny pebbles. Those must be the tokens. Of *course* Master Amery wanted her to walk past the sleeping beast and retrieve a pebble without waking it.

Even coiled up, the wyrm was several times larger than a person, its long reptilian head resting on its scaled front feet as it snored lightly. Curved claws protruded from each foot, while hints of sharp fangs were visible when its nostrils dilated, and a rumbling growl escaped its throat. She wasn't doing herself any favours by standing there waiting for it to wake, but her feet refused to obey her commands.

A droplet of water splashed onto her head, making her jerk back in surprise. Her limbs were still functioning, then. *Relax. It can't see you. Move as quickly as you can, and for Gaiva's sake, don't touch anything.* Wyrms swallowed their prey whole, according to the stories she'd heard, and she had no intention of learning if it was true.

Evita took in a deep breath of the musty air then approached the sleeping wyrm. The stalagmites and rocks left very little free ground to tread on without making a noise, while Master Amery had purposefully positioned the tokens directly underneath the wyrm's sleeping head. If it woke when she was that close, she wouldn't have the chance to scream before its jaws closed on her head.

As she drew closer, a thin stream of light illuminated the wyrm in all its fearsome glory, its head crowned in the brightest green she'd ever laid eyes on. Wyrms had no need of camouflage or other trickery. If by some miracle their prey dodged their snapping teeth, their saliva contained a paralytic substance that rendered the target powerless to move.

Why in Gaiva's name did I have to remember that? Evita very much regretted listening to so many stories of monsters from the villagers who cared for such things. They'd seemed fanciful even to her, but it seemed Master Amery hadn't been exaggerating when he'd claimed they'd witness marvels unheard of outside of tall tales. *Curse him. May an eagle shit on his head every time he walks outside for the rest of his days.*

Her foot kicked a loose stone. Evita froze, her eyes on the wyrm's crowned head, but it didn't move. Another water droplet hit her head. Fighting the urge to flinch, she looked down at the gleaming stones within its nest...

...and a small, fanged face looked back.

Evita choked back a startled noise, her legs sliding out from underneath her. The little creature's eyes followed her as she caught her balance before she fell. *Impossible.* Somehow, the small beast had seen right through her disguise to the person beneath. A pair of batlike wings stuck out from its back, and its reptilian head appeared too short for its long, awkward body. What kind of creature was it? A lizard? No, it was a dragonet, a smaller cousin of the fearsome giant beasts that had once roamed the Range. Perhaps they still did.

No wonder it'd seen through the magic of her cloak. Though whatever power it possessed hadn't helped it avoid ending up captive in a wyrm's nest, pinned beneath its coiled body. Nausea rose in the back of her throat. *It's the wyrm's dinner, isn't it?*

The pebbles were within reach. One quick lunge and she'd be on her way to freedom... but the dragonet's gaze followed her every movement, its eyes pleading.

I can't help you, she silently told the creature. If she did, she'd take its place as the wyrm's next meal. Doing her best to ignore its melancholy stare, she reached out and lifted the nearest pebble from the nest. The dragonet feebly snapped its teeth at her hand and continued to look at her with those piteous eyes...

Oh, Powers help me.

After pocketing the smooth stone, she extended her hand towards the creature. Its head was free, but its lower body was pinned beneath the coiled flank of the wyrm. The beast seemed oblivious to its prey's squirming.

"Grab my sleeve," she breathed. "I'll pull you out."

Did the creature understand Zeutenian? Dragonets were said to be intelligent creatures, but they were also said to be mythical. Regardless, when her hand skimmed the wyrm's flank, the dragonet reached out its long neck and closed its teeth on the sleeve of her cloak. Drawing back, Evita gave a firm tug.

The wyrm's head moved in a blur, and its sharp teeth would have taken her arm off—had the dragonet not broken free in the same movement. The giant beast's teeth snapped over empty air as its smaller prey flew upwards and landed on the wyrm's elongated nose. Evita stared for a moment, dumbfounded, until her instincts kicked in and she sprinted for her life.

The wyrm roared behind her, and the sound of flapping wings came from the dragonet as it flew out of reach of the monster's teeth. Then, with a sickening certainty, she realised she'd run past the nest towards the back of the cave and the beast was now between her and the way out. With no way to turn around, all she could do was keep moving onward. A thin stream of light gleamed, shining through a gap in the rock. *Thank Gaiva. Thank you.*

Teeth snapped at her heels. Evita all but threw herself out of the narrow opening, tumbling off the edge of a cliff.

This time, she did scream. The ground gave way, her feet skidding on nothing, and if her cloak hadn't spread out behind her and caught on something, she'd have kept falling until her bones shattered against stone. As it was, she hung awkwardly in the air, the part of her that wasn't shrieking in terror glad that the cloak covered enough of her body that nobody could see her pitiful struggle.

As she dangled, she heard the sound of beating wings and fervently hoped the wyrm was too big to fit through the narrow passage she'd squeezed through. Though maybe then at least her end would be comparatively quick. Since her cloak seemed to have caught on something vaguely stable, she risked wriggling around to see if she could get a handhold in the cliffside. Her fingers wedged into the cracks between rocks, her feet scrabbling at the sheer wall. Then, to her horror, a gust of wind freed her cloak, sweeping it over her head.

Her grip faltered, just as the dragonet's face appeared over the cliff above.

"Come to have a good laugh, have you?" she gasped out. "Or to push me to my death?"

If the dragonet could speak, it might have said, *What did you expect when you provoked a wyrm in its nest?* She'd also set the small creature free from the prospect of a crunchy death, but the dragonet could fly. She most definitely could not.

The dragonet leaned over the ledge on which it stood, extending its long neck. *Wait. Is it returning the favour?* It wasn't like she had anything to lose at this point, though the creature didn't look strong enough to grab her. Gripping the cliff firmly with one hand, she swung the other upwards in an attempt to grab the ledge. She missed, but the dragonet's teeth snagged her sleeve.

The beast's teeth sank in, and it dragged her up the cliff face with strength that went far beyond its small size. In moments, she sat on the promontory, gasping for breath. Her fingers stung, both from cold and from gripping the sharp edge of the cliff, but she was alive, and so was the dragonet. Sitting down, the beast came up to her shoulder, but it was bigger than she'd assumed when she'd seen it pinned under the wyrm's coils.

The dragonet had saved her life. Why? The beast was intelligent, evidently, but she'd never quite believed the stories of them being one of the few remaining magical beings who'd been touched by the Great Powers themselves. Despite her suspicions that the Powers had largely forsaken her a long time ago, she was glad of its help. Was this an auspicious beginning to her career as an assassin or quite the opposite? Evita didn't know, but right now, she was glad to be alive.

———

The boy moved around the city like a ghost. He never spent more than a few nights in a row in the same inn, disappearing overnight before anyone caught his name or where he'd come from. Some said he was a demon, swept in from the unnatural storm out at sea that had had every seafarer reeling. No ships had left Saudenne's harbour in days, and none had arrived either—in one piece, anyway. As of yet, no survivors of the storms had been found... with one exception.

The housekeeper at Clove's Inn on Saudenne's outskirts, the latest place the boy had picked, was determined to catch him out. She watched the boy flit upstairs like smoke, carrying no personal belongings, and leaving her with a burning curiosity that couldn't be quenched. She'd heard the fearful rumours, of course, but the stranger seemed tied with the storm that had so vexed her fisherman husband, and if the boy knew something of the cause, it would settle her mind.

Later that evening, she tiptoed to the boy's room and lingered outside the door, which had been left slightly ajar. A soft voice spoke within, whispering words she couldn't understand. Yet every sound manifested sweat on her forehead and goose bumps on her arms and evoked images of the recent terrible fog creeping across the ocean. She forced herself to peer through the crack in the door and instantly regretted her decision.

A window had opened in the middle of the room, as though a piece of the world had been cleanly sliced away with the edge of a blade. The boy stood in front of the window, his slight figure masking the view of the other side, and he continued to speak in that strange tongue to someone who lurked out of sight.

A chill struck her heart. As a port town, Saudenne had seen more magic than most places in Zeuten but mostly in the form of Aestinian merchants selling fake Relics and the very rare visit from ambassadors when the Emperor visited the capital. This was different, and all her instincts urged her to run before the child realised he wasn't alone.

The boy's voice faded to a whisper, and then he rotated on the spot, his gaze locking on the housekeeper frozen on the other side of the door. She found herself quite unable to move as his mouth curled into a cruel smile before he glided across the room to her side.

"Would you like to speak to the gods, hmm?" he queried, now speaking accented Zeutenian. "I doubt a human like *you* has ever set eyes upon their realm."

"I—" She couldn't get the words out, could barely

speak past the fear clogging her throat. "Please—I didn't mean to pry."

"There is nothing wrong with curiosity." His eyes—darker than any she'd ever seen—considered her. "I will tell you my reason for visiting your fine establishment. I come seeking a man who they say perished in the ocean, whose body was never recovered. I sent storms to drown him, and yet my master tells me he survives. And so, I am here."

She licked her dry lips. "Your... master?"

His mouth twisted with disdain. "Or so he believes himself to be. I allow him that luxury, for he feeds me blood, and with each drop, I grow stronger."

Her vision wavered, a sense of unreality settling over her. "Blood?"

"Yes." He took her hand in his, and his palm was as cold as his voice. "Yes, I have a fathomless appetite, after being left buried and neglected for so very many years."

The boy's words might have evoked a thousand questions, but her curiosity was thoroughly eradicated. More than anything, she wanted to run as far away as possible from this boy, this *creature,* but her own body refused to obey her commands. Her mouth opened, speaking without conscious thought. "You seek the man who survived the storm?"

"I do." He leaned closer. "You know of him?"

Her thoughts tumbled over one another, making it hard to think. "They found a man on the beach some days ago... he was thought drowned."

"Oh?" The boy's grip tightened, his nails digging into her palm. "Do tell me more."

Threads of smoke crept through the window in the

room, and when she made the mistake of glancing in that direction, horrifying shapes appeared on the other side. Her mouth fell open in a soundless scream.

"Ignore them," the boy said softly. "Tell me about this man."

"I don't know anything else." Her voice turned high, pleading. "He never came here. I swear on my life. Please don't—"

The smoke moved forwards, as did the monstrous shapes. The last thought that flashed through her mind before the world faded into blackness was that she hoped the man had gone far, far away from here.

4

———

After leaving the stranger in the guest room, Zelle roamed the upper corridor outside the locked door to the Sanctum, looking for any signs of Grandma's presence. None materialised, while the urge to check on the stranger nagged at her like an itch. Had she made the right choice in bringing him inside? What would happen when he woke up?

He'd asked for a book. A *book*. Did they not have books in Aestin? Yes, the Sanctum was crammed with ancient texts but not ones a foreigner would be aware of, much less inclined to risk their life in a storm to get their hands on. She descended the stairs and paced to the window again, cursing under her breath at the sight of the mass of snow outside.

You might want to think twice about insulting the Powers when you're dependent upon them for your survival, the staff told her.

She scowled. "Why are you speaking to me, anyway?"

I am not speaking.

"I can hear your voice in my head." She could only assume the staff couldn't hear her actual thoughts, but the caustic, dry voice that replied to her comments certainly wasn't hers. "Anyway, you've never said a word to me before now, and I assumed I needed to have magic to be able to hear you."

No, you simply didn't interest me. Since you possess no magic, then what use are you?

"What use am I?" Rudeness aside, the staff hadn't asked her about herself until now, so perhaps it would be willing to help her out if she gave it a little more context. "As a matter of fact, I earn a living to help keep this place running. I work in my aunt's shop, and I sell... trinkets. Oddities. Things my ancestors have collected over the years."

You mean you sell your grandmother's old junk to foolish merchants.

"Nobody asked your opinion." How had her grandmother put up with the staff's judgemental voice muttering in her ears for decades? Grandma Carnelian had likely been a child when she'd been chosen, since her own mother hadn't inherited the gift. It tended to skip generations, jumping straight to Zelle's sister. While Aurel could make a living by performing Readings for private clients, Zelle possessed no such advantages, and being scoffed at by a mere hunk of wood for doing what was necessary to keep her grandmother and herself out of poverty tugged at her already fraying temper.

Instead of apologising, the staff said, *I should inform you that your honoured guest is awake.*

"How do you know that?"

Because I do.

Right. The staff knew everything that occurred here in the outpost… except, apparently, where her grandmother was. Abandoning the door to the Sanctum, she made her way back down the narrow staircase to the lower floor.

If she were a romantic like Aurel, she might have speculated on the possibility that the stranger might be able to point her to a way out of destitution which didn't involve marrying a diplomat or someone else with buckets of gold. Or he'd turn out to be here to kidnap her to take on some perilous adventure. Aurel's stories tended towards the dramatic side. Whatever the case, she had no intention of being taken unawares.

The stranger hadn't left his room yet, so Zelle headed in the direction of the guest bedroom. Hesitation stayed her hand before she turned the doorknob. He *might* be here to rob her, given his evident lack of funds. On the other hand, he couldn't harm her. The Sanctum's defences would see to that… or so she hoped. Before she lost her nerve, she opened the door.

The end of a wooden staff nearly hit her in the chest. When he found Zelle looking at him, the young man took a step back and dropped the staff, where it clattered to the floor. As if she'd taken him by surprise and not the other way around. His boots were off, but he still wore the same ragged clothes as he had before. Of course he did, because he hadn't brought anything else with him, including money. He must have grabbed her grandfather's old staff from the back of the armoire.

"What were you going to do with that?" She eyed the fallen staff, which bore none of the knotted marks of the one her grandmother carried. "I expected some gratitude for bringing you out of the cold, not an attempted assault."

"I apologise. You startled me." The young man's gaze travelled around the room, as though he was confused about where he was. The last time he'd been awake, he'd been sprawled headfirst in a snowdrift, so his reaction was understandable. "Who are you?"

"I'm Zelle," she told him. "What's your name?"

The young man started to speak and then cut himself off. "I don't remember."

Zelle gave an uncertain laugh. "You can't remember your name?"

He blinked slowly. "How did I get here?"

"I carried you." When he eyed her squat frame in puzzlement, she added, "All right, I dragged you. You passed out in a snowdrift on my doorstep. Why did you come here?"

"Whereabouts, exactly, is 'here'?"

Is he joking? "An outpost of the Sentinels." His perplexed expression didn't waver. "In the Range. Zeuten. The world."

"You're not very polite, are you?" His accent grew more pronounced, though his Zeutenian was flawless. Why a traveller from Aestin of all places would travel to the most desolate part of Zeuten was beyond her, but he'd clearly done his research.

"You called me a *witch* earlier, if you've forgotten."

"I did?" He looked at her in vague puzzlement. *Had* he forgotten their earlier conversation? Along with his name? No, it was far more likely that he was trying to make a fool of her.

"Don't pretend you've forgotten," she said. "You claimed to have climbed up here in search of a book."

"Is this a library?"

"No, it's a sacred site of the Powers." Really, he was lucky the Powers hadn't led him astray or simply tossed him off the mountain as they did to other would-be trespassers. "The only people allowed here are the Sentinels and Zeuten's royalty. Not that the Crown Prince has ever dragged his lazy arse up here, so it's just us."

His eyes widened as if in shock at her words. As far as she was aware, the Aestinian people did not hold their Emperor in particularly high regard, but their Invokers were treated with the utmost respect. Which meant he ought to have treated *her* in a more respectful manner, since the Sentinels were the closest Zeuten had to Aestin's magicians, unless her lack of talent was obvious from a simple glance. Yet if he was neither a magician himself nor an explorer looking for riches, why had he come here?

"If you're a thief," she added, when he didn't reply, "the Sanctum is the most heavily guarded place in the entire country short of the Royal Vaults, so I wouldn't try your luck."

His expression turned scandalised, as though she'd accused him of a crime. Which, come to think of it, she had, but she was at a loss to find a polite way to get rid of him without sentencing him to death outside in the blizzard. His next words were spoken in clipped tones. "I don't suppose you have any spare clothes?"

She cast a glance at the wooden armoire in the corner. "There are some old clothes in there, but I can't say whether they'll fit you or not. They'd be my grandfather's."

They'd been gathering dust for decades, but that was not her problem. Zelle left him to dig out some clothes and returned to the main room where she'd left her pack. She was glad she'd brought enough food for a couple of days, given the storm, but she'd never entertained any guests in the outpost before. Nor did she make a habit of doing so at home, come to that. Her Aunt Adaine had not been popular, and her family's reputation meant few visited her store except for eccentrics and collectors, none of whom she particularly wanted to be close friends with.

She glanced at the staff, which leaned against the armchair without uttering a word. Thinking to itself, maybe, if an inanimate object was capable of thought. Why had she let her conscience overtake her and bring a stranger in here at a time when she ought to be embarking on an urgent search for her grandmother? If he truly couldn't even remember his name, then he'd be more of a hindrance than a help, and if he expected charity from her, he was going to be disappointed.

There came a creak as the guest room door swung outward, and the stranger appeared in the doorway, dressed in a plain shirt and some trousers which were as dusty as Zelle had expected. He looked more alert than he had earlier, and if not for the vague expression on his face, as if he'd wandered into a foreign country by accident, she supposed most people would call him handsome. Given the way he stood—shoulders back, head high—she could almost picture him in a noble's wear.

Why would a noble from Aestin want anything to do with the Sentinels? Shaking off the thought, she dug into her pack for the bag of pastries she'd bought down in the village. They were a little squashed from the climb, but she could warm them up over the fire.

Sensing the stranger watching her, she looked over at him. "Hungry?"

He gave a nod without speaking, but he looked as though he hadn't seen a decent meal in a while. At her prompting, he took the armchair, while Zelle moved to the window seat after she'd distributed the pastries between them. She devoured her meal, watching swirls of snow dance in the darkness outside, and the stranger, who was surely used to better fare, did likewise. Neither spoke, but outside, the storm continued to roar. Even over the crackling fire in the hearth, she heard the howl of wind, which sounded like some great Power was trying to rip the mountain out by the roots.

Zelle brushed crumbs off her lap. "I don't suppose you remember your name now?"

The stranger, who'd been staring into the flickering flames, looked up at her. "Call me Rien."

Surprised, she studied his face. "Is that your name?"

"I think so. It has a certain… resonance."

That would have to do. "Okay. Rien. Do you remember why you came here? You mentioned a book…"

His vague expression was back. "No. You have books here, though, right?"

"We have a small selection compared to the libraries you have in Aestin, I imagine," she told him. "However, you've come to the right place if you're looking for texts from the time of the first settlers here in Zeuten. Our oldest resources date back over a thousand years, from when our ancestors came across the sea from Aestin. That's where you're from, right?"

He gave a nod. "Yes."

"Well, that's a start," she said. "The first Zeutenian settlers came here during the Aestinian civil war, when the main Invoker families, ah... murdered the royal family. I believe that's why you have an Emperor now instead, but the Invokers still retain possession of all your magic..." She trailed off. A strange look had passed over his face, a mixture of sadness and anger, that vanished as quickly as it came. His right hand, which had clenched over his left, loosened in the same instant.

"Are you all right?" she asked.

Rien started, like she'd woken him from a deep sleep. "I am sorry, Miss Zelle. Carry on."

"There's no reason to call me 'Miss'." Definitely Aestinian, by his manners, but his reaction gave her pause. Had her words awakened some buried memory? If so, then she might be able to jolt him into remembering his purpose here if she said the right words. Delving into the sparse memories of her schooling on the subject, she said, "Aestin has a lot more magic than we do here in Zeuten. The Sentinels are all that's left, and we brought our Relics with us across the ocean. That is, my ancestors did."

Now he was listening intently. "Do go on."

"So..." She hesitated, unused to having a captive audience. "They say the original settlers of Zeuten were concerned that Aestin's Invokers were getting too powerful, so a small group of them stole every Relic they could lay their hands on and were allegedly led to Zeuten by Gaiva Herself. They established the two outposts in the mountains, said to be the last creation of the nameless Shaper."

"Your ancestors." Comprehension dawned on his face. "Your family—they're the people who built this place? They were led by Gaiva Herself?"

"The Powers' actual involvement is up to interpretation, but I do belong to the family of the original Sentinels. You'd call them Invokers, but you have many of them, and we just have one family."

At the last word, he flinched, almost imperceptibly. "So you're the only Invokers left."

"Not me," she corrected him. "The current Sentinel is my grandmother. My sister is her successor, and she lives at the other outpost."

"Then why are *you* here?"

Zelle frowned, resisting the defensive impulse that rose at his words—it was a perfectly valid question, after all. "I'm here to visit my grandmother, but I got caught in the storm. Have you remembered what book you're looking for yet?"

"No," he said, "but I believe some Power guided me here. Like your ancestors."

Right. She snapped her mouth shut before she mentioned the lost Relic, because if he turned out to have come here for *that*, she might pitch him off the mountain herself.

His gaze found hers, his grey eyes piercing. "You said there were texts from the time of the settlers. May I see them?"

"I can't guarantee you'd be able to read them, but most of the ancient texts are inside the Sanctum. That's upstairs." In a manner of speaking. The dimensions of the upper level were nebulous, to say the least. "There's a comprehensive list of every text there too. You can read through that to gain an idea of what you might need."

He gave a short nod, frowning as though the idea of combing through an endless list displeased him. Serve him right for coming here without a plan. "Very well. You'll assist me."

She blinked, surprised at his presumptuousness. "I can take you to the Sanctum, but I can't promise it'll react well to me bringing a stranger inside. If you fall afoul of its magic, then there's little I'll be able to do. As part of the Sentinels' family, I'm protected. You might not be so lucky."

He opened his mouth to speak then closed it again. Wisely, because she was already having second thoughts about this venture. Could she trust a man who claimed not to know who he was? He'd braved certain death to be here, which certainly gave his claims some credence, but without his memory, he'd have a hard time achieving his goal. All the same, she'd prefer to keep him within her sight while she searched for her grandmother in the Sanctum. There was no telling what trouble he might cause if she left him alone.

After putting on her indoor shoes, Zelle picked up the staff again.

What is he? she asked it silently. She wasn't sure if it could hear her thoughts, but the temperature of the wood cooled a fraction, as if in acknowledgement.

A troublemaker, said the staff. *Take him to the Sanctum, but don't let him touch anything.*

5

Zelle hadn't set foot in the Sanctum in a long while. After years of absence, part of her expected not to be allowed in at all. She hadn't been joking when she'd said the place tended to be hostile to non-Sentinels, and the staff might not be able to protect her if the Sanctum designated her as a threat as well as the stranger.

"Where are we going?" Rien eyed the heavy wooden door at the end of the upper corridor. "What is this Sanctum?"

"The home of the Sentinels' secrets." Swallowing her misgivings, Zelle approached the door and began to undo the latches sealing it closed. With each one that opened, she cast a brief glance at the stranger. She didn't detect any malice beneath his vacant expression, though she'd be the first to admit she wasn't the best judge of character. In any case, she wasn't entirely incompetent at defending herself, especially against someone who was unarmed. If all else failed, she'd give him a swift strike with the staff when he wasn't expecting it.

Powers help me, I hope I'm not wrong to trust he isn't an enemy.

The door creaked in its frame as the last latch unfastened, and she picked up the staff again before opening the Sanctum, revealing a dark corridor ahead of them.

Instead of looking at what lay before them, Rien studied the staff in her hand. "What's that?"

The staff remained quiet, but she'd prefer not to tell this complete stranger she heard its voice speaking in her head. "A walking stick."

Excuse me? The staff's indignant tone told her it was listening to her every word after all, but she ignored the voice and pushed the heavy oak doors the rest of the way open before entering the corridor. Her footsteps echoed on the stone floor, while gloom surrounded them on every side. The place had always given her the creeps, but Rien walked alongside her without any apparent fear. Perhaps he'd been in similar places himself; for all she knew, they were commonplace in Aestin. The only source of light stemmed from a few lanterns hanging on the walls, and they walked a short distance until they came to another, smaller door, leading into the Sanctum itself.

Rien's eyebrows lifted as she grabbed a clawed instrument with her free hand from a grate next to the door. "What's that for?"

"The books." That ought to serve as enough of a warning to dissuade him from picking anything up. The staff gave a coughing laugh in the back of her mind as she applied herself to unlocking the second door, while letting him imagine what kind of monsters they might find on the other side.

What they found instead was an enormous amount of dust. Zelle screwed up her eyes as she finished unlocking the door, coughing, and then pushed forwards. A rattling noise greeted them, echoing faintly down the short corridor.

Rien squinted into the gloom. "Is someone in there?"

"No." The rattling did sound unnervingly like footsteps or a chain being dragged along the floor. "There's not a living soul here but the two of us."

He lifted his chin. "I definitely hear something."

"This place was created by the Powers themselves," came her response. "That same magic lives inside the very walls. Don't touch anything unless I tell you to."

She transferred the staff to the crook of her elbow so that she had a free hand to unhook one of the ornately carved lanterns from the wall, and then she handed it to him. Rien stared at the leaping flame, the light reflected in his grey eyes.

"Go on, take it," she told him. "And please watch your step."

He took it from her without a word, while Zelle gripped the clawed instrument in her dominant hand and held the staff in the other. Despite her confident words, worry whispered at the recesses of her mind. If anything attacked them, she had nothing to defend herself with except for a staff which spent more time mocking her than being of any help.

"Are you all right, Miss Zelle?" queried Rien, and she wondered if he read more in her expression than she intended to give away.

"Just Zelle," she reminded him. "Stay close and watch your footing. If you see anything move, tell me. Immediately."

He nodded, appearing less rattled by her words than she might have expected. Then again, she didn't know him, did she? The fact that he'd made it all the way here alone indicated he was a seasoned traveller, while she herself felt decidedly unadventurous as she walked aside him, through the long shadows the lantern cast on the grey stone. They passed under an archway carved with words written in the runes of old Aestinian—the language of the first settlers, before it'd morphed over time—and Rien halted beneath, his gaze roving over the symbols.

"I'm assuming it says, 'Welcome, traveller'," said Zelle. "Or 'leave while you still can'."

Apparently, Rien didn't find her comment amusing. He said nothing as they walked beneath the archway and into the main part of the Sanctum. There, oakwood shelves lined each wall, interspersed with alcoves lit by lanterns like the one Rien carried.

"What manner of sorcery is this?" he murmured. "How do the flames stay lit when nobody lives in here?"

She'd begun to wonder if ever-burning lights were commonplace in Aestin. "They say most of Zeuten's magic dwells in these mountains, and the outposts are designed to serve the Sentinels alone."

She spoke quietly, but their voices didn't disturb the silence; rather, the silence itself seemed to wrap around them like a cloak. The air tasted old, of parchment and oakwood as well as cool, clear mountain air. And dust—a great deal of dust. In any other old dwelling, rodents would have been a problem, but frankly, she pitied any rodent which made it into these halls. She hoped the rattling they'd heard earlier was simply another rattler-imp and not worse.

Rustling sounded, distinct and sharp. Zelle turned back to find that Rien had plucked a book from the shelves and opened it.

"By the Powers!" She snatched the book from him, replacing it on the shelf. "Don't touch that. Are you out of your mind?"

"I thought you said we wouldn't be harmed in here."

"That doesn't mean you're allowed to go around picking everything up," she reprimanded him. "Didn't I tell you that everything in this place has been touched by the Powers?"

Then again, he was from a land where magic was as commonplace as snow on the mountaintops, so for all she knew, such matters meant little to him. She nudged the book back into place and then withdrew her hand sharply when a claw snaked around its side.

Oh, Powers. Gremlins.

"What in the name of—" Rien choked off, an unspoken name ringing in the air. The fine hairs on the back of Zelle's neck stood up though she *knew* he hadn't actually said anything, and she made a mental note not to mention any of the Powers by name until they left the Sanctum behind.

Zelle raised the clawed instrument and used it to seize the gremlin's skinny arm, provoking an ear-splitting screech as she dragged the beast into view. It looked like a shrivelled, papery child, except with claws designed for gouging out eyes and freakishly long teeth that snapped at Zelle as she held the beast at arm's length.

Rien watched the gremlin struggle, dangling from the claw like a mouse in an eagle's grip. "I thought there was nothing alive in here."

"It's not alive," she told him. "Magical constructs thrive in this place. Why do you think we don't usually get visitors?"

The gremlin might have barely enough magic to stir a breeze, or it could bring the whole shelf crashing down. And she didn't have a jar handy like she had with the imp.

Fortunately, the Sanctum came with its own methods of disposing of unwanted guests. Zelle turned away from the shelves, the gremlin's body writhing in the clawed trap, and headed for a stone alcove. Before she'd taken two steps, an almighty crash came from behind her. Zelle whirled around, her heart sinking. A heavy volume lay on the floor, where it had fallen from the top shelf. As she watched, another came tumbling to join it, sending yellowing pages everywhere when it hit the stone floor.

"By the Powers!" She glared at the gremlin, whose tiny teeth were bared in a grin, and dodged another book that toppled from the shelf above her head. "Rien, don't just stand there!"

The staff clattered to the floor as she wrestled the clawed instrument and its haul towards the alcove, using her free hand to work the lever concealed at the side of a shelf. Before she could tug on the lever, however, the gremlin broke free with a glad cry.

Rien loomed behind her, a heavy book in his hand, which he slammed onto the gremlin's head. The beast stumbled, and Zelle hooked the claw around the creature again and lifted it into the air. More yellowed pages scattered to the stone floor, and she groaned. "That book is centuries old, Rien."

Rien said nothing while Zelle swung the claw at the stone wall, depositing the gremlin through the hatch the lever had opened. As she'd told Rien, the creature wasn't alive, so the fall off the mountain wouldn't kill it. *It's certainly not worth defiling ancient books over.*

When she turned back, two more gremlins crept into view, leaping at Rien from behind. He swung the book again, knocking one of them on the skull. Several pages fluttered loose, and Zelle bit back a wince as she lowered the claw over the gremlin. This one was too slow to react before she flung it out of the hatch, but the third realised the danger and tried to run.

Rien barred its path, and Zelle caught it up, hooking the scruff of its neck with the clawed instrument before carrying it to the hatch and propelling it out into empty air. After checking there were no more gremlins in sight, she closed the hatch, belatedly wondering why the sound of the storm wasn't as audible up there. Magic, she supposed, designed to keep the contents of the Sanctum in place no matter how dire the weather conditions might be. Although *why* it had let Rien inside when he'd just proven he had no respect for its contents was a mystery to her.

The staff lay several feet away, and she retrieved it before gathering up the books the gremlins had knocked off the shelves.

Do you think Grandma will notice? she thought.

I think you already know the answer to that, the staff replied.

Despite being the active Sentinel, Grandma spent little

time in the Sanctum or, indeed, using the staff at all. Aurel would have more of a use for it, though she could only imagine what Aurel would say if she learned Zelle had let a stranger into the outpost. Despite Zelle's own mixed feelings on her family's attitude towards collecting old things and then allowing them to gather dust, a surge of annoyance hit her at the thought of Rien's casual attitude towards the ancient tomes. Hadn't she told him that the Sanctum contained the few examples of settlers' texts on the continent?

Zelle took a couple of calming breaths. He didn't know any better, that was all. Still, she'd be keeping a close watch on him from now on.

———

Rien followed Zelle through the Sanctum, their footsteps echoing on the stone floor, the lantern's flame casting flickering lights ahead of them. The gremlins hadn't been particularly threatening, but he still found himself watching the shadows for any signs of a potential ambush.

This fear, he was reasonably sure, was uncharacteristic to him. Yet every faint sound scratched at his ears, each echo of the wind seeming to whisper in a language he didn't quite understand. The air was cold and musty and thick with secrets. It must be due to magic, he supposed, but there was a gaping hole in his mind where he was *sure* that particular word had held a certain meaning for him.

A similar certainty had driven him to reach out and pick that book off the shelf. It had been bound in red and written in a language he couldn't read, but once he held it in his hands, the sense of *rightness* had disappeared, to be replaced by disappointment. He had an image of a similar book in his mind, but he couldn't say where that image had come from either.

After the scandalised look that had appeared on Zelle's face, he'd regretted using the book to strike down the gremlin, even though it'd been all he'd had in hand save for the lantern. While he glanced to either side as they walked, no other books called out to him, and none offered any answers to fill the gaping hole in his memory.

Once or twice, it occurred to him that they'd walked too long a distance to possibly be in the same tower he'd observed from the outside, but Zelle didn't seem inclined to comment. When they came to yet another door marked with nothing but a metal ring, she used that odd clawlike instrument she carried to pull the metal ring, and the door opened with barely a whisper. The room on the other side was much smaller than he'd expected, almost cave-like, and contained nothing except for a pedestal on which a worn book lay open.

When he drew closer to the pedestal, a sudden tremor in his bones drew him off-balance, though Zelle seemed undisturbed. His heart began to beat like a trapped bird. His hand trembled on the lantern, and for a brief moment, faint lines appeared on the top of his left hand, light as spiderwebs. Another blink, and they were gone.

"Go on," Zelle told him. "That book contains an archive of every title in the Sanctum. I doubt any of them can tell you your name, but it might stir a memory if you look."

He stepped up to the pedestal and peered down at the yellowed pages of the book. At once, a wave of dizziness swept over him, and the book seemed to expand to fill every inch of his vision. Somehow, its pages appeared simultaneously as tall as the tower itself yet small enough to entirely fit within the limits of his perception. It was enough to give him a throbbing ache behind his right eye. *Magic,* he thought. *What in the name of... of...?*

The missing name bothered him more than the absence of his *own* name. Breathing hard, he let his gaze rove down the pages, but they were entirely blank.

Then, words appeared, scrawled in spiked hand-writing and written in symbols that hadn't been used in Aestin in centuries. He supposed it made sense for the original settlers of Zeuten to have used their system of writing before they diverged in future generations and formed their own. The letters were similar enough to the modern language for him to get the gist of their meaning, and alphabetically listed topics expanded before his eyes. The book held entirely no regard for normal dimensions. A list the length of a town should not have fitted into two pages, but it did.

"What magic is this?" he murmured to Zelle, who stood close to his shoulder.

"Sentinel magic," she answered. "Don't ask me how it works. I haven't a clue. The first time I came in here, I asked the same question, and it directed me to a story about a man who was too curious for his own good. I believe his eyeballs ended up melting in his skull. I was six, and it left quite the impression."

He lifted his head from the book, alarmed. "You might have warned me first."

"Oh, *that* book is perfectly safe," she told him. "Go on, pick your topic."

Rien hesitated before scanning the list again. His

eyeballs hadn't melted yet, so presumably, he was safe from that particular danger, but he barely knew where to start. His mind kept drifting to that forgotten name, and a title leaped out at him: *Almanac of the Powers.*

That, he was sure, was what he needed. The book seemed to know it, too, because the words expanded until they filled the whole page. He turned away, blinking as though he'd looked directly at the sun for too long.

Zelle's brow wrinkled at his choice. "You know, if you wanted to know about the Powers, you could just have picked up one of my storybooks from downstairs."

"The Powers aren't just stories," he objected.

Zelle squinted at him from the side of the book. "You seem more certain of that than about your own name. Are you *sure* you're unfamiliar with magic?"

"No." But he wasn't sure of much else either. "Not the magic in this room, anyway. Where's this almanac?"

"This way."

Zelle turned her back on the pedestal and led the way out of the room, closing the door behind her. Then they retraced their steps along the bookshelf-lined corridors, where Zelle led him down twists and turns until she came to a halt. From the shelf on their right, Zelle retrieved a bound book with yellowing pages, written in the same letters as the one back in the smaller room—though this book at least appeared to be normal sized.

"I've never opened this one before," Zelle remarked. "It's just a list of the major Powers, I assume. I'd have thought they would be common knowledge in Aestin."

An inexplicable sense of shame rose within him. "Let's assume I have no knowledge and go from there."

He took the book from her when she offered it to him.

The cover peeled back like dried wax, revealing a yellowed page beneath. Handwritten words filled its space. The names of the Powers... but before his eyes, they were vanishing, the letters fading. He stared at the blank page for a stunned moment before turning to Zelle, whose face had paled.

"That's not supposed to happen. What in the name of the—" She cut herself off, like she'd meant to say *Powers* and thought better of it.

Rien looked down at the page again. "How is that possible? It's just a book, isn't it?"

"The Powers' names are potent, even written down," she said. "And for some reason, they've hidden themselves from you."

Even in his state of total confusion, he detected her unspoken meaning. *Hidden. Whatever Power is in the Sanctum, it doesn't trust me.* "Why?"

"Who are you, really?"

His mouth parted, but he spoke no words. He didn't know.

"Bring that back with you, then." She jerked her head at the book. "We're getting out of here before those gremlins come back."

———

There was far too much blood on the walls.

The boy regarded the inn hallway critically and wondered if it would be worth writing that in the guest book. "Too much blood." Of course, since he'd just killed the owners, it'd be inconsequential. But he liked the idea of a memento. A reminder to the people of Saudenne that he was still here, and that they were trying his patience in failing to help him find his target.

I'm cultivating quite the reputation, he thought. Ghost Boy, they called him. He'd toyed with the idea of taking on the appearance of an older human, but in truth, it made no difference to him whether he pretended to be young or old, male or female or neither. Besides, the humans continued to offer him shelter no matter how many of them he killed, not believing a child could commit such atrocities. He spent his days wandering the crowded markets and listening out for rumours, and many people in Saudenne had walked past him already without even realising what he was.

Poor fools.

He opened the door to the small room he'd rented, leaving the mutilated bodies of the innkeepers in the hall-way, and set down the small bowl of water on the floor-boards before picking the blood out of his fingernails. A tedious task, keeping up his human appearances, but it wouldn't do for anyone to know who he was, nor that he required blood to keep his disguise intact.

The boy removed a thin knife from his pocket. Care-fully, he pricked his finger, blood beading on his fingertip as he held it over the bowl. A grin curled his mouth as the droplet of blood hit the water.

Mist curled from the bowl's surface as he whispered words in a language few humans would understand. Of course, since he'd killed all potential witnesses, there was no danger of anyone getting close enough to hear him whispering.

The mist took form, coalescing into several vaguely human shapes that swept into the room. The wraiths had taken more of his strength to summon than the storm had, but now he looked upon them, they seemed a little too... impersonal. The storm had failed to find its target so far—understandable, given its non-sentient and simple form—but if his wraiths were also unsuccessful, then he needed more allies.

Human ones.

A plan formed in his mind. He'd take a risk if he showed his face in front of anyone whom he intended to keep alive, but perhaps it would be worth making alliances here in Zeuten. He might need them in the future, after all.

At his command, the wraiths took flight, swirling above the floorboards, and vanished from sight.

6

Rien and Zelle walked back through the Sanctum in silence, Zelle examining the corridor for any more potential threats while watching Rien out of the corner of her eye. The Sanctum might be rife with magic, but it had never done anything beyond her understanding. Until today.

Until she'd brought *him* in here.

She gripped the staff and thought, *Why would the almanac hide its contents from someone?*

Why indeed? Perhaps he was looking for forbidden knowledge.

Why would it hide the names of the Powers, though? Everyone knows them.

The staff didn't answer her. She became aware of the eerie silence around them, save for the quiet whisper of something scuttling in the shadows... and footsteps.

She tensed. "We're not alone in here."

Rien came to a stop when another gremlin slid out from underneath the shelves, its papery claws snapping.

Two more followed. Where *were* they coming from? Zelle couldn't grab all of them at once, so she went for the biggest and most threatening-looking first. The clawed instrument closed on its neck, lifting it into the air, but the others swarmed her legs from below.

Rien swung the lantern at them, and they recoiled from the leaping flame. She gave him a reluctant nod of thanks and hauled the gremlin towards the hatch opening onto the mountainside. Several moments of struggling later, she managed to pry the lever open and drop her captive out into empty air.

Rien, rather foolishly, attempted to grab another one with his bare hands. He released the creature with a hiss of pain when it sank its teeth into his fingers, while Zelle moved in with her clawed instrument. The second gremlin toppled down the cliffside, and Rien drove the final one into her grasp.

"Won't they just come back in?" Rien eyed the sheer drop as the gremlin disappeared with a final shriek.

"No, they're magical constructs. They'll disappear as soon as they fall too far from the Sanctum."

Yet they kept spawning inside the room, as though the magic inside the Sanctum was on edge. *Because of him?*

She hadn't directed the words at the staff, but it replied, *I have no idea. I'm a staff, not part of the Sanctum.*

"I thought you both served the Sentinels," she muttered, hoping the echo of their footsteps kept Rien from overhearing. "And do stop reading my thoughts. I'll speak aloud if I want to be heard."

The possibility that every one of her thoughts might be accidentally heard by the staff was unappealing and had had begun to give her a headache besides, so she wanted to lay down a clear boundary if they were to continue to work together. Though she might as well have tossed it out along with the gremlins for all the use it'd been in their conflict.

You've hardly been useful yourself, the staff told her.

"Too bad," said Zelle, irked that the staff had ignored her intention to keep her side of the conversation verbal. "It looks as though we're stuck with one another."

Rien gave her an odd look. "I thought we established that already."

It was easier to pretend she'd directed the words at him, so she said nothing. If she hadn't taken it upon herself to visit her grandmother instead of making her sister shoulder the responsibility that should rightly have been hers to begin with, then Zelle wouldn't have had to worry about any of this. A true Reader would be able to track the source of the spell that had erased Rien's memory *and* discern his identity without relying on the staff at all. The thought put her in a bad mood that she took out on the other gremlins, which Rien helped remove without exhibiting any fear. No doubt his lack of concern was a side effect of losing his memory, which she had to admit she envied. She wouldn't mind her thoughts being a little quieter once in a while, though she couldn't imagine what he'd done that the very *books* didn't trust him to read them.

Once the last gremlin had vanished, she closed the hatch and led the way out of the Sanctum. Despite her failure to find her grandmother *or* a clue about Rien's identity, relief flooded her when she closed the door behind them. She took the lantern back and hung it on the wall, stubbing her toe in the process. A volley of curses escaped her, and she slammed the door firmly in case evoking the Powers' names brought more misfortune on them.

Rien stared at her. "You don't talk like a lady."

"I'm not one." Zelle smothered a laugh at his expression. It seemed she wasn't the only one concerned that cursing the Powers would bring their wrath down on the pair of them. On second thoughts, given what had happened in the Sanctum, maybe doing so wasn't the best idea right now. "You wanted the Powers' names, right? I just gave you about five of them."

"Oh." He lifted the empty book, a wrinkle appearing in his brow. "I heard you, but…"

"Everyone knows the names," she said. "You might have asked anyone down in the valley or elsewhere."

With the exception of the nameless Shaper, all the Powers' names were taught to children from the moment they could speak. He couldn't have simply forgotten them.

After redoing the padlocks on the outer door, Zelle opted to take the clawed stick with her downstairs in case more gremlins appeared. *Never mind the bloody Powers,* she thought. *The sooner I find a way to get rid of him, the better.*

Yet the storm persisted outside, and when she returned to the lower floor, Zelle saw that the blizzard had worsened, and the snow had piled up to the window ledge. *Powers above. I can't even open the door to look outside. When will it stop?*

Resigned to staying put for the night, Zelle removed her shoes and returned to the warmth of the fire.

"I'll see what other books on the Powers I can dredge up," she told Rien. "They shouldn't all turn blank when you look at them, surely."

Zelle scanned the shelf and picked out a storybook on the Powers that she vaguely remembered reading as a child. Brushing dust from its pages, she glanced over at Rien, whose gaze roamed over the map affixed to the wall near the window. "Is that a map of Zeuten?"

"It's a thousand years out of date, but yes." It was the only map of its kind, drawn by the original settlers, which mapped the northern reaches of the mountains all the way to the coastline. The Range extended up Zeuten's spine and then cut off the upper half of the continent, while the route back to the coastal capital of Saudenne had taken Zelle almost a full day in a carriage.

"Are we here?" He pointed at the small symbol of a miniature tower which sat between two of the Range's peaks.

"Yes, this is one of two main outposts," she told him. "My sister lives at the other, but this place is usually deserted. If you'd arrived any other day, you'd have found the tower locked and impassable."

Rien made a sound like *oh*. His eyes moved to the lower part of the map, which showed the upper curve of Aestin's coastline. She supposed maps looked very different where he was from, though in truth, her knowledge of modern Aestinian history was likely out of date.

"Whereabouts do the other Sentinels live?" Rien asked after a short pause.

"My sister lives there." She indicated a smaller dot on the opposite side of the Range's curving edge. "My grandmother lives in the village of Randel, but it didn't exist when this map was drawn."

"Your family must be important," he commented. "You came here before there was even a King. Are you rich?"

"Me? Rich?" She almost laughed, but she supposed the Sanctum would have given him a misleading impression. "No. The magical items in the Sanctum are all we have, and it's not like we can sell any of them. Our family's fortune has been in decline for decades."

Why the past Sentinels had never tried to gain more authority... well, Aestin itself was a prime example of what happened when magicians ended up in control of the government. Their Emperor was nothing more than a figurehead for the ruling families who supposedly kept them from killing one another with the Relics they wielded. Zeuten's founders had intended that this nation would not be the same as the one they'd left behind.

"What happened to your parents?" Rien asked.

"Dead," she replied. "My mother died of a sickness when I was a child. My father was a commercial fisherman before he died in a boating accident when I was three. I don't remember him. What about you?"

"I think my family's dead too."

"Oh." That would explain why he'd come here alone. "I'm sorry. You remember them, then?"

"No." His voice was clipped, and his gaze landed on the book in her hand. "Does that book contain the names of the Powers?"

"Yes, but I can tell you them myself if you think the pages might turn blank again."

"Go on." He gave her an expectant look, as if he'd hired her as a tour guide.

Already regretting her offer, Zelle said, "Nobody knows the name of the Shaper, of course, but the other two Great Powers are called Gaiva and Invicten. Gaiva is the mother of the human race and is thought to have created life itself. The second god, Invicten, is known as the god of illusion and typically appears as a trickster deity in stories. And then there's the nameless Shaper, who created the land itself, but She is otherwise little known. Gaiva is also said to be the ancestor of all the other minor Powers... and there are a lot of them."

There was more, of course, but he didn't need to know that Gaiva Herself was believed to have guided the original settlers to this base. In fact, the staff's power stemmed from Gaiva, too, though Zelle had a hard time matching the images of the benevolent mother goddess with the staff's caustic voice. Admittedly, the Changers were also claimed to have access to part of Gaiva's power for the purposes of protecting the Crown by means of assassinating Zeuten's enemies, but since the goddess Herself had long since vanished from the world, She had no input in how humans wielded what was left of Her magic.

Rien held out a hand. "Let me see the book."

I suppose it can't hurt. They're just fairy tales. Zelle passed him the book, and he flipped it open.

"These are children's stories."

"I told you they were." An idea occurred to her. "Here's an alternative. Have you ever played Relics and Ruins?"

"I don't—"

"Remember," she finished. "I'm told it's one of the few card games which crossed the sea from Aestin to Zeuten and the rules have more or less stayed the same for centuries. Anyway, I think I have a set of cards somewhere in here." She crossed the room to her pack and rummaged through it, while he continued to thumb through the book.

Her pack contained little but a few changes of clothes

and some food, but they'd run out of supplies if they were stuck here for more than another day or two. Should she really be entertaining her companion's whims when they had more pressing matters at hand?

You already know the answer to that, the staff said from where she'd left it propped against the wall.

She shot it a glare and whispered, "Stop reading my thoughts when I'm not addressing you. It's rude."

She'd assumed the crackle of the fire drowned out her words, but Rien looked up from his book and then walked to her side. He halted next to the staff, briefly examining its knotted wooden surface. "This is no ordinary walking stick, is it?"

"No." How much to tell him? If he'd seen Relics before, the revelation wouldn't be a surprise, but there was no telling how he'd react when she said *which* deity its magic came from. Her family held the only known Relics with a direct link to Gaiva Herself, while none existed in Aestin at all, and She was the only one of the three Great Powers believed to even *have* Relics remaining in the human realm. Who was to say he wouldn't attempt to pry it from her grasp?

"One of *them* is in there," he went on.

"Partly." She chose her words carefully, explaining to him as if he was a curious child. "Relics contain a portion of a deity's power. The Powers themselves aren't believed to have set foot in this realm in centuries, so the only traces of them remain in the Relics they left behind."

"A Relic." He lifted his head. "Yes. I think that's what I came here to find."

Zelle's heart sank. *Oh no.* "Did someone tell you about a legendary Relic buried somewhere in the mountains which would grant you anything you desired, or some-thing along those lines?"

He was silent for a moment. Then—"Yes."

Curse it. I should have known. There were too many wily merchants wandering around the coastal towns looking for foreigners to ensnare. Rien was a walking target, and it would explain why he had had no coin in his pockets. *He was swindled. He must have been.* It didn't explain why he'd left Aestin in the first place, of course... nor how he'd lost his memories.

"I don't know what they teach you in Aestin, but the lost Relic is a myth," she informed him. "It doesn't exist. My family have lived in the Range for generations and have never seen so much as a hint of any Relics. There's magic inside the Sanctum, true, but that's all."

"What about the staff, then?" he asked. "You implied that was a Relic."

"Yes, the Sentinels are the closest Zeuten has to Aestinian magicians," she replied. "Or Invokers, as you call them. Our own Relics are the last in the country, though I frequently have to stop tourists getting themselves killed looking for the mythical ones from the stories every time I come to visit the Range. They generally either give up or die in the attempt."

She hoped he wouldn't take that as a challenge. The image of those two tourists returned to the forefront of her mind, along with the messenger she'd found slain in the forest. She never did find out who'd killed him.

"I know why I came here." He spoke with renewed certainty. "Perhaps the Relic is the reason I lost my memory."

She stifled a sceptical snort. "Look, the stories have

been around for centuries. They sprang up as a result of the mountains being uninhabited for centuries before the Zeutenians first settled here and the fact that the region is said to be the last place in the realm that the nameless Shaper created. There are dragonets, magical beasts, constructs... but no Relics."

"What does the staff do, precisely?" he asked.

Talks to me in an unhelpful manner, she thought.

Aloud, she said, "A Reader can use the staff's magic to trace an object's history. If you gave them an object that belongs to you, the Reader would be able to trace exactly where it came from and therefore work out your identity. Any object. Like that medallion of yours."

Rien's expression shifted from confident to perplexed when Zelle pointed at the string around his neck, just visible under his collar. He took it in hand, examining the medallion, his brow furrowing. "I don't think this is mine."

"You've been wearing it since you arrived," she said. "That suggests it's yours. Unless you stole it."

"No," he said, his tone clear and certain. "I didn't steal it."

"Do you have anything that originally belonged to you?" She hadn't found anything when she'd searched him for weapons except for those cheap knives. Zelle wasn't sure if her sister could use her Reading magic without an object belonging to the person. Even Grandma might struggle.

Rien said nothing. His right hand had clenched over his left, and for some reason, she remembered him making the same odd motion earlier. "If I knew, I wouldn't be here. Where is your grandmother?"

She considered him for a moment. Even if he'd once known of her grandmother, he'd forgotten her along with everything else. Did it matter if he knew the truth, especially if he might be able to help her? "She's missing."

He regarded her for a moment. "Does she have a successor? You mentioned one."

"My sister can use the staff, too, but she's at the other outpost."

"Then we'll see her," he said decisively.

"You'll wave a hand and the storm will go away, will it?" She rolled her eyes at him. "We'll have to wait until morning at the very least unless we want to meet an unpleasant end. You almost died coming here, in case you've forgotten."

It struck her that she was being a little harsh on him, but worry gnawed at her insides at the prospect of being stuck here for a day or more with her grandmother's whereabouts unknown.

His eyes narrowed, his grip loosening on the storybook. "You're quite obnoxious, you know, and frankly condescending, for that matter. What's to stop me finding the information myself?"

A flush crept up her face. "Nothing aside from whatever caused the Powers' names to vanish before your eyes. Besides, this is the Sentinels' quarters, not an inn or a public library."

"I gathered," said Rien, his lip curling in a manner that didn't fit with the way he'd behaved until now. "Then we'll wait out the storm, and I will speak to the Sentinel's heir in the morning."

You're welcome. She managed to refrain from saying the words aloud. Instead, Zelle left Rien with the storybook and took the staff with her into her grandmother's bedroom, more to get out of his line of sight than anything else. The sight of the dust-covered furniture unnerved her all over again, while the staff looked doubly out of place in her hand and not in its owner's.

"What do you have to say?" she whispered to the staff. "You're being quiet."

I thought you wanted to speak to your guest. You're clearly getting on well.

"Hilarious," she said. "He wants to speak to Aurel, but that's not happening if the weather is against us. Can't you banish the storm?"

I'm designed to defend the Sentinels. I can't control the weather conditions.

"You also can't find Grandma, allegedly." She jabbed the tip of the staff into the wooden floor of her grandmother's room. She hadn't left anything else behind at all. "You know leaving the outpost means I'll have to bring you with me, don't you? Unless you're happy to stay with the gremlins instead."

It's him. He's attracting the trouble. Take him with you and the problem will leave.

"Of course he is." She drew in a breath. "The storm too?"

Maybe.

"Then perhaps I'll throw you outside and see if you can figure it out."

What do you want me to say? The storm is a magical creation?

"It *is*, isn't it?" *Aha.* "So—he created it himself and blew out his memories in the process, did he?"

How should I know? He has no Relic of his own. In Aestin, that means he is less magical than a rock.

Regardless, if he hadn't caused the storm himself, then it wasn't a stretch to say he'd brought it with him. The question was, had he seen her grandmother before he'd lost his memories? He'd come here seeking the Sentinel, or someone who knew of the lost Relic at any rate... or so he claimed.

"He's heard the rumours of the lost Relic, too," she muttered. "Where would an Aestinian get that idea?"

Stories spread. Even when books cage them, the words slip out and into waiting ears.

"I wish someone would retire that particular story," she said. "Because there is no Relic. Not the one in the stories, anyway."

Besides, it made no sense for him to have sailed across the ocean then hiked across Zeuten to the Range in pursuit of a legend that most believed to be nonsense. If he'd wanted power, the logical step would surely be to seek out a source of magic in his own country. Not unlike the Sentinels, most of Aestin's magicians preferred to pass their Relics through the family lines, so perhaps he'd missed out on that particular inheritance, but coming to a foreign country was even less likely to yield results. Let alone one with as little magic as Zeuten.

If it stops him from griping at you, it's best to let him have his way.

"He's not a child. He's a snooty foreigner with no memory and an elevated sense of self-importance." She tapped the staff on the floor again. "Do you trust him, then? What kind of magic would have stripped him of his memories?"

The Sanctum's defences are designed to act against a threat, so they might have sensed his intentions and neutralised them.

"Wait, you think the *Sanctum* blocked his memory?" Zelle asked. "Wouldn't it be easier just to kick him out?"

It's a more pleasant alternative to letting him die in the storm.

The storm. Which might well be the result of a spell itself... perhaps a spell someone had placed on the stranger to ensure he never left the mountains alive. It was as good a guess as any, and it further implied that his presence put her at risk. Still, if the Sanctum had indeed been responsible for his memory loss, then she wanted to find out why.

7

A fter sitting on the cliff's edge for a long moment to catch her breath, Evita looked at the dragonet crouching beside her. "Can you speak?"

The dragonet made an odd squeaking sound. No, then. *It might be magical, but it's not human.* As for why it'd helped her... that was a mystery. Maybe it'd believed it owed her for saving it from certain death under the wyrm's fangs.

She felt for the reassuringly round shape of the token in her pocket and shakily pushed to her feet. Over her dead body was she going back through the cave, so she'd need to find another route back to the starting point to hand the cloak of Changing over to the next recruit. Master Amery would not be thrilled at her for using the wrong exit, but she'd be dead if she hadn't run out of the cave. She ought to have still passed the trial, since she'd left the cave with the token. That ought to convince the Master to let her transgression slide, right?

Evita found a rocky path hugging the mountainside

that she sincerely hoped would lead her back to her starting point. Out of any other ideas, she began to walk with one hand on the cliff's side for balance. As she did so, the dragonet launched into flight, its wings casting a shadow from above.

"Why are you following me?"

No answer came, of course. Perhaps the dragonet was worried the wyrm would come back to finish it off unless it stuck closer to its rescuer. Armed with a view from underneath, she identified it as a juvenile male. Other than that, her experience was limited to sheep and chickens, not mythical mountain beasts. The dragonet's short stubby wings looked hardly capable of supporting his own weight, and each strong gust of wind threatened to blow him off course.

Wait. Why am I calling it 'him'?

If she wasn't careful, she'd end up giving him a name, which would only make her feel more obligated to let the creature follow her. As tempting as the idea might be, putting an innocent creature in the path of the Master's fury was not an appealing notion.

The dragonet flew down, hovering close behind her, and a surge of pity hit her. The two had already helped each other once, and she hadn't a single friend among the assassins. Who was she to turn her back on someone who'd saved her life?

Ah, damn. She beckoned to the creature with her free hand and carried on down the path, which soon brought her within sight of the shivering group of novices perched on the cliff outside the cave. They hadn't noticed her, and it struck her that they probably thought she was dead. The impulse seized her to take the cloak and run while she had the chance, but where could she possibly go? Her village was a pile of ashes, down to the last house. Besides, she'd come here for a reason, and she'd sworn not to run away again.

Halting, she turned to her new companion. "You have to leave. Stay out of sight, or else the others will see you."

She'd prefer not to find out what the other recruits would do if they set eyes on her companion. Use him for target practise, probably.

The dragonet squeaked then flapped his spindly wings and flew upwards out of sight. Feeling a slight pang of regret, Evita turned back to the path and the inevitable punishment that awaited when she showed her face in front of Master Amery. Hopefully, it wouldn't be too heinous. From her observations so far, the actual death rates amongst candidates didn't seem to be as high as the rumours had suggested, but crippling injuries accounted for at least half the dropouts. She had no intention of becoming one of them, so if the Master turned on her, she'd have to break her word and run after all. Especially with Vekka still lounging among his followers, smirking to himself as though amused at her apparent demise.

After the wyrm, Vekka hardly compared as a threat. Evita cleared the short distance between herself and the others, and then she whipped off the cloak. "Having fun?"

Several people jumped. Even Vekka jerked back from the cliff's edge with an oath, while the Master whirled on her.

"You!" Master Amery's eyes bored into hers. "What kind of trick was that? Did you cheat?"

"No, Master." She removed the token from her pocket,

draping the cloak over her arm. "I took a wrong turn in the cave."

"The cave is far too small to get lost in," he growled. "I think you're lying."

"I'm not. How else could I have found my way back here?" When he continued to scowl at her, she added, "The wyrm woke up and chased me to the back of the cave. I had to escape through a gap in the back wall, otherwise the wyrm might have followed me. I didn't think you'd want it roaming out here."

"Wyrm?" asked one of the novices who had yet to complete the challenge.

"Give me that." Master Amery all but snatched the cloak out of her hand and threw it at the next novice. "And get out of my sight."

"The token?" She held up the round, gleaming stone, but Master Amery was already turning away to haul the next unfortunate novice towards the cave.

Sidestepping him, Evita joined the others who'd survived the trial and picked a spot that wasn't anywhere near Vekka. A cold breeze swept overhead, making her shiver, and she fervently hoped the dragonet had hidden himself out of sight. Despite his annoyance, at least the Master hadn't failed her outright.

Tucking the token into the pocket of her thin cloak, she rested her back against a rock and tried her best not to look over at the cliff's edge. Truth be told, after the wyrm, the sheer drop didn't unnerve her nearly as much as before, but that didn't mean she was looking forwards to the walk down to the base.

"What did you really do?" whispered the boy on her left. "Did you sneak off and explore the mountains alone?"

"No," she murmured. "I took a shortcut."

"Some shortcut that was." Vekka spoke from somewhere on the boy's other side. "You took twice as long as the others. Thought you were dead."

She heard *pity you weren't* in his words, and several of his friends exchanged snickers. At any other time, she might have challenged him, but she had little energy to preserve for the climb down and a dwindling supply of luck. Luck had been more responsible for her survival than any Power that might dwell within the mountains, though it'd been the dragonet who'd looked out for her in that cave, not the deities.

The mutters died out as another, taller boy stepped lithely around their group and came to sit in front of Evita, his long legs dangling over the cliff's edge. "Hey, Evita. I'm glad you got through the trial."

"Hmm," came her eloquent reply. She ought to have known Ruben would take an interest in her strange detour, and sure enough, he inched closer to her.

"How'd you get back here?" he whispered. "Is there a secret? I won't tell anyone."

His tone carried a suggestive hint, and her heart sank. His flirting had started almost from her first day with the Changers and had only increased the less attention she paid. She'd been dreading the moment when it inevitably came to a head and he wanted answers from her that she couldn't give. If it was anything like what had happened with her former best friend, Tansel, she could say farewell to their burgeoning friendship, such as it was—except at least Tansel hadn't been an assassin-in-training.

"Nothing," she answered. "The wyrm chased me to the back of the cave, and I found another way out."

"Stop talking," snapped Master Amery, and they all fell into silence.

Relieved, Evita returned to contemplating where the dragonet might have come from in the first place, while doing her level best to avoid looking at the drop.

When the final contender had left the cave, the novices travelled back to the Changers' base at the foot of the mountain. Only two among their number had failed the trial—and both had fled the cave rather than risk being chewed on by the wyrm. Evita might have saved a couple of lives when she'd accidentally let the nature of the challenge slip in front of the remaining novices, and despite the day not *quite* going as planned, she'd passed the test and evaded a nasty fall to a grim death. As far as she was concerned, that was enough reason to celebrate.

Master Amery never had requested the token back, so she decided to consider it a trophy of sorts and kept it in her pocket throughout the climb. At long last, they reached the camp at the foot of the mountain where the novices spent most of their time. The lone building in the area was the single-storey wood-frame building where the Masters lived, and even that was rather austere. Compared to the freezing caves where the novices slept on their thin cloaks on the hard floor, though, its wooden walls looked positively luxurious.

Evita's insides growled as the smell of cooking drifted across the camp, and a familiar ache clamped her lungs when the inevitable sense of homesickness returned. She waited for dismissal and tried not to think of her old life. Waking to the smell of her mother's cooking and the sound of her father's chatter as he brought in the day's catch seemed as distant as the stars, even if they lingered on in her mind while she listened to Master Amery's grumblings. Her life before joining the Changers hadn't been perfect, of course. There'd been floods and storms and fallen trees and freak accidents, but it brought a bitter taste to her mouth to know that she'd only attained the chance for the adventure she'd always craved after her home had been scorched to ruins.

In fact, her wandering tendencies had saved her life that day. She'd been swimming in the sea early in the morning when she'd glimpsed someone approaching the shore. Since the figure appeared to be walking *on* the water, he'd immediately drawn her attention, and she'd hastened to warn the villagers.

Nobody had believed her, not even her parents, but she'd returned to the beach to watch for any signs of the strange figure. When the boy had reached the shore farther down the coast, the screams drifting across the sea had sent her running with a second warning. This one they'd believed, but it was too late.

The creature was already upon them.

As the first buildings had caught ablaze, she'd swum across the estuary to safety, hoping her fellow villagers would follow—but nobody had. She'd wandered through the woodland, alone, before she'd stumbled upon the gutted ruins of the neighbouring village on the coast. That was when she'd known there was no point in turning back.

Chattering voices brought her back to the present as the other recruits dispersed at Master Amery's command. She had no desire to return to the caves, so she walked around the camp instead, picking a winding path that stayed firmly on ground level instead of taking her up the mountainside. The thought occurred to her to look for the dragonet, but she highly doubted the beast had followed her all the way back here. Not if he had any sense, anyway.

As she walked, she spotted Vekka and his friends sitting on some nearby rocks, shooting arrows at passing birds, so she veered off down another path where she might get some peace. Most routes eventually ended up back at Saudenne, which was where the more ambitious of her fellow recruits had come from. The capital of Zeuten was said to produce the best Changers, perhaps because living on the streets of the city required a special kind of cunning. She'd debated staying there herself, for a bit, but she'd make a terrible pickpocket. She'd failed to sneak up on a wyrm while wearing a Changer's cloak, after all, and between living on the streets and sleeping in a cave, the cave narrowly won out. Even if the odds of having her throat slit in the night were about even…

A shadow crossed her path and brought her to a halt. A strange man—boy, really—stepped in front of her. He had startlingly blue eyes, brighter than she'd ever seen before, and wore finery which looked out of place against the austere backdrop.

"I want to speak to your Master." He spoke an odd accent that she couldn't place, his words bringing her to a halt. "It's a matter of great urgency."

"Who are you?" she asked.

"Nobody of your concern."

By the Powers, those eyes were bright. Almost unnatural. "He's busy."

She didn't know if he was, but she doubted Master Amery wanted to be disturbed by an oddly dressed child who spoke in a strange accent. His pale skin suggested he was from the northern regions of Zeuten or perhaps the Isles of Itzar, but the formal cadence to his voice gave the impression of someone older than he appeared. And the way he dressed suggested he belonged to the nobility, which made no sense. Unless...

Powers above, was she talking to a representative of the Crown? Had someone finally come to check up on the Crown's elite assassins? That didn't sound right, either, especially given his evident youth.

"Do I have to emphasise my point?" His gaze bored into her. "I want to speak to your Master."

The breath drained from Evita's lungs. She looked into his eyes, and she saw oblivion. "I..."

"Take me to him," he ordered. "Now."

———

Master Amery sat in his tiny office in the Changers' base, cursing the Powers and the Crown alike for putting him in charge of these useless recruits. *Damned novices. They'll be dead in a year, the lot of them, and good riddance.*

He tapped his fingers against the desk, surveying the stack of papers on its wooden surface. Letters to the Crown Prince, mostly, asking for financial aid. The royal family seemed indifferent to the need to send supply carts this far up into the mountains, and while he had more than enough hapless recruits to run errands, it would be nice to have a little respect for once. The Crown Prince of all people ought to understand that they needed to confine themselves to this region to maintain their repetition as elusive, mysterious, and dangerous. More crucially, they needed the magic present here in the mountains to effectively train using the cloaks of Changing.

A knock sounded against the wooden surface of the door. He growled through his teeth, "Come in."

A novice slipped into the room, tall and gangly and forgettable. Her dark hair was a windswept tangle, and he vaguely recognised her as the recruit who'd nearly absconded with the Changers' cloak during the day's trials. What was her name again?

"There's someone here to see you," she told him. "Says it's urgent."

"Tell them to go away."

She fiddled with a loose thread on her coat. "He says he's important. I think he is... and dangerous too."

Master Amery paused for a moment. He'd been moments from devising a suitable punishment for insubordination, but the girl appeared more afraid of this *visitor* than she did of him. Now, that wouldn't do at all.

"Send him in, then. If he's not important, you'll be sleeping outside tonight."

"Yes, Master."

The girl slipped out of the room while Master Amery watched, his suspicion rising. Not only had she behaved improperly during the test, but she seemed to have no understanding of how to comport oneself as a representative of the Crown. Many of the Changers were recruited from distant villages, like her, but she acted disinterested at best. Her work with a bow was appalling, as was her habit of getting into fistfights with her fellow recruits. He'd been sure she'd cheated during the test, and he resolved to keep a closer watch on her. He'd catch her out next time.

Another rap on the door drew his attention. "Come in."

He fixed a derisive expression on his face, intending to put this unwelcome visitor in their place. A young man strode into the room, dressed in finery the likes of which Master Amery hadn't seen outside of the Royal Palace. Red and gold embroidery covered a cloak clasped with buckles, and his black boots had been polished so fiercely he could almost see his reflection in them. But it was the seal on the arm of his cloak that rendered the Master wordless, for it depicted a circle of red thorns. That was the seal of Astiva, the Power which belonged to the Astera Family—the most prominent family in Aestin and the most powerful magicians in the world.

"State your name." Master Amery did his best to keep the apprehension out of his voice. The most elite families in Aestin had no reason to consult the Changers, so why would Volcan Astera send an emissary here, of all places? Why not go directly to the Crown Prince himself if he wanted to discuss diplomatic matters?

"My name is not of consequence." The boy spoke in a voice surprisingly chilling for such a baby-faced creature.

The Master frowned at him. "Why do you wear the Astera seal? You serve the noble house, am I correct?"

"The noble house is no more," said the boy, in the same matter-of-fact tone. "The master of the house is dead, and I thought it was a shame to let these fine clothes perish in the fire that devoured his home."

"He—what?" Amery looked at him blankly, quite unable to conceal his surprise. *Dead?* He'd thought Volcan

Astera was invincible. *Did you kill him?* he almost asked, but this boy... no, he couldn't have been capable of such a thing. He didn't carry Astera's staff, for a start, even if he seemed to have pillaged his wardrobe. Schooling his features into an expression of mild surprise, he went on. "Pity. I'm told the Astera family's cache of Power was deeper than any in the nation."

"They do not lie. You might call it fathomless." The boy was positively grinning now. In any other circumstances, Amery would have clipped him around the ear for impertinence and possibly left him overnight on a glacier, just to drive home the lesson, but the boy's revelation had knocked him off-balance. This child must have been close to the scene of his death if he'd managed to steal Astera's clothing, but who was it that now wielded the staff of Astiva?

"What is your purpose here?" If this boy was deceiving him, then Master Amery would ensure he paid dearly, no matter what kind of magic he might have. *We have magic, too, boy. You're on our territory, and we will protect the Crown by any means necessary.*

"Power," said the boy, in tones that brought a chill to Master Amery's skin. "I hear it runs through the mountains like blood through a person's veins. That is what I seek."

"The Changers alone are able to use the magic of these mountains," Master Amery told him. "If you wish to hire one of my assassins, I will gladly dispatch them anywhere you see fit. Do you have enemies?"

If the boy named an enemy or two, Amery might be able to discern his identity through the process of elimination. The number of families who had access to the strongest Powers was limited, after all, and he knew all their names.

"There is a particular individual who has been eluding me for weeks, and I have grown impatient," the boy replied. "So has my master."

"Your master?"

The stranger smiled chillingly. "We wish to engage your services to dispose of this individual."

Master Amery's fingers trembled, ever so slightly, as he picked up a piece of fresh parchment before dipping his pen in the inkwell on the desk. "The name?"

"Arien Astera."

Master Amery's hand froze midmotion. "You said the Astera family died, did you not?"

"One of them slipped through our clutches," said the boy. "Several witnesses confirmed that they saw the Astera family's youngest son leaving the country on a ship bound for Zeuten. We believed him to have hidden himself in Saudenne, but he's proven quite impossible to find, and we've recently obtained evidence that he might have come to the mountains. He's powerless, of course, but my master will not risk being challenged."

Powers above. If this master of his had been the one who'd killed the rest of the Astera family, he was a dangerous man indeed. Exactly the kind of individual Master Amery usually delighted in doing business with. He'd killed many a nobleman's son or daughter in his time but nobody from the major families of Aestin. The Crown Prince would never have asked him to risk a war with their magic-rich neighbour by taking sides in their power struggles. The Crown maintained a friendly relationship with the Aestinians, but everyone knew the

Invokers were the real seat of authority, not the Emperor.

All the same, this Astera boy might have some magical talent remaining, and Master Amery had absolutely no intention of risking any of his top recruits on someone who'd once held the staff of Astiva in his hands. Conversely, if this Astera child was truly as powerless as the boy claimed, he might not need to send in a full-fledged assassin at all. Not at first, anyway.

He finished writing down the name. "And his presumed location? You must know the Range is rather extensive."

"Don't you condescend to me." He slammed a palm on the desk, and a blast of wind struck, pinning Amery to his seat.

Master Amery couldn't speak a word. *He has access to magic of his own. Powers above, how did a mere child get his hands on such power?*

"I... I need to know where to send my assassins." Master Amery hadn't spoken with a tremor in his voice since his father had beaten his stuttering habit out of him as a child. "If, that is, you know the general area where this young Astera might be hiding."

Astera. The name inspired at least as much awe as the name of the Changers, among those who knew what it stood for. How could Volcan Astera be dead? He'd thought the man was immortal, or as close to as possible for a human. Thorn-hand, they'd called him.

Who carried Astiva's staff now?

The boy studied him coldly, his eyes such an intense shade of blue. "The ship young Astera was travelling on fell victim to an unfortunate act of nature. We believed him dead, but it sounds as though the Powers protected him somehow, and he made it to shore. He can't have travelled far from Saudenne."

"Saudenne is a fair distance from here." The Changers made their home at the very end of the Range, but on foot, it still took several days to travel there unless they used their Changer's cloaks to fly. The novices, of course, had to walk until they earned that right, but he still shied away from the notion of sending away one of his more valuable assassins. "We deal in death, not searching for missing persons."

He quailed as the boy raised a hand and several shards of ice formed in front of his palm. Sharp as glass fragments, they hovered inches from Amery's petrified face.

"I'll send someone, right away," he breathed. "On Gaiva's name, I swear it."

"That vow will soon mean very little." Yet the boy lowered his hand, and the shards immediately melted. Water droplets soaked the papers on Amery's desk, but better that than his own blood. He hardly took in the boy's next words. "You will dispatch an assassin immediately, and you have one week to deliver the body of Arien Astera directly to me. I am staying at the following address." He placed a fragment of parchment imprinted with an address in Saudenne in spiky handwriting upon the desk.

"Saudenne?" read Master Amery, his voice sounding odd, distant. "You're staying in Saudenne yourself?"

"Yes, I am," replied the stranger. "I have a rather unpopular reputation among the smaller inns, so I decided to dip into the Astera family's coffers and find more appropriate lodgings."

Light-headedness swept over the Master, and he wondered if he might faint. "Do... do you know what the young Astera might have come to the mountains to find?"

Few ventured to the Range without a plan. Of course, he'd heard many tales of tourists meeting unfortunate ends, but this boy was running away, not seeking adventure.

"I believe the young Astera will be in search of magical assistance," said the child. "He has no power remaining of his own, after all."

He doesn't. He could still be dangerous, though, and even the most elite of the Changers would be hard-pressed to take on an Aestinian Invoker in combat. No, stealthily taking him out was their best option.

"So he's likely to come here?" Master Amery asked.

"No," the boy said. "If he seeks any kind of Power, he'll search for the very best."

Ordinarily, Master Amery would have been insulted at the insinuation that his Changers weren't worthy, but he could hardly summon up a retort.

"We *are* the best that Zeuten has to offer." Inwardly, he cursed the tremor in his voice. "We select only the most promising to join our ranks."

Admittedly, the last part was a lie. Standards had slipped somewhat, though he fully intended on culling half the novices before the summer was over. Half the rest would meet a sorry end when winter came. That wouldn't help him replenish the dwindling higher ranks, though, and he wouldn't give up any of them to this futile hunt. Neither would he forfeit his own life to this boy and his strange, terrifying power. Who else had magic on this gods-forsaken continent? He cast his mind around and recalled his last formal meeting with the Royal Family, in which an elderly woman had reprimanded him for some reason or other and had hit him in the kneecaps with her staff. A Relic...

The Sentinels. The last descendants of the original settlers in Zeuten. The old woman might not even be alive, for all he knew, but he was fairly sure her family had made their home elsewhere near the Range. If the Astera boy wanted magic, they'd be his first point of contact.

"Then you should have no trouble finding him," said the stranger. "Send your assassin and dispatch the target within a week. I will be waiting."

Master Amery heard the unspoken promise beneath those words, because he'd used the same tone often enough himself. *By the Powers.* This boy was dangerous, and his master must be worse, but he couldn't shake the feeling that he'd agreed to a fool's errand. Chasing the son of the most powerful family in Aestin seemed a spectacular way to end up dead or worse. On the other hand, the young Astera was a stranger in a foreign country, and he would doubtlessly leave behind a conspicuous trail. If anyone had seen an Aestinian in this isolated region, people would talk.

"And..." He hesitated. "What if the assassin fails in their task? If Astera kills them instead?"

"Then send me their name, and I will have them punished accordingly... if they survive." The boy turned back, treating Master Amery to another flicker of those cold blue eyes. "I will be waiting in Saudenne."

Master Amery nodded, thinking hard. Who could he spare? Certainly not his best; the majority of them were off fighting raiders in the Isles of Itzar on behalf of the

Crown. The rest would need to watch for more potential trouble from Aestin, since the balance of the families had presumably altered after its Power changed hands. He knew nothing of the new wielder of Astiva, of course, but they must have uncommon skill to have bested the Astera family. It wouldn't do to make an enemy of them, but it would take several days to make contact with the elite Changers, and there were no guarantees any would return within a week as the boy demanded.

As today's trial had made clear, he *did* have an excessive number of wet-nosed overeager novices keen to prove themselves. One would need to seek out the Sentinel, for a start, to ask for her assistance in tracking Astera. Once they had his location, he could send any number of novices to perform the actual deed. If any of them died in the attempt, then another would take their place. As long as he picked novices who wouldn't be missed if they failed... and whose background would give them little choice but to obey his commands to their bloody conclusion.

A face came to mind. The newest recruit, who'd returned late from her trial with a look in her eyes that he didn't like. Where better to start than with someone he already wanted out of his sight? "I think I can provide the perfect candidate."

8

Closing the bedroom door behind her, Zelle returned to the main room. From the armchair, Rien gave her a curious look. "Who were you talking to?"

"Nobody," she lied. "I think the storm is magical in nature."

He rose to his feet and crossed the room to the window, surveying the mass of whiteness outside. "It is?"

"Did anyone follow you here?" she asked. "From Aestin?"

Maybe that was why he wanted the Relic—to defend himself against whatever or whoever had pursued him— but even then, he'd come on a false errand. Rien was silent for a moment, contemplating the flurries of snowflakes. "You said your grandmother disappeared?"

"Yes," she replied. "I arrived at the outpost to find her gone, shortly before you showed up."

Since he hadn't been near the outpost at the time, he couldn't have caused her disappearance, but if someone had conjured the storm to prevent him reaching his goal, had they also targeted her grandmother in the process?

Rien remained quiet for a long moment. "I have no memory of anything before I reached this place. If someone followed me..."

"You wouldn't know," she finished. "I thought not."

That didn't mean it was untrue, of course, which left her in a dilemma. As long as he had no memory of his past, she could only guess how much of the current situation was his fault. She'd already made the choice not to throw him back into the storm, but was she right in treating him as an ally?

Rien remained by the window, saying nothing, so Zelle walked into the guest room and whispered to the staff, "If he made Grandma disappear, now's the time to tell me."

No, he didn't.

The clicking sound of a door opening echoed, and Zelle ran out of the guest room as a rattling gust of wind swept into the main room.

He's opened the door. The fool!

She ran to the door to find Rien staring into the heavy snowdrift blocking the tower's entrance.

"What in Gaiva's name are you *doing*?" she called to him.

"There's someone outside."

Zelle cursed expressively. She couldn't even see past the thick snow, but she reached over his shoulder and yanked the door closed.

Or tried to. The wind snatched the door from her grasp, causing her to overbalance straight into the wall of snow. Wetness soaked through her clothing, while her vision filled with white. Coughing, she backed up a step and raised the staff, as if to sweep the blizzard aside.

To her astonishment, the next blast of wind *did* clear the whiteness before her eyes, revealing the rocky path winding away from the tower... and three figures standing there, watching the tower as though waiting to be invited in.

No... they weren't standing but instead hovered above the path, tall and translucent and not even close to human. They resembled blurred smudges on the path, drawing closer with each blink of her eyes.

Zelle's legs had turned to blocks of ice, unable to move, and a flicker of alarm travelled through her when Rien stepped past her, striding down the path towards the approaching figures. As he did, they stirred, their bearing becoming more humanlike as three arms, three hands, three fingers pointed directly at Rien.

Three voices echoed, speaking one syllable: "You."

"What kind of monstrosities are you?" Rien demanded, sounding nothing like himself. Zelle swayed on the spot, convinced that she was seeing things, or having a *very* vivid dream.

Yes. I'm dreaming. That's it.

She didn't really believe it, but the thought unstuck her legs, allowing her to walk down the path to stand beside Rien.

"You can't come in here," she told the shadowy figures. "This tower belongs to the Sentinels, at the behest of the Great Powers themselves. Whatever you are, you have to leave."

The shadowy figures pointed at Rien again and chorused, "He is ours."

Someone had sent them after him. *I knew it.*

"That, I very much doubt."

What in the name of the Powers were these creatures? She'd seen nothing like them in the Sanctum before, yet the staff in her hands remained awfully quiet when the three figures moved closer, leaving no imprint in the snow.

A shiver rattled her teeth in her skull, but she forced her jaws apart. "Leave, in the name of the Sentinels."

"You are not the Sentinel." They seemed to turn towards her, their indistinct forms shifting, and icy cold washed over her as if she'd plunged into a fathomless snowdrift. These creatures must have come for Rien and taken her grandmother in the process, and they knew she was no threat to them. She gripped the staff in both hands, though its wooden surface felt too solid to leave an imprint on creatures that seemed to be made entirely of shadow or fog.

Rien had other ideas. He vanished into the tower behind her, and when he emerged, he carried a stick in his hand, its end alight with flames. He must have jabbed it into the fireplace until it caught ablaze—but even in the past few moments, the creatures had moved farther up the path, closer to the tower.

Rien ran straight past Zelle, brandishing the burning stick. A rebuke died on Zelle's lips, because the creatures recoiled from the flames with inhuman hissing noises. It seemed they were not fond of fire, and they slithered back down the path to avoid the heat of the flames.

Rien grabbed her shoulder. "We need to get inside. They're magical constructs. As soon as we leave their line of sight, they won't know where we are."

"How do *you* know that?" He'd had no knowledge of the magical constructs they'd encountered in the Sanctum, but the man who stood beside her seemed a total stranger compared to the person she'd been dealing with earlier. Regardless, she pulled out of his grip, unwilling to turn her back on the creatures in case they slipped into the tower when their backs were turned.

"I've seen them before." He spoke in a low voice. "They're wraiths, I think... constructs designed for a purpose. They can only obey basic commands."

If he spoke true, then had *they* taken her grandmother? How could mere constructs have laid a finger on the Sentinel, especially when she was armed with her staff? Or had they meant the person who was commanding them was responsible for her disappearance? "I'm not leaving them outside."

She grabbed the flaming stick from Rien's grip and gave it a swing in the direction of the wraiths. The fire made the three figures recoil once again, and an idea struck her. Drawing back her arm, she threw the stick at the snow, where it landed near the wraiths' feet.

As she'd hoped, they drifted back down the path, vanishing amid the haze of the storm. The stick wouldn't burn forever, but a lantern would do the job nicely instead.

Glancing over her shoulder, she saw Rien had withdrawn into the tower. She gripped the staff and whispered, "He was the wraiths' target, wasn't he? Whoever he is, he pissed off someone important and then conveniently forgot who it was."

No answer came, but she'd have time enough to ask questions later. For now, she ran to the tower herself and went upstairs to grab a lantern from the Sanctum. She'd have preferred to leave the doors firmly locked, but it couldn't be helped. Every moment it took to unlatch the door gave the wraiths another chance to approach the tower, and while she had ample experience with magical constructs, she'd never seen ones designed with such purpose before.

Lantern in hand, she returned to find Rien waiting for her at the foot of the stairs. "They're after me. I brought them here."

Yes, you did. She didn't speak the words aloud, but he seemed to hear them all the same, because he held out a hand for the lantern.

She gave it to him. "Put the lantern directly in front of the door."

He obeyed, while she released a shaky breath. If not for the snowstorm, whoever had sent these constructs might have come in person... but who was to say they hadn't sent the storm too? She bit her tongue when a gust of wind entered through the partly open door, then glared at the staff. "You're useless. What would you do if we'd got killed, eh? Sit and watch?"

The staff made no response. Then she saw Rien had returned and was looking directly at her. Oh, Powers. He probably thought she was talking to him.

"Not you," she clarified. "Close the door. If it's true that they'll give up if they can't see us, then if we don't open the door again, they might go away."

She didn't believe it would be that simple, not for an instant. The wind roared outside, rattling the door in its frame, and Zelle had the vivid mental image of the lantern toppling off the cliff's edge. If the storm came from the same source as the wraiths... this wasn't over. Not at all.

The staff's voice whispered in her ear: *The storm will not abate until he is dead.*

———

Rien spun around when the door shook behind him, trembling within its frame. When he turned back to Zelle, she lifted her head. "The storm is trying to kill you, if you haven't already figured it out. Don't open the door again."

"I wasn't planning to." He followed her as she ran to the window, where the storm seemed to have worsened in the past few moments alone. Whirling clouds battered the tower as though trying to knock it to the ground.

"Powers," Zelle whispered. "What have you brought after us?"

I don't know.

Though he hadn't spoken aloud, she turned on him with her eyes narrowed. "Either those wraiths took my grandmother or the person who was commanding them did. Who was it? A magician—an Invoker?"

Invoker. His blood stirred at the word, and an odd prickling sensation travelled up the fingers of his left hand. As he glanced down, an odd, spidery pattern appeared on the back of his hand, as though the veins glowed beneath the skin. Then he blinked and the impression was gone. When he lifted his head, Zelle gave him a questioning look, though she seemed not to have noticed the strange marks herself.

"Yes," he responded. "Wraiths are constructs, so only someone with a Relic could have summoned them."

Zelle lifted the staff, which she'd propped against the window ledge. "And they conjured the storm too. They must have *really* wanted to be rid of you."

The wind's howls grew in volume, along with the clatter of rocks falling. Or the lantern, perhaps, which wouldn't make any difference if the storm had the same source as the constructs did. His head pounded, as though the wind rattled against the inside of his skull as well as the tower's door.

The next gust of wind caused the door to swing open, inviting a flurry of snowflakes into the room. Instinctively, Rien sprang over to the door and scrambled for the handle, attempting to pull it inwards.

The storm seemed to tug back, as though an invisible figure stood on the other side, intent on entering the tower.

With a desperate lunge, he yanked the door closed and held it there. The wind tugged back, each tremor causing his teeth to rattle in his skull. *Invoker.* That odd feeling came over him again, and as he gripped the door handle, a prickling began in his numb fingers. As if something should be there, within reach... but it wasn't.

Another blast rattled his whole body, and Rien staggered back, letting go of the door. The tingling in his left hand continued with no apparent cause, and his legs felt unsteady beneath him. There was a gaping hole where his memory should be, but that wasn't all that was missing.

A horrible aching sense of loss knocked the breath clean from his lungs, and his vision wavered, darkness sweeping him away.

He stood on a ship's deck, the vessel rocking beneath him as blue-green waves broke against the hull. In the distance, a coastline beckoned, but dark clouds gathered above, growing closer by the moment. Coldness pressed against his chest, and every so often, pain would jolt through his entire body as if a gaping hole within him sapped away at his strength. His hands clenched on the railing, the fading lines on his knuckles reminding him of what he had lost.

He needed to stay alive for long enough to find another Relic. To claim the allegiance of another Power.

The storm broke, the clouds opening like a curtain. Thunder crackled, and raindrops pelted the ship's deck, soaking him to the skin in an instant.

The waves turned rough, tossing the ship between them like children tossing a ball. Two men fell overboard, their screams swallowed in another roar of thunder. He clung to the rail, but the slippery surface grew harder to grip. A short distance away, a whirlpool formed, grabbing small boats and dashing them to pieces, tossing debris upon the waves. There was no way to turn back.

I'm dead, *he thought.*

And yet, somehow, he couldn't accept it. Not after he'd got this far and he'd beaten the odds so many times already.

The ship tilted forwards, and screams mingled with the crashing and crunching sounds of the sea consuming its prey.

"Please," he whispered, pressing himself to the ship's rail as the swirling waters drew closer. "Please, spare me. I'll do anything."

The whirlpool opened its maw and pulled him under.

9

---

*Z*elle saw Rien collapse against the wall, the door handle slipping from his hands, and her heart sank into her shoes. If she didn't think of a plan, they were dead. The wraiths, he'd claimed, would cease their attack if they could no longer see their target, but the storm itself had no such limitations. The door swung open and closed at the wind's behest, while more snow piled in the entryway.

"Do something!" she hissed at the staff, which made no response.

Zelle stepped over Rien's prone form and grabbed the door handle as another blast of air slammed into the wooden surface, as though the mountain itself was trying to shake them off. Zelle pulled the door back into its frame, but she hadn't the strength to hold it shut until the wind ceased its raging.

The staff whispered, *I told you, I can't stop the storm. Magical or not.*

"Then what use are you?" Zelle's gaze fell on the door

19

handle, and an idea occurred to her. She held up the staff, measuring its length against the gap between the door handle and the floor. It should just about fit, and from the way the snow hadn't left a single mark on the staff earlier, it plainly did have some level of defence built into its wooden surface. The staff was a Relic, after all, as unbreakable as the foundations of the earth.

What are you doing?

"Saving our lives." Zelle pushed the staff underneath the door handle and then angled it so that the staff's tip was wedged between the handle and the frame and its base was firmly pressed against the wooden floor. The instant she released it, the wind slammed into the door, causing the staff to tremble... but it held firm.

Breathing hard, she took a step back. The staff would be furious with her for using it in such a disrespectful manner, no doubt, but she'd had no other options available. Rien sat slumped with his back to the wall, and his lips moved, muttering a few inaudible words to himself. She crouched beside him, wondering if he even knew she was there.

"A red book," he slurred, his Zeutenian barely understandable. "A red-bound book with thorns..."

"A book with thorns?" she echoed, nonplussed and a little impressed that he could speak another language while in his current state of semiconsciousness, even if his words made no sense to her. His eyes were closed, and he spoke as if he was in a trance.

"They're dead," he whispered. "They're dead. He killed them."

Chills raced down her spine, and when the door rattled in its frame again, she jumped to her feet. The staff kept the door from flying open, but the chill breeze crept in and made Zelle aware that her clothes were soaked through. So were Rien's, which couldn't be doing his current state any favours.

For the second time that day, Zelle grabbed Rien's shoulders and dragged him closer to the fireplace before collapsing into an armchair. Her whole body ached, while part of her wished she'd simply thrown him outside before he'd brought the mountain crashing down around them. On the other hand, the person who'd sent the storm and the wraiths might know where her grandmother was... which meant there was a good chance that their identity lay within Rien's missing memories.

No wonder the names of the Powers had vanished before him, but why would the outpost have erased his memories when they might have helped her to identify whoever chased him? More to the point, why would a magician have gone to such lengths to find Rien when he held no Relic of his own? Nobody could work magic without one, even in Aestin, though her knowledge of the specifics was hazy. The families of Invokers guarded their secrets at least as well as the Sentinels did, after all.

In any case, she didn't truly believe Rien's intentions were malicious. He'd come here as a last resort, mistaken or not, and he'd little expected to bring this level of chaos with him. He hadn't lied to her.

Rien stirred, sitting upright with an expression of confusion on his face. "What...?"

"Oh, good." Zelle did her best to keep the relief out of her voice. "You're awake."

Rien sat up slowly, rubbing the back of his head. His

eyes were unfocused, but they sharpened as they locked onto her. "What happened?"

"You passed out," she said. "The storm almost killed us both, but I barred the door."

"I did *what?*"

"You fell unconscious and started talking to yourself. You mentioned a red book covered in thorns. And..." She trailed off as he moved, his right hand clenched over the left so tightly that she wondered if it hurt. "And you said someone was dead."

Had he been recalling some part of the memories he'd lost? A red-bound book with thorns was a rather specific image, but the rest of Rien's ramblings were far more worrying.

They're dead. He killed them.

Had he witnessed something so distressing, his mind had somehow erased the whole experience? She'd heard of such things in tales from those who'd been involved in war and horrifying events, but Rien seemed to recall nothing of his life in Aestin at all. Not even his own identity.

"Did I?" His hand unclenched, brushing several strands of dark hair from his eyes. She found her gaze lingering on the medallion around his neck. It *looked* like a Relic, but the staff had told her it wasn't magical. The staff wouldn't lie to her, right?

When she looked up at his face, she caught him staring at her. "What is it?"

"You called me *useless,*" he said. "I'm fluent in your language, you know, and I can tell when you're muttering about me."

"What...?" A flush rose to Zelle's cheeks. "Oh. I wasn't

talking to you. I was talking to my—to my grandmother's staff."

She'd made up her mind: there would be no more secrets between them. If they wanted to survive the storm, they had to be honest with one another.

"You were talking to the staff?" His voice was flat, as if he didn't believe her.

"Yes, I was. Is that so strange?"

"You said you weren't magical. That you had no Relic of your own."

"It's not mine," she said. "It's my grandmother's, and it's sentient enough that I would have expected it to make more of an effort to keep us alive. That's why I yelled at it. Anyway, I did find a way to use it in the end."

"Oh." His gaze went to the staff, which still lay wedged beneath the door handle. "If your grandmother is the wielder, then why did she leave it behind?"

"Even the staff didn't seem to know." Zelle sighed, leaning back in the armchair. "You'd think it would have been more cooperative, since I'm probably the only person who might be able to get it back to Grandma."

"But we're not dead." Rien's gaze swivelled towards the window. "I can't hear the wraiths anymore either."

"They might still be lurking outside." She rubbed her shoulder, sore from where she'd tugged the door shut. "This kind of thing might be second nature where you come from, but I've never seen a wraith before. Do you remember where you learned about them? What exactly are they?"

"Wraiths…" He trailed off, as though searching his thoughts. "I remember they're constructs sent to commit a task, but I can't remember how I learned."

"They were sent by a magician." She eyed the window, a chill racing down her spine. "Invoker, I mean."

"Yes." He inclined his head. "They can only follow basic commands, but they're persistent. They tend to avoid fire, though... I think the heat burns through whatever magic is keeping them alive, so to speak."

She stared at him for a moment. Did they teach every child in Aestin about magic, or had he learned elsewhere? There was no use in asking him specific questions about his education, she knew, and yet curiosity seared her mind all the same.

As for the storm... Zelle found herself hoping it *did* have the same source as the wraiths, because if one foreign magician was too much to deal with, two or more would be downright impossible. The storm might have failed to rip the door open, but it continued to beat away at the windows, as though it intended to reach into the tower itself and grab its target.

Rien.

He saw her watching him. "What is it?"

"You're the target," she said. "Is the storm like those wraiths? I mean, does it have to be able to see you to know your location?"

"Possibly," he acknowledged, "but I've already shown my face outside, and the storm isn't repelled by light or heat. It's not conscious, though, not like the wraiths are. It's likely been designed to persist until..."

"Until you're dead." She thought hard. "Can we convince it you *are* dead?"

"If you want me to lie outside until it believes I've died, then there's a fair chance I'll freeze to death anyway."

Zelle frowned. They were inside a tower created by

magic. If anywhere contained answers as to how to trick a magical storm into leaving them alone, it was here. "Would that work, though?"

"You seem rather keen to send me to my death." Rien paced to the window, peering through the glass. "The command the Invoker gave to the storm will have been simpler than the one given to the wraiths. They're constructs, so they have some level of intelligence..."

"Constructs." Her gaze fell on a glass jar she'd left on a shelf several hours beforehand. *Hang on a moment...*

"What's that?" he asked, as she strode over and picked up the jar.

"I found a rattler-imp lurking in here earlier," she explained. "They're constructs which can use basic shaping-magic to imitate any form."

She gave the jar a shake, and the imp woke up. Rien's eyes widened as the little creature flung itself against the glass, its mouth open in a shriek. "Is it alive?"

"No more than those gremlins, but it has quite a nasty bite."

The imp screeched and beat its tiny fists against the jar.

"Listen," she said. "Be quiet, or I'll put you back on the shelf until you expire."

With another shake of the jar, the imp fell mute, glaring up at her.

"If you want to get out of that jar, you'll do as I ask," she said. "You can imitate anything, right? Can you pretend to be *him*?" She pointed at Rien, and the imp shook its little head.

"I know you can imitate a person," she said. "I remember the time one of you pretended to be Aurel and lured me into the Sanctum when I was eight and terrified of the dark."

She sensed Rien watching her curiously, but she didn't particularly care what he thought of her childhood exploits. The imp was part of the Sanctum, and if she could convince it to play a part in defending it, then they might have a chance of getting out of here after all.

"If you turn into him, then I'll let you out of this tower," Zelle told the imp. "Otherwise, you're going back in the jar. Indefinitely."

The little beast gave a nod. Constructs such as the imp were fairly simple creatures, but ultimately, they were born of the Sanctum itself and ought to have enough respect for the Sentinel to obey even Zelle. She hoped so, anyway.

Here we go. With a twist of the lid, she opened the jar. The imp leapt out, screeching for freedom, and bounded towards the door.

Zelle barred its path. At a warning look from her, it grew to the height of a man. Shoulders broadened; hair grew past its chin; even its clothes looked just like Rien's.

"Rather uncanny," she murmured. "Right?"

Rien seemed struck speechless at the sight of the creature. "I never knew how much I looked like…"

He trailed off as though unsure how to finish that sentence. Zelle, meanwhile, beckoned the imp to follow her towards the door, her heartbeat quickening. If she removed the staff, the storm might well rip the door off its hinges this time. She had one chance.

"This is the way out," she told the imp. "When you leave, run as far as you can. That's an order."

She laid her hands on the staff and gave a sharp tug. At

once, a horrible screeching noise echoed in her ears like some rabid beast, and the door flew open in the same instant. A gust of wind caught Rien—or rather, the imp—and then he was gone. The staff fell from her grip, that awful screaming still ringing in her skull.

"Did you hear that?" She pressed her hands to the side of her face, not quite daring to retrieve the staff in case it yelled at her again. Or worse. Angering a potent magical object had not been part of her plan, but despite the echo of its shout, the storm already seemed quieter, the wind less fierce.

"Aren't you going to close the door?" came Rien's answer.

"Yes." She gave it a firm tug back into its frame and then crouched to pick up the staff. This time, no strident cry answered her, but she propped it against the wall in case she needed to use it to bar the door again.

Rien halted beside the window. "Look out there."

Zelle crossed the room and peered out, disarmed to see that the view had cleared. While she didn't see the Rien-like form of the imp, the swirling snowflakes had shifted away from the tower in pursuit of their new target. When the construct vanished, the storm wouldn't realise it'd been tricked. With any luck, it'd assume—as far as a force that couldn't think for itself was capable of assuming, anyway—that he was dead. *I hope.*

She found herself smiling. "Good teamwork, if I do say so myself."

10

W ithin an hour, the snow had mostly melted into puddles. The staff, after its screaming fit, had fallen into a stubborn silence, while Zelle and Rien watched the clouds retreat from the tower until she could see past the mountain to the pine forests below. The moon became visible, a silver coin peeking over the mountains, and while the impulse hit her to leave the tower while she had the chance, she'd never climbed down the mountain in the dark and the snow had left the path slippery and dangerous.

Besides, it would be better to be certain their enemy had gone before leaving the security of the Sanctum.

Her gaze drifted to Rien, who looked more alert than she'd ever seen him, as though the storm lifting had also sharpened his mind.

"Do you remember what you dreamed about now?" she asked him. "When you were unconscious? You mentioned a red-bound book." Now she thought back, the book he'd lifted from a shelf in the Sanctum had been bound in red. He hadn't read it, though, and he'd had the audacity to use it to hit a gremlin instead.

Rien shook his head. "If I recalled anything, I would have told you."

"We'll leave tomorrow, then," she decided. "Your pursuers might send some new surprise in the morning, so we should make our move as soon as the sun rises."

"Yes, you're right." His gaze remained fixed on a point somewhere outside. "But as long as I'm here, there's a chance that whoever is chasing me might show up in person. If they already took your grandmother..."

That's what I'm afraid of.

"If you want to walk down a sheer drop in the darkness, be my guest," she said. "Besides—I think you should come and see my sister." Aurel might be able to get some sense out of the staff or at the very least use her own abilities to discern Rien's identity—and that of his pursuer.

"Who is your sister?" he asked. "You haven't told me anything about her."

"Aurel and I aren't close." As siblings close in age, they'd been rivals for the position of Sentinel, and Zelle's prospects of being anything other than the spare had vanished when she'd lost out. "Anyway, she'll be the next Sentinel, so she might be able to use her powers to figure out who you are and who is chasing you."

"If you're sure," said Rien, sounding doubtful. "I don't want to bring trouble to your family."

It was a little too late for that. "She's one of the only magicians... Invokers... in Zeuten. If your enemy took Grandma to keep her from getting in their way, they might go after my sister next. Besides, it's her job as

Sentinel to take care of any magical problems that might threaten the Crown."

"Who selected your sister as the next Sentinel?"

"Nobody did. She has the gift, and I don't." She did her best to keep her tone pleasant despite the flicker of old resentment stirring within her. If Aurel had been here and not her, then events would have turned out very differently for all of them. "There's only one Sentinel per generation, if at all. We're kind of… obsolete."

"Obsolete?" he echoed. "Why? You said the Sentinel deals with any problems that might threaten the Crown."

"There haven't been any since before I was born," she explained. "It's a mistake that I even ended up involved in this. I live in Saudenne, but I come to visit my grandmother every so often, and I happened to be in the area when she disappeared. My sister's the one who's supposed to check up on her, not me, but the two of them have a difficult relationship."

He paused for a long moment as though to consider her words. "There's magic here, in these mountains. Doesn't it belong to your family?"

"Magic doesn't *belong* to anyone, even those who hold Relics." She could understand why he might have had that impression, being from Aestin, but it couldn't be farther from the truth. "It's on loan from the Powers. They own it, and they can take it back at any moment."

"That's strange. In Aestin, it's…" He cut himself off for a moment, as if searching for the right words. "Magic is our whole identity."

Their identity? While her aunt had often grumbled that the Aestinian magicians' worst trait was their tendency to believe their magic to be their right to wield, without any regard for the Powers to whom they owed their Relics in the first place, Zelle hadn't realised that they might have framed their entire existence around them.

"Most of us don't have any Relics to speak of," she reminded him. "You can't make an identity out of nothing."

"The mountains, though," he went on. "They contain lost Relics, right? You told me your ancestors brought them here."

Not this again. "There is no lost Relic. It's a story."

"How do you know?" The intensity of his expression startled her. It reminded her of the man who'd crawled face-first up a sheer path in a blizzard, in search of something he wanted badly enough to risk bringing the wrath of Powers-knew-what upon both of them.

"Because I've watched people die while looking for those Relics." She tried and failed to keep the tremor out of her voice. "Half my *family* died on adventures in the wildest parts of the world, trying to get their hands on any magic that might restore our fortune. If a lost Relic would appear to anyone, it would be one of the Sentinels, but none of them ever found anything but a grim death."

"I'm sorry, Miss Zelle," he said. "Zelle, I mean. I didn't intend to disrespect your family."

"You didn't know," she acknowledged. "When you first came here, you said you were looking for a book. Perhaps you heard the rumours when you first arrived in the country, and the stories of Relics merged together with the real reason you came to the outpost."

That was a more reasonable explanation than some of the alternatives, but he shook his head. "A Relic is all that can defeat whoever pursues me."

"And you seek to claim it for yourself?" Did he know how arrogant and presumptuous that sounded? "If I were to sail to Aestin and demand my own Relic, do you think the Invokers would happily let me do so?"

"There are no unclaimed Relics in Aestin." He spoke as though reciting a passage from a book.

"And there are none here either." She met his stare defiantly. "But if there were, that doesn't give *you* the right to take them for yourself. I don't know or care what enemy is following you."

His mouth parted. "You're angry with me."

"Did you only just figure that out?" Ignorant or not, he'd have a rude awakening if he made such suggestions in front of Aurel. Or her grandmother, come to that. "Most treasure hunters want to collect or sell Relics, not use them to fight their battles. Powers above, do you know nothing of your own country's history?"

The last part was a little unfair, she'd freely admit, given the gaps in her own historical knowledge, but she did know that all the major wars Aestin had been involved in had featured Relics wreaking devastation on the battlefield. Even the current era of stability had been founded on the main Invoker families using their Relics to murder the reigning monarchs, for the Powers' sakes. Hardly comparable to Zeuten, which had been founded by magicians and had then promptly forgotten they'd ever existed.

Rien's gaze clouded. "I wish you wouldn't keep bringing that up. I want to remember, but every time I try, it's like something in my mind blocks me from thinking."

"I'm sorry." She rubbed her forehead, annoyed both with herself and with him. "I know you didn't intend for any of this to happen. Finding a Relic won't solve your problems. It probably won't bring back your memories either."

"No, but I did remember something else from my dream, or vision."

"Oh?" She glanced up, intrigued.

"I remember a ship," he said. "I came here over the sea."

Zelle had come to the same conclusion, since there was no other way for him to have travelled there, but he must still have had his memories at that point. "Do you remember anything else?"

He grimaced. "It hurts if I think too hard. I don't even know who did this to me."

"Aurel will find out." She hoped so, anyway. "Grandma would have been able to do the same. I wish I knew where she was."

Rien faced the window again. Outside, the storm might never have happened, and barely a dusting of snow sprinkled the ground. "I keep thinking of a name, like it's on the tip of my tongue, but it vanishes whenever I try to recall it."

"Your name?" She watched his profile, his blurred reflection appearing in the glass. "You wanted to know the name of one of the Powers, right? Didn't you find them in that book?"

His brow crinkled, frustration underlying his tone. "I can't grasp them. I see the words, but it's like they slip away as soon as I read them. Like my memories."

A jolt of unexpected pity went through her. He might have hit a nerve or two with her, but it must be infuriating for him to know the answers lay in front of him but be unable to read them. "I think we should find out who *you* are first, then. That ought to lead us to the person who erased your memories."

It occurred to her briefly that if the outpost's magic had indeed erased his memory, then the spell might lift when they reached the village. She had her doubts that they'd be that lucky, but the more she talked to him, the more Zelle burned with the need to know the truth. For curiosity's sake, yes, but also because Rien needed help. *Her* help. She was the one who'd found him, saved his life even, and she couldn't remember the last time anyone had asked for her assistance without making it an obligation.

"Perhaps," he said. "Or if I read every book in the Sanctum, one of them might show the words to me."

"That would take all night." She gave a strained smile. "I have another way, though."

She returned to her pack, which she'd opened to search for her set of playing cards before she'd been distracted earlier. After rummaging through the pack, she pulled out the bundle, and Rien gave her a curious look when she unbound the scrap of material keeping them together. "Cards?"

"I mentioned a game called Relics and Ruins." She gave the cards a quick shuffle. "I'll teach you the rules."

She began dealing out cards. The game was fairly intuitive, so Rien ought to be able to get the hang of it without too much difficulty, but her real purpose lay in the illustrations on each card. They were made to represent the various Powers, so one of the images might jolt his memory without him having to read the names. When each of them held five cards, she left the remainder facedown in a pile and gave a quick explanation.

"There are five suits, one named for each of the children of Gaiva," she said. "Each suit contains cards numbered one through ten, and the goal is to assemble a hand that beats your opponent's. I can explain the rest as we go along."

As she'd predicted, Rien was a quick learner. Each turn, they drew one card from the deck and then chose one to discard, and while she had started the game with three successive numbers in a single suit, she had so much trouble finding the others that she wondered if Rien might have already drawn them. They were so intently focused on the game that when a door rattled somewhere within the tower, they both jumped and then tried to pretend they hadn't.

"Sounds echo in here," Zelle remarked, picking up a card. Her skin prickled. She'd drawn the Shaper card, of which there was only one in the entire deck, and which forced both players to shuffle their hands back into the deck and redraw them from scratch.

If Rien *was* trying to outdo her hand, she'd just scuppered him. She played the card, to be rewarded by Rien's expression of tight-lipped annoyance. Then they redrew, and he stared at his cards for a moment. "I think I win."

"You did what?" That couldn't be right.

He flipped his hand over, revealing the cards—numbered one through five, from the suit of Gaiva's first child, Astiva. The birds painted on each card seemed to shimmer in the firelight, and as she watched, faintly glowing lines appeared on the exposed skin of Rien's left wrist. A breeze swept through the room, and she shivered, part of her expecting to hear the door break under the assault of the storm once again.

Rien opened his palm, and the cards fell to the wooden

floor. His wrist looked normal now, but she could have sworn she'd seen markings that hadn't been there beforehand—and a glow that didn't come from the fireplace.

She put down her own cards. "I think that's enough. I also think we should avoid looking at anything so much as linked to the Powers until we're out of these mountains."

He nodded slowly. "I agree."

Zelle gathered the cards together before bundling them, hiding the illustrations from sight, but the image of how the glowing lines on his wrist had seemed to connect to the cards in his hand was slow to leave her mind.

11

Evita's nose had turned blue with cold. The night had been a particularly fierce one, with the wind howling in the background and rumours sweeping among the novices of an unnatural snowstorm elsewhere in the mountains. She'd worried for the dragonet, having to spend the night outside, but she had no doubt the beast had an abundance of cracks and crevices to use as hiding places.

Evita had more pressing problems when she was confronted with the looming presence of Master Amery as she left the cave after breakfast.

"You. Come with me."

Evita's stomach plummeted while Master Amery turned away, beckoning her to follow him. *He's going to kick me out.*

She ought to have seen it coming after yesterday's trial. She'd been too brazen, and her run-in with the strange boy who'd shown up the previous day hadn't painted her in a stellar light either. But she couldn't leave. She had nowhere to go.

"I didn't cheat in the trial," she blurted. "I didn't go out of the cave. I mean, not until after I fetched the token, anyway. Did you want me to give it back?"

"Quiet," he snapped. "This way."

She followed Master Amery towards the building that housed the elite Changers, excuses rising in her mind like steam from water. If he exiled her to die in the mountains so, too, would die her hopes of finding the monster which had killed her family. Besides, she hadn't broken the rules, and there was no way he could possibly know about the brief moment when she'd contemplated stealing the cloak of Changing and running off into the mountains alone.

The Master's office was as austere as anywhere else in the base, containing little more than a crooked wooden desk and chair, a stack of shelves lined with scrolls, and a rack of weapons, mostly arrows. She wondered if he spent his free time forging them or if he just brought them in from Saudenne. Papers littered the desk, but since Evita couldn't read, she didn't pay them much attention. The smell of ink and parchment hung in the air, along with an undefinable lingering chill that exuded images of sheer cliffs without an end in sight. For some reason, she found herself thinking of the eerily bright-blue eyes of the strange boy who'd visited the previous day.

Master Amery positioned himself behind the desk before addressing her.

"Candidate Evita," he said. "You have been selected to represent the Changers on an urgent mission. You'll leave immediately."

Evita stared, certain that she'd misheard him. "Master

Amery, I haven't even passed all my trials yet. I don't have my own cloak or anything."

Master Amery rubbed the back of his neck, giving a brief glance over his shoulder. It struck Evita as oddly out of character. He was always perfectly assured, but now his whole demeanour was different. Shaky, almost. Was it to do with the stranger who'd visited yesterday? The boy had scared the life out of her, but she'd assumed a full-fledged Master Changer wouldn't have been afraid of him.

"A noble from Aestin has requested our services," he told her. "We are to dispose of a certain individual. His name is Arien Astera."

"Dispose?" she echoed. "You mean—I'm supposed to kill him?"

"I doubt you can." His confident manner returned, and his unblinking eyes dared her to flinch. "He is a known traitor to the Crown, and a magician at that. You are to depart immediately for the village of Tavine, where a certain family is known to reside, and ask for their help tracking down this individual. If they refuse to cooperate, then you may use any means necessary to make them see that helping us is essential."

"But—" She broke off, certain she glimpsed his hands trembling under the table. "Who is this family?"

He thrust a scrap of parchment at her. "The name of the family's representative is Aurel Carnelian. The young woman is close to your age and is untrained in combat, so she'll be an easy target."

"Is she magical?" Carnelian. The name didn't sound familiar to her, but if this person was supposed to know whereabouts a dangerous magician from Aestin was hiding, she must have some kind of expertise.

"Her family are simple historians," he said. "They spend their time arguing over the value of fossilised dung. It's not real magic, certainly nothing as practical as ours—and it goes without saying that if you accept this mission, you'll have full access to all the Changer's equipment, including your own cloak."

Evita's mouth fell open. She hadn't expected to gain access to a cloak of Changing for a long time—or at all, after the disastrous trial yesterday. Why had he chosen her? *Something's not right about this,* a voice in the back of her mind whispered to her. But a louder voice said, *So what? You're getting a second chance. Besides, the quicker you advance in rank, the quicker you'll get what you want.*

More to the point, he was sending her away on a mission *with* the cloak. If she wanted to, she could take the cloak and leave and then hunt down the creature who'd killed her family. With the aid of a magician, her goal might not be so impossible after all.

"I accept, Master," she said.

His eyes narrowed, and she wondered if she'd spoken too quickly. Then he nodded, a peculiar expression softening his features. Relief. He *had* been scared of that child. So had she, of course, but he must have been responsible for this unexpected mission. The Changers didn't typically take orders from strange outsiders, and that boy had been the very definition of the word. At the memory of his creepy eyes, prickles of unease trailed up her spine like cold fingers.

"Gather your belongings and come back here," he said. "I'll give you a pack of basic survival equipment and weapons—and the cloak."

"Yes, I will. Thank you, Master."

She all but ran back to the cave where the other novices slept to gather her belongings. Not that she had much to gather aside from a couple of changes of clothes acquired when she'd first arrived at the base. She hoped the Master would see fit to furnish her with more warm clothing if she was to venture out into the wilderness alone.

"Evita?" At the voice behind her, she suppressed a groan. Ruben leaned against the cave wall, eyeing her curiously. "Where are you going?"

"On a mission." She rolled up her bedroll and put it into her pack along with her clothes. The token from the previous day's trial was still in her pocket, but Master Amery had yet to ask for it back and she'd prefer not to remind him of how much she'd irritated him yesterday.

"Oh, really?" A smile tugged his lips upwards. "Tell you what... if you're running, you don't have to go alone."

"I'm not running away," she said, a little put out that he'd make that assumption despite the warning tug in her gut. "I really do have a mission."

"You're a novice," he said. "You haven't passed all your trials yet."

"I had no idea." She tried to sidestep him, only to find him barring the way out of the cave. She tensed when he rested a hand on her arm. "What are you doing?"

"I meant it," he said quickly. "I've had enough of all this. Sleeping in a cave, shitting into a hole in the ground... there's no glamour to this."

"Did you expect to find glamour in killing people?" She winced as her voice echoed loudly enough that a couple of the other novices looked in their direction. "Why didn't you leave after the first week?"

He was silent for a moment too long. "I stayed for you, of course."

"Me?" Her heart sank somewhere below the cave floor. She'd been afraid of this. "You didn't have to. I mean, I didn't expect you to. Can I leave now?"

He remained awkwardly standing with one hand on her arm as though he didn't quite know what to do with himself. It occurred to her that he was making as much of a fool of himself as she, but she wasn't the one who'd had anything to gain. She just wanted to leave on her mission before Master Amery changed his mind and made her spend the week cleaning bat guano off the floor of the cave instead.

When Ruben didn't move, she cleared her throat and gave a gentle push on his arm. He sidestepped, his face falling. "I thought you—liked me."

She had, at first. They'd been friends, but she'd never understood why the men in her life always tried to complicate their friendships with touching and kissing and were then upset when she turned them down. Whenever someone took an interest in her, they acted as though they were speaking to another version of her who didn't actually exist. Someone who desired them back. But she didn't. Ever. And they were always so *hurt* when she told them so.

"I…" She had to say *something*. "I have to take part in this mission. I'm going to kill a god."

His mouth fell open. She'd successfully rendered him speechless, except she hadn't the faintest idea of where she was supposed to go from there. Instead, while he stood there gawping at her, she ducked under his arm out of the cave and hurried away, towards Master Amery's office.

This is it. I'm really going to be a Changer.

As for killing a god? She might have to survive killing a man first.

———

She'd said yes. Master Amery shouldn't have been surprised, given that Evita was nothing more than a simple village girl who wouldn't recognise the name of her target. Most Zeutenians had no idea who the Aestinian families were, and his assumptions of her ignorance had been on the mark. As for convincing her this impossible mission was achievable—he hadn't even had to try. She'd been eager to please him. Almost too much so.

A momentary suspicion flared. She'd wandered off the proper path in yesterday's trials and had demonstrated insubordination he'd usually punish severely. But this mission would be punishment enough, and while she was gone, he'd send other Changers to scour the mountains in search of her target in case she failed. Either way, he wouldn't have to look upon her face again.

Master Amery sat back with a smile and waited for Evita to return. In the meantime, he took a spare scrap of parchment and scrawled the Changers' symbol—three circles within one another with an arrow drawn through them from top to bottom. He folded the paper several times and snapped his fingers. A fluttering noise sounded, and a mountain eagle soared through the open window and landed on his shoulder.

"You know what to do." The bird took the folded paper in its beak. "Take this to the Sentinels' home in Tavine."

When the bird took flight, Master Amery allowed himself a smile. The eagle would give the family a warning—he was kind enough to offer them that—before Evita showed up and informed them of the Changers' need of their help. And if the young Astera was with them, then Master Amery's note would grant him the courtesy of forewarning him of his impending death.

———

Crossing the mountains towards Tavine was worse than Evita's first journey to the Changers' base, despite her warmer, sturdier clothes and better equipment. And her cloak. She occupied her attention by admiring the silvery folds swirl around her ankles as she walked down the steep, rock-strewn path, unseen by anyone. Not that any of the other novices had come to say goodbye. She doubted they knew she was gone at all. Except for Ruben, and she'd so thoroughly astounded him that she doubted he'd tell the others of her true goal. If he even believed her.

Never mind them. You're the one with the mission. A mission that might even be optional if this Reader could point her in the direction of the creature responsible for the deaths of her family.

The weather, on the other hand, left much to be desired. She'd never appreciated how the Changers' base had been low enough to avoid the frequent blizzards which struck the highest peaks, but clouds masked the area ahead of her in a raging white maelstrom. As far as she knew, no one else was foolish enough to live *in* the mountains, but Tavine was hidden somewhere in the pine forests on the western side of the Range, and the storm raged close to her path.

She had only three days, Master Amery had warned. Three days to find this Carnelian girl and convince her to find Arien Astera's location... or help her find the location of the creature which had murdered her family. Even with the cloak, she sensed Master Amery's eyes on her back, so she didn't dare commit until she was back on steady ground.

Assuming she went ahead with the mission and found this Arien Astera, the Master didn't want her to do the actual killing. When it came to it, she wasn't sure she could—and besides, an Aestinian magician who also happened to be a traitor to the Crown was hardly a fair opponent for someone without magic, even with her new cloak. If she'd had Master Amery's ability to change forms, she'd be able to become a bird and fly over the mountains to save time, but she had yet to figure out the extent of the cloak's capabilities.

Besides, she was being followed.

Occasionally, small pebbles would fall from the ledge above her, along with a flutter that reminded her of wings. She wondered if the dragonet had found his way to her again, but she saw no signs of his reptilian form, nor anyone else. She found herself reaching beneath her cloak to check her weapons were in place. Two daggers were strapped to her waist, while a bow hung over her shoulder along with a bag containing a few ordinary arrows and three spelled ones that she'd been ordered to save for her target and nobody else. Her weapons wouldn't do much good against a beast like the wyrm, but she ought to be able to frighten off any pursuers.

Evita kept walking until an arrow whistled overhead, bringing her stumbling to a halt. Laughter echoed on the path above. *That's not Master Amery.*

"Come on, you can do better than that," said a male voice, and Evita tensed for an instant before she remembered she couldn't be seen. Neither could the speaker, though, and given the bare rocks to either side of her, her pursuers must have been wearing cloaks just like hers. Yet the voice… it was Vekka's. *Did Master Amery give* him *his own cloak?*

"This is pointless," said his companion, whose voice she recognised as belonging to a heavyset girl called Izaura. "There's a bloody great blizzard in the way. How're we meant to hit anything?"

"What part of the words 'spelled arrows' don't you understand?" Vekka chuckled under his breath.

Stumbling footsteps gave away Izaura's location. "I think Master Amery wants to get rid of us. First he sent that girl off to Tavine, and now he has us shooting arrows at the clouds."

Vekka snorted. "He doesn't want to get rid of *us*, but the girl cheated yesterday. Of course he wants her gone."

The pair of them were making enough noise that it was easy enough for her to guess their approximate location, but it seemed that even a top-secret mission wasn't enough to get Vekka and his hangers-on to leave her alone. It was lucky she had the cloak, but a sinking pit opened in her stomach at their words. *Of course he wants her gone.*

They shouldn't even know of her mission, but the

Master wouldn't have given her the cloak if he thought he was sending her to her death. Would he?

Another arrow whizzed overhead, snapping Evita out of her dismayed thoughts. Her eyes followed its progress as it sailed through the air and straight into the mass of clouds ahead of them. Who were they supposed to be shooting at?

"What's with the storm?" Izaura muttered. "I've never seen weather like that in summer before."

"You wouldn't. You're from the city." Vekka lumbered along without a trace of stealth, and Evita felt a surge of irrational satisfaction that if she'd been sent away to keep her out of Master Amery's sight, then the pair of them certainly had too.

Are they shooting at Arien Astera? Did he send more than one of us? The Master had asked her to deliver a message, not actually kill him, but assigning Vekka of all people to commit the actual deed didn't strike her as the wisest of decisions.

"I'm not joking." Izaura came to a halt. "The Master is acting—weird. Since that creepy kid came to the base yesterday. Did you see him?"

"No." Vekka spoke in a disinterested tone. "I don't care about some kid. I care about hitting our target. Even a magician can't dodge spelled arrows."

Her blood chilled. So they *were* shooting at someone out in the storm... and if it turned out to be Arien Astera, then Evita might not be needed at all.

"Why would the Crown want to get rid of a foreign ambassador, anyway?" Izaura said. "It's not right. I don't like it."

"You don't have to like it. Orders are orders."

Evita's foot kicked a loose stone, and she held her breath. Those arrows were lethal and never missed, but if they were aimed at *her* target, why was the Master sending her directly into the heart of the storm when he'd already sent two other recruits after the same target?

Questions swirled around her head, and no answers awaited. The sensible thing to do would be to leave while she could and head back to Saudenne, but that was the coward's way out, and besides, the Master had specifically sent her to see this Aurel Carnelian first. Neither of the others had mentioned her. If nothing else, perhaps the Reader might be able to answer some of her questions.

Such as the identity of the child who'd given Master Amery orders. *Creepy* was the right descriptor, but he'd also seemed oddly familiar to her in a way she couldn't explain.

"C'mon," said Vekka. "The storm's on the move, look. I don't wanna get caught out in it."

Neither did she, but Vekka at least had Izaura's company. Evita had been sent out alone, and if those arrows truly never missed their targets, then she might be on a fool's errand. Unless the storm threw them off course.

The storm *was* moving, clouds scudding across the mountaintops in a way that didn't seem entirely natural. Whatever the case, though, she was heading right for it. Hoping her new cloak was waterproof, Evita pulled up her hood and walked on.

12

Zelle's night was restless, punctuated by dreams of the door breaking under the pressure of the raging storm. Sleeping in her grandmother's bed didn't help, because she kept thinking she saw her squat outline lurking in the corner of the room, holding the staff and prepared to reprimand her. The staff itself stood unsupported against the wall; Zelle had been reluctant to turn her back on it even though she'd angered it so badly.

Aurel would be stunned if she knew Zelle had had the gall to use the staff as a tool to keep the door closed, but she hadn't seen the storm with her own eyes. If she hadn't kept it from ripping open the tower door, she and Rien might have perished without ever finding a way to the reunite the staff with its owner. There was no telling how long it'd take Aurel to realise her grandmother was missing. Given her past record, it might be seasons before she thought to pay a visit to the other outpost, and even then, she might not decide to travel down to the village. Aurel left that to Zelle, most of the time, except on the rare occasion when she needed Grandma's advice.

Granted, if whoever had taken Grandma caught up to Aurel before they did, then she'd find out the hard way that someone was intent on taking down any would-be magicians who stood in their way.

The morning greeted them with blue skies and sunshine when Zelle looked out of the small, dusty window in her grandmother's room. Though the snow had cleared, the idea of traversing the mountain paths remained unappealing, especially when it meant leaving the Sanctum behind. If the protections on the tower were the only thing keeping both of them safe, then another storm or worse might await them outside. Especially as they were none the wiser as to who—or what—had caused it. For all they knew, they were right in the middle of a power play between rival Invokers. If Rien was one of the players, losing his memory had been a major drawback, but she was the one who had the most to lose by leaving the outpost.

Staying here wasn't an option, though. They were almost out of supplies, for a start, and it would take the better part of a day to reach the village of Tavine and the second outpost. After Zelle had dressed in her travelling clothes, she picked up the staff and found it resolutely silent. It'd been refusing to communicate with her since the incident yesterday, but she'd hoped that by the morning, it would have been willing to forgive her. No such luck.

Zelle left the room to retrieve her pack, finding that her thick socks and boots had dried out after a night by the fire. She dug out her waterskin—it would need refilling soon, especially as she'd given her spare to Rien—and found a handful of stale pastries in the bottom of the pack. Better than nothing, but she couldn't deny that she looked forwards to a proper meal when they reached the village.

The guest room door opened and Rien emerged, dressed in travelling clothes he'd presumably found in the back of her grandfather's armoire.

"There's nothing for breakfast except stale pastries, I'm afraid," she told him. "The day looks clear, though. Ready to leave?"

A curt nod was his only response, and he took the pastry from her without enthusiasm. Had he been dreaming again, or was he concerned that his pursuers would be waiting for him on the other side of the door? She finished putting on her coat and boots before retrieving the staff and her pack. Then, before she lost her nerve, she opened the door. A thin breeze ruffled her hair, and she tensed automatically on the threshold, scanning the path for any potential ambushes.

"I don't see anything out there," she said to Rien. "Do you?"

"No, I don't."

When they were both outside, Zelle closed and bolted the door before leading the way down the path that had been covered in snow the previous day. Her destination was an opening concealed in the side of the cliff that would lead them to a shortcut across the mountain to the Sentinels' second outpost.

The thought of seeing her sister seemed much less appealing than it had the previous day, especially when Zelle would be forced to admit that she'd taken Grandma's staff and had no real explanation for her disappearance. She could only imagine what Aurel would make of Rien, too, but she'd worry about that when they were out of the Range. The path dropped steeply downhill, and she held onto the side of the cliff with her free hand as she climbed, eyes open for the cave opening that lay nearby.

A fluttering sounded overhead. Zelle glanced up in the hopes that it was just a bird, and Rien hissed out a breath. When she looked down, a piece of crumpled parchment lay on the path in front of them, marked with faded ink. She crouched down to pick it up. "What in Gaiva's name—?"

Air whipped past her face, and the paper was whisked from her hand. An arrow pinned it to the rock wall, and Zelle jerked back, her heart thudding frantically. "Where did that come from?"

"I don't know." Rien snapped the arrow between his fingers, freeing the parchment, and then tilted his head back to look up. She did likewise, but the sheer cliffs gave nothing away. "There's nobody up there."

"There must be." Zelle grabbed the scrap of parchment on impulse, stuffing it into her pocket. "Come on. We're too exposed here."

They descended the slope as fast as they could without tripping. Partway down, another gust of wind brought a second arrow that passed so close to them that it grazed Rien's sleeve. He caught his balance, alarm flitting across his face when a third arrow brushed against Zelle's jaw. The sting of pain jolted her into action. Seizing Rien by the arm, she felt the cliffside with her free hand until she found the hidden switch concealed from the naked eye.

With a faint noise, the rock wall slid open to reveal a narrow tunnel. "Come on in."

Rien stared at the tunnel for a heartbeat, then he followed her inside. Zelle didn't breathe until she released the mechanism which caused the cliff wall to slide back into place, cutting off all outside light. Instead, ever-burning lanterns lined the path ahead, similar to the ones inside the Sanctum.

"What is this place?" Rien's voice echoed around them.

"Sentinels' shortcut." Her heart thudded in her ears. "Someone just tried to kill us. Did you not see anyone up on the cliffs? Because unless we have invisible assailants on our tail—"

Rien cut in. "What's on that parchment?"

Zelle removed the scrap of parchment from her pocket and smoothed out its crumpled edges. The ink had faded, perhaps washed out in the storm, but Zelle recognised the symbol that had been scrawled on its surface.

"The Changers. Oh, *Powers*."

The Changers. The name was usually whispered rather than spoken aloud, especially in villages like Randel or Tavine, as though speaking the name of the notorious assassins would attract their notice. The Changers worked directly for the Crown, but the rumours surrounding them outnumbered even those concerning the lost Relic. Whether they had Relics of their own or not, no one could be sure, but that arrow had seemingly come out of nowhere.

"What in the Powers' name did you do?" she demanded of a stupefied Rien. "The Changers don't send assassins after petty criminals. They send them after enemies of the Crown."

"Assassins?"

She threw the parchment in his face. "The Changers work for the Crown Prince, who is a close ally of the Sentinels. I think it's a safe bet that it isn't *me* they're firing arrows at."

Comprehension dawned on his face. "They're mercenaries?"

"Not exactly. They're also rumoured to have... abilities."

His brow furrowed. "I thought you said your family were the only magic users in Zeuten."

"Now is not the time to be a pedant." She moved a few steps through the tunnel, her heart continuing to lurch against her ribs. "First cursed storms and wraiths, now assassins. Clearly you've pissed off someone very important."

Someone allied with the Crown, apparently. Which would make him *her* enemy. *Powers. Why did I ever trust him?*

Rien's footsteps echoed behind her. "Can you tell me more about these Changers?"

She walked on into the gloom, glad of the lanterns that lit their path. "People say a lot of things about them, mostly unpleasant. They're the only professional killers in the whole of Zeuten, and they're good at their jobs. Whether they use magic or not is up for debate, but the Crown Prince of Zeuten himself dispatches them against the most dangerous enemies on the continent."

"Oh," said Rien.

"Yes, *oh*," echoed Zelle. "They can't follow us in here, but the Powers alone can help us if they're lurking on the other side."

Rien turned the arrow over in his hands as they walked. "This is a spelled arrow. It's not from here. I think they're manufactured in Aestin—"

"It's sharp and it nearly killed me. I don't care for the details." She touched her hand to her face, and her fingers came away damp with blood.

He dropped the arrow. "What are we going to do now?"

"Walk to the outpost and hope we don't get killed on the way," she said. "Alternatively, we can stay in here until we starve to death. Up to you."

Maybe she was being unfair, but she had no desire to perish at the hands of the Changers because this man had somehow made enemies of every magical force in Zeuten and beyond. If anyone found out she'd offered him shelter, she might well find herself hanged for treason against the Crown.

Yet the Changers couldn't have sent that storm. They were assassins, not Invokers, and they didn't carry Relics. The Changers couldn't possibly have taken her grandmother either. Perhaps they'd been after another target entirely and Rien had simply got in their way, or there'd otherwise been some kind of misunderstanding. A misunderstanding that might cost her her life, admittedly, but she had two options remaining. Either she sent him back to the Sanctum and risked bringing yet more misfortune upon the tower, or she accompanied him through the passageway and then got rid of him as soon as they reached the other side.

Questions circled Zelle's mind as they walked, not speaking, for an hour or more. Thick stalagmites jutted from the floor, while the lanterns were their only source of light.

"Are we inside the mountain?" Rien asked after a while.

"Yes, but once we reach the other side, we'll be out in the open," she replied. "The path leads directly to Tavine, where my sister lives. I only hope the assassins will know better than to attack *her*."

The Changers never did anything by accident, but she'd done absolutely nothing to aggravate them *or* the Crown, except being in the wrong place at the wrong time. The presence of her grandmother's staff might lend her some credibility, since the Changers must have met her grandmother at some point. If they'd been present at the Crown Prince's coronation after he'd officially stepped in to take over from his father in diplomatic matters, they certainly would have spoken, but Zelle had stopped paying attention to such things after the gift had passed her by and she'd been shunted off to her aunt's shop instead. She wished the staff would offer a word of encouragement, to reassure her that she'd made the right decision in allowing Rien to walk alongside her rather than simply knocking him out and leaving him to his fate.

Rien was silent for a long while. Then he said, "I brought this on you."

Yes. You did. But really, she couldn't lay the blame on someone who had no recollection of why someone would want to kill him, could she? Not until he had his memories back, at any rate. She couldn't send him back to the Sanctum, and so the only path was onward. Once they reached the end of the passageway, she'd have to make a choice.

Soon, the wind whistled from ahead of them as the path flattened out, signalling that they were close to the exit. Zelle almost wished the storm was back, but as long as she stood at Rien's side, she'd be equally vulnerable.

"We're here." She halted, glancing at Rien. "Once we're outside, we'll be exposed. Better hope the Changers don't know where the shortcut ends."

Zelle couldn't hear any movement on the other side of the wall, but she held her breath as she found the mechanism that unsealed the cave entrance. Part of the cliff wall moved aside to reveal a narrow opening identical to the one they'd entered through, but no assassins waited for them out in the open. She drew in a breath and then walked out onto a steep, rocky path.

The cave's opening rumbled closed behind her, while a driving wind lashed at the cliffs, though not as wild as the storm the previous day. The path wound downhill, and the dusky shapes of pines formed a dense forest below. The village of Tavine was somewhere down there, nestled in the mountain's shadow. She glanced sideways at Rien. Taking him to her sister was a risk, but up until the moment the Changers' arrows had crossed their paths, she hadn't truly believed he'd done anything to harm anyone. Would Aurel have made the same choice? Until they knew his identity, she had nothing to go on but instinct and the knowledge that if she sent him away now, she might never learn the truth.

Mind made up, Zelle descended the path, having to clamber over boulders and slide down steep rises. Zelle's thick coat soon became suffocating, sweat running down her forehead, her hands covered in tiny cuts from pulling herself over rocks. She had no breath to speak to Rien, though they paused a few times to check no one followed them. Aside from the occasional bird's call, not a single living thing disturbed them. This was a trail no sane hiker dared to follow. Hopefully, it'd slow even the Changers down, though Zelle had heard rumours that the most elite among their number could transform into animals like snow leopards and eagles. Hence their name. She'd never seen it for herself, but given what she'd seen of them so far, anything might be possible.

A rumbling sounded from the peaks behind them, like thunder. *Not another storm!*

No—worse. Zelle barely had time to grab Rien's arm and pull him under the nearest overhang before a water-fall of snow came tumbling down the path. The rocks shook with the force of the avalanche, and Zelle found herself gripping Rien's arm convulsively, certain the ground would give away and they'd plunge to their deaths. *At least all that snow would provide a soft landing,* she thought, seized with a bizarre desire to laugh. She dug the staff's edge into the path with her free hand and focused on keeping her balance. While the trembling ground should have caused her to stumble, the staff remained upright like a solid force, unmovable. Zelle braced herself against the wooden surface as the trembling slowed, breathing hard.

"I can't feel my arm," said Rien.

"Sorry." She let go, feeling ashamed for her moment of panic and equally abashed that her instincts had over-come her reservations about Rien's involvement in their misfortune. "That wasn't the Changers."

It might not even have been magic but simply nature setting itself against them. Nevertheless, she couldn't help wondering if the staff *had* helped stop her from being swept away. Perhaps the Powers hadn't forsaken them after all.

Rien peered out of the overhang. "That was close. Is it safe to walk?"

"I think so." Zelle inched out onto the path, which was now almost entirely buried in thick whiteness. One slip might carry them over the edge to their deaths, but she'd climbed down here countless times before, even as a small child. As long as they were careful—as long as no one else tried to kill them—they might safely reach the bottom.

"Come on," she muttered to Rien. "Watch where you tread. There are rocks under the snow."

"I know," he said. "Are you an older sibling, by any chance?"

"Yes. What does that matter?" Did he have siblings himself? He'd mentioned his family being dead, so she didn't want to probe the issue, but she had to wonder whether his words came from his own experience even if he didn't realise it.

"You seem very... responsible."

"I have to be," she said. "Those of us who aren't Sentinels have to make our own way."

Rien gave her a sideways look as if he sensed there was more that she might have added, but he didn't speak. Instead, they continued to climb down the slippery path until the treetops were on a level with their feet and the valley closer than the peak. Not for the first time, she found herself wishing the Sentinels had picked a more accessible location, though they might have been much worse off if they had.

How close were they to the Changers' base from here?

EMMA L. ADAMS

She was fairly sure the Changers were based at the southernmost peak, near Saudenne, but they must have their own shortcuts through the mountains. It would explain how they'd caught up to the pair of them so quickly, though for all she knew, they'd been chasing Rien for days.

They walked until Zelle's feet were numb, her legs burning from the steep trek. Rien made no complaint, so neither did she, and they stopped only to refill their waterskins from rivers or streams. Her insides ached with hunger, but she consoled herself by imagining a hot meal waiting on the other side.

Tavine was widely considered the first settlement on Zeuten, but it'd never developed beyond a village. Perhaps because the dense forests made it tricky to find without a detailed map. That didn't deter any would-be tourists, of course, but they had even less luck on this side of the peaks than they did in Randel.

As the path steepened, the pines towered above their heads while they often had to brush thick swathes of leaves out of their way. Soon they'd be within sight of the village—but Zelle could have sworn she saw movement within the trees. She kept watch as they walked, nearly slipping a couple of times.

She came to a halt when a dark shape rose from among the trees, resolving itself into several shadowy humanlike forms.

The wraiths, it seemed, had been waiting for them all along.

13

Master Amery closed the door to the cloakroom, the key turning in the lock with a soft click. They were down several cloaks of Changing, but it couldn't be helped. His novices wouldn't last long without them, and even then, some of them claimed that their spelled arrows had been lost in the storm that had struck the Range earlier that evening.

A storm that had vanished as swiftly as it had arrived.

He hadn't the faintest clue whether the storm had been a natural occurrence or otherwise, but his simple plan had turned into quite the headache. Not only had the novices he'd sent after the young Astera failed to return, but it had taken far too long for him to realise that the Sentinel's outpost might be the ideal spot for an Invoker on the run to hide. Whether the Sentinels could actually help with the Astera boy's dilemma was beside the point, but it would explain why he'd been so blasted hard to find. On one hand, the Astera boy might have made the Changers' job easier if he had indeed joined forces with the

Sentinels, because there'd be no need for his hapless novice to request that the Reader track Astera herself. On the other, if the Astera boy had convinced the Sentinels that he was a victim and not a criminal on the run, then it would put another unwelcome obstacle in his path.

He looked out the window at the darkness filling the base, unease flickering within him. The Sentinels were the oldest family on the entire continent, and the notion of angering them was not an appealing one. They were allies of the Crown, and while their magic was known to be inconsequential, few would dare to trifle with them. He'd sent that girl to convince the Reader to help, but night had fallen by now and no update had reached him from the village of Tavine. She might benefit from a reminder to get a move on, assuming she was still alive.

Upon returning to his office, Master Amery scribbled a quick note, marking the back of the parchment with the Changers' symbol. He then opened the window and whistled softly.

A rustling of wings followed before the eagle he'd tamed flew through the open window and landed on the desk, looking up at him expectantly while Master Amery folded the scrap of parchment. "Take this to... what's-her-name. The girl. Evita."

The eagle's wings flapped again as it clamped its beak over the note, and Master Amery stood back and watched it fly out of the open window.

"Nice bird."

He jumped violently. The strange black-haired child stood in the doorway, watching him. Powers above, the boy moved quieter than the elite Changers. Who had even let him into the building?

Recovering his dignity, Master Amery said, "I sent several of my assassins after young Astera. Our arrows are specially imported from Aestin and designed not to miss, but I believe this Astera boy has magic, does he not?"

The entire room chilled when the boy met his eyes. "He shouldn't have magic. Not anymore."

No. Someone took it from him. And not this boy either. Whoever it was, Master Amery didn't want to meet them.

"No, of course not," he said quickly. "Still, there's been some odd happenings. That storm, for instance..." He trailed off as the boy gave him a sharp, knowing smile.

"Whatever happens, the Astera boy will die," he said. "Perhaps I've failed to make myself clear as to the consequences to the rest of you, should you fail to meet my demands. I hoped we could make an alliance with one another, but you're trying my patience."

Master Amery's words died in his throat as the boy walked away, leaving only the blurred impression of a human-shaped shadow. Except the Master was starting to doubt he was human at all.

Despite knowing the eagle wouldn't be back until the morning, he sat watching the window until long after the boy had departed.

———

Evita's new cloak was definitely *not* waterproof. Cold rain drenched her to the skin until she'd lost all sensation in her limbs, while the mountains had disappeared beneath a mass of thick clouds, as though giant hands were pummelling the peaks and hurling torrents of snow at the cliffs. Trying not to think about avalanches, she walked on, hoping to find shelter before nightfall.

Her route took her directly through the mountains, at the expense of anywhere to shelter aside from a few rocks, and she found herself wishing she'd forsaken the cloak of Changing and exchanged it for a fur coat and hat instead. A chill wind blew her hair back, sharp and biting. When she lifted her head to check her bearings, the clouds lifted from the peak as though some unseen force had plucked them out of the air. The swirling storm clouds drifted westwards over the mountains... right towards Evita.

Oh, Powers.

She swore, looking around for shelter, but she found nothing more than a narrow overhang to stand underneath while the clouds veered over the path as though they'd spotted some irresistible prey to chase down. Specifically, her.

"Gaiva's tits," she said.

The storm roared over her hiding place, driving rain pummelling her black and blue. She backed up against the cliff, the jagged edge digging into her back. The wind howled on, and a torrent of snow slammed into the path only to be swept away by the gale—and then, as suddenly as they'd arrived, the clouds departed. Perhaps to find some other poor soul to chase.

Evita pried herself loose from the rock wall, breathing quickly. A skittering sound drew her gaze downwards, and she yelped when a reptilian foot stepped out of the shadows next to her. The dragonet crawled into view, emerging from a crevice at the foot of the cliff, his tail flicking Evita's leg on the way out.

"We've got to stop meeting in situations of dire peril." A hysterical laugh bubbled in her throat, and the dragonet tilted his head as though confused by her reaction. "No, really, you should probably leave me behind in case that storm comes back to finish me off."

The storm, however, must have been chasing another target after all. When she emerged from her hiding place, she glimpsed the clouds scudding across the valley and out of sight. It was surely no ordinary act of nature, but she'd never heard of the Changers being able to control the weather conditions before. Who, then, was responsible?

The dragonet took flight with a beat of his spindly wings, occasionally overtaking her as she continued along the path, moving as quickly as the slippery rocks allowed. The upside to her ordeal was that she hardly noticed the sheer drop anymore, at least until it vanished, the path flattening out. She'd made it to the other side of the Range.

Now all she had to do was find the village where the Reader made her home, which lay... somewhere in the thick forest on the other side. Darkness merged the pines into an impenetrable mass, and the muddy trail she followed had no landmarks to speak of. Twice she had to hide when some predator or other slinked out of the trees, before remembering the cloak rendered her unseen. When the sound of branches cracking overhead brought her to a halt, she stiffened, hands moving towards her bow—then a clawed and feathered shape exploded through the canopy.

A giant bird of some kind. An eagle? Before she could do more than blink, it dropped a piece of parchment at her feet and circled her, once, its claws digging into her shoulder through her cloak.

By the Powers. It can see me. Evita leaned against the nearest tree, feeling faint. Her shoulder throbbed, but she didn't dare remove the cloak to check on the damage. How had it known she was here? She hadn't been making a particular effort to be quiet, true, but she knew Master Amery had a pet eagle. If he'd sent it after her with a message... then she couldn't read it. She'd never had formal lessons, and when she scooped up the parchment the eagle had left behind, the only words she could make out underneath the Changers' symbol were "kill" and "three".

Evita crumpled the parchment in her hand, dread crawling down her spine. Three days she'd been given, and one had elapsed already. Another animal noise sounded, this one like a cross between a cough and a growl. Her hands brushed her bow, and a long reptilian head popped up from the bushes.

Evita stared at the dragonet in disbelief. "You followed me?"

The dragonet made a chirping sound as if to say "yes".

"Didn't you hear me say that you'd be safer if you avoided me?" She rubbed her tired eyes with the hand clutching the note Master Amery had sent her. "I have three days to find my target or else I'm dead, and I can't even find the bloody village."

The dragonet chirped again.

"What does that mean?" She shoved the note into the pocket of her cloak. "I need to get to Tavine and find the Reader, but I'm pretty sure you don't understand a word I'm saying."

The dragonet let out a sound halfway between a hiss and a grunt.

She blinked. "You can?"

His head dipped. So he *did* understand her, though he couldn't speak Zeutenian himself. The dragonet had taken a liking to her, for some inexplicable reason, and considering he was the only one who'd given her any help in the past two days, she'd be a fool to send him away.

Evita gave him a considering look. "Do you have a name?"

The dragonet made the same odd chirping noise and shuffled his wings.

"Can I call you Chirp? That might be easier for both of us." Not least because she was fairly sure she couldn't imitate the noise he'd just made without sounding as if she was being strangled.

The dragonet's chirps gained an enthusiastic hint, which she took as an affirmative.

"Let's go, then, Chirp."

Evita continued through the forest, Chirp padding beside her. When the trees thinned a little and she found the mountain's shadow looming over her again, she groaned. "Did I just spend half the night walking in circles?"

The dragonet squeaked and then jabbed his tail to the left. Did he want her to follow him? She had nothing to lose by this point, so Evita turned left and walked on. The trees continued to thin out, and soon, she came to a low wooden fence. A *man-made* fence. Beyond, she glimpsed several stone buildings between the trees. Dawn crested the tops of the pines surrounding the village, painting the skies in shades of pink and gold.

EMMA L. ADAMS

"Thank you." She breathed out. "I don't know how I'll repay you... though I suppose I already saved your life, didn't I?"

The dragonet chirped, while Evita resisted the impulse to leap and cheer. She still needed to find the Reader, and while Tavine appeared to be even smaller than the fishing village she'd grown up in, the simple stone buildings all looked similar. After parting ways with the dragonet, Evita found a gate leading into the village and hesitated for a heartbeat before removing her cloak. Her clothes were soaked and rumpled, and she probably looked like a half-drowned goat, but it couldn't be helped.

Folding her cloak under her arm, Evita went looking for someone to ask for directions. Her gaze caught on the local tavern, whose owners might be knowledgeable on the latest news, but on second thoughts, it wouldn't do to attract too much attention. Taverns bred gossip, and besides, it was too early in the morning for her to ask questions about the Reader over drinks with the locals.

Instead, she stopped a teenage farm boy with the pale complexion of an inhabitant of the Range. "Hello. Can you point me to the house of Aurel Carnelian, the Reader?"

He pointed over his shoulder. "She's in that house right at the foot of the mountain, but that won't do you any good. She's not at home."

"She isn't?" She couldn't keep the disappointment from her voice. "Where is she, then?"

"She went to the Sentinels' cave." He pointed towards a path leading out of the east side of the village. "Said she wanted to see what the cause of that odd storm was. You know the Readers, they're more in tune with magic and such than the rest of us are."

Evita would have to take his word for it on that, because all she remembered about the Sentinels was the little Master Amery had told her. He'd said they weren't powerful but they had magic of some kind that would enable them to help her find her target. Yet doubts trickled into her mind like rainwater. Why would Master Amery send Vekka and Izaura after the same target? He'd delivered her a warning, so perhaps the others had failed, but did that mean Astera had found them first? Had he killed them?

She shut down the thought. She'd come all this way, after all, and the Reader might be able to help her with her other task... finding her family's killer.

Evita traipsed over to the fence and found the dragonet sitting on the other side, concealed in a thicket between pine trees. "Turns out she's up in the mountains. Still sure you want to come with me?"

The dragonet chirped in answer, while Evita resigned herself to following the dirt track that circled the village back to the shadow of the Range. The trees were a tad thinner there, affording her a view of the towering peaks ahead of her, while she fervently hoped the cave wasn't too high up. At this rate, her first question to the Reader would be to ask if she had somewhere for her to sleep.

Yet Master Amery's face appeared every time she closed her eyes. He'd sent her on this mission, and if she failed, she'd face punishment at his hands. Or worse—that child.

Worse than being thrown off a cliff? Powers above, she

was tired, but that child had evoked a different kind of fear than the Master's stark brutality. A deeper one.

Chirp continued to follow her as she came to a path sloping up the mountainside. Not the same route she'd come in by, but the dragonet seemed to know it well. Flapping his wings, he led her up the steep path. The climb exhausted her already weary bones, and when her steps started to falter, the dragonet slowed to keep pace with her and made chirping noises of encouragement. Finally, the path ran out, and she found herself looking at a solid cliff. It didn't look much like a cave. The dragonet knocked against the cliffside with a clawed foot and then paced away.

"The Reader's in there?"

Evita sank into a sitting position with a groan. What was she supposed to do now? Wait in the tunnel for the Reader's return or find another way in? She needed to rest her eyes first, though, just for a short while.

Throwing the cloak over herself, Evita sank down and leaned against the side of the tunnel wall, and she was unconscious in moments.

———

Humans truly were noisy. Especially when you were killing them. They always screamed and flailed and generally made an unnecessary fuss. And the blood— again, such a mess. Still, that was a problem for whoever had to peel what was left of the family off the stable floor and mop up the crimson smears.

Actually, the boy thought, tilting his head on one side

to consider the effect, it was an improvement. Red was a good colour. Bloodred.

He wanted to make Arien Astera bleed. The blood of an Invoker, even a broken one, would sate him for long enough that he wouldn't have to keep killing peasants to maintain his form, and besides, he was out of patience with people refusing to comply with his entirely reasonable demands. Perhaps the fault lay in the childlike form he'd chosen to wear, but he suspected that the error was more a flaw of humanity itself. The people of this continent had grown complacent, lazy, and had forgotten their history. Aestin might have its own significant flaws, but some of its people retained a sense of their old greatness. The one who'd found him, for instance, and who'd given him access to this form.

It wasn't until he'd walked in the skin of a human that he began to understand their tendency to act upon impulse at any given opportunity. Their lives were so short, fraught with danger, and it was no wonder they let their emotions get the better of them. As he began to clean the blood off his hands, he sensed one of the horses watching him. The beast snorted as though unimpressed by the violence inflicted on its former masters, but it calmed at the boy's whispered command. He'd always had a way with animals. He was, after all, a distant descendent of Gaiva Herself.

And it was past time for him to take what was due to him.

The youngest Astera had eluded him for too long, and when the wraiths he'd sent the previous day had informed him that the Sentinels themselves had got involved, he'd lost his grip on his remaining shred of patience. That inept assassin's empty promises had been the last straw. As usual, he'd have to take care of matters himself.

A window opened before him, and he addressed the shimmering outline of the wraith waiting on the other side. "Lead me directly to the Sentinels' outpost."

He'd kill the Sentinel first. Then he'd slaughter Arien Astera, spill his lifeblood, and be done with this whole wretched continent.

14

Z elle tightened her grip on the staff, but she might as well have held nothing but a stick. Three wraiths detached themselves from the trees, semitransparent and emanating coldness that put her in mind of looking into the depths of that terrible storm. There was nowhere to run, unless they hurled themselves from the cliffs and hoped the thick canopy of tree branches broke their fall.

Bracing her hands on the staff, she faced the wraiths. "I thought I told you to go away."

"You should be dead." The wraiths' hissing voices addressed Rien. "The storm should have killed you."

"We tricked it." Rien lifted his chin, defiant. "The storm had no intelligence, and neither do you."

The wraiths took no heed of the insult. They spoke as one: "We have orders. We will obey."

"Good for you," said Zelle. "Whose orders, exactly? Not the Changers?"

She'd spoken without real thought to her words, but

the wraiths hissed in response. "No. The Changers' arrows cannot pierce the defences of the Sentinels... but we can."

"Arrows?" Rien echoed. "You know who sent them. They sent you too."

Zelle's breath caught. No, that was impossible. The Changers served the Crown, and while they did possess some magic of their own, she'd never heard of them using constructs before. These monstrosities weren't their creation... but how had the person who'd sent them got hold of the Changers' arrows?

The Changers' arrows cannot pierce the defences of the Sentinels. If they'd been anywhere other than here, then the first arrow would have found its mark and Rien would be dead. As it was, the wraiths drifted towards the pair of them, a wave of icy air chilling Zelle's blood.

Rien drew back and hurled something at the wraiths. An arrow—or rather, a piece of the arrow he'd snapped earlier. Zelle expected it to have no effect on the semi-transparent shadowy creatures, but it pierced the central wraith through the centre.

All three fell back, emitting a hissing noise of pain that reverberated in the air.

Zelle whispered to Rien, "I didn't know they were vulnerable to spelled arrows."

"It was a hunch," he murmured back. "Pity I only had the one."

The hissing stopped. As they watched, the three wraiths merged together, becoming even more indistinct as their cloud-like forms melded into one being. The arrow Rien had thrown lay on the other side of the single large wraith, and Zelle had nothing to hand but the staff.

"Perhaps you shouldn't have thrown away the one thing that can hurt them."

"The thought did cross my mind." His didn't budge, his gaze on the arrowhead lying near the wraith's hovering form. There must be a way for her to distract its attention.

Pointing the staff directly at the wraith, Zelle raised her voice. "I wouldn't threaten the Sentinel's family if I were you."

"You aren't the Sentinel," said the wraith.

Ignoring the cold feeling in her chest, Zelle took a step towards them. "The staff contains the magic of a Great Power, did you know? Are you afraid of it?"

The wraith drifted closer to her, its shadowy form skimming the path, and Rien seized his chance. Diving behind the wraith, he seized the fallen arrowhead and flung it at the wraith from behind.

The arrow struck the wraith in the spot where the top of its spine would have been, had it been human. The wraith staggered forwards as though something larger than an arrow had pierced its nonexistent flesh, and it lacked its former grace as it turned on Rien.

The creature's voice rattled in Zelle's ears. "My master will see to it that you regret this."

"Who?" Zelle demanded. "What master do you speak of?"

The wraith spoke no more, its form fraying at the edges like worn fabric, and Zelle watched in disbelief as the wraith dissolved into mist.

Rien reached down and picked up the worn shard of arrow. "This is more useful than I thought. Next time someone fires one of these at me, I'll try not to break it."

"Ha." Zelle rested the staff on the ground. "I think it's

safe to say the person who ordered the arrows to be fired at us also sent those wraiths. This master of theirs."

But the Changers' own symbol had been on the note they'd sent with the arrows. If the person who'd sent the wraiths was working alongside the Changers, then what had possessed the Crown's assassins to turn against the Sentinels? Or had they named Rien as an enemy of the entirety of Zeuten and Zelle as guilty by association?

"We should keep going" was all Rien said. Perhaps he'd had the same thought.

Zelle continued to walk downhill. She found herself wondering if the wraiths had been reluctant to attack her because of the staff or if Rien had been their only target. If they feared the staff, they couldn't have been responsible for her grandmother's disappearance, could they? She was no closer to answers on the Sentinels' location, and while finding her sister would lift the burden of seeking answers from her own shoulders, she couldn't imagine turning her back on Rien when she reached the village.

Zelle hadn't the faintest clue what Aurel would think of her bringing a stranger to her home, let alone a stranger who might just have brought the Changers, the wraiths, and the wrath of some unknown Aestinian Invoker upon them, but she'd take Grandma's disappearance seriously enough to listen to her. Whether she'd be able to make sense of the situation, though, remained to be seen.

The path steepened as they drew closer to the forest below. Somewhere on their right lay the entrance to the Sentinels' cave and the second outpost itself, but thankfully, her sister lived on more solid ground. When they reached the beginning of the track connecting the mountain to the village of Tavine, Zelle asked Rien, "Can you remember anything of your past now?"

Rien's brow furrowed. "No. Why?"

"I thought the memory loss might have to do with the magic around the Sentinels' outposts," she explained. "We just left the second outpost behind, but I suppose we're still close enough to its magic that its effects would linger."

"You think so?" Rien's head tilted. "Why would your magic erase my memory?"

"I don't know," she said. "It's not *my* magic, anyway. As you're about to see, when you meet Aurel."

The dirt track had turned into a swamp in the aftermath of the storm, and she had to test the ground with the staff before taking a step. She expected—almost hoped—the staff might raise a fuss, but it remained resolutely silent.

"Do the Sentinels' outposts often erase visitors' memories?" asked Rien.

"No," she replied. "Which is why I wasn't sure that was the reason. The other possibility is that the spell might have been used before you came here and caught up with you at the Sentinels' quarters."

There hadn't been anyone else out there in the storm, so if the mountain itself hadn't been responsible, she could think of no other explanation.

He seemed to consider her words. "You think your sister might be able to help? You mentioned her power works by Reading someone's possessions…"

"But you don't have any." There was that slight issue, but she'd been too fixated on getting off the mountain to think about how they'd handle the next obstacle. Namely, her younger sister.

Thinking back to her last visit to Aurel, there was no guarantee she'd even be at home. Her sister was just as likely to have been lounging in the guest room of some out-of-town traveller instead. Zelle had no patience to chase her around according to her whims, not when someone wanted them both dead.

Zelle's gaze dropped to the staff. *Any suggestions?*

No answer. Zelle released a sigh and murmured aloud, "Would it help if I said I was sorry for using you to bar the door? You were all I had."

Yes, they'd figured out how to get rid of the storm in the end, but the staff had won them time they wouldn't otherwise have had. While the staff might have helped prevent her from being swept away in that avalanche earlier, she couldn't believe it was still maintaining a stubborn silence even now they'd reached their destination.

"Fine," she murmured to the knotted wood. "We'll find Aurel soon, and we'll get your owner back. Soon you won't have to deal with me any longer, and you can go back to keeping Grandma company on her ill-advised jaunts into the woods."

No response came, but Rien gave her a sideways look. "The staff doesn't have any advice, then?"

"No, but I have an idea." Her gaze swept the path ahead of them and the sloping route to the second outpost. "We're going to the Sentinels' cave."

15

"What exactly is the Sentinels' cave?" Rien asked Zelle as they began to climb the path again, this time angling to the right.

"It's kind of like the Sanctum, in that it only lets Sentinels in," Zelle answered.

Plainly unsatisfied with that explanation, Rien frowned. "Yes, but what does it *do?*"

"It shows you the truth," she replied. "Like the Sentinels, it has the ability to Read you but without the need for an item of yours. Instead, it requires direct contact. Fair warning... it can be painful."

She'd only set foot inside the Sentinels' cave a handful of times before, and each of those occasions had been permanently etched in her mind.

His brow furrowed. "What do you mean by contact?"

"You'll see."

Taking him into the cave was as risky as taking him to the Sanctum, except worse, because now she had more idea of the extent of the enemies he'd made. She didn't have any excuses this time. If this went wrong, then the fault was entirely her own. Yet the wraiths' appearance had solidified her certainty that Rien wasn't the guilty party in whatever feud he'd brought across the ocean with him. Whatever the reasons for the Changers' apparent involvement, whoever had summoned the wraiths must be tied to her grandmother's disappearance. It couldn't have been an accident that she'd vanished at the same time as the storm's arrival, after all.

Zelle didn't relish the idea of staying in the mountains for any longer after their narrow escape, but the cave wasn't as hard to reach as the Sanctum, and there wasn't so much as a single cloud in the sky now that the storm had passed. She picked a direct route until the ground flattened out, where Zelle reached for a hidden lever in the cliff wall in front of them.

As she did so, she spotted several footprints in the churned-up mud at the entrance. Had someone been here recently? Grandma? No, Aurel was the more likely candidate. Perhaps she'd noticed the oddness of the storm after all. The sense of being watched pursued Zelle into the narrow tunnel burrowing into the rock. Like in the Sanctum and the other Sentinels' passageways, lanterns had been affixed to the walls, their ever-burning flames lighting the way through the short tunnel.

At the end, a large cavern waited, with stalagmites jutting upwards from the rocky floor and a sizeable rock dominating the centre. Jet black in colour, the rock glowed as if lit from beneath, exuding a chill that felt like a cold breath on her face. Zelle's gaze dropped briefly to the staff, but it didn't speak a word to her. Below her feet, the path was flattened by countless footsteps from previous generations of Sentinels who'd made regular treks to consult the rock that lay in the centre of the room. Including Aurel, but if she'd been here earlier, she wasn't now.

Shivers chased each other down Zelle's spine when she forced her mouth open to speak. "We seek an audience with the Sentinel."

Rien shot her a sideways look. "Is one of the Powers inside that rock?"

"In a manner of speaking," she said. "The rock is capable of answering any question you ask, if it so desires, and it communicates through images rather than words. Put your hand on it and ask it to show you your identity."

Rien's eyes widened a fraction. When he didn't move, Zelle took the staff in one hand and pressed her other palm flat against the rock.

"Show me our enemy," she murmured to the Sentinels' rock. "Show me where Grandma is."

Rien reached out and pressed his own palm to the rock, his breath quickening. "Show me who I am."

The rock remained still and quiet for an instant, but the feeling of being watched intensified. Zelle had a brief moment of shock when her gaze shifted and she saw a pair of distinctly *human* eyes watching her from behind the rock—and then the world disappeared.

———

Arien faced his father, who stood with his left hand resting on the top of his staff. Thorns trailed down its wooden length, while its crimson colouring was vivid enough to make the polished wooden surroundings look washed-out. Though Arien carried

181

an identical staff of his own, he'd never quite achieved the same level of assuredness his father held in his posture. Volcan Astera's hand flickered with crimson streaks, thorny vines snaking up and down his wrist as they always did when he was agitated.

"Your brother is missing," said Volcan.

"No, he's more likely to be drunk in an alleyway," Arien told him. "It wouldn't be the first time. Shouldn't you be more concerned with the Trevains? I told you about their scheming yesterday."

"The Trevains are why I'm concerned," said Volcan. "I'd rather have your brother here where I can keep an eye on him." He ran his hand over the staff again, more thorns flickering at his fingertips. By Astiva, he really was worried. Yes, the Trevains were one rank below their own family in terms of their magical prowess, but it was Torben who'd first noticed them selling Relics at the local market.

"I didn't believe him at first," Arien said to his father. "I'm sure that's why he took matters into his own hands, but that doesn't mean he's run into any trouble."

Unable to restrain his curiosity, Torben had disguised himself and tried to buy one of the Trevains' Relics. They'd caught him in the act but not before he'd confirmed that the Relics they sold, at a premium price, were the genuine artefact.

"He went after them again, Arien. You know he did."

He wasn't wrong. Torben had talked Arien into coming with him to interrogate them the following day, but the Trevains hadn't shown up at the market. Torben had marched off in frustration, and that was the last Arien had seen of him.

"I'll go and look for him," said Arien. "This is a waste of time, you know. He's probably in some village girl's bed again."

Volcan sighed. "Yes, but it's better to be sure."

"Then I'll be back in an hour."

Arien left the room, tightening his grip on his own staff. This would be far from the first time his impulsive younger brother had gone astray without telling his family, but his father's concern was understandable.

After departing the house, Arien walked towards the market, its stalls wreathed in colourful banners. The scents of fried seafood, baked apples, and other delicacies filled the air along with the briny smell of the sea. Sellers thronged the street corners, handing out flowers—and in some cases, Relics, in the form of jewels and decorative rocks. Arien would bet his family's fortune they were all fake, but the Trevains' business ventures had left even his father baffled. Relics had been the domain of the main Invoker families for a thousand years or more, and selling pieces of their own power to commoners went against their very nature.

Arien did his best to ignore the stares his staff drew as he wove through the crowd, and he inwardly cursed himself for taking such a direct route. He fixed a smile on his face and managed to shake off a contingent of giggling teenage girls by offering a gold coin to anyone who'd seen his brother recently. Volcan would reprimand him later, but word spread through the crowd like a forest fire, rippling back and forth along with Arien's brother's name.

Then the voices were abruptly silenced, buried beneath the sound of an almighty blast. Arien spun around, his shoulders stiffening when he glimpsed smoke billowing over the rooftops. Clouds of thick blackness blotted the sky beyond the market, from the direction of the Astera estate.

From his home.

Rien felt his conscious body stirring, yet he was unable to look away from the vision. Not even as Arien Astera turned back and began to push through the market's crowd, no longer paying them any attention, his gaze fixed on the sky.

I am Arien Astera, son of Volcan Astera. The name ricocheted around his head. *Arien Astera. Arien Astera.*

The vision faded out. Back in the cave, Rien let go of the rock, reeling backwards. His hand burned with cold, while a sharp pain reared up in his chest, a reminder that he'd never seen his family alive again after that day... but he hadn't seen it all. Not yet. He needed to return to the vision to see the remainder of his memories.

At his side, Zelle stood frozen, her palm pressed to the rock and the edge of the staff resting on the ground at her feet. Her mouth was pressed tight in an expression of concentration, and her eyes were closed. He reached out to touch her arm, and the sensation of being watched pressed upon him like a knife to his throat.

Rien turned on his heel, and the numbness of the vision was replaced with a fresh wave of shock. In the cave's opening, visible through the tunnel, a shape he could only describe as a *door* had opened. On the other side, he glimpsed the vague impression of blurred white, like clouds—until a person stepped out into the tunnel and smiled at him knowingly.

Rien was fairly sure he'd never seen this boy in his life. He couldn't be older than twelve or so, slight and pale with black hair. He was utterly unremarkable aside from his eyes, which were as blue as a frozen lake. Combined with his even white teeth, which bared in a smile, they brought a chill to his skin. They weren't human eyes.

"You've been waiting for me, haven't you?" the boy asked, his voice soft, lightly accented.

Rien swallowed, his throat dry. "Who are you?"

Why did this child look so familiar? He wasn't part of the vision the rock had shown him, Rien was sure, but he was equally certain that whatever lay behind that doorway wasn't part of the regular world at all.

Still smiling, the boy reached behind his back and withdrew a staff, crimson and decorated with thorny vines. A jolt of recognition pierced him to the core.

"This was your brother's staff." The boy continued to smile. "The poor fool screamed for you to come and rescue him, but I told him you weren't coming."

Rien's heart contracted. *Torben.* He'd run straight back home when he'd seen the flames, abandoning his task to find his brother, but he'd already been too late to save the others.

The boy raised the staff. "I expected to find the Sentinel here, not you, but this makes it so much easier."

Rien's limbs remained locked into place despite his instincts urging him to move, to attack, to scream, to fight —anything other than waiting to die. Yet the boy didn't move an inch. Could he not enter the cave? Zelle had mentioned it being magically protected... which meant Rien was safe as long as he didn't leave.

As long as Rien remained a coward.

"It was pointless of you to run," the boy said softly. "You should have known I'd catch up to you."

The chill spread to his core. The staff had turned the same icy blue as the boy's eyes.

That's not right, he thought. *The staff should be red. What did he do to it?*

The boy watched him for a moment. "I'd hoped this would be more enjoyable, but you're no challenge to me while you're in this state. I wanted to kill Arien Astera. Not you."

Rien wrenched his jaws apart. "Who *are* you?"

A glow alighted in those blue eyes. "They call me Orzen. You should know the name of the one who sent me."

The ice-cold feeling in Rien's chest weighed him down and pushed him to his knees. Zelle remained frozen, captured in whatever vision the stone had shown her, oblivious to her surroundings. Even to the wraiths sweeping into the cave, their icy hands reaching for Rien.

How can they be in here? Even the boy couldn't enter… but the wraiths who'd attacked them earlier had claimed they were able to get around the Sentinels' defences.

He backed up against the rock, Zelle standing motionless at his side. Either he let the wraiths kill both of them or he left the cave to confront the boy and meet his own end that way. Whatever the case, he'd be dead before he had time to consider what the rock had shown him.

Or to recall the name of his true enemy.

He took a step forwards, and a rock clattered to the ground a moment before a winged shape with sharp teeth lunged across the cave, crashing into his adversary. The spell relinquished its grip on Rien when the boy staggered under the weight of his attacker, releasing a stream of curses in a language Rien didn't know.

What in the name of the Powers?

He hurried over to the tunnel entrance, where the boy had shaken off his attacker and was bleeding from several deep-looking cuts to his face.

"You will bleed for this," he growled, sounding quite deranged. "You will bleed, Arien Astera."

Another voice shouted from outside the tunnel, "Get out of my cave!"

A grating noise sounded, as of rock sliding against rock, and the cave entrance began to close—with the boy standing directly in its path. Rien might have imagined the dragon-like creature, but he didn't imagine the flash of incredulous disbelief in the boy's eyes an instant before the tunnel sealed itself in front of him, dust and rocks scattering in its wake. Rien coughed, hand outstretched as if to close around the staff the boy had been holding—

The staff.

A pain struck him in the chest, sharp and sudden. His forehead hit the cave floor, and he knew no more.

16

The world was ending. Or so it seemed to Evita, anyway. A howling wind swept through the cave, and she clung to the side of the stalagmite, hoping the cave's ceiling wouldn't give way and crush her to death. The dragonet was nowhere in sight. He'd probably been swept away, poor thing.

And it'd all been going so well. Admittedly, she'd fallen asleep outside the Sentinels' cave for rather longer than she'd intended, but when she'd woken up at the sound of voices, she'd seen two strangers dressed in thick travelling cloaks approaching the cliffside. One of them had operated some kind of hidden lever, and they'd walked into a tunnel.

Curiosity had got the better of her, so Evita had followed them in, studying them from behind. The woman was short and broad and carried a thick wooden staff. Might she be the Reader, Aurel? Her companion, tall and dark and long-haired, looked foreign to her eyes, and imposing. They exchanged words in low murmurs, facing the large rock in the cave's centre.

Intrigued, she trod closer, pulling up her hood to ensure her face was hidden. The man pressed his palm against the large rock. What was he doing?

Evita ducked behind the rock herself, and her hand accidentally brushed against it. A sudden chill shot through her palm. Despite the cloak hiding her from sight, Evita felt as exposed as if a pair of unseen eyes looked straight through her disguise. A depthless cold penetrated her limbs, and a sharp voice spoke in her mind. *Who are you?*

Evita recoiled with a gasp, and to her horror, the hood of her cloak fell back. She briefly met the wide eyes of the woman on the other side of the rock before she yanked the hood back into place, the remnants of the strange voice echoing in the back of her mind.

Holding her breath, she kept an eye on the two strangers, but neither of them was paying her any attention. Both stood frozen on the spot before the large rock. Was *that* where the voice had come from? She ought to escape before the woman recovered and told her companion of Evita's presence, but her legs refused to cooperate with her.

As she moved, the man stirred from his frozen state. He withdrew from the rock, holding his hand at an odd angle as if it pained him.

That was when events took a decided turn for the bizarre. At the cave opening, light bloomed in midair and enfolded into a shape that resembled a doorway. Fog pressed at its edges, and Evita was seized with the inexplicable and yet undeniable realisation that the door led to somewhere that wasn't the outside of the cave—or indeed near the mountains at all.

A figure stepped out of the doorway. Cold blue eyes surveyed the cave, and recognition seized her. *He's the one who wanted to see Master Amery. He's the reason I'm here.*

The boy didn't notice her. His gaze was fixed on the long-haired stranger, whose companion remained frozen at his side.

"You've been waiting for me, haven't you?" His voice was soft yet chilling.

The man responded in a deep, accented voice. "Who are you?"

Evita's instincts screamed at her to run, but the one escape route was barred by a door to nowhere. If she moved, the boy might notice her, though he seemed to only have eyes for the stranger. When he spoke, a familiar dread curled through her stomach. A staff appeared in his hands as he addressed the man, patterned with crimson vines and sharp thorns. Her breath caught. Was that a *Relic*? Evita recalled the way the boy's piercing stare had frozen her when she'd seen him at the Changers' base. Whatever power he possessed was impossible to resist, and the stranger had no visible weapons of his own.

"I'd hoped this would be more enjoyable, but you're no challenge to me while you're in this state," said the boy. "I wanted to kill Arien Astera. Not you."

Arien Astera.

Powers above. The boy *was* the person who'd hired the Changers, except he'd seemingly decided that he didn't trust them to do their jobs after all. He'd come after Arien Astera himself. And while Evita had been chasing the same target, the notion of hiding behind a rock and watching the man die was repellent. She barely caught the boy's name—Orzen—before a faint clattering sounded behind her, and her gaze snapped onto the crouching shape of the dragonet, hiding behind a nearby stalagmite. Relief filled her, turning almost immediately to dread. She'd hoped that Chirp might have escaped, but he'd followed her in here, and now they were trapped together. She had little doubt that when the boy had finished with the two strangers, he'd realise he had more company.

Evita's hands fumbled for her bow and arrows, though frankly she wasn't certain even the Changers' spelled arrows would leave a mark on the boy. She also had a sinking suspicion that if he looked past the rock, he would be able to see through her disguise as thoroughly as the dragonet had.

Speaking of the dragonet—his legs bunched as if to jump, and before Evita could breathe a word of warning, Chirp had leaped at the boy.

He stumbled back into the tunnel in evident surprise, while Evita's limbs stirred to action. The man—Astera—moved first, his movements jerky, but the boy hadn't expected the assault. Evita hissed out a breath when he managed to dislodge the small beast, but Chirp's short wings carried him out of harm's way. The boy spat out a stream of curses in no language Evita knew, and then he froze as a voice shouted from outside the cave.

Rock slammed against rock. Evita glimpsed the boy leap through the open doorway and into the fog beyond a moment before the tunnel entrance slammed closed.

Trapping them all in here together.

The dragonet landed in the shadow of a stalagmite, and Evita hurried over to check if he'd sustained any injuries. It didn't look as though that was the case, though Chirp's spindly body shook violently. A thud drew her attention to the man, who'd fallen to his knees, his eyes closing. Evita entertained the brief notion of waiting for him to wake up and asking him if he truly was Arien Astera, but there seemed little doubt that was the case.

Would Master Amery care if she brought him her target whole and intact after all? Did it matter when the person who'd hired the Changers had already found Astera and failed to catch him? The boy might have fled, but he'd be back. And if she had any sense, she'd flee while she had the chance. If she knew how to open the cave entrance from the inside, she would, but she didn't see any hidden levers. Perhaps only the cave's owner was able to find them.

Evita trod over to the woman's side, peering up at her face, but her gaze remained distant, unseeing. As for the other voice she'd heard outside—who did it belong to?

A roaring wind struck Evita in the small of the back. Spinning on her heel, she saw that the doorway lay open once again, in front of the closed tunnel. Fog seeped from within, forming tall, elongated shapes that filled the cave, bringing a chill that penetrated her to the bone. The man remained unconscious on the cave floor; the woman stood in a trance at his side... and Evita and the dragonet were the only remaining targets.

Chirp whimpered, batting at the shadowy forms with his claws. His attacks made no impact upon the creatures, which must have been made of something other than flesh and blood, but it was hardly fair for them all to attack him at once.

Reaching for her bow, she called out, "Over here!"

The creatures turned her way, and her hands wavered on the bow. How was she supposed to aim at a creature that didn't have any recognisable features? She had only three arrows, not enough to bring them all down—and that was assuming an arrow could leave a dent in a beast that appeared as solid as smoke.

A roaring gust of wind shook the entire cave, and the dragonet shrieked as his wings were caught in the maelstrom. Evita, meanwhile, stumbled against a stalagmite, struggling to maintain a grip on her bow. Her feet fetched up against a solid surface, the large shape of the rock preventing her from falling.

At this point, she'd rather face an unknown presence living inside a piece of rock than those monsters, so Evita pressed her palm to the surface in an imitation of the woman who stood in an oblivious trance at her side, and gasped, "Help me!"

That cold, sharp voice spoke in her mind again: *You should not be here.*

She stifled a wince, acutely aware of the ghastly creatures descending upon the rock. "You're being attacked!"

Another gale swept through the cave, yet she remained upright, unable to pry her hand loose from the rock. The voice spoke once again. *You dare to trespass on the property of the Sentinels?*

Panic blotted out her thoughts. "I'm here to speak to the Reader. I'm not here to steal from you."

I speak for the Reader, said the voice. *You are in the cave of the Sentinels. Ask your question.*

It wanted her to ask a question? If that meant she'd be allowed to live, she'd gladly do as the rock asked. Groping beyond the terror dominating her mind, she asked, "Can you show me who destroyed my home?"

At once, the cave and the rock disappeared, and Evita knew no more.

17

Zelle tumbled into emptiness, but the fog was deceptive. The rock was Reading her, and she'd sworn to herself never to let that happen again.

It wasn't the first promise Rien had forced her to break.

When Zelle's vision cleared a little, she found that she hovered amid a foggy blur that would have reminded her unpleasantly of the storm if it wasn't for the dreamlike sensation that pervaded the visions the Sentinels' rock provided.

No physical harm could befall her in here, but the real danger was the way the rock could reach for her dreams and crush them into dust.

The first time she'd been in here, as a child, she'd asked, *will I ever be the Sentinel?* The Sentinels' cave couldn't see into the future, but Reading a person showed the very essence of them, and the rock had sensed no magic within her. In a heartbeat, the revelation had stripped her to the core. She wasn't destined for adventure. She wasn't destined for anything at all, except loneliness or a marriage that might postpone her family's destitution for a while. Her sister would carry on the Sentinels' name, and she would be forgotten by everyone.

This time, she hadn't asked anything about herself, but nothing in the nebulous fog around her displayed Grandma's location or her enemy's nature. Even with the staff in her hands, she had failed to be worthy of the cave's notice, and the thought brought a rush of indignation. She might have no magic, but she'd retrieved the staff and kept herself alive for long enough to bring it here in order to return it to its owner. The cave might at least try to help her a little.

"Go on, send me back," she told the empty fog. "If you aren't going to answer my questions, there's no need to waste my time."

A cold, empty voice echoed around her. "They wake."

Zelle might have jumped if her feet were on solid ground. The voice came from everywhere and nowhere at the same time, and she couldn't have described the speaker if she'd tried. The voice did not sound particularly young or old, masculine or feminine. It did not, in fact, even sound human.

She forced her mouth open. "Who wakes?"

"The forgotten ones," the voice answered. "The lost. The dismissed. The damned."

"I have no idea what you're talking about." Her voice shook, but a disconnected thrill travelled through her at the notion that the presence within the rock had finally noticed her. "I asked you to show me the nature of my enemy. Is that you? What *are* you?"

"They wake, and there is nothing we can do to prevent it."

Nothing we can do? The rock itself contained a fragment of magic rumoured to belong to Gaiva Herself, but what could a piece of the creator deity possibly be powerless to stop?

"Who is waking?" She felt as though she stood on a precipice, and one wrong move would send her plummeting into an abyss.

"There is a crack in the world," said the disembodied voice. "A crack between our realm and yours has opened."

Our realm and yours. There was only one realm other than the human world... which meant she truly was talking to one of the Powers.

"Does this have to do with what happened in Aestin?" she whispered. "The magician... Invoker, who summoned the storm and the whirlpools... but a lone human can't be responsible for that much chaos, can they?"

"No," the voice answered. "They had help from elsewhere."

"Elsewhere?" Surely not the realm of the Powers... but that seemed to be what the voice was implying. Unless she was mistaken. Her family's lessons had always made it clear that the realm of the Powers was beyond reach and no traces remained behind but their Relics, even in Aestin. The voice speaking to her was nothing more than an echo, like the staff's. Right?

"As you asked... this is the nature of your enemy."

The fog vanished, and a vision filled her mind's eye. A vast ocean spread below her, and a figure walked on top of the water as though it were a solid surface. The strange figure—a boy, with dark hair and eyes as blue as frozen water—continued to walk until he reached the shore beside a sleepy-looking fishing village.

Shadows followed him, forming ghastly and inhuman shapes. While she wanted to shout a warning to the villagers, she knew it would go unheard. The boy reached the shore, and the wraiths fell upon the unfortunate humans who'd seen his approach.

Blood sprayed the sand, running in crimson streaks. The boy followed the shadows' path through the village, leaving a trail of death in his wake.

It's him.

He was the person trying to kill Rien. Except he wasn't a person at all. No human could tread upon the water as if it were ground and open windows in the air from which more wraiths rose to strike down anyone in their path. Let alone someone with the appearance of a child. But how could one of the deities be here, in the human world?

"Other deities will wake, too," said the cave's voice, echoing in the background of her vision. "Unless, that is, you stop them."

"What can *I* do?" She was no Sentinel. She had no magic of her own. How could she stand up to one of the Powers themselves?

"Close the doors," said the voice.

Light bloomed behind her eyes, and Zelle emerged from the vision in time to see several wraiths rising around her, formed of smoke and shadow. Tendrils of icy cold brushed against her skin, and she recoiled.

They weren't a vision. They were real. Worse, Rien lay on the cave floor, unmoving. The creatures had crept up on them both while she'd been ensnared in the rock's vision.

How did they get in here?

Zelle rotated on the spot, finding that she'd maintained a firm grip on the staff even while she'd been in a trance. Likely, that was the only reason the wraiths hadn't killed her where she stood.

"Get out," she warned the wraiths. "This is a sacred place."

The monstrosities hovered above the cave's floor, their shadowy forms close enough to touch Rien's prone body. Images of the same wraiths ripping villagers apart filled her mind, and she tasted bile in the back of her throat. That boy, that Power, had sent them to kill Rien. Zelle, though... they hadn't touched her. They didn't see her as a threat.

Close the doors, the voice had said. She hadn't the faintest clue what that meant, but the rock had seemed to think *she* could handle this. The Powers only knew Rien wasn't in a position to do so.

Zelle lifted the staff with both hands. "I told you to get out of here. This cave belongs to the Sentinels at the blessing of Gaiva Herself. Does whoever summoned you have no respect for the Great Powers?"

The wraiths moved towards her, and the blood froze in her veins. This was it. She'd pay for her moment of bravery with her life.

She stumbled back against the rock, and the staff stirred in her grip. The hairs on Zelle's arms stood on end. What in the Powers' names was going on? A burning sensation ran between her palms and the staff's wooden surface, but it felt more like coldness than heat. A bright glow came from somewhere behind her—from the *rock?*—but she didn't dare turn to look. When she raised the staff between her and the wraiths, a blazing streak of bluish light flared up from its surface.

Wraiths hated light and heat, as she'd discovered yesterday, but the light that emanated from the staff in her hands was no colour she'd ever seen in a flame before. From the similar glow pulsing from the rock behind her, she suspected the Sentinels' cave was loaning her its strength in the only way it could.

Seizing her chance, Zelle swung the staff at the wraiths, causing them to flail towards the cave opening. Or rather, the spot where the cave opening was supposed to be.

In its place, a patch of whiteness blocked her way, like a scrap of parchment suspended in the air. The voice seemed to whisper in the back of her mind—*There is a crack in the world.*

Dread gripped her at the sight of the emptiness looming on the other side, and then more shadows blurred its surface, moving towards her.

The wraiths had brought allies. They were constructs, formed of pure magic, but the person who'd summoned them had yet to show their face.

"Get back," she told the wraiths, her voice startlingly clear despite her trembling hands. "Leave."

She raised the staff so that its tip brushed against the rock, and its brightness intensified. Dazzling light flared outward, pushing the wraiths backwards. They fled, blurring into the whiteness and disappearing as if through an open window.

She took a step forwards, and the patch of fog contracted. The window's edges folded inwards, collapsing in on itself until nothing remained.

"What did that?" Her voice echoed through the cave, but nobody answered.

Zelle staggered, exhaustion washing over her. At her feet, Rien lay unmoving on the ground, so she crouched down beside him. His lips were blue as if with cold, his face deathly pale. Veins stood out on his left hand, which was clasped over his chest. No, not veins but lines, like faded ink, spreading across the back of his knuckles. She grabbed his wrist, feeling for a pulse.

The staff spoke loudly in her ear. *Get out, you fools, before they come back.*

Zelle startled. "You're talking to me again?"

You humans never cease to astound me with your skewed priorities.

"You almost left me for dead," she said accusingly. "Where'd that window go? Or rather, where did it come from to begin with?"

Its owner fled, said the staff, in what she thought was a tone of satisfaction. *He got more than he bargained for.*

"What does that mean?"

A grating noise came from the cave's entrance, indicating someone had pulled the lever, opening the cave from outside. She hadn't even noticed it was closed, but she broke into a run, raising the staff—and found herself staring at her sister. "Aurel?"

It couldn't possibly be anyone else. Aurel's hair was auburn where Zelle's was red-tinted, which made her stand out among the other villagers, and her broad frame was stronger than Zelle's. While she didn't wield a staff like Grandma did, when she walked into a room, she turned heads. Aurel's brows drew together in confusion as she took in her sister's appearance. "What *are* you doing in here?"

"Did you shut us in?" She must have, but not intentionally, given the bemusement on her face.

"I thought you were intruders." Aurel peered over Zelle's shoulder and caught sight of Rien. "Who's that?"

"An ally. He needs help, I think... how long have you been here?" Had Aurel spoken to the cave herself recently? Had she heard—*no, that's enough, Zelle. Think about what the rock told you later.*

"I was on my way down to the village when I saw movement up here," Aurel replied. "I thought I'd accidentally left the cave open, so I closed it, but... look, one of you is going to have to explain everything, because I'm lost."

Rien sat up so suddenly that Zelle jumped back with an exclamation of alarm. "Powers! You're alive."

Rien ran a hand over his forehead as though checking he was still in one piece. "Yes, I suppose I am."

"I thought you were dead. Those wraiths..."

"The dragon killed them," he said. "I think."

"A dragon?" Had he been dreaming again? "No, I got rid of them. Or the staff did, anyway. Come on, we'd better move."

He looked around the cave, doubt etched on his face. "I'm certain I saw a dragon."

"The rock showed you a vision, right?" In truth, she hadn't the faintest idea how he'd survived the attack. The wraiths had already been close enough to touch him when she'd come back to her senses. "Never mind. Aurel wants to know what happened, and I assume you saw some of it yourself."

His mouth parted, and he shook his head. "No... not all of it."

Aurel scoffed, looking between them. "Well, both of you tell me what you saw and we can figure it out."

Rien blinked in surprise at the sight of Zelle's sister, but he pushed to his feet without argument. Zelle, meanwhile, followed her sister out of the cave before the wraiths returned. They would, she had little doubt.

Rien walked behind her, not speaking and not offering an explanation as to why she'd found him unconscious on the floor. What had he seen in the vision the rock had shown him? She wanted to ask, but she herself was reeling over what the disembodied voice had revealed to her.

Close the doors... as she'd done to the window the wraiths had come out of. No, it had closed by itself, and besides, Zelle would never have been able to scare the wraiths away without the aid of the staff. Even with Grandma missing, the staff was supposed to be Aurel's, not hers. Right?

When they emerged from the cave, Rien addressed Zelle, indicating Aurel. "You haven't introduced us."

"Right, of course." She ignored Aurel's slight smirk at her lapse in manners. "This is my sister, Aurel Carnelian, also known as the Reader. Or the next Sentinel, depending on who you talk to. Aurel, this is Rien. We came here from the other outpost. I take it you've had as much trouble as we have?"

"Trouble?" Her gaze fell on the staff. "What's that doing here?"

"Grandma is missing," Zelle said. "That's the first part. The second is that we were attacked by wraiths inside the cave itself, and I'd quite like to be back on solid ground before I tell you the rest."

Aurel pursed her lips. "I'll hold you to that."

They walked downhill, following the dirt track to the village. Rien said nothing, and when Zelle gave him a glance, she saw that his head was bowed and he was turning over the medallion in his hands. She turned back to the staff instead.

"I take it you accepted my apology, then?" she murmured.

No, the staff said, *but I thought it was prudent to keep you alive.*

"Has the rock forgotten who the Sentinel is?" she whispered. "Why not ask Aurel instead?"

This is out of the realm of the Sentinels' responsibilities. The doors between worlds are open, and they need to be closed.

She forced a laugh, a sinking sensation in the pit of her stomach. "Maybe that's what Rien saw too."

He didn't look up at the sound of his name. A flicker of unease stirred within her. What had he seen in his own vision? Had it been anything like what she'd seen in hers?

Only then did she realise the Sentinels' cave had neglected to show her where her grandmother had been taken, or even if she was alive. They might have found her sister, but they were farther from answers than ever.

18

A vision unfolded before Evita's eyes. The ocean filled her line of sight, and homesickness rocked her like a boat tossed upon the waves. When she recognised her village, a gasp escaped her.

Especially when she saw the boy walking atop the waves, approaching her home and flanked by creatures not unlike the ones that surrounded her in the cave.

I have to go back... but the vision refused to let her go. Evita's mouth stretched in a silent scream as the boy walked onto the shore, shadows swirling around him and forming monstrous shapes.

Nobody stood a chance. The creatures tore them apart, the boy walking through their blood and smiling that horrible inhuman grin. Evita could do nothing but watch as he walked through the bloody remains and followed the road to Saudenne.

There, he became more cautious. He approached an inn and rented a room, using the coin he'd taken from the villagers he'd slaughtered. Evita could do nothing to warn the proprietors that the lone boy they'd so kindly offered shelter to was not what he seemed. There was a method of sorts to his bloodlust, if you could call it that—he always killed before he summoned up those ghastly creatures, or before he opened one of those odd doorways in the air and stepped through to some other place entirely. Evita began to wonder if she was dreaming after all, at least until the boy stepped out of a doorway and appeared on a mountain path she recognised all too well.

Evita's attention sharpened when she saw him approaching a gangly novice wearing a plain black cloak, and she watched their own conversation replay itself in stunned disbelief. How could the rock possibly know all this? Could it see into her thoughts? A thousand more questions exploded in her mind, but her mouth wouldn't move to voice them aloud. Instead, she watched the thing that wasn't a boy enter Master Amery's office and convince him to send his assassins to kill Arien Astera. After leaving, he stepped through a crack in the world and vanished.

The spot where the boy had disappeared resembled a door or a large window, and on the other side, she glimpsed nothing but a wall of solid grey. The vision dragged her closer, even as she fought to escape back to consciousness, and she found herself looking into a space shaped like a small room, recognisable only as such by the elderly woman sitting on the floor, an aggrieved expression on her face.

What is a person doing in there?

The woman was short and broad, as far as Evita could tell, with tawny skin and dark-grey hair tangled around her narrow face.

"You should be scared," growled a voice that came from just out of sight. "You complain too much."

"You try being stuck in here at my advanced age," the old woman grumbled back. "I've been positively well-behaved, considering there isn't a decent chair to be found in this accursed place. I suppose *you* wouldn't understand such things, but by human standards, I'm old enough to be in need of certain comforts. The least I deserve is a little respect, even from the likes of you."

It belatedly occurred to Evita that if the woman was human, her companion was something else entirely, but that was the least of her present worries. The rock might have shown her the beast who'd destroyed her home and killed her family, but if she never got out of the cave, then her revenge wouldn't matter.

As though prompted by her thoughts, the vision faded into nothingness. Cold spread across her palm, and she came back to alertness. Breaking away from the rock, she fell to her knees on the cave floor.

The rock *had* answered her questions, but it'd only confirmed what part of her had already begun to suspect... the person who'd hired the Changers and the person responsible for her family's deaths were one and the same. Never mind the Reader—the boy was her real target, and the reason she'd joined the Changers in the first place.

Chirp tapped her with his tail, startling her upright.

"You're all right," she breathed. "Where did those creatures go?"

The cave was empty. Not only had the shadowy creatures vanished, but the man and woman had gone too. Had the rock itself somehow got rid of her attackers, or had her companions recovered and driven the beasts away themselves? She didn't know, but the doorway into nowhere no longer barred her exit. Instead, a wall of rock did.

"Oh, Gaiva's tits." Evita lurched to her feet and approached the rocky barrier, while the dragonet scampered ahead of her and indicated a lever buried in the rock with his tail. "What... you want me to pull that?"

The dragonet chirped, while Evita fiddled with the lever until the cave wall slid open. Nobody else was waiting on the other side, by some divine miracle, and the others hadn't seen her at all. Except for that brief moment when her cloak had slipped and she and the woman had locked eyes—and if the rock had shown her anything like it had Evita, she might have dismissed the sight as part of the vision.

Evita hurried through the tunnel, unable to believe her luck. She had no idea how long she'd been gone, but the sun was still up, and the path ahead was bare. Chirp left the cave behind her and prodded another lever with his tail, causing the tunnel to seal itself behind them.

"Good idea," she murmured. "We don't want to get on the Reader's bad side."

Not now she might be their last hope. In fact... the truth of Evita's predicament sank in as she looked down the dirt track leading to the village.

"What am I supposed to do now?" She directed the question at the dragonet, who'd continued to follow her on foot, chirping occasionally. "I'm here on a false errand."

If the vision the rock had shown her had been the truth—and she had no reason to doubt what she'd seen—the Changers had been taking orders from the very creature that had killed her family. He wanted to kill Arien Astera, and while he hadn't finished the job himself, he plainly had no faith in the Changers to do so. As for the Reader... well, who else might be able to help her at this point? Aurel Carnelian might well slam the door in her face when she learned the Changers had sent her, but Arien Astera and the Reader were the boy's enemies, which meant they were on the same side. If Evita explained her situation, she might even be able to help them.

As she continued down the sloping path, her thoughts returned to the impossible things she'd seen in the vision —and outside of it too. Like that doorway to nowhere and those voices she'd heard on the other side. When darkness fell, she found herself quickening her pace, half expecting more shadowy beasts to rise from the trees to attack her. She still had no explanation for what had caused them to vanish in the first place.

As she neared the forest, more doubts crept into her mind. Sneaking up on the Reader at this late hour might not be advisable, but she wasn't sure she had the energy for another confrontation. The rock had claimed to speak for the Reader, and it hadn't thrown her out of the cave. That ought to mean Aurel should trust her, right?

Reaching the ground, Evita followed the dirt track leading back to the village. The dragonet followed, though he didn't seem to like the marshy ground. A faint growling escaped him whenever his small feet stuck in the thick mud, and when the village came within view, Chirp swung around, his scaly body blocking her path.

"What is it?" she whispered.

Chirp flicked his tail. She turned to the left, at first

seeing nothing but thick pines. Then she looked closer, and an odd flickering caught her eye at the top of the fence. The image of an arrow appeared and disappeared just as quickly, pointing towards the village.

She stifled a gasp, recognising the concealed shapes of several other Changers. They were wearing cloaks that hid them from sight, but they couldn't hide their weapons, pointing over the back of the fence that circled a large stone house at the rear of the village. The Reader's house, Evita was willing to bet.

It seemed that the other Changers had made it there first.

19

A urel strode ahead of Zelle, while Rien walked alone, his head bowed. Among the trees, Zelle began to spot the outlines of some stone cottages ahead of them, but her sister's house lay beyond the rest of the village. Twice as big as its neighbours and flanked by two thick oak trees, the stone house sat behind a low wooden fence that belied the genuine magical defences built into its stone walls.

They'd made it to Tavine, albeit not in the circumstances she'd ever have expected. No sign of any wraiths lurked outside the house, and nor did the Changers, but Zelle didn't release her breath until her sister unlocked the door and revealed the lower floor of the Reader's home.

Aurel stepped aside, muttering something about checking the defences around the property and allowing Zelle and Rien to enter the house first. The living room contained the remnants of their family's antique furniture, with embroidered armchairs sitting between cabinets of what the staff had charmingly referred to as "junk". Like her grandmother, Aurel insisted on acquiring more and more oddities and trinkets every time Zelle visited.

Beyond the living room lay the kitchen—judging by its neglected state, Zelle's hopes of a hot meal might have been wishful thinking—and another door led into the room in which Aurel met with customers who wanted her to Read for them. Grandma frequently griped about Aurel using her gift for such mundane purposes, but Zelle was more concerned by the fact that she didn't seem to have used her earnings to hire a new servant to keep the house clean and tidy. Even the Reading Room overflowed with dusty shelves, while the Book of Reading lay open on the desk next to a deck of Relics and Ruins cards.

Rien leaned over to examine the book. "The pages are blank."

"They're supposed to be," said Zelle. "Only Readers can use the book, and like the Sentinels' rock, it shows images rather than words."

Rien turned over the page before closing the book with a snap.

"You have no respect for old books, do you?" Zelle reached over and opened it again, though she doubted Aurel would notice. "I suppose in Aestin they're as common as mud, but I can count on both hands the number of people who can read the ancient language our ancestors brought across the ocean."

"Doesn't everyone here know how to read?"

"Not the old language," she said. "I can read a little, as well as modern Zeutenian, because my grandmother insisted on teaching me. Generally, reading ancient texts isn't seen as a useful pastime."

Rien looked up from the book and stiffened, his gaze catching on a painting on the wall behind the desk. "Who's that?"

Zelle peered up at the painting, which depicted a beautiful woman with a row of birds sitting on each arm. "Gaiva. Or... one interpretation of Her, anyway."

The birds must be the lesser Powers. Her children, and Her children's children, and so on. Zelle found her skin crawling at the memory of the boy she'd seen in the vision. If he was truly a lesser Power, then she'd never heard of one wearing the skin of a human child before.

She gave Rien a sideways glance. He regarded the birds with a frown, perhaps not used to seeing the children of Gaiva depicted in such a manner. No doubt Aestin had its own perspective on the Powers, and besides, they were generally believed to be able to shapeshift into any form they chose. As for why such a beastly creature had chosen the innocent form of a mere boy... a quiver of unease travelled through her. "Right. We need to tell Aurel... everything."

After leaving the Reading Room, Zelle removed her boots, stretching her blistered feet, and shrugged out of her coat. She would have happily handed over the meagre collection of coins in her purse for a decent bath, but not until Aurel knew the truth. Besides, Rien's taciturn state made her edgy. He followed her out of the Reading Room without speaking and didn't sit down.

Aurel entered the house, closing the door behind her. "I don't see any more intruders, but they won't be able to get past the fences anyway. We're safe."

"Haven't you managed to find a new servant yet?"

Zelle brushed some dust off the back of a chair before sitting down.

"The last one quit," Aurel replied. "Besides, I'm not made of money."

"You'd have more money if you sold some of this junk." The words came out automatically, as if part of her was driven to speak as if nothing was wrong, as if the very foundations of her world hadn't shifted beyond recognition. The lack of food and rest and their near misses with death didn't help, and when Aurel gave Rien one of her winning smiles, Zelle felt her temper rise.

"Do sit down," Aurel said to Rien. "I'm sure Zelle is going to tell me all about how you ended up in the Sentinels' cave... unless you want to talk to me somewhere more private?"

Zelle shot her a warning look. "Aurel, he can't even remember his own name."

Aurel ignored her sister. "I thought your name was Rien."

"It is." He didn't quite meet her eyes, however. "I'm told you're the Sentinel's heir and a Reader."

Aurel beamed at him. "Yes, I am. You're Aestinian, aren't you? Your Zeutenian is faultless."

This time, Rien did look directly at her. "Thank you."

Zelle cleared her throat. "To start off with, Grandma is missing."

"Went for another long walk in the forest, did she?" asked Aurel.

"No, she vanished, apparently from the inside of the outpost itself." She picked up the staff from where she'd leaned it against the chair.

Aurel's smile faded, and she addressed Rien again. "She is lying, isn't she?"

"Not as far as I'm aware," said Rien. "I reached the outpost in the mountain not long after Zelle did."

"And she let you in?" Aurel arched a brow. "You must have appealed to her softer side, if she has one."

"Aurel," Zelle said, a bite of impatience in her voice. "He was out in the storm, unconscious and half dead. As soon as I got him inside, we were attacked by gremlins and then wraiths. Even in the Sanctum—"

Aurel's eyes widened. "You took him into the *Sanctum?*"

"It's a long story." Zelle already regretted mentioning that part. It would help if Rien would add his own contribution, but he seemed more interested in the contents of the overflowing cabinets. Under other circumstances, Zelle might have found that amusing, seeing as her sister was doing everything she could to get his attention, but she found her grip tightening on the staff.

"I want to hear it." Aurel kept her gaze on Rien rather than Zelle. "Wraiths? Who'd send *wraiths* after Grandma?"

"The same person who sent the storm. You must have seen it down here."

"I *knew* it was magical," she said in triumphant tones. "I actually went to consult the Sentinel's cave myself earlier, but you know how cryptic that place can be."

"I have an inkling." At least her sister had made *some* effort to handle the situation, but she wished Aurel would stop looking at Rien as if he was a delicacy she wanted to sample. "But you weren't in the cave when we went up there ourselves."

"I can't believe you took him into the cave as well."

Amusement flickered in Aurel's expression. "I might have come to meet you at the outpost myself if I'd known you'd brought a dashing foreigner here."

"I took him into the cave because he hasn't a clue who he is," said Zelle, feeling oddly defensive. Perhaps because Rien had saved her life, when she hadn't exactly been civil to him at times, she wanted to keep him from being yet another victim of Aurel's flirtatious tendencies. "He was lying in a snowdrift when I found him outside the tower, and when he woke up, he had no memory of his name or why he'd come to the outpost."

Aurel's eyebrows climbed higher with every word she spoke. "With or without his memories, he was clearly being pursued by someone magical, and yet you let him in anyway? Who are you, and what have you done with my sister?"

"The staff spoke to me," she retaliated. "Told me that he had no magical gift and that it might have been the outpost's own magic which erased his memory in the first place. I wasn't going to leave him outside after that."

"Powers above," Aurel said. "The staff spoke to you?"

"Yes, it did, and it was the staff who told me Grandma vanished," she said. "Leaving it behind. Has she ever done that before?"

Aurel shrugged one shoulder. "It's hardly the first time she's inconveniently wandered off."

"Whoever sent that storm nearly ripped the doors off the outpost," Zelle retaliated. "We had to coax an imp into mimicking Rien to drive it away."

"You convinced an imp to do *what*?" Aurel snorted.

"Can you take me seriously for once?" Zelle asked. "If I

hadn't got rid of that storm, I wouldn't have survived to come here and warn you. Or to give you the staff."

Aurel blew out a breath. "I do take this seriously, thank you very much. I've dealt with Grandma's nonsense for years, remember? I've also told her a thousand times that I'd have more use for the staff than she does, but she never listens."

Powers give me patience. Zelle had known seeing her sister would end in one of their arguments, but not this soon. "Well, you're in luck. The staff's yours until Grandma comes back. As for Rien, he wanted you to Read his identity. That's the only reason he came here with me."

Unless he'd found out the truth in the cave, but she didn't blame Rien for being reluctant to share his deepest secrets with her overbearing sister.

"He wants me to Read his identity?" Aurel's expression turned calculating, and she turned towards Rien. "Do you have a personal possession I can borrow?"

Zelle glanced at Rien, who said, "No, I don't. I assume I lost everything at sea."

"Lost at sea?" Aurel blinked. "Powers above, you're full of surprises. We should go to the tavern for a drink, and you can tell me all about them over a mug of ale or three. I knew my sister was exaggerating when she said you forgot everything."

"The only memory he has is of being shipwrecked," Zelle informed her sister. "He doesn't want to talk about it."

Rien's brows shot up with disbelief, while Aurel tutted. "If you're trying to make him sound less endearing, that's not very nice of you, Zelle. I can help him."

"Not after a mug or three of ale, you can't," Zelle said. "That won't do either of you any favours."

"Oh, I think he needs it even more than I do," she said. "You know, I've never seen an Aestinian here before. Though I suppose you prefer to take your holidays to the Eastern Isles, not this miserable rainy country."

"Aurel." Zelle lost her grip on her last fragment of patience. "In the Reading Room. Now."

Her sister rose to her feet, her expression half surprised, half exasperated. "All right, all right."

"Not you," she told Rien, who watched Aurel as though quite unsure what to make of her. That didn't help Zelle's temper in the slightest.

Once she and Aurel were in the Reading Room, she closed the door. Aurel grinned at her. "Is there something you want to tell me alone?"

"Do you remember what Aunt Adaine used to tell us about not pissing off the gods?" Zelle asked her sister. "Rien did exactly that. Several times over, by the sounds of things. If he hadn't nearly died in the cave, I wouldn't have brought him here." That and she wanted to find out what he'd seen, but every word her sister spoke brought back the urge to walk as far away as possible.

"Says the person who let him into the *Sanctum*."

"I didn't know that at the time." Zelle found herself gripping the staff in both hands. "All I knew when I found him was that Grandma was missing and he was on the verge of freezing to death in a storm. He told me he wanted to find a book."

"He climbed the mountain in a storm in search of a *book*?"

"That's what he told me," Zelle replied. "Unfortunately,

the next time he woke up, he didn't remember anything at all. I took him into the Sanctum in the hopes that it might help him recollect his reasons for coming to the outpost, but instead, the books hid their contents from him. Ever heard of that before?"

Aurel's lips pursed. "No. Also, I can't Read him if he doesn't have any personal possessions. You'd think someone as highborn as he is would have brought a Relic with him."

"Highborn?" she echoed. "He had nothing but the clothes on his back, and he's not magical."

"Obviously, your Aestinian friend met some misfortune on the road," said Aurel. "But yes, he's clearly highborn, which means he's an Invoker. The two are inseparable."

"He's not an Invoker," Zelle argued. "Only the ruling families have magic, don't they? The staff told me he had no Relics or anything."

Aurel snorted. "He's an aristocrat if I ever saw one. The upper class wear their hair long in Aestin. It's clear from the way he speaks too. He's educated."

"So are most people in Aestin," said Zelle. "He doesn't have magic. If he had, he wouldn't have ended up lost in a storm with no memory."

"Maybe he conjured the storm and accidentally wiped out his own memory."

"Don't be absurd," said Zelle. "The storm nearly killed him. Nearly killed me too. The wraiths came from the same source."

"I wonder if it was the same person who summoned up a whirlpool in the middle of the main trading route with Aestin?"

"A whirlpool?"

In answer, Aurel pushed open the door and reentered the living room, where Rien had finally sat in an armchair, waiting for their return. She wondered if he'd heard some of their discussion, but he offered no comment of his own on Aurel's assumptions.

"Haven't you heard?" Aurel addressed both of them. "The whole south coast of Zeuten is out of bounds thanks to that whirlpool. No ships can leave Saudenne."

"Really?" Zelle glanced over at Rien. "Didn't you mention you were shipwrecked here?"

She didn't recall hearing any rumours before she'd left Saudenne, but she hadn't been paying attention at the time.

Rien inclined his head but said nothing more.

"What else did you hear?" Zelle asked her sister. "The whole coastline is out of bounds? What will the fishermen do?"

"I don't know, but I spoke to a merchant from Saudenne who was at the tavern the other night," Aurel said. "He said there's some downright disturbing reports coming from all over the region. Horrific murders, ghastly apparitions, entire villages vanishing overnight..."

A chill raced down Zelle's back at the memory of the vision... of that boy. "Did they say who was responsible?"

"No." Aurel looked at the staff in Zelle's hands. "I can't think why a foreign magician would target the Sentinels, but as for working out your friend's identity... if the Sentinels' cave wasn't able to help, then I have no idea."

"The cave..." She drew in a breath. "It showed me something, and I'm going to need you not to interrupt while I tell you. It's... it's going to be a shock."

"I'll grab a drink." Aurel ran to a cabinet and opened it, revealing several bottles of expensive-looking wine.

Rien, meanwhile, was back on his feet. When he approached the Reading Room again, Zelle followed. Her gaze landed on a large scroll leaning against the desk, depicting the edge of a map showing a curving coastline.

"I knew we had a map of Aestin here somewhere." She retrieved it and held it out to Rien. "This might help us pinpoint where you came from."

He looked down at the map without comment, but Zelle brought it back into the living room anyway. Unfurling the scroll gave her something to do with her hands, so she spread out the map in the little free space available on the floor while her sister dug in the cupboards for some dusty wineglasses.

Unlike most Zeutenian maps, this one only showed the very edge of their country where it met with the ocean, and Aestin took up most of the page. In contrast to Zeuten, whose urbanised areas dominated the coastline and whose rural areas were thickly forested, Aestin's cities were more spread out and its forests had been cut down in swathes to make room for farmland. The southern edge was bisected by a thin line of mountains but nothing so large as the Range.

Rien's attention lingered on the northwest coast of Aestin and the capital, Tauvice. He traced a line with his fingertip across the ocean towards the southernmost point of Zeuten, where Saudenne sat at the tip, prompting Zelle to ask, "Is that the way you came?"

He didn't answer. His head was bowed, an expression of total concentration on his face as he traced the route with his fingertip before moving his attention back to

Aestin. The map was doubtlessly a little out of date by now, but most of the cities would be in the same places, as would the line of mountains at the very bottom of the map that cut off the nation from the uninhabited lands in the south. The lands where Aestin's worst magical wars had been fought.

He rose to his feet, not looking at Zelle. "I'm going for a walk."

Zelle's mouth parted. "While we're being hunted? Really?"

Aurel waved a wineglass in their general direction. "Anyone want some?"

"No," Zelle and Rien chorused, before the former strode across to the door. Zelle watched him leave, wanting to call him back but feeling as numb as she had in the cave.

When the door closed behind him, she turned back to her sister, who wore an odd look on her face. "What did you say to him?"

"Nothing. I was trying to help." She rolled up the map again, more to avoid making eye contact than anything else. Her hands had begun to tremble, and when her sister offered her the wineglass again, she accepted.

It was time to reveal what the cave had shown her.

———

Rien walked through the village listlessly. Each glimpse of his reflection in the puddles appeared less and less familiar to him, even as the pieces of his identity continued to slide into place.

His family was dead. The person who'd taken his

magic had slaughtered them, and he could hardly believe he'd forgotten his name. *Naxel Daimos.* The Daimos family had been exiled for conspiring against the Emperor, and they'd been stripped of their Relics as a consequence. The other families, including Rien's own father, had seen to it that the Daimos family would never set foot in Aestin again.

He'd never have guessed one of them would have survived, much less gained enough power to topple the Astera family. He must have found a Relic, somehow, and bargained with the deity whose power lay within it. Daimos had left Rien's entire family dead, but that hadn't been enough. Rien himself had no recollection of how he alone had survived, but his escape must have prompted Daimos to send all the forces he could muster to hunt him down. After he'd nearly drowned at sea, he should have suspected Daimos would find another way to reach him even across the vast ocean separating the two continents.

Yet his memories of entering the Range were still blurred, and for all the rock had showed him, the answers as to how he'd lost them to begin with remained in as much doubt as ever. And to add insult to injury, he'd failed to stand up to that mere *child.* If not for Zelle and Aurel's intervention, he'd have died without ever avenging his family.

Anger clenched his fists. Was he not the son of Volcan Astera? No, according to that demonic child, he was nobody at all.

He couldn't tell Zelle. She'd react with nothing but pity, and besides, his enmity with Daimos was personal. He'd come in search of a new source of power to replace what he'd lost—a new Relic—and even losing his memories hadn't erased that certainty from his mind. But to learn more, he needed to return to that cave.

When he walked past the fence bordering the village, an arrow shot past him, jolting him out of contemplation. *The assassins.* Rien turned, seeing no traces of his attackers, but the arrow lay discarded on the path. Not a spelled one, like the arrows from the mountains, but maybe Daimos had sent the Changers too. If he had, and Zelle had mentioned they served only the Crown... he didn't like the implications, but right now, he'd seize on any distraction from his own thoughts.

Rien snatched up the arrow, his gaze skimming the bushes. His attackers must be well-hidden, because he didn't see so much as a hint of whoever had shot at him. Stalking towards the trees, he hurled the arrow into the bushes and was rewarded by a shuffling movement that gave away his adversaries' location. Were they using some kind of sorcery to render themselves unseen?

A second arrow whistled past his face, reminding him that they were armed while he was not, and they had the advantage of being able to aim without him seeing them. With a curse, he backed up several steps.

A reptilian shape flew through the trees and landed amid the bushes, drawing a series of shrieks and curses. Its claws lashed out, and the scrambling sound of two or three people fleeing filled the background as Rien watched in confusion. An instant later, the dragon-like creature landed on clawed feet and chirped at him.

"You," he said. "You were in the cave too. I didn't imagine you. Are you following me?"

Weren't dragons supposed to be bigger than that? None had been seen in Aestin in centuries, but it made sense that some might have survived in Zeuten's wilder areas. He hadn't known they lived this close to humans... but why had this one defended him?

Instead of answering, the dragon-like creature stalked towards the bushes, where the sounds of movement came from deeper in.

There are more of them. Hunting unseen enemies without any weapons of his own was the height of folly, and so was leaving the village to begin with. He ought to have known better, and when the sound of bows being drawn echoed from the treetops, the first stirrings of panic filtered into his mind.

More arrows flew, aimed directly at him.

———

Evita crouched near the fence of the Reader's house, doing her best to ignore the discomfort of the hard ground and the icy wind cutting through her coat. At each small noise, she suppressed a flinch. Her cloak kept her hidden, but her nerves stood on end after that awful vision she'd seen in the cave. That child who wasn't a child and the destruction he'd wreaked on her home.

And the mission he'd pressed Master Amery into giving her.

The other Changers hadn't acted against the people inside the house yet, but when Evita had tried to climb the fence, she'd found some kind of unseen barrier preventing her from accessing the Reader's property. She'd have to go through the gate, assuming it wasn't also equipped to keep her out. In the meantime, she peered over the fence and through the window to the Reader's house, trying to see her target. There were two women, she was sure, and she didn't know which of them might be the Reader. The taller red-haired woman with the loud voice and the confident stride was the obvious choice, but the shorter one held the same staff she'd brought into the cave. Granted, it was difficult to be certain of what she saw through the thick layer of grime on the window; it seemed the Reader was not taken to cleaning her house on a frequent basis.

A chittering sounded behind her, and Evita's heart leapt when Chirp crawled out of the bushes. She pressed her finger to her lips, urging him to stay quiet, but silently glad of the company.

Chirp prodded her in the spine with his tail. She heard movement behind the fence and lifted her chin when she saw the young man from earlier leaving the house. Alone.

What's he doing?

At Chirp's urging, she backed deeper into the woods, but the man aimed straight for the nearest gate out of the village. He couldn't know the other Changers were waiting, ready to strike, but if Evita defended him against them, she'd all but announce herself as a traitor to their cause. Following the fence circling the village, she kept an eye on the man as he walked out of the gate—and an arrow shot out of nowhere, narrowly missing his face.

Evita's mouth went dry. The man stopped in his tracks then seized the arrow from the path and scanned his surroundings. He didn't plan to fight off the assassins single-handedly, did he?

She had an answer to that question when he flung the arrow into the bushes and sent the hidden Changers scurrying out of range. One of them shot a second arrow, which came even closer to finding its mark. Evita gave the dragonet a nudge from behind and whispered, "Help him."

The dragonet flapped his wings and launched himself into the bushes. The resulting cries of alarm showed Evita the Changers' location as they fled the dragonet's sharp claws, and she glimpsed two cloaks flickering as they ran. *Only two?* No others should be here at all, but with the dragonet's help, she and the stranger might be able to drive them off.

Evita gave chase, her hands on her own bow, though she wasn't sure she wanted to fire at her former comrades. They didn't know they followed a false errand, after all, but they also might not want to listen to her explanations. Who would believe her? Aside from Master Amery, she was the only person who'd seen their inhuman visitor.

The dragonet positioned himself in front of the man, hissing at the bushes, while Evita heard the distinct sound of more bows being strung. Their owners were up in the trees. *There are more of them.* Flickering shapes of arrows— she counted three—pointed directly at their target.

Evita drew in a breath and let out a shriek, in an imitation of a mountain eagle. One of the arrows missed the man by a hair's breadth, while the dragonet's tail whipped up and deflected another. The man dove to the ground to snatch up an arrow for his own and hurled it into the trees, causing one of the Changers to lose their balance. A painful thud echoed in the air, while Evita stared at the man for an instant. Unarmed or not, he knew how to defend himself, and he'd done an impressive job picking out the outline of the hidden assassin amid the canopy. While the Changer lay groaning in the bushes, she heard the others climbing down to help their fallen comrade.

The dragonet chose that moment to launch forwards in a sweep of wings. A second assassin lost their foothold in the branches, while the other dropped their bow outright in their scramble to avoid being struck by Chirp's talons.

Instead of running, as she'd assume would have been his instinct, the man snatched up the discarded bow and nocked an arrow, aiming at the unseen figures in the bushes.

Unfortunately, that also included her. Now was not the time to announce her presence, but if she wasn't careful, she'd find herself skewered by the very man she'd come here to find. Arien Astera pointed an arrow directly at the bushes and fired a shot that drew a cry of pain.

Heart lurching, Evita backed into the surrounding trees, beckoning to the dragonet. Another yelp from the Changers told her that the young Astera had the situation in hand... and that Master Amery had severely underestimated his target.

No wonder he sent so many assassins to take him out.

And no wonder even that boy-who-wasn't-a-boy hadn't managed to finish him off in the cave.

Evita held her breath as Arien Astera left the prone assassins and returned to the village, casting a last distrusting look around the forest as he did so. She hesitated before following—if she was in his position, she'd be ready to tell the Reader to shoot down the next Changer who set foot near any of them. No, she'd have to approach them as Evita, not as a Changer.

A rustle of wings sounded above her head, and instinct

drove her to throw herself flat to the ground. Not a moment too soon, because a flurry of feathers and claws slammed into her from above, pinning her to the ground.

Master Amery's eagle. It hadn't even been a day since its last visit, but the urgency was clear.

"Get off me!" she hissed, her mouth dry with panic.

The eagle's claws dug into her shoulders, drawing a strangled cry. Had it seen her try to thwart the other Changers? If so, then she was as good as dead.

Evita scrambled underneath her cloak for her weapons, but her position made it impossible to aim her bow. Instead, she one-handedly grabbed an arrow and stabbed blindly in the eagle's direction.

The bird released her, enabling her to roll onto her back. The dragonet swooped in, shrieking, and the bird flew sideways into the nearby trees. She watched it disappear into the canopy and out of sight, breathing hard.

Evita lifted her head and pushed into a sitting position. The cloak didn't have so much as a mark on it from the bird's claws. It might even have helped to save her life... but she had no doubt that the eagle was on its way to tell Master Amery of her treachery.

20

Zelle finished updating Aurel on the vision she'd seen in the cave, leaving a concerned silence in her wake. Rien had declined to relate his own experience, so it would have to wait until he returned, but her own was revelatory enough.

Aurel blew out a breath. "You're seriously telling me there's a crazed child rampaging through Zeuten, leaving a trail of bodies behind him?"

"He's not a child," she said. "He's some kind of Power, one who's happy to slaughter any human who crosses his path."

"There's actually a door between our world and theirs?" asked Aurel. "How'd that come about?"

"I don't know. The Sentinels' cave wasn't very clear on that one."

"Damn," said Aurel. "The first Power to set foot in this world in centuries. No wonder he's so pissed off."

"Aurel." Zelle rubbed her forehead, a headache brewing. "He's not the only Power to interact with humans, is he? Look at Aestin's Invokers and their Relics. And what about the Changers?"

"I doubt *they've* ever spoken to a Power," said Aurel. "These days, half their recruits don't think what they do is real magic. No wonder they're becoming irrelevant. Anyway, the Powers haven't *directly* interacted with humans in centuries."

"Except the staff," added Zelle. "And the Sentinels' cave."

"They don't count," said Aurel. "They're fragments. Like the pieces of the Powers that reside inside Relics. Doesn't mean they don't have their own personalities, but they aren't whole beings."

"Not like that boy," Zelle concluded. "And—the rock told me that now this crack between the worlds has formed, more of them are awakening."

"Wonderful," said Aurel. "Well, we need to get rid of *that* one first."

"Easier said than done," Zelle murmured. "As for where this crack opened, it must have been in Aestin. That's what brought Rien here."

"Of course it started in Aestin," said Aurel. "Those families are never satisfied. Plainly, one of them decided they didn't already have enough power of their own and got more than they bargained for."

Zelle peered out of the window. "I should find Rien. I shouldn't have let him walk off alone, not when…"

Not when there was something he wasn't telling her. Had he decided to strike out on his own? He hadn't told her anything of what he'd seen in the cave, but if he'd gained any sense of his purpose here, he might have changed his mind about asking for Aurel's help after all.

Given how many enemies he had, it was almost a guarantee that he'd run into trouble again.

Zelle grabbed her boots and shoved them on. As she was fastening her coat, however, someone rapped on the door. Zelle suppressed a flinch, but Aurel simply shot her a smirk. "There he is. Told you he'd be fine."

"You didn't say any such thing."

"I knew what you were thinking." Zelle watched her sister open the door, and sure enough, Rien stood on the other side.

He took a step into the house, revealing an arrow in his hands. "The Changers are hiding in the forest. I drove some of them away, but they might have the village surrounded for all I know."

Her heart sank. "The Changers came back?"

"The *what*?" said Aurel.

Powers above. She hadn't mentioned that particular complication yet. Resigning herself to facing her sister's irritation, she said, "The Changers are involved with the people chasing Rien, somehow. Some of their spelled arrows almost hit us in the mountains, and they sent a warning note marked with the Changers' symbol to make sure we knew it was them."

Aurel's eyes narrowed dangerously. "All right, both of you, get in here and tell me what's going on."

Zelle removed her coat and shoes, while even Rien didn't object to being ordered to come back in. He held onto the arrow, though, and his expression remained dark, distant. Whatever he'd seen in the cave had rattled him so much that he hardly seemed bothered that there were assassins potentially watching the house. How had he driven them away without any weapons of his own? That question would have to wait, because Aurel's expectant stare would accept no more delays.

"I told you, someone using the Changers' symbol fired arrows at us," Zelle said to her sister. "Did you actually see them in the forest, Rien?"

"No, but they were hiding... using magic, I think." His jaw tensed. "Some kind of wild animal attacked at the same time as they started firing at me."

"A... wild animal?" What had come after them this time?

He shook his head. "That's not the important part."

"No, it isn't," said Aurel. "The person who sent the wraiths and the storm also hired the *Changers*?"

"To ensure they didn't miss their target, I suppose," said Zelle. "I know the Changers are supposed to work for the Crown Prince, but I have a hard time believing Rien made an enemy of *him*."

"Maybe he insulted his fashion sense."

"Aurel." Her sister cracked jokes to cope in times of distress, she knew, but she wasn't in the mood for levity in the slightest. "Are the Changers likely to be able to get inside the house?"

"Absolutely not." Aurel strode across the room and peered out the window. "They're good at hiding, aren't they? You didn't see them outside?"

"No, we didn't." Zelle slumped back in her seat, exhaustion tugging at her limbs. She desperately needed a bath. And a hot meal. "I assume, since you sent your last servant away, that you've learned how to cook during the last year?"

"I usually eat at the tavern."

"And you wonder why our family's money is running out."

Aurel scowled, casting a glance at Rien. "Our family's finances are in tatters because our parents died without leaving us a single coin, not because of anything *I* did."

Here we go. It was an old argument, and not one Zelle particularly wanted to have. "Our family has pissed away more money with each passing generation. Besides, nobody in our mother's generation had the gift."

Aunt Adaine had taught Zelle how to handle money from the moment she'd been old enough to help out at the shop, but since Grandma had taken Aurel away to train her as the new Reader, she'd neglected to give her proper instruction on how to manage her family's remaining resources.

Rising to her feet, Zelle walked into the kitchen to see if her sister had any decent food in stock. The answer, it seemed, was no.

"What are you doing?" asked Aurel.

"Unless you want to leave your house unattended with assassins watching the doors, one of us has to cook."

"Oh, Powers above, the Changers won't attack us in the middle of the village," Aurel scoffed. "They stalk their prey when they're alone."

"It's already dark outside."

"Don't be so uptight, Zelle," she said. "We can get food at the tavern for far cheaper than a simple meal in Saudenne. Frankly, I don't understand why you even live there."

Zelle shrugged, not wanting to revisit *that* old argument either. She'd stayed in Saudenne after her aunt had died, partly out of habit and partly out of reluctance to move closer to her other two surviving family members and end up spending all her time watching over Grandma or arguing with Aurel. Besides, she *liked* Saudenne, and the view of the sea from the window of her aunt's shop and the familiar briny scent of the fresh wind off the ocean felt like home to her.

Rien spoke. "The Changers won't come back. I injured at least two of them, and they'll have more sense than to attack us while we're in a group."

"You injured them?" Zelle asked. "With what?"

Rien lifted one of the Changers' bows from inside his coat in answer, while Aurel chuckled to herself. "Resourceful, aren't you? What else do you have in there?"

"No coins," Zelle said bluntly. "You'll have to pay for our meals."

"Done." Aurel bounded to the door and grabbed her coat, still smirking. "I knew you'd give in."

Zelle gathered her coat and boots, her insides grumbling at the potential of getting some substantial fare. She didn't relish the prospect of potentially running into the Changers again, but she believed Rien when he claimed to have scared them off. Something about his current manner set her nerves on edge, and he'd barely spoken since their arrival. It was a different kind of silence to the confusion that had followed the loss of his memories—sharper, somehow.

Aurel strode into the lead, not even bothering to check the shadows for any lurking threats. "Relax, Zelle. Nobody is going to attack us out in the open."

"Aside from wild animals?" She glanced towards Rien, but he didn't seem to be paying them any attention. "Or Changers. If they use magic to render themselves completely invisible, there might be any number of them out there."

"We're not defenceless." Aurel indicated a dagger strapped to her waist. "Also, the Changers aren't as competent as they pretend to be."

"Are you certain?" Zelle recalled their spelled arrows' potency, which had even managed to make an impact upon the wraiths. "How did someone who isn't connected to the Crown hire the most notorious assassins on the continent to commit murder for them, anyway?"

Aurel snorted. "Notorious? They might have been back in Grandma's day, but they're obsolete now."

Some would say the same of the Sentinels. She managed to keep that thought to herself, however, as she followed her sister along the path connecting her house to the rest of the village. Rien brought up the rear of their group, not speaking to either of them, while Zelle and Aurel speculated on whether someone had paid the Changers to hunt Rien down or threatened them instead. Either would fit.

"The actual person hunting him might not even be here in person," Aurel said. "That's why they're acting through intermediaries."

"That boy is here in person," she reminded Aurel. "Relatively speaking, anyway. Nobody from Aestin has ever attacked Zeuten before, right?"

"No," answered Aurel. "Didn't the cave say the boy came from elsewhere, though? Through a crack between the worlds?"

"It was implied, but... I don't know." The boy was answering to someone else, she was sure. "It can't have happened by accident, and I think someone sent that child here. He has a will of his own, true, but he moves with purpose."

Zelle spotted Rien out of the corner of her eye, falling farther behind with each passing step, but he made no effort to catch them up. Had the cave shown him anything at all? Would she have to wait until Aurel wasn't within hearing distance before she convinced him to confide in her again?

"Maybe he just likes killing people," said Aurel. "The Powers were downright bloodthirsty when they used to walk between the worlds whenever they liked. When they weren't mating with humans and having half-divine offspring, they were slaughtering us in brutal ways and waging war."

"This isn't like the old days." A lone deity walked among them, not thousands. Besides, this was Zeuten. Powers and humans had never coexisted on this continent at all. "They're supposed to have vanished from the world entirely more than a millennia ago, aren't they?"

"Nobody knows for sure," said Aurel. "Their influence faded, yes, but there's nothing to suggest that they permanently disappeared from the world."

"The Sentinel's cave told me they were waking up," Zelle murmured, the hairs on her arms standing on end. The warmth of the tavern beckoned them, and she pushed away all thoughts of the cave, intending to return to them later when she had a hot meal in her. "Never mind the deities. The assassins are the more immediate threat."

"They're after your friend. Not us."

"You don't think they'll notice we helped him?" asked Zelle. "If they've been watching us all along, they'll know I'm the reason he got here in one piece."

"Yes, I know." Aurel lowered her voice. "First thing tomorrow, he has to leave."

"What?" Zelle halted, frowning at her sister. "I thought you wanted to help him."

"If the Sentinel's cave showed him anything, he's not talking," she said. "And his enemies will also be *our* enemies for as long as he's under my roof."

"Are you forgetting that they took Grandma first?" asked Zelle.

"Not the Changers," Aurel said. "When he's gone, they'll leave the pair of us alone."

"He's Aestinian, Aurel." She lowered her voice in case anyone within the tavern could hear snatches of their conversation through the partly open door. "He also has no magic. I'm not saying he can't take care of himself, but the Changers... if they're working with the enemy, they might be able to lead us to Grandma."

"Unlikely." Aurel advanced towards the tavern. "Not if they were bribed to keep their mouths shut, for instance."

"And if you convinced them otherwise?" Zelle didn't know where the words came from, but the idea of sending Rien away didn't appeal to her in the slightest.

Aurel's brows shot up. "Excuse me? Weren't you lecturing me about unnecessary expenses?"

"The Changers officially work for the Crown," Zelle reminded her. "Don't you think they might change their minds about hunting Rien if you gave them a talking-to for shooting at the Sentinel and trying to assassinate a foreign ambassador?"

Aurel's expression turned calculating. "Might work. I wonder..."

"What are you talking about?" Rien interjected.

"The Changers," said Zelle. "I think if we can get one or two of them alone, we might be able to convince them to see things our way."

Rien's confused gaze landed on her. "You *want* us to be attacked again?"

Zelle smiled. "I'm counting on it."

vita didn't return to the Reader's house until she was sure the Changers—and Master Amery's eagle—had gone. By now, night had fallen, and she thoroughly regretted not following the occupants of the house to the tavern. Her remaining rations were soaked through, and after a meagre supper of soggy bread and hard cheese, she'd waited for their return to the house before preparing to show her face.

She hadn't counted on the dragonet following her. When the three travellers returned from the tavern, the dragonet's tail shot out and tripped her before she could approach them.

"What is it?" she hissed. "You defended him earlier. Why don't you want me to speak to them?"

The dragonet made a quiet chittering noise. Then a rustle came from above her head and a net descended from the trees, a solid weight of rope crashing on top of her.

Intruder, the staff barked in Zelle's ear, scarcely a moment after they'd entered the house. She spun on her heel and reached the door first, following the sound of scuffling to the area below one of the oak trees flanking the house. Her sister had taken some convincing to set up several nets in the trees surrounding the house, but after Rien's tale of the assassins concealing themselves up in the branches, it seemed an ideal way to catch one of them.

Zelle approached the net, squinting at the tangled ropes before she gave them a prod with the staff. The net yelped, squirming. *Alive.*

"Who's there?" Zelle hissed, to be met with silence. She wasn't fooled, however, and she raised the staff warningly. "I know you're there. You can't run."

The net shifted a little. Zelle lowered the staff and used her free hand to grab a handful of rope. A fluid substance brushed against her hand. She released the rope, instead gripping the strange material beneath until it came free of its wearer, folds pooling on the ground. The cloak gave her the impression of cloud stitched into fabric, and when she tossed it aside, she found a girl of around Aurel's age under the net, with long limbs and lank, dark hair.

"*You're* the assassin?"

The girl lay sprawled in a tangle of ropes, her eyes flickering from the staff to Zelle's face like a mouse caught between two cats. "Please don't kill me! I wasn't trying to murder you in your sleep or break into your house or steal anything."

Zelle cut through her babbling. "Then what in Gaiva's name were you trying to do?"

"I need to talk to the Reader." The girl lifted her chin, with difficulty. "That's you, isn't it? I'm here to talk to you."

"You came here to ask for a Reading?" Zelle said in disbelief. "You're not fooling anyone. You were wearing that cloak for a reason."

Aurel appeared behind her. "What's going on?"

"I caught our assassin," Zelle told her sister. "She says she wants a Reading."

Aurel eyed their captive. "*This* is our assassin? She looks like she's never seen a weapon in her life."

The girl's face flushed. "I'm new to the Changers. Anyway, I'm here to speak to the Reader."

"Who exactly sent you here?" asked Aurel.

"I came here on my own," she said. "Not at first. I was sent here to ask the Reader to help me find someone the Changers were hired to kill, but that was before I realised the person giving the Changers orders wasn't... well, I'm not working for the Changers anymore. I quit."

Questions exploded in Zelle's mind, but the only one she voiced aloud was, "Who did they send you to kill?"

The answer confirmed her suspicions. "Arien Astera."

———

Master Amery paced at the cliff's edge. Everything was falling apart around him. He strongly disliked losing control, and this week had been by far the most disastrous in all his long years of working for the Changers.

Not only had his recruits failed to take out Arien Astera, but three of his best archers had been found brutalised on a mountain path, pierced all over by their own arrows. Reports had come in of similar incidents in surrounding villages of messengers meeting unpleasant ends on the road. In addition to the flood of bad news from outside, his nerves were on edge with the anticipation of waiting for the boy who'd hired him to return. His second visit had confirmed that Master Amery had made a terrible mistake in holding back in his efforts to track down his adversary, and if he wasn't careful, he would be the next to face the brunt of the boy's wrath.

Master Amery came to a brief halt, looking out across the dark pines of the forest visible in the distance, the same direction in which he'd sent that hapless girl. If by some miracle she did reach her target, or one of the others did, would the death of one man make this agent of misfortune go away? Where were the Sentinels in all this? They were supposed to deal with magical threats, and such threats seemed rampant at the moment.

Granted, despite what he'd seen, Master Amery had a hard time believing some of the locals' reports of some malevolent entity who walked through the countryside, slaughtering anyone who dared to cross his path. Paranoia was rife, and a fair bit of it seemed to be directed at his own people. Yes, the Changers had unique abilities, but most of the citizens of Zeuten held no true belief in magic. *Real* magic, like the Invokers wielded in Aestin. Why should they start now? If some beast had made its way down from the wild regions in the north, it was hardly *his* fault it had developed a taste for human flesh.

All the same, the mountain had never felt as isolated as it did now, and the urge struck him to leave the base for the first time in over ten years. Perhaps he should visit his surviving family in Saudenne, if any held the slightest desire to see him again. Anything rather than waiting for another grim report...

Master Amery's heart jumped into his throat. One moment, he looked out at an overcast sky over dark forest; the next, the strange blue-eyed boy stepped out of the air in a whirl of icy wind. Master Amery stared, dumbfounded, at the outline of what appeared to be a window, a squarish patch of cloud from which the boy had stepped.

The boy spoke. "You failed to honour your bargain."

Master Amery took a step back, suddenly all too aware of the sheer drop in front of him. "It hasn't been that long."

"I found Arien Astera before any of your assassins did."

The sensation that hit Master Amery felt rather like tumbling over the edge of the cliff, but his feet remained on steady ground, and a dark stirring in the patch of clouds behind the boy warned him that whatever was on the other side of that doorway might make his worst imaginings seem tame.

"Good," he said hoarsely. "You wanted him to die. Right?"

"I wanted him to suffer." The boy's feet touched down on the cliff's edge, directly in front of him. "I wanted to cause him pain, for all the trouble he's caused me."

Master Amery swallowed hard. "He's still alive?"

"Yes." The boy fixed his piercing blue eyes on him. "Your Changers still have a chance of finding him before I kill him myself."

Relief splintered the cold fist clenching around his heart. "They won't fail. On Gaiva's name, I swear it."

"Gaiva." The boy snorted. "*She* isn't here. You should find yourselves a new Power."

Master Amery didn't have the slightest clue what he was talking about. "A new Power?"

"There are more of us than ever before." He grinned, showing his even, white teeth. "We have been forgotten, true, but not for much longer."

"You... you're..." Master Amery's skin chilled all over. He'd thought there was something inhuman about the boy. But a *deity*?

"Yes," he said, softly. "Do you understand? I am the first to come here to take what is due to me, and I will not be the last. You waste your gifts."

"What?" he squeaked. "We use Gaiva's magic to protect the Crown. It is the highest honour in the whole of Zeuten."

"How limited." The boy's grin didn't waver. "I tire of you, human. Have you told anyone you met with me?"

"I—" He hadn't. Who would believe him? "I don't want to die."

"Isn't that all you humans are good for?" whispered the boy.

The world turned red.

22

The instant the assassin said "Arien Astera", Aurel grabbed her, ropes and all, and hauled her into the house. Zelle remained outside, the name ringing in her ears. *Arien Astera.*

She found herself gripping the odd, fluid coat she'd taken. She'd heard rumours of the assassins' gift for sneaking in the shadows, but now she had one of their tools in her grip, it didn't look too impressive. The staff had still picked up on the intruder's presence regardless of how well she'd been hidden.

"Arien Astera," she said to the staff. "Tell me who he is."

The staff was quiet for a moment. Then it spoke. *Aestin's dominant Power is Astiva, son of Gaiva. The Astera family holds the Relic of Astiva and has wielded it for a thousand years.*

"Rien's family." Arien Astera. Arien. *Rien.* He'd remembered part of his name but nothing else.

Yes, and you'll find out more if you check those books of yours, said the staff.

While she might have been relieved that the staff was finally answering some of her questions without complaint, she had more pressing concerns. The history books Aurel had in the house must have a record of the Astera family, considering they'd been one of the first established Invoker families in Aestin. Rien's family had held their Relic longer than the Sentinels had *existed*.

Reeling, Zelle entered the house behind her sister, who was attempting to wrestle the squirming assassin across the room without knocking any of the cabinets over. Rien, who'd gone straight to the upstairs guest room upon their return from the tavern, hadn't shown his face yet. Which was probably for the best, given that Zelle wouldn't be able to stop herself from confronting him about his true identity the next time she set eyes on him.

"Are you going to put her in the Reading Room?" Zelle asked her sister, overtaking her and ducking through the door to the smaller room before scanning the shelves on either side of the desk.

"If you get out of the way," came Aurel's response.

"One moment." Picking up a book on Aestinian history, she moved aside to let her sister push the assassin into the room. The young woman fell to the floor in a tangle of ropes, gasping and cursing.

Aurel reached over to the desk and grabbed the Book of Reading. "Nicely done. If I do say so myself."

"Don't forget it was my idea." Admittedly, her sister was the one who'd found the net, which had belonged to some kind of trap that had been abandoned in the forest by some hikers, and which Aurel had naturally added to her collection of junk.

After leaving the Reading Room, Aurel closed the door

on the would-be assassin. "I'd call it a joint effort. Not counting that friend of yours. He didn't even bother leaving the guest room."

Zelle made a noncommittal noise, unwilling to share her new revelation and face her sister's triumph at being right about Rien being highborn. The strongest of all Invokers, in fact, though such hierarchies didn't apply here in Zeuten.

"What do you want to do with our assassin?" she asked her sister. "Question her now or wait until morning?"

Aurel dragged a chair in front of the door. "Might as well wait until it's light outside. Besides, her friends might come after her."

Zelle didn't think so, somehow, but she was not in the right frame of mind to interrogate the assassin when it was Rien she really wanted to talk to.

After climbing the stairs, she glanced at the door to the guest room that Rien occupied, which remained closed. She didn't think it was likely he'd already fallen asleep and missed the disturbance, but she was reluctant to walk in on him until she'd figured out what to say.

Returning to her own room—which was usually where Grandma stayed when she visited—Zelle lit a candle and opened the book she'd grabbed from downstairs on Aestinian history.

It didn't take long before she came across the first mention of the major families—the Asteras, the Trevains, and the Martzels. The former owned the Relic of Astiva, and like most of Gaiva's direct descendants, the Relic's power was centred around nature. A full-page illustration depicted a staff with thorns wrapped around the hilt.

Words came to Zelle's mind. *Thorns. A red-bound book with thorns.*

"Arien Astera," she whispered. "Oh, Gaiva. I should have known."

By the Powers, he was equal in status to the Crown Prince. Higher than Aestin's Emperor, who everyone knew followed the commands of the Invokers himself. Or he had done, before whatever catastrophe had led Rien here to Zeuten.

The staff stood propped against the wall, and Zelle addressed it in a low voice. "You said he wasn't magical."

He isn't, the staff told her.

"He's from the family who owns the most powerful Relic in the whole of Aestin. What changed?" The major Invoker families had held the country's Relics in balance for a thousand years, and none more so than the Astera family.

Ask him yourself, said the staff.

"I will in the morning." She nearly dropped the book when the door handle turned and Aurel entered the room. "Haven't you heard of knocking?"

"Who were you talking to?" Aurel's eyes went to the book in her hand then the staff. "You know you'll have to give that back to Grandma when we find her, don't you?"

"Of course I do." Irritation prickled beneath her skin. "If you're still awake, why not interrogate the assassin?"

"I thought you wanted to wait until Rien was awake."

"Or Arien Astera." She held up the book, all notion of keeping secrets from her sister fleeing. Rien had some serious explaining to do to *both* of them. "That's who the Changers sent her to kill."

Her sister's jaw dropped. "Of course. Astera... they're

249

one of the major families. I think Grandma *met* Volcan Astera, years ago."

"Who's Volcan Astera?" asked Zelle. "Head of the family?"

"Last I heard," said Aurel. "The Asteras split the Power between several of their members, but Volcan's the one with the reputation. They call him thorn-hand over in Aestin because of that staff of his. Grandma said he could summon the thorns to attack his enemies, and he even used the staff to dispose of a rival family a few decades ago."

"Then how would one of his relatives end up alone and powerless in a foreign country?" Zelle whispered, hoping Rien couldn't hear them talking.

"I don't know," said Aurel. "Nobody has ever challenged the Astera family and walked away unscathed, as far as I know. Not that I've ever met one of them... until now, apparently." She chuckled under her breath. "I knew he was part of the aristocracy but not that he was *that* renowned."

"But he has no magic." He hadn't lied, though, when he'd admitted to forgetting his identity. Zelle herself wasn't an accomplished judge of character, but Rien hadn't struck her as the type to maliciously deceive her. The memory loss had been real. "No Relic... but he said he came to find one."

She thought they'd got to know one another a little over the past couple of days, but she couldn't connect that person with the one whose family occupied a full chapter of every history book which so much as mentioned Aestin. All the same, she ought to have guessed sooner. Rien could speak fluent Zeutenian and even read the old form of the language, while most Aestinians preferred to ignore their eccentric neighbours across the ocean altogether. In fact, it wouldn't surprise her if knowledge of their language was restricted to the nobility.

Invokers. Powerful. Dangerous. And if she believed the stories, barely tolerant of one another, unforgiving, and liable to hold grudges for generations. Her relatives might have been biased on the subject, but Powers above, she'd been a fool. How many Aestinians could afford the steep cost of hiring a boat across the ocean to chase a rumour?

"He came to find one?" asked Aurel. "That would explain why he visited the Sanctum. Volcan Astera knew its location, even though it's been years since he set foot on the continent. He probably told his whole family."

Zelle glanced down at the book. "He was looking for *the* Relic. The one from the stories."

Aurel snorted. "I doubt he was. He probably forgot the specifics when he lost his memory. Anyway, he's made one persistent enemy, to have followed him all the way here."

"You'd think the Crown Prince would have noticed."

"The Crown Prince doesn't care," Aurel said. "When was the last time he spoke to Grandma or me? He's forgotten the Sentinels, and he leaves the Changers unsupervised."

"Might be a mistake, given what's coming." Zelle thought her sister sounded far too relaxed about the notion that they might be among a handful of individuals in the whole of Zeuten who had the faintest idea of the kind of danger they were in.

Aurel's expression lost its casual air. "Did the

Sentinels' cave really tell you more of them were coming? The Powers?"

"Yes," said Zelle. "As if the one hunting Rien isn't enough."

Aurel swore under her breath. "I think Aestin is in worse trouble than we are, personally, if he isn't the only Astera to have misplaced his Relic."

"Misplaced?" If the families' Relics were anything like the staff, she couldn't imagine them being easily lost. Zelle put down the book on the bedside table, thinking of Rien's grim expression when they'd left the cave. "I thought no magician could survive being separated from their Power."

"I thought not, too," her sister replied. "But it takes a strong individual to wield a Relic of one of Gaiva's children."

Zelle rested her forehead on her palm, her elbow propped on her knee. If Rien had survived such an ordeal, then no wonder he'd wanted to forget. Unless he'd recovered all his memories, there was no way to know for certain what had transpired, but he'd definitely seen *something* in the vision the Sentinels' cave had shown him. "It's not possible for someone to just pick it up and wield it, then."

"No," said Aurel. "They say the effectiveness of one's Relic comes from the cooperation of the deity. The closer your wishes align with the deity you control, the easier it is to use the Relic's power."

That would explain why the staff had been so reluctant to cooperate with her, then. Turning her attention towards it, she thought, *Is it true? Do you think Rien is actu-*

ally Arien Astera? Is it possible for him to have lost his Relic and survived?

It's certainly possible, answered the staff.

Aurel's gaze followed Zelle's to the knotted wooden surface. "You know, I've never known that staff to speak a word to anyone except Grandma before. Let alone a non-Sentinel."

Zelle's head snapped up. She should have known her sister wouldn't last through an entire conversation without making one of her belittling remarks. "I've never known of a door opening between our realm and the world of the Powers either. Anything is possible, however unlikely it might be."

"Powers above, Zelle, I wasn't trying to insult you." Aurel hesitated, then she backed up a step and shoved her palm against the door, revealing Rien's tall shadow outside the room. He'd been listening to their conversation. How much had he heard?

"I heard voices." He didn't meet Zelle's eyes. "What are you talking about?"

Zelle rose to her feet. "We caught one of the Changers' assassins outside and locked her in the Reading Room. I assumed you wanted to be left alone, and I didn't want to disturb you."

"You thought wrong." He said no more, but the silence that followed was as thick as mud.

Aurel, to Zelle's surprise, slipped past him and out of the room. "I'll see you in the morning, Zelle."

Zelle beckoned to Rien before she lost her nerve. "I want to talk to you alone."

Rien still didn't look directly at her face when he

entered her room and closed the door behind him. "What is it?"

She lifted the book from the bedside table and opened it to display the name of his family.

"Arien Astera." Her tone came out more accusing than she'd intended. "When were you planning to tell me your name, exactly? How long have you known?"

He was silent for a long moment, his gaze fixed on the floor. "Since the cave."

I knew the rock showed him the truth. "So you're from the most powerful family in Aestin, yet you came all the way over here in search of a Relic? Why not go looking for one at home?"

"My family is dead," he said tonelessly. "Nobody was spared, even those with no Relics at all, and my home was reduced to rubble. The killer took every Relic we owned."

Zelle's spine stiffened in shock. *The person who stole his Relic murdered his entire family and destroyed his home?* Then perhaps there *was* nobody for him to turn to in Aestin. His family's killer must have taken all the magic he had, leaving him with no choice but to leave or else suffer the same fate. "You remember it all?"

"Most of it. I remember taking a ship to Zeuten, but after that... it's a blur." His right hand was clenched over his left, so tightly that the veins stood out. "I can still hardly think of his name."

"Who?" The Power who had once served his family. The name he'd been trying to find. "As—"

"Don't *say* it," he snarled. "You have no right to."

"Rien!" Zelle stared, shocked. Rien's entire demeanour had changed, and his eyes were somehow clearer, more piercing. He wouldn't look out of place with a staff in his hand.

"My family's dead, and I—" His hands clenched at his sides. "I have to go."

"What?" Zelle said, disarmed by his change in tone.

"My family is dead, and it's up to me to destroy the one who took them from this world."

"It's late," she returned. "You're not thinking straight. Your enemies almost killed you several times already, remember?"

Rien moved towards the door, and Zelle strode past him, barring his way out of the room. "Are you going to keep getting in my way, Miss Zelle?"

"I told you not to call me 'Miss', Rien." If she'd been feeling more vindictive, she might have called him 'Arien', but that was unnecessarily cruel, and besides, she could hardly blame him for wanting to act immediately upon remembering what had happened to his family. "And yes, I am. You'll only get yourself killed if you go out into the forest at night. Don't you at least want to read up on your family history first? Do you remember all of that too?"

His jaw tensed. "No. Some of it, but not all."

"Try this." She held out the book towards him. "I don't know if this will help, considering it's an outsider's perspective on your country, but I'm pretty sure you family's killer isn't going anywhere if you wait until morning."

His hand closed around the book. "Are you always so blunt when you deliver bad news?"

"Only when I'm dealing with spoilt nobles." Powers above, she might have to re-evaluate how she spoke to him if he truly was an equal to the Crown Prince. "I hope you won't develop an attitude of entitlement now that you remember who you are."

He frowned at her. "Would that make you let me leave any faster?"

"Let you?" Was he trying to make a joke or being serious? She honestly couldn't tell. "You're welcome to walk into a nest of Changers if you're so inclined, but I might remind you that you brought your magical feud to my country to begin with, and the Crown won't be thrilled if you die and then leave the rest of us to clean up the mess you left behind. I know you Invokers think you own the earth, but you don't own Zeuten."

"I'm sorry." His hands were clenched around the book, and Zelle felt a spasm of guilt for making light of his pain. Her own family had had a cavalier attitude to death and dire peril—a necessity born from the number of them who'd met premature ends—but someone like him, who'd likely thought of himself as invincible before he'd learned the hard way that he was anything but, would have found it harder to accept.

She lowered her head. "I'm going to bed. If you're still here in the morning, we're planning to interrogate the assassin."

"Right." His gaze went from her face to the staff. "I apologise again, Zelle."

He walked away and returned to his own room, leaving her wondering how many more revelations she could take—and wondering which Power had managed to bring down the most magically potent family in the entirety of Aestin. As she made to close the door, Aurel sprang into view, making her jump.

"Powers!" she said. "What is it now?"

"I wanted to wait until you'd finished your little heart-to-heart before I gave you this." Aurel pressed another book into her sister's hand. "Thought you'd find it interesting."

"What?" Zelle glanced down at the book, which was titled, *The Art of Changing*.

"The Changers," said Aurel. "Our friend has some interesting talents at her disposal. Or her cloak does, anyway."

Zelle flipped open the book onto a double-paged illustration of what appeared to be a winged man. When she looked more closely, she realised the wings weren't growing from the man's back but were attached to him some way, and they resembled the folds of the cloak she'd snatched from the assassin downstairs.

Zelle scanned the page. *The Changers use cloaks infused with divine power to aid them in their goal to protect the Crown. Their talents range from being able to hide themselves from human sight to flying, and some can even transform into animals. The cloaks themselves are something of a mystery but are believed to be created from the remnants of Gaiva's own power...*

Zelle lifted her head. "So they're like Relics. All of them have Relics."

"Including the one we brought into my house," Aurel added. "Never mind waiting until morning. I'm going to talk to our captive now."

23

E vita lay on the floor, cursing her terrible luck. Not that she'd expected luxury treatment as a prisoner, but she hadn't come in here intending to get locked up by the Reader before she even had the chance to ask her any questions. The thick ropy net tangled around her limbs as she flopped around like a fish, trying to find an opening to free herself. Why hadn't she removed the cloak before approaching the house?

Powers. The cloak. They'd taken it. While she'd told the Reader she intended to leave the Changers behind, she'd been counting on keeping the cloak in order to evade attention. Granted, the cloak hadn't kept her safe from Master Amery's giant eagle. Even the eagle might not be able to get into the Reader's house, of course, but either way, she was trapped.

Evita managed to get herself into a sitting position and studied her surroundings to distract herself from the creeping sense of dread. This room must be a study of some kind. Worn, old paintings covered the walls, and books filled the shelves to each side of the desk. No lights shone inside the room itself, but a trickle of moonlight pooled on the desk from the grimy window half hidden in a corner.

As Evita began a fresh struggle with the ropes, she heard the door open. Lifting her head, she struggled to make out the shadow entering the room. It wasn't the woman she'd seen in the cave but the other, the taller one with striking auburn hair who looked younger than her companions. She also held a book in her arms. Evita couldn't see the cover, although even if it hadn't been dark, she wouldn't have been able to read it anyway.

The woman gave her a long, measured look. Evita tried to stand, tripped, and fell into a sitting position again. "Are you here to kill me?"

"I might ask you the same question. You approached my house wearing a Changer's cloak, after all."

Evita blinked. "You're Aurel Carnelian."

"And you're with the Changers, aren't you?"

Evita swallowed, her throat dry. "No. Where is my cloak?"

"It'll be a nice addition to my collection," said Aurel. "I've never owned a Changer's cloak before."

"I…" Evita hadn't expected her to be so… irreverent. She tried to move the ropes away from her eyes so she could properly see her companion, without much luck. *Aurel Carnelian.* Who was the other woman, then? "There's been a misunderstanding."

"Really?" Aurel said. "If you truly did come to ask for a Reading, then you shouldn't have shot arrows at us."

"I'm not the one who did that." Evita racked her thoughts for anything which might make the Reader set her free. "The rock talked to me. In your cave."

Aurel's brows shot up. "Talked to you, did it? So you broke into the Sentinels' cave as well as my house?"

"No." Evita wished she hadn't mentioned it at all. "It was an accident. Anyway, the Changers aren't... I mean, I don't think they're taking orders from the Crown."

"What makes you say that?"

At her apparent genuine interest, Evita found the whole story pouring out of her, from the slaughter of her family to her journey to join the Changers and everything she'd seen in the vision in the cave.

Aurel considered her for a long moment. "So you joined the Changers to avenge your family?"

"I did," said Evita, "but I was supposed to complete my training before I was given a major mission. Instead, Master Amery sent me..."

"To ask for my help tracking Arien Astera," finished Aurel. "Someone hired the Changers to do their dirty work. Not the Crown Prince, I assume, unless Astera has done something to mortally offend him."

"I don't know." Evita knew she ought to be careful what she said, but she was so relieved that Aurel seemed to be listening to her that she couldn't seem to control her mouth. "I don't think he has. Master Amery was taking orders from someone else, but it wasn't the Crown Prince."

"He can't have trusted you to do your job, though," she said. "We found more of you in the forest earlier. Are they still here?"

"I don't know, but I'm not with them," said Evita.

"They don't know it isn't the Masters who are giving the orders, but I do. The person who hired them... he looks like a child, but he isn't one. He's a monster."

"I've heard the same about the Changers," said Aurel. "Right... what should I do with you?"

"Please don't kill me." Her voice quietened to a whisper. "I can help you. I'm on your side. We're after the same person."

Not a person, a voice whispered in her mind. That child was far more. She'd always known it, on some level, but the vision she'd seen in the cave had stripped away all doubt.

"I'll believe that when I see it," said Aurel. "I know. Tomorrow, you'll take us to speak to the other Changers, and we can verify who's giving them orders."

"I can't," said Evita. "The Master will have me killed for giving away our secrets instead of completing my mission. I have only one day left before they come after me. Besides, the others don't know that they're taking orders from someone other than the Crown—"

"That isn't my problem." Aurel reached for the door handle. "Look, I feel for you, but I have a distinguished guest who won't be thrilled if I let you walk free. He'll probably want to talk to you himself, come to that."

Arien Astera.

Evita opened her mouth to protest, but Aurel had already slipped out of the room. Now she was in trouble. If Arien Astera didn't kill her himself, then the other Changers would. It didn't matter who they answered to when she'd be dead before they realised they'd been tricked.

———

Rien turned the page of the book under the light of the candle on the bedside table.

He'd stayed up for hours to read up on his family history, yet the stories might have belonged to a stranger despite the return of his memories. It didn't help that the book wasn't written in his own language. He was familiar with modern Zeutenian, but it'd been several years since he'd last read one of their texts, especially a dense book like this one. He found himself with the sensation of trying to glimpse the sky through heavy fog. As long as the disconnect remained between his memories of his time in Aestin and his arrival at the Sanctum, he'd remain severed from his past as surely as he was severed from his deity.

He'd lost more than his memory, after all.

His left hand throbbed again. The marks stood out starkly, pale and sharp lines across the back of his knuckles. The godsmark had covered his entire hand and wrist, and now he knew what he'd lost, he sensed the absence like someone had torn out his beating heart.

Astiva serves the enemy now. And yet he couldn't accept it. His family had been the only wielders of Astiva's Relics for a thousand years. How could anyone have stripped that away so easily? How could Daimos have brought him to the brink of death?

He couldn't believe he'd forgotten his enemy's name, until the boy had repeated it to him in the cave. Until he'd remembered… but not enough. He didn't know how he'd survived to cross the ocean to Zeuten. Had Astiva been watching over him, or was his deity no longer able to see him at all? Had he already forgotten his previous wielder?

Astiva. Every time he read the name, it blurred before his eyes, but he knew it as surely as he knew his own.

I am the son of Volcan Astera. Astiva is my deity.

Yet a void had crept in to fill the space Astiva had left behind. No human was supposed to be able to survive the separation, and yet he was still breathing. Even the book of his family's history held no answers as to why, and neither did it mention any Relics hidden in Zeuten. No surprise, since he'd read about them in the Astera family's collection of obscure texts, but Daimos had probably burned their library to the ground along with the rest of the house.

Don't think about it. He couldn't get home. Not until he had the ability to challenge Daimos directly, and besides, the chaos at sea made it impossible to contemplate taking another ship back to Aestin. Yet despite Zelle's common-sense remarks, a burning desire for vengeance roared inside his heart. A need to punish the one responsible for his pain. If not Daimos, then the deity who acted in his name. *Orzen.*

An image flashed before his eyes: a book bound in red and covered in thorns. Even the vision he'd seen in the cave hadn't told him what *that* meant. His chest tightened and his hand clenched over the medallion. He couldn't remember exactly when he'd taken it from his brother's body, but he recalled slipping it around his neck as he crawled from the ruins of his family's home, his fine clothes soaked in his own blood, the godsmark an open wound on his hand.

He shouldn't have survived. Shouldn't have survived

sinking into that whirlpool, but he held no explanation for either. There were still gaps in his memory. Maybe there always would be, but the Sentinels' cave must have the answers.

He turned the page and waited for dawn.

24

Evita jolted awake. She'd fallen into a fitful doze, still tangled in the pile of ropes on the floor, and they'd left painful welts on her arms and neck. For a moment, she wondered what had woken her, since she didn't remember falling asleep. With difficulty, she sat up in her net, rubbing the sore spots where the ropes had rubbed her skin. A chill crept across the back of her neck, a sudden certainty that someone watched her. A soft noise sounded near the desk, and then the dragonet appeared in a flutter of wings. Evita stifled a yelp of surprise. "What are you doing here?"

More to the point, how in Gaiva's name had he got inside the room? Chirp tilted his head towards the door, made a chittering sound, and flapped his tiny wings.

"You... you opened the door?"

She'd suspected the dragonet was intelligent but not that he was attached enough to her to risk his own freedom for her sake. Chirp ambled over to her, turning the net's ropy edges over with his head.

"Can you help me get out of here?" she whispered.

The dragonet sank sharp teeth into the net and hacked away at the ropes, while she moved the net with her hands until the dragonet had chewed a sizeable hole in the net that was big enough for her to step out. Discarding the net, she breathed out. "Thank you."

Evita knew that escaping was not likely to end well, but she would have preferred to die in a slightly more dignified position than pinned underneath a ropy net in the Reader's study. It was only a matter of time before Arien Astera demanded a face-to-face conversation with her, and she would rather not be unarmed when he did so.

The dragonet bounded to the door and nudged it open, revealing the now-dark living room. The window was too grimy to let in any moonlight, and Evita didn't dare move too fast for fear of knocking something over. Dusty cabinets loomed against each wall and crooked furniture filled the rest of the space. Where might the Reader have put the cloak? She hadn't seen it downstairs, though the translucent material was difficult to spot. More likely, she'd taken it to her room, and she'd heard the way the stairs creaked with every step. How to get it back without alerting the Reader's attention.

Chirp bounded onto an armchair and nudged the window open. *So that's how he got inside.*

The dragonet crawled through the gap in the dusty glass. Dawn had yet to penetrate the black sky, so if the others were deeply asleep, she might stand a chance of sneaking past the Reader and taking back her cloak if she got in through the open window.

Taking in a deep breath, Evita placed one booted foot

on the windowsill and did her best not to look at the drop as she climbed awkwardly through the narrow gap and scrambled down to solid ground. Then Evita turned to face the house, her gaze travelling to the upper floor. Short of overpowering a Changer, she was unlikely to obtain another cloak, and it'd saved her life too many times to count. Besides, after her experience in the past few days, scaling a wall and climbing through a window seemed a simple matter.

Evita reached for the wooden fence and pulled herself on top, perching in an awkward crouch. The nearby oak tree's branches almost reached the windows, and her heart lurched when a gust of wind hit her from behind and nearly caused her to overbalance. Gripping the top of the fence with both hands, she willed herself to calm down. *You're only on a fence, not a sheer cliff. This is ridiculous.*

Then an ice-cold chill crept over her, one that had nothing to do with the cool night air. Her hands fumbled and lost their grip, and she landed in the overgrown grass alongside the house, looking up into a sudden burst of light.

The air flew from her lungs. A window had appeared in the air, slightly above the fence, and the boy stepped out, smiling down at her. He stood on the air as if it were a solid surface, a wicked grin curling his mouth. His eyes were startlingly blue, and red stained his hands and arms to the elbows.

It's him. The boy hovered in front of a doorway to nowhere, and Evita knew with certainty that if he got inside the house, there was nothing to stop him from killing every single one of them.

He spoke. "Your name is Evita, is it not?"

He's talking to me?

She managed an indistinct sound, no more. Chirp had disappeared, but she didn't blame him for hiding. Unless he was preparing to pounce on the boy as he had in the cave, but luck alone had spared them that time. Luck, and Aurel's quick intervention. If she called loudly enough, she'd wake the Reader, but the boy—or rather, god— might crush the breath from her lungs before she could utter a word.

"At least you're quieter than the others," the boy muttered to himself. "I am tired of listening to you humans scream and beg for mercy, and even more tired of waiting for my orders to be fulfilled."

"You just killed someone." The blood on his hands spoke for itself. "Is that why you're here—to kill us?"

"Eventually." He looked down at her, his feet resting on the air as if it was solid ground. In fact, if she tilted her head a fraction, she might have thought an invisible barrier prevented him from stepping over the fence and into the Reader's grounds. That must be wishful thinking on her part, surely. "I heard you have one day remaining to complete your task. Since your Master is no longer around, I took it upon myself to see to his last wish."

He killed Master Amery. He's going to kill me. And yet he made no move to attack her.

"You can't get into the house, can you?"

The boy's blue eyes narrowed a fraction, and Evita felt a surge of giddy relief. *He can't get in.* He hadn't been able to get into the cave either. The Sentinels' magic kept him out.

The boy shrugged one shoulder. "You can't lock yourselves up indefinitely. Perhaps I'll give you an incentive to leave. For instance, I know where the Sentinel is."

Evita blinked in confusion. Aurel Carnelian was still here, but she wasn't about to start an unnecessary argument. "I thought it was Arien Astera you wanted."

"It is," said the boy. "You have one day to deliver him to me. I will be waiting."

He stepped through the doorway in the air and disappeared. So did the door-like gap in the world, leaving nothing but the cold night sky and dark trees behind. Evita stood in the grass for a long moment before the dragonet's long nose poked her in the side. Chirp hadn't abandoned her after all.

She straightened upright and shook her head. "I can't leave."

If she stayed, she'd end up locked back in the Reading Room, but anything was preferable to meeting a grim death at the hands of that deity. What was his name again? Orzen, he'd said in the cave. The name meant little to her, but the idea of running for freedom felt more like a death sentence than the alternative.

————

Zelle couldn't sleep. Her limbs ached from the road, and while she'd intended to take a bath upon her return, the assassin's arrival had cast that plan aside. She'd given Rien the book without reading much of it herself, but her thoughts ignited like flint with each new realisation. She was sleeping in the same house as an Invoker. An Aestinian magician. Someone with power which had once ruled almost the entire world... and which might well have ended up in the hands of someone who intended to use it for that very purpose.

Zeuten had never been invaded before and would be ill prepared to handle a threat from Aestin's magicians. If the Changers were involved too—Powers above, if she kept thinking about all the possibilities, then she'd never fall asleep.

Instead, her thoughts landed on the person who'd somehow overcome the entire Astera family. Astiva was one of the five children of Gaiva Herself, so it would take uncommon skill to defeat the wielders of his Relics. That or the wielder had relied upon the element of surprise to take out the Astera family.

What do you think? she asked the staff.

In order to stand a chance of defeating a single member of the Astera family, the challenger must have had the aid of another Relic, the staff replied. *Also, one person cannot possess the Relics of more than one Power. It's too much for a lone human to handle. For most, one is too many.*

"Meaning me?" She rubbed her forehead. "So the person who stole Astiva's Relic must have had the help of another, but... it sounds like that in order to properly claim Astiva's allegiance, they'd have had to give up the other Relic they held. Do I have that right?"

Yes. Now go to sleep.

Zelle ignored it. If the thief had yet to win over Astiva, that might mean there was hope left for Rien to recover what he'd lost, but did Rien himself know? She hadn't asked for the details of his vision, but she suspected he must be awake, like her. She slid out of bed and walked out into the landing, turning towards the other guest room.

"Astiva…"

Zelle halted at the sound of a quiet voice from behind the door, speaking what she assumed must be Aestinian. Though she couldn't understand the language he spoke, she guessed that Rien was praying to his deity, for all the good that would do.

The words stopped, and she heard the faint, unmistakable sound of someone quietly crying. Zelle froze, her hand inches from the doorknob. Now definitely wasn't the time to speak to him. She couldn't imagine what it would feel like to lose her whole family at once, let alone forget and then relive the whole experience. What kind of comfort could she possibly offer? No, she'd talk to him tomorrow. They'd figure out a plan, preferably one which didn't involve any of them going off to confront the assassins alone.

A distinct scuffling noise came from outside, followed by a thud. Like a person crawling out of a window. The assassin, it seemed, had figured out how to escape her net.

After ducking into her room to retrieve the staff, Zelle walked downstairs, not bothering to quieten her steps. Sure enough, the door to the Reading Room lay open, revealing the tangled remains of the net. The living room window was open, too, and a cold breeze rattled the contents of the cabinets. As Zelle firmly closed it, a bright flash came from outside.

Zelle gripped the staff tighter and headed to the door, finding it bolted from the inside. Aurel's work, no doubt. Cursing under her breath, she ran to the window instead. She wasn't as lanky as the assassin and climbing out was a bit of a struggle, especially with the staff in one hand. Her feet touched the ground on the other side next to where Evita crouched in the bushes.

The girl let out a startled cry, her hand colliding with the staff. Her eyes were wide in the gloom, showing more terror than was ordinary for someone who'd simply been taken by surprise.

Zelle gave her a suspicious look. "What are you doing out here?"

Evita was silent for a moment, and a scuffling noise sounded in the grass. A small animal—or so Zelle hoped, anyway. "I have to talk to the Reader."

Zelle regarded the taller girl with suspicion. "Whatever it is, I'll tell Aurel when she's awake."

"They're coming," she blurted. "The assassins are coming, and—he *killed* the Master. Orzen did."

"I'm sorry, what?"

Evita drew in a breath, and Zelle listened in increasing alarm as the assassin gave the story of her escape attempt and the person who'd thwarted her. Zelle had no doubt that Evita was telling the truth, since she'd seen what the boy was capable of with her own eyes, and now she had a name to put to that childlike face. *Orzen.* It wasn't familiar to her.

"So Orzen is commanding the Changers?" Zelle asked.

"Directly, now that he's killed their leaders," said Evita. "I don't think he could get past whatever barrier the Reader put on the fence, but he ordered me to hand Arien Astera to him in person or else he'd kill us all."

"So he's the one who originally sent you to find Aurel in order to track down Rien," Zelle surmised. "It seems a tad unnecessary to keep you involved when he's already here."

"I don't think he's really here," said Evita. "He walked through a doorway and went somewhere else."

"By all the Powers," she murmured. "If you're telling the truth…"

Then what? Rien had no magic, and Evita didn't either, while Zelle herself had nothing but the staff and a vague instruction from the rock in the Sentinels' cave. Hardly enough to stop a bloodthirsty deity intent on total destruction. Even Aurel's own talent was limited to Reading someone, not doing battle with the gods.

"I am," Evita insisted. "He also said something odd, though. He told me he knew where the Sentinel is, but Aurel is here, isn't she?"

Zelle's eyes widened in disbelief. "He can't mean my grandmother?"

Evita wouldn't have known who the boy was talking about, of course, but Zelle should have guessed that Orzen had been involved in the Sentinel's disappearance.

"He didn't give any more details," said Evita. "You're related to the Reader, then?"

"She's my sister." Zelle couldn't help taking pity on the girl. She looked utterly lost, her former bravado melted away by the sheer terror of her encounter with Orzen. "I'm Zelle. My grandmother is the current Sentinel, and she's been missing since… since just before I met Rien."

"Arien Astera," said Evita. "I never wanted to kill him, you know. I only joined the Changers to find the person who murdered my family, but… but their killer was there all along."

"That boy," said Zelle. "Or rather, deity. Orzen."

Fear flickered through Evita's features. "I don't suppose you know how to kill a god?"

273

Zelle considered her. Despite her evident terror, the young, aspiring assassin held an air of determination. Or resignation, at the very least. "We're going to find my grandmother. I'm pretty sure she's the one person left who can help get us out of this mess."

25

Zelle rose early the following day, having snatched a few hours of rest despite her encounter with the assassin during the night. She didn't know if Evita had taken her advice to move back into the Reading Room, but then again, she'd been in genuine terror for her life yesterday. The boy—Orzen—had threatened to kill her if she didn't bring him Rien. Zelle didn't entirely trust Evita's word, but her tale had been too outlandish *not* to believe.

As for her comments about the Sentinel? Zelle couldn't begin to guess where Orzen had taken her grandmother, but the Changers would be a good starting point. If he hadn't specified where he wanted Evita to meet him, then he must be with them.

Rubbing the sleep from her eyes, she changed out of her nightshirt into a fresh outfit from her pack—or as fresh as it was possible to be after a trip through a snowstorm over the mountains, anyway. The staff remained propped against her bed as she got ready for the day.

"You're being quiet," she muttered to it. "Aren't you excited about finding Grandma?"

You don't know for sure that you'll find her, the staff put in.

"It would help if you offered me a clue about her location," said Zelle. "You saw her vanish, didn't you? I'm fairly sure you must have some idea where she went, but you let me run all over the mountains and almost face certain death rather than telling me."

Instead, the Sentinels' cave had answered her questions—and raised a lot more. The rock surely didn't expect *her* to close the doors between their realm and that of the Powers. No, her grandmother needed to be the one to do it, if not her sister. Speaking of Aurel, Zelle needed to give her an explanation as to why the Reading Room door was unlocked.

Pushing to her feet, she picked up the staff. The knotted wood felt familiar enough in her grip that she suspected that it'd be quite the adjustment to hand it over to her grandmother again, but the relief would doubtless outweigh any pangs of regret.

Downstairs, she found Rien sitting at the kitchen table, poring over the same book she'd given him last night. Presumably there had been spare clothes left in his room, because he wore a clean white shirt several sizes too big for him, with the chain of the medallion visible beneath. His dark hair was tangled as if he'd been running his fingers through it, and he looked as if he hadn't slept all night.

"Got anything out of that book?" she asked, more to be polite than anything. She couldn't entirely forget she'd heard his grief the previous night, nor their mild argument over his temporary concealment of his experience in the cave, but she suspected that he didn't want to discuss the subject.

He looked up at her with bloodshot eyes. "You spoke to the assassin, didn't you?"

So he'd heard her come downstairs after all. "Yes. Is she still in the Reading Room?"

"I assume she is." His gaze was piercing, oddly intent. "Did you unlock the door?"

Zelle cast a glance in that direction. "No, I didn't. She got out herself, but she ran into trouble outside."

She relayed what Evita had told her during their encounter the previous night.

"She went to the trouble of escaping only to come back?" asked Rien.

"Did you miss the part where she came face-to-face with that child?"

"The lesser Power, Orzen," said Rien. "Who, I suspect, was summoned to this realm by Naxel Daimos."

"That's his name?" she asked. "The one who—?"

"The one who killed my family." His tone was dispassionate, but emotion glittered in his eyes. "Yes. The Daimos family used to be as prominent as my own until not long ago, but they overstepped their boundaries and went as far as to threaten the Emperor himself, so the other three families worked together to banish them from Aestin altogether."

"Then he's out for revenge?" she guessed. "That's why he went after your family."

"Precisely." His hands clenched on the table. "He must have known I'd survived and sent Orzen to track me down."

"Do you remember anything else?" she asked. "Anything more than you did yesterday, that is?"

He blinked several times, no longer meeting Zelle's eyes. "I remember Daimos chased me through Tauvice relentlessly, and my only option was to leave Aestin for the one place I knew still had magic that he hadn't reached yet."

"Zeuten," she said. "Do you remember whereabouts you heard of the outpost?"

"My father came here once, many years ago," he said. "I never asked for the details. We were too preoccupied with our own affairs, as were the other families. Our petty power struggles seem insignificant now."

Zelle didn't know what to say. "So you came here..."

"To look for the Sentinels," finished Aurel.

Zelle's sister stood in the doorway, watching the pair of them. She carried a heap of packages in her arms, and Zelle forgot about questioning Rien. "You went out?"

"Don't look so scandalised." Aurel heaped the packages on the table. "I went to buy supplies for you and your friend. You're welcome."

Zelle reached for the nearest package and opened it to reveal a pile of neatly arranged handmade clothes. "Aurel, how much did you spend on these?"

"Always so grateful." Aurel gave an eye roll. "I bought clothes, food, even weapons."

Zelle's eyes widened at the sight of an ornate knife hilt poking out from one of the parcels. "Aurel..."

"Don't you start. It's far cheaper than shopping in Saudenne." Aurel opened another package, revealing several freshly baked pastries which she must have bought from the local bakery. Selecting one, she bit into it. "I wanted to get all our errands done before I speak to our guest again."

"Ah." Zelle jumped to her feet, forgetting her own hunger. "Speaking of whom..."

Evita chose that moment to sheepishly emerge from the Reading Room and clear her throat. "I—"

"You let her out," Aurel said to Zelle. "Really?"

"No," said Zelle and Evita at the same time.

"I let myself out," Evita added. "But when I got outside, that boy showed up again."

Aurel's eyes rounded, and she spun to Zelle. "He came back? He was here?"

"I didn't see him myself," said Zelle. "According to Evita, he couldn't get past the boundaries around the house. You were asleep, and I didn't want to wake you. That's why I was worried about you going out."

Aurel swore under her breath. "I didn't see any signs of the little demon child while I was out shopping, so I'd guess he's lying low."

"Or hiding on the other side of one of those doorways of his," added Zelle, with a glance at Evita.

The girl's eyes darted over to Aurel. "I saw him step through the doorway and disappear. I think he can use them to get anywhere, even the Changers' base."

"Ah yes, the Changers," said Aurel. "Your friends. I notice they didn't come back overnight."

"They'll be around," said Zelle. "Turns out it's not the leaders of the Changers they're taking orders from, though. That thing that looks like a boy *killed* their leaders and has taken the rest of the Changers under his command. If Evita doesn't bring him Rien today, he'll kill her."

Rien himself rose to his feet, his eyes on the assassin. "Orzen commands the Changers? Directly?"

Evita nodded frantically. "I don't *want* to take you to him. I want to help you. If I can."

Zelle cast a glance at Aurel, who looked as sceptical as she'd expected. "Seems a little too neat to me. You decided to hunt down Rien and then changed your mind?"

"She didn't know the Changers had stopped taking orders from the Crown until recently," Zelle put in. "Anyway, Rien's their target."

"Then I'll go to them," said Rien.

"Excuse me?" said Aurel. "You'll do no such thing."

Rien gave her a flat stare. "You don't get to give me orders."

Zelle winced inwardly. "Don't start arguing. Evita doesn't know whereabouts the deity... Orzen... will be waiting, but she expects him to be with the Changers."

"Orzen." Aurel frowned. "Doesn't ring a bell. A lesser Power, is he?"

"There's nothing lesser about his abilities," Zelle said firmly. "Evita, whereabouts are the Changers based?"

"That... I don't know," she admitted. "They were in the forest, but I think Rien chased some of them off..." She trailed off, as if she'd intended to add more but had stopped herself at the last instant.

"We'll find them," Zelle said. "The boy—Orzen—won't want to let his target escape."

"He was angry that he couldn't get into the house." Evita lowered her gaze. "Like the cave too."

"Right, you broke into the Sentinels' cave," said Aurel. "Are you *sure* we should take her word for it, Zelle?"

"I didn't know it wasn't allowed," Evita protested.

"Once I was in there, I couldn't get out. That doorway was right in front of the exit."

"It was." Zelle cut off her sister's objection. "Evita, did you see anything else in there?"

She'd momentarily forgotten that the assassin had been in the cave, too, but she wondered what the rock might have revealed to someone who wasn't a Sentinel. Evita was lucky the cave had done her no harm.

"Nothing I haven't already told you." Evita paused for a moment. "Oh, except one thing. I saw one of those... doorways in the vision. And there was someone on the other side. A human."

Zelle frowned. "You mean in the realm of the Powers?"

"I think so," Evita said. "An old woman, and she seemed quite annoyed at being there."

Zelle's mouth fell open at the same time as her sister's did. Both of them spoke, almost in unison: "*Grandma?*"

"It has to be her," Zelle added. "Who else could have travelled into the realm of the Powers, much less survived?"

"Not to mention without her staff." Aurel eyed the knotted wood in Zelle's own hand before turning her attention back to Evita. "You're full of surprises. Why'd the rock show *you* that?"

"I don't know." Evita ran her teeth over her lower lip. "Yesterday, Orzen said he knew where the Sentinel was. I didn't realise he meant your grandmother."

"Orzen knows." Aurel swung her gaze over to Zelle. "Right, now we have twice the incentive to find the bastard."

"Not unarmed." Zelle moved to the packages on the

table and unearthed two simple but sturdy daggers. "Unless you have another net we can use to trap him."

"A net won't hold him," Evita said firmly. "And he'll have the Changers with him too. We'll be outnumbered."

"It's me he wants dead," Rien said. "At the command of Naxel Daimos."

"Daimos is the man who stole Rien's Relic," Zelle said, for Aurel's benefit. "He isn't here in person... I assume he isn't."

"I don't think he is," said Rien. "I also don't think he realised I left the country at first. The ship didn't sink until I'd almost reached Zeuten, and I was the only survivor."

"Then he sent the boy to finish the job," Aurel surmised. She seemed less enamoured with him than she'd been the previous day despite the revelation that he *was* a member of the nobility after all. Perhaps it was simply the distraction of everything else going on and the knowledge that the instant they left the house, they'd become targets.

"He can't be here simply to kill Rien, though," said Zelle. "He also banished the Sentinel into the realm of the Powers and took over the Changers, which seems an excessive way to take the life of a single man."

"He wanted to tie their hands," Rien said. "They're locked into an agreement now, and Daimos and his allies have the most powerful assassins on the continent at their disposal for any other purposes they need them for. I suppose it's fortunate that they didn't send their best after me."

"That might have been deliberate," said Zelle. "The assassins might have wanted Evita to fail."

"Why would they?" asked Rien.

Zelle glanced in Evita's direction, hoping she and Rien hadn't hurt her feelings with their comments, but she simply shrugged her thin shoulders. "Because Master Amery has had it in for me from the start. He didn't care if I died in the attempt."

"Regardless, Grandma's gone," said Aurel. "And I can't think of anyone else in the area who might be able to reach her except for Orzen and his army of Changers. Who's coming with me?"

"I am—and Evita." Zelle turned to Rien. "Coming?"

He inclined his head. Intensity simmered in his eyes. "Yes. I'm coming."

———

Evita held her breath when their group passed beyond the gate of the Reader's house, but nobody fired upon them. They'd set off after a hurried breakfast and a briefer discussion of their plan to draw out the Changers. Evita hadn't mentioned her own idea, since it depended on the dragonet choosing to stick around after their close call the previous night. He wasn't waiting outside, anyway, though they reached the forest without seeing any of the Changers either.

"Nobody's here." Aurel took the lead through the gate out of the village, sounding slightly put out. "Have our assassins gone home?"

Evita cleared her throat. "I might know someone who can take us directly to them, but it depends if he's still in the area."

283

"He?" echoed Zelle, nonplussed. "You have another ally in the forest?"

"Not a human ally. I think you've already seen him, Rien." She faltered when Rien looked directly at her, his brow furrowing in confusion. "When the assassins attacked you…"

"That dragon?" His expression cleared. "That was yours?"

"He's not mine. I think he's a wild rock dragonet, and… well, he seems to do whatever he likes, but I saved his life up in the mountains, and he's been following me ever since."

"He drove the Changers away," Rien explained to the others. "I thought I imagined him in the cave…"

"I thought you drove the Changers away yourself," said Aurel. "Exaggerating your achievements, were you?"

"Aurel." Zelle spoke in the exasperated tones of someone used to having to rein in an unruly sibling or friend. Evita's own family members had used the same tone on her often enough in the past.

"Not an exaggeration," Rien said. "I did drive them away… and I don't think they're here."

Neither was the dragonet. Worry fluttered in Evita's chest. Had he abandoned her after all? Perhaps their second encounter with the deity had been the last straw. Chirp had wanted Evita to escape the house, though, and she hadn't been willing to put herself at risk.

Orzen didn't kill him, did he? No, the dragonet was too clever to be caught, but she felt alone and exposed as she walked along the dirt track circling the village with the others. She tried to tell herself she was making the right choice in leading the others to find the Changers. If they really had Zelle's grandmother as their prisoner, then she owed it to them to help, and she might even be able to convince the Changers to turn against the deity giving them orders. More allies certainly couldn't hurt.

Besides, her own life hung by a thread, and staying with the Reader and her companions was her best chance for survival. The fact that the enemy wanted them *all* dead pointed to how dire her odds truly were, but at least she had her cloak back. Aurel Carnelian was no enemy, and she didn't think Arien Astera was either. However this ended, she wouldn't be going back to the Changers.

They walked along the dirt track until they came to the path sloping up the mountainside. Evita tilted her head up and glimpsed movement near the Sentinels' cave. "Did they make camp up there?"

"Probably thought it'd be safer." Aurel gave a derisive snort. "I'd appreciate it if people stopped using my cave as a camping spot."

"Aurel," Zelle hissed. "We aren't alone."

Cloaks rustled, and the Changers appeared from nowhere, their bows at the ready. Evita's heart pitched downwards when Ruben stepped to the front of their group.

"Master Amery is dead," he said to Evita. "*You* killed him."

"I didn't," Evita insisted. "I wasn't even there."

"Then are you going to explain what you're doing here with the Reader and the man you were sent to kill?" Vekka spoke from within the group of Changers. He'd lost some of his usual confidence since she'd last seen him, and his eyes carried a newfound wariness. What had happened to the Changers while she'd been gone?

Evita lifted her chin. "I found out the Changers are taking orders from an impostor who murdered your Master and who isn't answering to the Crown at all."

"Also, I want you to return my grandmother," Aurel interjected. "Your allies kidnapped her."

"We did no such thing." Ruben sounded affronted. "But if you want to try and best ten of the Changers at once, then you're welcome to try."

The Changers closed in around their group with their bows taut, arrows ready to fire.

"Stop!" Zelle shouted. "We don't want to hurt anyone. We just want to explain—"

Aurel stepped forwards with no fear in her expression. "Do you really want to make an enemy of the Sentinels? We were the first people to settle in these mountains. Attacking us will bring calamity upon your own heads."

"We've had enough calamity already," Vekka said, but a faint tremor sounded in his voice. Despite her own fear, Evita felt a faint twinge of satisfaction to see him unnerved.

"Because of that boy," said Aurel. "He's giving you orders. *He* killed your Master… and he isn't even human, is he? You're serving a deity."

"Then you know why we can't disobey him," said Vekka. "We have to give him Arien Astera."

They know the truth. But they'd chosen to stay with the Changers anyway.

"No," said Zelle. "Absolutely not."

"I'll go." Rien stepped forwards. "If I'm the one Orzen wants, then I'll go to him, and you'll leave the others alone."

The urge hit Evita to intervene, but what could she

possibly say? If Rien didn't go with the Changers, she'd be the first to pay the price for his refusal. He had more of a chance of besting Orzen than she did, and he'd always been the intended target.

"No," said Zelle. "I want to talk to him too. Where is he?"

"Waiting for you." One of the Changers pointed uphill towards the Sentinels' cave, where two more assassins flanked an old woman dressed in a lime-green travelling cloak.

Zelle's gasp told Evita everything she needed to know. *That's her grandmother.*

"Orzen has agreed to a trade," said Vekka. "We'll give you the old lady if you give us Arien Astera, and nobody else dies."

"No." Yet Zelle spoke with less heat in her voice than before, her gaze fixed on her grandmother.

"Agreed," said Rien.

Evita didn't hear any more. A pair of hands closed over her shoulders, yanking her backwards. "Oh, and we'll take her too."

A sack was thrust over her head, blocking out her vision, before the Changers dragged her away.

26

Zelle's grandmother looked down at her from outside the Sentinels' cave, where a Changer stood on each side of her. Had they held her captive all along and Evita had lied to them? No—Evita looked stunned too. In fact, she was paying so little attention that she didn't see the two assassins sneaking up on her until they lowered a sack over her head and hauled her away.

One ally had gone, and Rien looked sure to follow her. His jaw was set in determination, and Zelle knew he wouldn't hesitate to go with the Changers if it meant getting closer to avenging his family. There was nothing she could do to convince him otherwise, though admittedly, he stood a far better chance at besting the deity than she did.

Aurel, on the other hand, had eyes only for their grandmother. "We have to get up there."

Grandma didn't seem to have noticed either of them. Her gaze was fixed on her feet, and Zelle knew she must be furious to have been captured. If only Zelle could get the staff into her hands, she might be able to free herself, but to do that, she had to follow the Changers up the steep slope towards the Sentinels' cave.

Rien stepped forwards. "Don't intervene. I will go with them alone."

A protest rose to Zelle's tongue, but she cut herself off. Deep down, she'd been thinking of her grandmother as the indomitable Sentinel who'd outlived most of her relatives. Instead, she was at the Changers' mercy, and the sight of her knocked the wind from her.

Zelle had lost her parents young. She'd nursed her aunt as she wasted away from sickness. She'd heard tales of all the other unfortunate accidents which had befallen her other relatives—drownings, falls, disease. She and her grandmother might not always see eye to eye, but she refused to watch someone else she cared for die.

She drew in a breath. "If you're sure, Rien."

"I will deal with the Changers myself," he said. "Take your grandmother and get out of here."

"You—" Zelle broke off. "You can't go up there alone."

He was already striding up the path, his eyes on the Sentinels' cave. Aurel swore under her breath and then hurried after him, followed by Zelle.

Before he reached the cave, the assassins released Grandma, who tottered downhill towards them. Zelle quickened her pace, as did Aurel, who caught the old Sentinel's arm to prevent her from slipping on the path.

Zelle, meanwhile, held out the staff towards her. "I found this at the outpost."

"Good." Grandma all but snatched the staff from her hands, which left Zelle with a stark feeling of emptiness that seemed entirely at odds with the panic hammering in her chest. "I wondered if you cared I was missing at all."

Aurel flushed. "I didn't even know until Zelle told me."

"Zelle told *you*? Not the other way around?"

"Yes." A familiar annoyance flickered inside Zelle, displaced by her worry for Rien when he approached the Changers outside the Sentinels' cave, his shoulders back and his head high.

Grandma chuckled. "Made a friend, did you?"

"He just condemned himself to set you free," Zelle hissed between her teeth. The rising tide of anger inside her felt more like despair. How could she do anything to help Rien now? The Changers outnumbered them all, and without the staff, she had no means of overcoming them.

Aurel cursed under her breath. "Zelle, take Grandma back to the house."

"What are you doing?"

Instead of answering, Aurel climbed uphill towards the Sentinels' cave. Zelle watched her, surprised at the raw pain of seeing the others risk their lives while she turned her back—but someone needed to make sure Grandma returned to the safety of the Reader's house.

"Come on." She beckoned to Grandma Carnelian. "Let's go."

The Sentinel didn't move. "You should have gone with them, girl."

"I had to help you."

"I don't need your help," her grandmother returned.

"We risked everything to save you," Zelle told her. "You mean to say you were perfectly happy as the assassins' prisoner?"

"I don't need your help *now*," Grandma clarified. "Your sister does, and that Astera boy."

"He..." She looked up at the cave and the assassins surrounding Rien. "There's no help I can give them. I don't have—"

"Magic?" she interjected. "Neither does that Astera boy, and if he faces that creature alone, there can only be one outcome."

"You let Aurel go to help him."

Aurel's strengths lay in Reading, though, not combat. She didn't have the staff, either, and when brightness flashed from somewhere up the hill, Zelle's heart contracted.

No. She couldn't turn her back. She had to help them.

———

The Changers had Rien surrounded the instant he reached the path near the entrance to the Sentinels' cave. He glimpsed Aurel hurrying uphill behind him, but she stopped walking as soon as he did.

Zelle hadn't followed. Sensible of her, because he had an inkling the deity would soon make an appearance.

He wasn't disappointed.

A doorway opened in the air amid the Changers, and the boy stepped out. Rien looked directly into Orzen's icy-blue eyes. "You're going to pay for what you did."

The boy smiled. "Remember your history now, Arien Astera? Are you ready to face me as your true self?"

"Yes." He withdrew a sword from its sheath—a sword Aurel had bought for him that morning, simply made but adequate for his needs—and raised the gleaming blade. "Orzen, I will avenge my family by spilling your blood."

"I cannot be killed," said the boy. "I can maintain this form as long as I take in the blood of those I slaughter. Like your father's."

Hate spread through his body, as insidious as slow-acting poison. *This* was what he'd been waiting for. "Yet you still want more? You still want me?"

"Yes," said Orzen. "I dislike being cheated, you see. I was promised your lifeblood, and I have dreamed of the taste for weeks."

"The last time we spoke, you accused me of not being the person you wanted." His grip tightened on the sword's hilt. "Am I enough for you now?"

The blade swung down, slicing through the boy's chest. The boy smiled at him, blood trickling between his teeth... and then his face warped and changed before Rien's eyes. Growing older, craggier, and turning into someone Rien knew well.

Volcan Astera. His father.

A gasp lodged in his throat. He couldn't move an inch; his hands froze on the sword's hilt.

Swirling darkness descended behind him, and Aurel cried out in alarm. Wraiths formed from the darkness, and Rien knew he should fight them off, but he was unable to look away from the mirror image of his late father.

The fake Volcan Astera transformed into the boy again, the blood already vanishing from the wound in his chest.

"No mortal blow can wound me," he told Rien. "I'm not convinced you truly remember who you are at all."

"I remember." An unwelcome sense of fear began to rise inside him at the sight of the wraiths gathering behind the boy. He'd destroyed them with a Changer's arrow before, but the Changers themselves had understandably vanished from sight. A sword wouldn't touch those monstrosities. Only magic would, and Aurel had all but disappeared behind a curtain of shadow.

"Do you remember everything you did after you fled Aestin?' whispered the boy. "I don't think you do."

"You're lying." Coldness rooted him to the spot, radiating from a deep ache somewhere inside his chest, the place where Astiva had once resided.

"You survived for a reason," said Orzen. "You couldn't have done so without the aid of another deity."

Memories flickered behind his eyes. A whirlpool opening like a gaping maw... crawling desperately up a mountain pass... collapsing inches from his destination...

But whose strength had he drawn on to save his own life?

"Enough of your games," Rien told the boy. "Face me like a man."

Orzen laughed. "I am more than a man."

The wraiths swarmed over to him, bathing him in darkness. Rien's vision dimmed, and then a familiar staff appeared in the boy's hands, glowing against the dark.

The staff of Astiva.

"That's mine," he ground out.

"No," Orzen breathed. "I don't think so."

He swung the staff, and Aurel appeared from the smoke, a knife in her hand. She thrust the knife at the deity's side, but he shook her off as though swatting a fly. Her intervention gave Rien the chance to back up against the cliffside. Near the Sentinels' cave... but the fog was too thick to see the hidden lever.

Orzen advanced on him again. The sight of the crimson staff in his hands brought a spasm of sharp pain to his chest, as if the sight of the staff had reminded his body and spirit of what he'd lost. And for all his imaginings of enacting revenge, he hadn't managed to deal a killing blow.

Crimson thorns flickered in front of his vision. His chest ached as though it was full of glass splinters, and Orzen's cold smile suggested he knew exactly the effect his staff had upon Rien.

Ignoring the pain, Rien thrust outward with the blade, which pierced Orzen through the chest. When he withdrew the sword, the deity's expression tautened with annoyance. "I told you, I cannot die... and if you continue to wound me, I will replenish my strength by taking your allies' lives."

His hand thrust into the fog and seized the nearest Changer. The cloaked figure squirmed in his grip, and the wraiths descended. Aurel released a choked noise of horror when blood splattered the path and the body turned limp in his hand.

Orzen turned to Aurel next, but the Reader backed up to the cliff and slammed her fist against the rock wall. A rumbling sound came from their backs, and the cave entrance slid open. Aurel darted behind Rien and grabbed his arm, hissing, "Get in here. We can't kill him."

Rien didn't budge. He had no desire to be trapped in the cave again—but when Orzen advanced, another stab of pain pierced his chest. Instinct drove Rien to step backwards, into the tunnel. Orzen fetched up against the unseen barrier, his teeth bared in a snarl. "You can't escape me forever, Arien Astera."

"You can't get in here, Orzen... whatever you call yourself." Aurel gave the deity a defiant stare. "Damn the Powers, he really does look like a child."

"Don't goad him," Rien said out of the corner of his mouth. "The cave... can it tell us how to get rid of him?"

"I hope it can." Aurel backed down the tunnel, Rien following, fighting the urge to turn and face Orzen again. He couldn't be killed, and if Rien wounded him again, he'd kill another person to rebuild his strength. Like Aurel... or Zelle.

They halted before the rock, and he dug his fingers into its surface in a desperate attempt to stay upright when another spasm of pain hit his chest. Why was the lost bond with his deity bothering him at a time like this?

"You survived for a reason," Orzen had said. *"You couldn't have done so without the aid of another deity."*

Rien needed to know what his previous vision in the cave had failed to show him, but if he asked the rock that question, he'd lose his chance to learn how to defeat Orzen.

Aurel reached a hand towards the rock. "I'll ask how to kill him. You don't have to ask a question. You look like you need to lie down instead."

"No." He addressed the rock. "Show me... show me how I survived Daimos's attack. Show me how I reached the outpost."

Memories exploded behind his eyes, pouring into his head like a waterfall. Once again, he stood in the street of Tauvice as his family's home caught afire, but this vision prompted more details he hadn't remembered the last time. Such as the way he'd run back from the market and found his brother's lifeless body outside the Astera family's estate, with the medallion he'd always worn hanging from his palm. Rien had picked it up and continued through the gates to see his father lying in a puddle of his own blood—and Naxel Daimos carrying his staff.

Daimos had barely toyed with Rien before striking him down with his father's staff and his own, yet the blow had somehow failed to kill him. Perhaps some fragment of Astiva's magic had recognised him as an ally in spite of it all, but he'd woken from unconsciousness to find himself alone in the ruins.

Then he'd run. He'd had no choice but to flee like a coward, heading for the docks. All he'd had left was a story from his childhood, a tale of a place where the deities slept and where a Relic lay that could grant any wish he desired.

He'd used his last coin to buy passage on a ship, but even then, he hadn't been safe. When the shore had appeared within sight, a whirlpool had threatened to drag him to certain death. Grasping his brother's medallion, he'd called on the Power hidden inside it.

His next memory was of waking up on the shore sometime later. Nobody else had survived, but the medallion had been wiped clear of the name once etched upon it. A miracle had saved him, but he didn't know to whom he owed his thanks, and he knew he wouldn't be able to ask them again.

His last hope lay in the Range, so he'd headed in that direction, aiming for the tower where the Sentinels were supposed to live...

Before he could recall the rest, he became aware of the

cool surface of the rock pressing against his hand and the copper taste of the blood flowing into his mouth from where he'd bitten his tongue. A familiar chill swept into the cave behind him, and the pain in his chest throbbed anew, sharper than ever.

Am I dying?

He'd grown accustomed to the possibility in recent days, but that didn't make him any more eager to depart this world. Not with the creature which had seen to his family's deaths still walking.

He lifted his head, forced his eyes open, and saw that wraiths surrounded him and Aurel, trapping them against the rock. They had nowhere to run.

27

Zelle ran up the steep incline past the spot where she'd parted ways with Aurel and Rien, hardly stopping to breathe until she neared the Sentinels' cave. A person with the slight build of a child stood outside, and her heart leapt into her throat at the sight of Rien swinging his blade.

She saw Orzen stagger back, bleeding—and then he reached out and grabbed one of the Changers by the scruff of his neck. Wraiths descended in a cloud, and Zelle's stomach lurched when the Changer's blood splattered the path.

Orzen, who'd been bleeding from Rien's blade an instant beforehand, no longer appeared to be wounded at all, and behind him, she glimpsed Aurel and Rien ducking behind the barrier of the tunnel's entrance. They had to know the wraiths could reach them even in there, but they had no other escape routes available.

Orzen can't be killed. Nor even permanently wounded,

by the looks of things. In another instant, he'd realise he had company.

Grandma caught up to Zelle. A bluish glow suffused the air around her, and the wraiths recoiled from both of them. Orzen, meanwhile, turned his back on the cave, a scowl appearing on his face. "You again? I thought you had the sense to return to your home comforts, human."

"As if I'd let you run rampant all over the mountains with your dirty little feet, Orzen," said Grandma.

She knows his name?

Before Zelle could blink, Grandma raised the staff, and a wave of bluish light spread throughout the wraiths. The boy released a hiss of displeasure when the fog turned transparent, the wraiths dissolving into a fine mist. Zelle watched in growing disbelief as her grandmother made short work of the boy's companions.

No wonder he'd wanted the Sentinel out of the way. But had she truly been with the Changers the whole time? Evita hadn't thought so—but she was gone too. The Changers had taken her with them, and the remaining few seemed to have fled or hidden nearby. Not a surprise, given that Orzen seemed to have little value for his allies' lives, but he was enough of an opponent on his own. Blood splattered the path around him, and as Zelle watched, it *moved,* travelling towards Orzen's slight form and creeping up his feet in a haze of crimson.

"Blood." Grandma scoffed. "Of all the things to choose to feed on to maintain your form. You deities are always so *dramatic*."

"Grandma," Zelle hissed, her heart in her throat. If Orzen needed blood to keep his human appearance, then two more targets stood directly in front of him. Could even the staff bring him down? Even if it could, she was no longer the wielder, and the sense of helplessness was akin to being stranded on a raft at sea.

The boy faced them, his icy-blue eyes narrowing. "Your friend is not long for this world, and I was promised the lifeblood of the youngest Astera to sate my hunger."

Rien. "You'll never touch him."

"No." Grandma raised the staff. "I would advise you to consider your next move very carefully, Orzen."

"You do realise I cannot be killed, don't you?"

"Yes, I spent time in your realm, remember?" Grandma shuffled towards him. "Conjure a wraith and I will destroy it. Summon a storm and I will banish it with ease. You've made a powerful enemy, and it looks as if your allies have fled."

"You forget I have help from beyond this realm." A doorway opened at Orzen's back, and wraiths surged out to join him in a tide of rippling shadow.

Then Orzen hissed in surprise. The wraiths didn't attack Zelle but instead turned upon their summoner, pressing against him like an icy shroud. A laugh sounded, and it came from the Sentinel. Beyond the doorway, Zelle glimpsed a pair of shadowy forms that resembled large human-sized birds. *Deities.* Had someone else come to their aid?

The wraiths swarmed Orzen, driving him farther down the path and away from the cave. While he had command over the others, Grandma had obliterated them with one wave of the staff. As long as Rien remained in the cave, they'd be at a standstill, and from the calculating expression in Orzen's eye, he knew it too.

"You will pay for this." The boy cast a glare towards Zelle and her grandmother. "I will come back for you, Sentinel."

With one step, he vanished into the whiteness along with the doorway.

"What did you *do*?" Zelle asked her grandmother.

The old Sentinel positively cackled. "The deities are as easily swayed as humans are, for the right price."

"You bribed the deities?" Zelle moved towards the cave entrance, while Grandma shuffled up behind her.

"Go on," she snapped at Zelle. "Run in there and find your sister."

Zelle pushed her questions aside and followed the tunnel into the cave. She broke into a half run and skidded to a halt in front of the large, gleaming rock, where Aurel crouched beside Rien. He lay inert against the rock, while Aurel lifted her head to meet Zelle's eyes. "I don't know what's wrong with him. What happened to the wraiths?"

"Grandma." Zelle leaned over to Rien, whose eyes were closed, his free hand clenched over his chest. "Rien... what have you done to yourself?"

A groan escaped him. "Not... me. Astiva."

"I have no idea what you're talking about."

Rien's hand twitched, his eyes flickering open. "Zelle," he croaked. "I made a terrible mistake."

"What the—?" She broke off, alarmed at the sight of the vine-like scars creeping over his left hand. "Rien, what did you do?"

"Forgive me," he said and then passed out.

"Get him out of here," Grandma called to them from the cave entrance. "Before that deity comes back."

Aurel surveyed him. "I hope we're strong enough to carry him between us."

Aurel was stronger than Zelle, but she staggered when she lifted Rien's shoulders and Zelle took his feet. After carrying him to the cave entrance, they had to lie him on the ground to manoeuvre him through the gap in the cliffside.

"You're taking this far too calmly," Zelle said to Grandma, who waited outside the cave. "Do you know who he is? Rien, I mean?"

She didn't know where to begin explaining how she'd come to cross paths with Rien, much less how his true identity had come to light.

"I see the resemblance," Grandma responded. "He has his father's look."

"You *met* him?" asked Zelle.

"Volcan Astera," said Grandma. "He visited Saudenne a long while ago, before *his* father died and gave Volcan's children his share in the family's Power. They pass their Relics through the family line in that way, from generation to generation."

Not anymore. Zelle's heart contracted as she helped Aurel lift Rien into the air again. "It doesn't seem possible that one person could just steal the entirety of his family's magic. I don't know how Rien even survived it."

"He didn't," said Grandma. "His godsmark is broken. He should be dead."

"Clearly he isn't." Zelle's breath puffed out as they walked, her shoulders protesting.

"How intriguing," Grandma muttered to herself, leaning on her staff as she hobbled down the path. "Few can survive being parted from their Relic, and his family's been bound to that Power for a thousand years."

"Astiva," said Zelle before she could stop herself.

Rien shifted, his right hand gripping the left one and nearly causing Aurel to drop him. Zelle stalled, allowing her to readjust her grip before they continued downhill.

"He bore a left-handed staff?" Zelle guessed.

"All of them did," Grandma said. "The Asteras always had the left hand marked, too, without exception. Frankly, I don't know how he's alive after his own mark was broken."

"He's been alive for days, if not weeks," Zelle told her. "He escaped drowning at sea too."

"Well, there's lucky and there's impossible." Grandma hobbled past them. "Ask him the details when he's awake."

Zelle peered at Rien's unconscious face, a quiver of dread travelling up her spine. She and Aurel struggled on until the path evened out when they reached the forest. Tiredness dragged at her limbs, and Aurel stumbled several times, too, though Rien didn't so much as utter a groan when his head bumped on the low branches. Grandma, meanwhile, walked ahead down the dirt track, as though she hadn't spent the past few days held captive Powers-only-knew-where. Zelle's list of questions she intended to ask grew by the moment, and she released a breath of relief when the Reader's house came into view.

Grandma used the staff to push the gate open before delving into the bushes near the front door for the spare key and unlocking the door. "Come on, get him into the house."

"Shouldn't we take him to a healer?" Zelle asked.

"It's too late for that," said Grandma.

Zelle nearly dropped him, but Aurel took most of his weight as they carried him through the doorway. Upon laying him down on the rug, Zelle slumped against the nearest armchair in exhaustion. "What do you mean by too late?"

Aurel lifted the medallion around Rien's neck and let out a hiss of surprise. "What in the name of the Powers is this thing?"

Grandma stomped over to her side. "I thought so."

"What?" Zelle squinted at the medallion, which appeared no different to her eyes than it had before. "You know what this is?"

"It's a Relic… or it *was* one." Grandma peered at the medallion. "He's drained it dry."

"What are you talking about?" asked Zelle. "The staff said it wasn't a Relic."

"Did it now?" Grandma sounded intrigued. "Were you going to tell me the staff spoke to you?"

"I was, but we were preoccupied." To say the least. "The staff told me you vanished through a door but not who took you. Was it the Changers?"

"Oh, the Changers couldn't catch a rat in a trap." She scoffed. "I saw the storm from down in the village and knew it must have a magical cause, so I went to the Sanctum to check on the situation."

"And?" Zelle prompted. "Who captured you? Was it those wraiths?"

"Hardly," said Grandma. "One of them showed up at the outpost and tried to threaten me, but I frightened it into fleeing through a doorway. Orzen must have accidentally left it lying open after summoning the ridiculous thing."

"You didn't follow it." Aurel frowned. "Did you?"

"Who wouldn't?" Grandma said. "It was right in front of the outpost, so I decided to see who'd had the nerve to open a doorway to the gods' realm outside my home. The staff insisted I had to leave it behind in case its protection was needed, but I little expected *you* to find it, Zelle."

"The doorway wasn't there when I went up to the outpost," Zelle said. "Let me guess... Orzen made it disappear, and you got stuck."

"He's not very observant," said Grandma. "It took him long enough to notice I was there."

"How did you even survive?" Zelle asked. "The realm of the Powers—from what I saw, it doesn't look habitable."

"I found it lacking in certain necessary comforts, but it was an educational visit," Grandma said. "It seems many of the deities are not impressed with the way the original three Great Powers exiled them from the human realm. I gather they were somewhat fond of us."

"And one of them helped you?" Zelle guessed. "Was that how you drove Orzen away?"

Rien chose that moment to startle awake. His body convulsed, his right hand gripping the left, and he writhed for a moment before he fell into unconsciousness again.

Zelle leaned over him, her heart racing. "What's wrong with him?"

"He's dying, of course," said Grandma. "The odds of surviving the loss of one's Relic are about the same as the odds of drawing a winning hand in a game of Relics and Ruins."

Zelle jerked upright, recalling their game... and

recalling the deity whose cards Rien had drawn out, seemingly at random. "He can't be dying. He was fine."

"He wasn't fine, not if he had to bargain with another deity to keep himself alive." Grandma flicked the medallion with her fingertip. "Aestinian magicians see all the deities as their personal servants. If young Arien here was close to death, I would guess he begged a Power to save him in exchange for a debt."

"I didn't know such a thing was possible." Was that how he'd survived this long without his Relic?

Aurel made an approving noise. "I can't decide if he's really brave or really foolish. Maybe that's why he lost his memories too."

"Did he now?" Grandma asked.

"When he first showed up, he didn't even know his name," Zelle explained. "It was as if his mind had wiped itself clean. Until he touched the rock in the Sentinels' cave, he had no recollection of anything, including the name of his family's Power... but he wanted to find out. Is that why it's getting worse for him? Now he remembers?"

Grandma inclined her head, and horror hit Zelle's heart. "Yes, but his family has been tied to that deity for so long that it's become part of their very identity. To forget that..."

...was to forget everything he was. A lump stuck in her throat, and Zelle swallowed. "But why... oh, Powers. Is there anything we can do for him?"

"The only real cure is to find a substitute for the Relic he lost," said Grandma. "He'll die without it, no matter what bargains he makes. No doubt that was his intention in coming here."

"He was looking for Relics in the mountains," she said. "He heard the stories, but they're not true."

Rien stirred, groaning a little.

Zelle crouched beside him. "I'm sorry. I shouldn't have mentioned his name. The Power, I mean."

His eyes opened a fraction. "Not... your fault."

She was conscious of the others watching both of them, but she hardly cared. "Grandma said you made a bargain with a deity. Which one? Are they as strong as— as Gaiva's children?"

He shook his head then grimaced. "A minor Power... I don't quite recall the name yet."

"That doesn't sound good." She knew her perspective on the deities was vastly different than his, but becoming indebted to an unknown Power struck her as an excellent way to end up mired in utter disaster. *Don't bother the gods and they won't bother you,* Aunt Adaine had said... but she'd well and truly disregarded that advice herself, hadn't she?

Rien's hands twitched. Now Zelle looked closely, she made out a web of lines across the back of his left hand, spreading to the ends of each fingertip and disappearing up his wrist under his sleeve. Faint white streaks, like faded scars. The godsmark, she assumed.

She looked up at her grandmother. "He'll be all right, won't he?"

"Unless the deity he bargained with comes to call in their favour." Grandma tutted. "The fool. Now, Zelle, are you going to tell me what bargains *you* made with the gods?"

"Me?" she said. "None. The staff spoke to me, and so did the rock in the Sentinels' cave, but I wouldn't say any bargains were made."

"Really?" asked Grandma. "What did the Sentinel's cave tell you, exactly?"

Zelle sat back against the armchair, her pulse beginning to race. "The rock told me to close the doors."

Grandma's gaze was piercing. "Tell me everything."

28

Rien remained unconscious throughout Zelle's explanation, so she alone had to tell her grandmother the story of her and Rien's experiences at the outpost and their journey over the mountains to Aurel's house.

"The other Powers will wake if the crack between realms remains open, the Sentinels' cave told me," Zelle finished. "And—it said that I had to close the doors myself, but I'm guessing that it would have handed the task to you instead, if you'd been there."

"No," said Grandma. "Our job as Sentinels is to safeguard Zeuten's magic, not to meddle with the Powers."

"That isn't my job either," Zelle pointed out. "I'm not even a Sentinel. I've also never set foot in Aestin, which I'm pretty sure lies at the centre of this."

"You aren't wrong," Rien murmured, making her jump. She hadn't realised he was awake. "Daimos is in Aestin. He did this."

"If you're thinking that you're going there right now,

then you're mistaken," Zelle told him. "You barely survived your encounter with his ally." To say nothing of Grandma's remarks about his time being limited without his deity.

Rien's mouth turned down at the corners. "I didn't think that creature was capable of resisting a mortal wound."

"Of course he is," said Grandma. "His humanlike form is simply a construct in itself. He requires sustenance—blood— to sustain it, and he is able to regenerate indefinitely, I imagine, as long as he can travel between here and the realm of the Powers."

"The cave told me the same, when I asked how to beat him," said Aurel in sour tones. "So we're letting him win? We're going to allow him and his Changer friends to rampage around the continent, killing everyone in their path?"

"Certainly not," said Grandma. "Why do you think I spoke directly to the Powers myself?"

Zelle gave her a sharp look. "You really did make a bargain with them?"

"You did *what?*" Aurel spluttered.

Grandma regarded them with a calm expression. "When you get past their undying nature, the Powers are as prone to petty squabbles as we are. Most of them are partially human, or so they say."

"Not the three Great Powers," said Zelle automatically.

"They're long gone, even Gaiva Herself, as Her descendants know well," said Grandma. "Two of them agreed to oppose Orzen, though they might be regretting that decision."

"That's why he left." Nausea crawled up Zelle's throat. "Do you think he killed them?"

"Killing a deity isn't as easy as killing a human," Grandma said. "I won us time, but once he's finished with them, he'll come back to find his target."

Rien grimaced. "Me. And I have no deity to bargain with this time."

Zelle's gaze went to the medallion around his neck. "That was a Relic?"

He lowered his head. "It was my brother's. He said only to use it in an emergency, and Daimos didn't see it as worth taking. Its power enabled me to survive the shipwreck that struck before I reached Zeuten, but now... it's worthless."

"I thought so," Grandma said. "No, you need a new Relic to survive."

"Do you know where to find one?" Zelle asked, not daring to hope. "Grandma, did you learn anything in the realm of the Powers that might help us?"

"No," said Grandma. "Though I find myself wishing I'd found out which of the deities the young Astera boy owes a favour to. Some of them *want* their Relics to be found. Especially the deities whose Relics were lost in remote regions... such as the Range."

Zelle frowned. "I thought that was nothing more than a story used to trick gullible tourists."

Rien's gaze briefly travelled over to her, but he didn't voice a comment.

"Stories have a tendency to change over time," said Grandma. "That one has been remarkably consistent, however. The tale of the first settlers who came to

Zeuten, guided by Gaiva Herself, and who hid Relics somewhere in the mountains."

"And founded the outposts, I know," added Zelle. "What about all our ancestors' failed attempts to find those Relics, then? Some even died in the process."

"Oh, that might be true," said Grandma. "I had quite the interesting discussion on the matter with a certain ambassador from Aestin some years ago. Someone who had written records from the time, preserved for a thousand years."

Rien's gaze turned piercing. "You mean—?"

"Volcan Astera," her grandmother said. "I imagine you've seen the records yourself, and that is what brought you here."

"Are you trying to tell us there *are* hidden Relics in the mountains?" Aurel asked. "How can nobody have found them in all this time?"

"Did you think the nameless Power would have made it easy?" asked Grandma. "The Range is brimming with magic. Don't look at me like that, Zelle. There has been no need of any Relics in Zeuten before now."

Zelle's throat went dry. "Do you understand what this means? If we're not careful, Zeuten will become another Aestin."

"Not if you keep your mouth shut," said Grandma. "Tell nobody of the Relics and they won't be any the wiser."

Rien straightened upright. "There truly are unclaimed Relics in the mountains? Might I be able to claim one?"

His hesitancy was a stark contrast to his earlier certainty that a Relic would submit to him. Recent events had shaken him, no doubt, but Zelle might say the same for herself too. If this was the only way for him to survive... but how would they find these hidden Relics with Orzen out there, waiting for Rien to leave the sanctuary of the Reader's house?

"I have a more pertinent question," said Aurel. "Whereabouts *are* they hidden? I think I'd have noticed if any other Relics were inside the Sentinels' cave. Or the Sanctum."

"The best hiding places are often the more obvious ones," said Grandma. "The Sanctum is certainly the place I'd choose to hide a Relic I didn't want anyone to find."

"But—it's all the way on the other side of the mountains," Zelle said. "We barely got here in one piece, and this time, I won't have the—"

"Take the staff with you."

Zelle stared at her grandmother. "You can't be serious."

"Take it," she repeated. "You're younger and faster than I am, and you stand more of a chance than I do of reaching the Sanctum in time to outrun that Orzen's wraiths."

"I won't leave you unprotected," Zelle protested.

"This house is well protected," said Grandma. "Also, Aurel will stay with me."

"What?" asked Aurel. "No. I'm not sitting at home with Orzen out there threatening our family."

Zelle's mouth parted. She'd never heard her sister admit to wanting to use her magical talents to protect their family before. Despite their frequent arguments, she'd always known that her sister did retain a sense of responsibility both towards her family and the Sentinel title that awaited her when Grandma retired, but she tended to bury sentiment in jokes or irreverent comments. In a situation of peril like this, however, it was understandable that she'd speak plainer.

"Orzen will expect the Sentinels to go looking for him again," said Grandma. "One person is enough to escort the Astera boy, and that honour goes to Zelle, since they already trust one another."

Her face flushed when Rien swivelled to face her. Did she trust him? They'd had to rely upon each other for their own survival and had even saved one another's lives a few times, but they'd butted heads just as frequently, if not more. Zelle startled when Grandma pushed the staff into her hands.

You again, it said to her.

"That's me," she said, not particularly bothered that the others could hear her talking to it. "Are you going to cooperate with me this time?"

I suppose it would be a waste of all our time if you were to perish this close to your goal.

"What goal?" She studied the knotted wood. "You weren't exactly keen on helping Rien beforehand."

The staff didn't answer. Zelle rolled her eyes. "Not this again. If you're going to give me the silent treatment, I'm going to assume you don't know the answer yourself."

That is untrue.

"Right." Zelle shook her head, fighting an inexplicable smile. With the staff in her hands, a strange sense of rightness bolstered her, despite her deep-seated certainty that it would never truly be hers. Did she have a right to challenge the word of a fragment of a Great Power, though? However unlikely it might be that the deities would need help from the likes of her, the Sentinels' cave *and* Grandma seemed to think that the job was hers.

The gods don't care for your intentions, she told herself. *Look what happened to Astiva.* Aestin's entire history was rife with tales of the Powers fighting with one another, alongside mortals or otherwise, but Zelle had never consciously believed the Powers had ever existed as actual, physical beings. Not when they hadn't been seen in this world since before accurate written records were widespread. They didn't even know the *name* of one of the three Great Powers, and nobody was clear on how their realm had been severed from the human world to begin with.

"Go on," said Grandma. "Go and fetch that friend of yours."

Zelle spun on her heel, groaning when she saw the door lay partly open. Rien must have slipped out as stealthily as a Changer while she'd been conversing with the staff.

Yes, go on, the staff told her. *We have no time to waste.*

———

Rien walked out through the gate leading to the Reader's house and into the village itself. He knew it wasn't wise, but he wanted to clear his head. The cold air certainly helped; he'd known that Zeuten's summer months were comparable to winters in Aestin, but he hadn't had direct experience of its temperamental weather conditions until he'd visited in person. The continuing recollection of his lost memories was a dizzying assault on the senses, and he hadn't had time to process that he was a visitor to a foreign country who'd come to take something that Zeuten might not willingly part with. Even if the

Sentinels seemed willing to help him, it didn't guarantee that his quest wouldn't end in failure.

Zelle had the staff back, and despite her obvious efforts to hide it, she was thrilled at the idea of holding it in her hands again. As for him? He had no magic of his own, and even with a sword in his hand, he'd failed to destroy Orzen. Worse, he owed his survival to at least one minor Power who might come to call him to repay the favour at any moment. Even the prospect of finding another Relic didn't quell his fear that Astiva's loss had damaged him too badly for him to ever recover.

Until the last few weeks, he couldn't recall a day without Astiva at his side, his deity guiding his hand with every swing of his staff, a part of his soul that he hadn't even known was there until it'd been ripped away.

It was enough to drive one to madness.

Yet that hadn't been his only loss. His father, his brother... every member of his family had met the same end, and nobody was alive to avenge them but him.

He needed to find another deity, another Relic. To save his own life, yes, but above all—to kill Naxel Daimos.

Footsteps pounded behind him. Zelle came to a halt, breathless, the staff in her hand. "Don't leave without me. Orzen's looking for you, remember?"

"Yes, I remember." Yet defeating him seemed as much of an impossibility as ever. How to kill someone who couldn't die and who regenerated as long as he slaughtered others to spare his own life? "Are you certain we'll find what we need up in the mountains? I know now that I came here chasing a rumour designed to trick the foolish."

"You didn't," said Zelle. "You never heard the story

from a merchant you met on the road. You read it in your family's records. Someone in your family must have known the Relics were here. They were acquainted with the original settlers, weren't they?"

How did she know? Well, it was a reasonable assumption to make, given her grandmother's revelation that she'd met with Rien's own father. Yet he'd never shared anything about his family with an outsider before. His father had impressed the importance of secrecy upon him. He knew the price of another of the Invoker families gaining access to sensitive information.

Such as hidden Relics on another continent.

A fist clenched over his heart at the thought of Torben, once his best confidant, and he swallowed hard. He sensed Zelle waiting for an answer, and so he attempted to find the words.

"There were records," he began. "Correspondence between my ancestors and the settlers. It wasn't constant, and they occasionally dropped out of touch, but my grandfather kept the tradition alive."

"He kept in touch with the Sentinels?" Zelle's eyes widened. "Directly?"

"I don't know. He died when I was a child." He shook his head. "Besides, not all my ancestors kept meticulous records. A thousand years is a long time."

"That it is," said Zelle. "My family's own records... well, to be honest, they don't exist for the most part. We're supposed to be historians, but a few centuries after we settled here, nobody bothered to write anything down. We don't enjoy the prestige that the Invoker families do, after all."

"There were times when I wished I could escape my

responsibilities." He found himself speaking without intending to, admitting truths he'd never voiced aloud to his family. "The attention, the constant obligations…"

"Oh, poor you." Her lips pressed together. "That was callous. Sorry. I keep forgetting—I mean, my aunt used to say that all the Invokers did was wage war on one another."

Grief reared its head within Rien's chest, and he averted his gaze. "My father never wanted war. He didn't even like disputes with the other families; he preferred to resolve matters diplomatically. There were other families, long ago, who destroyed themselves and each other through their need to maintain dominance. In my father's view, we were originally meant to be peacekeepers."

"The Sentinels were, too," said Zelle. "Granted, I'm not one of them, but I can't sit by and watch that deity destroy everything my ancestors wanted to protect. I'm willing to do anything to stop him, and—I hoped you might be too."

Shame rose within him for becoming wrapped up in his own dilemmas when Zelle had risked her life on his behalf. More than once. And now she was offering to do the same again.

He saw Zelle watching him, a faint blush on her cheeks, and cleared his throat. "All right. I'll come with you."

29

The Changers dragged Evita along the path for an indefinite amount of time. When they came to a stop, they bound her hands with ropes and left her in the darkness. Presumably inside a cave, judging by the way the wind echoed above her head and bit through her travel-worn clothes. They'd removed her cloak and taken her weapons away, too, leaving her entirely vulnerable.

A short while later, the sack was pulled from her head, and she found herself looking up at a familiar face. Ruben frowned at her, and with a rush of embarrassment, she recalled telling him of her intention to kill a god in order to make him stop flirting with her. How typical that he might be her only hope for getting her freedom back.

"Ruben," she said hoarsely. "Nice to see a friendly face."

The grim set to his mouth told her that he remembered their last encounter as well as she did. As she'd suspected, the Changers had thrown her into a cave, but it wasn't one of their own. Light filtered in from behind

Ruben, but he moved to prevent her from peering behind him. "I shouldn't be talking to you, Evita, but I have to know... what were you thinking?"

She straightened upright, the ropes pulling at her wrists. "You must know I didn't kill Master Amery. I was away on a mission when he died."

"I know," he said. "You were sent to find the Reader, but instead, you turned your back on us."

"You were keen to flee the Changers with me before." She kept her voice low. "What changed?"

Instead of answering, he held out her cloak. An unexpectedly kind gesture, but she couldn't put it back on with the ropes binding her wrists together. There was a new wariness in his expression that hadn't been there the last time she'd seen him, and Evita had a feeling she knew exactly who was responsible.

"It's *him*, isn't it?" she asked. "Your new master."

Ruben gave a nervous glance behind him. "We're being picked off one by one. More Changers have died in the last few days than in the last decade, I heard. That—that thing that looks like a boy—" He cut himself off with a shudder. "I shouldn't be telling you this."

"Keeping me here won't make him any more likely to spare you," she pointed out. "He killed Master Amery, don't forget."

He shuddered again. "The others don't see it that way. They think helping him will win them favour with the gods."

"Helping him do what?" Evita asked. "He's perfectly capable of hunting down Arien Astera himself."

In fact, Evita had half thought Orzen had already killed him. As she'd seen before the Changers had dragged her away, Arien had willingly handed himself over in exchange for the old woman—Zelle's grandmother. *Why was* she *with the Changers, anyway?*

"He got away." Ruben shook his head. "Back to the Reader's house."

Evita's heart leapt. If he'd survived, then Zelle and the others must have too. "Where am I, then? This isn't the base."

"No... we set up camp here so we could see down to the valleys and look for the—" He cut himself off.

"The what?" she pressed.

"Evita, we can't talk about this."

"You're not supposed to be talking to me anyway." She shuffled into a more upright position. "If he's looking for something, maybe I know where to find it."

Ruben studied her face for a moment. "Have you ever heard a story about a lost Relic in the mountains?"

She opened her mouth to say no, but it wasn't true. When she thought back to the time when she'd eagerly collected stories of adventure from any travellers who passed through her village, she did recall a tale or two of old Relics from long-forgotten deities buried in the mountains. Everyone said the Range was the most potent source of power in the whole of Zeuten, after all.

Did the Reader know what Orzen was looking for? Evita was hardly in a position to warn her, but maybe she could use this situation to her advantage.

Inspiration struck. "Yes, I've heard the stories. I heard them from the Reader herself, in fact, and she said that nobody can touch the Relics without suffering a horrible death."

His brows rose. "Really?"

"Yes," she went on, hoping that she sounded convincing. "The Relics were hidden by her ancestors, a million years ago."

He blinked. "I thought the Sentinels only came to the mountains a thousand years ago, not a million."

Evita never had learned much of history, but she suspected he was probably right. "A thousand years ago, then. The point is, they'll kill you if you lay a hand on them. Your skin will melt off your bones, and your eyes will dissolve in their sockets."

Ruben shuddered. "The Reader told you that?"

"Yes," Evita improvised, sprinkling in a little truth. "That boy—he doesn't care if you all die. I bet he's planning to have you dig up the Relics with your own hands and then take them from you after you're dead."

Ruben watched her for a moment. Then he reached for a knife at his belt and began hacking away at the ropes on her wrists. Evita remained absolutely still, her body tensed with the anticipation of the others' return—but they didn't come back, and the ropes fell away when she shook her hands.

"Thanks," she breathed. "I owe you one."

"That so?" A tentative smile crossed his face. "If you *do* want to run away with me, then I'm still open to the idea."

"No," she said firmly. "Put it out of mind. I'm not—I'm not interested in you in that way. Or anyone like you."

"Men?" he said.

"Anyone." She stretched her sore wrists and reached to pick up the cloak he'd brought her. "But I appreciate your help."

"I don't know what they did with your weapons," he murmured. "But I have one of these left."

He held out a spelled arrow. Even without a bow, it was better than nothing. She nodded and stashed the arrow in the inside pocket of her cloak. "Thank you."

"Better move fast," he warned. "Before they come back."

After pulling on the cloak, Evita hurried towards the cave opening and emerged into the open, squinting at the brightness of the sky. Despite the sunlight, a thicket of dark clouds gathered around the distant peaks.

"You should run, too," she whispered to Ruben, but he shook his head, looking up at the dark peak.

"Go," he told her. "I'll only draw attention to you."

Right—he didn't have a cloak of his own. He might have taken hers, but he hadn't. She really did owe him a favour—if they both survived, that was.

The other Changers were nowhere to be seen, but the winding path carried a hint of familiarity. Her relief at her newfound freedom surpassed her fear of the drop, so Evita hurried along and didn't look up until a shadow fell over her from above.

A cloud scudded across the sky, oddly silvery in colour, and hovered above her for a moment. She thought of those ghastly creatures the boy had summoned and threw herself flat to the ground, behind a rock. *Please tell me they aren't looking for me.*

The cloud shifted onward, above the peaks, and Evita lifted her head to look at the underside of the cloud and saw humanlike shapes moving within. They *were* humans, but they were cloaked in silver that formed overlapping wings. It couldn't be possible...

Changers.

————

Zelle waited for Rien outside the Reader's house, her nerves tensed in anticipation. She was putting an awful lot of faith in her grandmother's theory that they'd be able to reach the Relics without running into trouble as long as they stuck to the established routes. They'd done the same on their journey here, after all, and they'd been lucky to make it to the Reader's house in one piece. Granted, they were armed this time, but she'd seen Orzen shake off a mortal wound as if it were nothing.

Rien walked out of the door, looking unusually—she had to think for a moment to remember the word—regal. He'd changed into a fresh white shirt and some well-made trousers that he'd found in the packages Aurel had bought, but it wasn't just the new clothes or the weapons he'd equipped himself with. When he looked at her, there was a clarity in his eyes that hadn't been there before.

If she hadn't seen him unconscious not long earlier, she would never have thought he was slowly dying.

Zelle did her best to put that thought out of mind when they left the village behind and followed the dirt track through the forest directly to the mountain path. Aurel and Grandma had stayed behind in the Reader's house in the hopes that its defences would keep any potential attackers out, but Zelle would have to rely upon the staff and hope that Orzen didn't have the patience to have stayed near the Sentinels' cave to wait for his target to return. He seemed impulsive enough that she couldn't imagine he'd want to stay in one place when there was no guarantee that Rien would willingly return.

Unfortunately, that also meant he was as likely to

appear from nowhere and confront them as not. Zelle kept both eyes open for any potential attackers as they emerged from the forest and began the long climb uphill. The Changers might not know Rien had survived, but it was only a matter of time before they unknowingly walked past one of their hiding places. Assuming the deity didn't have them all running around doing his bidding instead, but what else was he doing if not hunting Rien?

Zelle's heart sank when she spotted a mass of dark clouds circling the peaks overhead.

"There'd better not be another bloody storm on the way," she muttered, wiping the sweat from her forehead. "Magical or not."

She glanced behind her, seeing that they'd come a long way, but they had a fair distance left to go before they reached the shelter of the passageway through the mountains.

"I doubt Orzen would have summoned another storm," Rien commented. "Not if he's actually here in person this time."

"That's not reassuring, Rien."

The staff chose that moment to speak up. *That's not a storm.*

Zelle swore under her breath. "What is it, then?"

"What is what?" Rien asked.

"Ah—I was talking to the staff," she clarified. "It claims the cloud isn't a storm."

We're too far away for me to tell what it is. Unless you're willing to get close enough to see for yourself.

"No thanks," she said. "Whatever it is, we'll deal with it when we get there."

After this next stretch of the climb, they'd reach the

passageway through the cliffside, which would help protect them both from potential assassins and acts of nature, but they'd neared the spot where the avalanche had almost swept them off the mountain. Had that had a magical cause too? Zelle hadn't been certain, but it didn't necessarily matter. There was such a thing as an accident, given the scrapes she'd seen tourists manage to get themselves into, but to her knowledge, no tourist had ever managed to incur the wrath of a deity.

As they walked beneath the overhanging cliff, Zelle talked to Rien to take her mind off the memory of their near miss. "Where do you think the deity is, if not here?"

"In his own realm, no doubt," Rien answered. "Even Invokers know little of the realm of the Powers, but I think those doorways must allow him to get around faster. It's an effective place to hide too."

"I bet that's why he was sent here to find you," she said. "It's far more efficient than travelling by boat."

Or walking. Their path seemed longer than it had before, and Zelle's nerves spiked every time she looked up to see the clouds had shifted closer to their position.

Close the doors, the Sentinels' cave had told her, but that deity seemed to be able to open doors between the realms whenever he liked. Not only that, but Grandma had said the boy was effectively immune to physical damage and was able to heal any injury. How, then, were they supposed to best him?

Find the Relic first, she told herself. If the Sanctum could lead Rien to a new Relic, then perhaps it could also tell her how to rid the world of Orzen.

As they emerged from the overhang, the clouds awaited on the other side, directly above their heads.

They didn't look like ordinary storm clouds, magical or not, as their colour was closer to silver than grey. In fact, now she looked closer, they reminded her of something else entirely.

Zelle's heart plunged as if she'd taken a wrong step on the path. The cloak Evita had been wearing had enabled her to hide from sight, but Zelle hadn't known it was possible to use one to fly. Yet unless her eyes were deceiving her, the mass of cloud was in fact formed of a number of overlapping Changers' cloaks, their owners flying close enough together for their cloaks to merge into a single cloud.

"Rien," she hissed. "I think the Changers are up there."

Of course it's them, chimed in the staff. *I sensed that there was magic at work, but those cloaks of theirs are vexing and hard to detect.*

What were they *doing* up there? Had they seen her yet? She couldn't see any individual faces amid the clouds, but they were close enough that they'd only need to glance down to see the pair of them.

"They aren't watching us," Rien murmured. "I saw those clouds before we left the forest. They've been here for ages."

"Then what…" She trailed off, another unwelcome realisation crashing down on her head like an avalanche. They weren't looking for the Relics, were they? Had the deity heard the rumour, too, and guessed the truth?

If Orzen found the Relics before they did, then they'd truly be lost.

30

Evita carried on walking, the cloak hiding her from sight. Knowing the Changers flew directly above her head didn't help her nerves, but they weren't looking for her. She'd never seen the Changers mobilise in such a way before, moving as a single being to hunt down their target.

Or looking for Relics. According to Ruben, anyway. She hoped he'd found somewhere safe to hide, because he'd carried no cloak of his own. Evita felt very small and insignificant beneath the raging clouds, and vulnerable despite the cloak masking her from sight. After all, while the Changers wouldn't be able to see her, their leader would.

Her family's murderer. She'd sworn to avenge them in whatever way she could, but she never could have guessed where that road would lead her. Nor did she know how to enact revenge upon a being who couldn't be killed.

The clouds whirled, changing direction abruptly, and a gale swept in their wake. Evita's feet stumbled, her hands

flailing for something to grab onto, but the wind intensified, dragging her downhill. Evita tumbled and tripped
until she came to a halt near the edge of a cliff. The wind
ceased as suddenly as it had begun, but she squeezed her
eyes shut and dug her fingers into the ground until a soft
thud at her shoulder prompted her to open them again.

A chirp sounded in her ears. *The dragonet.*

"Get out while you can," she whispered. "Fly away. It's
not safe."

Chirp's clawed foot brushed her shoulder. Evita raised
her head to the sky and saw that the cloud had descended
above a spot where two figures stood on the mountain
path.

Rien and Zelle.

The dragonet nipped at her wrist. Evita snatched her
hand away. "You want me to help them? You can fly, but I
can't. With or without the cloak."

Chirp's spindly wings fluttered in the breeze. She was
somewhat surprised that he hadn't already been blown off
the path, though the wind had died down now that the
Changers had moved in on their target.

I have to do something. But if she got too close, even her
cloak wouldn't stop her from being caught in the gale and
swept off the mountain. She had no weapons save for the
single arrow Ruben had given her earlier. That wouldn't
help her against such a large group of assassins, much less
ones who'd acquired the ability to fly.

Chirp reached out and hooked a claw into the back of
her cloak, yanking down the hood.

"Don't do that." She pulled the hood up again, but the
dragonet's claw remained lodged firmly into the part of
her cloak at the back of her neck. A second front claw

joined it. "Wait. When I said you could fly, I didn't mean—"

The dragonet chirped, his wings spreading outward. The next gust of wind caught them, and then they were flying.

Evita's scream lodged in her throat as the path dropped away beneath her, her legs dangling perilously as Chirp's claws maintained a firm grip on the back of her cloak. The dragonet oughtn't be strong enough to lift her, but he didn't seem to be struggling with her weight.

Was this what it felt like when the Changers shifted into birds and flew? She doubted most Changers looked this undignified, nor did they fight the constant urge to scream and flail as they rode the wind currents upwards. It took every scrap of willpower she possessed to keep from making a sound when they neared the cloud of darkness gathering above the path where Zelle and Rien were located.

Evita kept her eyes on the cloud instead of the sheer drop, counting nine, maybe ten Changers within the blur of silvery material. Their cloaks appeared to merge together, giving the illusion of the cloud being much bigger than it truly was, and they entirely masked Rien and Zelle from sight.

The dragonet beat his wings, nearing the cloud. She didn't dare make a noise that might draw the Changers' attention, but when Chirp came to an abrupt halt, she couldn't suppress a whimper. Her legs dangled, the world spinning beneath her—but in another instant, she forgot about the sheer drop altogether.

A doorway had opened in the air, and the boy-who-wasn't-a-boy stepped onto the rocky path below. The clouds masked Rien and Zelle from sight, but had they seen the doorway too? She'd admittedly rather be stuck in a cloud of Changers than face-to-face with the deity, but that wasn't much of a choice to start off with.

The boy extended his hands, and shards of what appeared to be icicles formed in front of his palms. When he lifted his arms, they shot like spears through the clouds, straight into the mass of Changers.

The cloud roiled and warped as the Changers panicked—the boy didn't seem to care about hitting his allies—but everyone seemed entirely oblivious to the dragonet hovering nearby. Evita's heart raced. She wouldn't have a better chance than this.

"Fly behind him," she breathed, hoping the dragonet understood her. "Then let me go."

Chirp circled the boy from behind, careful to keep out of sight. When Evita's feet brushed the path, she lifted a trembling hand to search her pockets for the spelled arrow Ruben had given her. Her entire body quaked, and her sweaty hand gripped the arrow tightly while Chirp flew her closer to her target.

When his claws released her, she took aim. In training, Master Amery had taught them to find a spot on the spine which, if hit, would instantly kill the target. Of course, she'd never tried it out in practise, much less against a deity instead of a human, but he didn't seem to have heard her approach. Step-by-step, she drew closer, her grip tightening on the arrow.

Evita gave a lunge, burying the arrow in the tip of the boy's spine. He shuddered, the slightest motion, and blood trickled from the wound.

Then he turned around, fixing his icy-blue eyes on

Evita, and smiled. "You've turned out to be quite the nuisance."

He reached out a hand and shoved her off the cliff.

———

The Changers surrounded Zelle and Rien, their silvery cloud enveloping the pair of them until the rest of the path was lost to sight. Within the cloud, a number of arrows pointed at her and Rien.

"Hang on." Zelle lifted the staff warningly. "You don't want to make enemies of the Sentinels."

"We've come for the Relics," said one of the Changers. "You know where they are, don't you? Tell us."

"There aren't any." She'd guessed right, then. Orzen knew of the Relics hidden in the mountains, and he'd sent the Changers to find them. Zelle momentarily forgot she was speaking to a group of deadly assassins and instead channelled all her pent-up annoyance from years of directing tourists away from certain death. "Powers above, every outsider who comes to the mountains wants a piece of the mysterious lost Relic, yet none of them has ever found anything. You should know better than to believe lies told by merchants to trick travellers into wandering to their doom."

"What are *you* doing here, then?" asked another Changer.

"Helping the Sentinel," replied Zelle. "By stopping intruders from trampling all over our outposts. She's a ninety-five-year-old woman, in case you were unaware. She deserves to be treated with courtesy, not to be kidnapped and then hassled about Relics that don't exist."

She'd hoped to distract them for long enough to allow Rien the chance to run for the entrance to the hidden passageway, but the dense cloud made it impossible to see the path beneath their feet, and one wrong step might send them plummeting to their deaths.

Besides, she couldn't help wondering what the deity could possibly need the Relics for. Didn't he already have enough power?

As though conjured up by her thoughts, a flash of white lit up the clouds. A doorway opened, and Orzen stepped out onto the path. He raised his hands, and a flurry of icicles shot towards Rien. Zelle swung the staff on instinct—for all the good it would do—but it went cold in her hands, and a dazzling flash of bluish light emanated from its wooden surface. The icicles shattered into pieces at once, while the Changers scattered in alarm. Even Orzen had turned away and seemed to be conversing with an unseen foe, so Zelle seized on the chance to escape.

Zelle and Rien ran through the mass of Changers, emerging onto the other side of the cloud intact. A short distance away lay the route into the hidden passageway. Without pausing to breathe, Zelle hurried up to the cliff face and slammed her palm against the lever. The wall slid open, and she and Rien ducked inside. Another strike of her palm, and the exit closed behind them.

Rien gave the wall a doubtful look. "I highly doubt a mere rock will stop that creature from following us."

"Or he'll be waiting on the other side." Zelle began to walk all the same, relying on the lanterns to guide their way. "Once we're outside, we'll have to run straight for the Sanctum."

The staff's voice spoke in her head. *Walk towards the wall.*

"Walk towards the—?" She broke off as a thumping sounded from behind them, as if someone was trying to break through the wall. "Tell me Orzen can't follow us inside."

He can. This passageway isn't like the Sanctum or the Sentinels' cave, and even a wall of solid rock cannot keep him out forever.

Rien gave her a quizzical look. "Is the staff talking to you?"

"Yes." She looked down at the knotted wooden surface. "It's telling me to walk towards the wall. As opposed to the way out."

There's no time for you to wander for hours under the mountains. The enemy is at your back.

"Really, I had no idea," she said. "Unless you can make me fly, like those cloaks, we can't move any faster than we are."

A pang hit her at the thought of Evita, who she hadn't seen among the other Changers. She hadn't thought to look for her either. Even if she was their prisoner, Zelle hoped she was out of harm's way, because one of them deserved to get out of this in one piece.

As for Zelle, she still hadn't the faintest clue what the staff was talking about. "Which wall?"

You're as impatient as the Sentinel.

"Thanks." She took a step back when the nearest lantern swung of its own accord, as though caught in a breeze. Rien reached out to steady it, and a rumbling reverberated through the tunnel. In the light of the lantern, she glimpsed a line of symbols etched into the wall.

"What is that?" asked Rien. "Those markings look familiar."

"They're everywhere," Zelle said. "I assume the previous Sentinels enjoyed writing their names on things."

"That's the ancient language of our common ancestors, isn't it?"

"Yes, but I can't read most of it." The writing, she realised, stretched all along the wall, and while she couldn't read every word, it resembled the text written on the Sanctum's entryway.

The staff spoke again. *Are you going to do as I say?*

Zelle startled when the staff jerked forwards in her hands, its edge touching the wall. Then the wall shifted before their eyes, sliding open to reveal another entryway to what appeared to be a similar passage to the one they stood in.

"By the Powers," murmured Zelle. "Was that always there?"

Yes, and no, said the staff. *Go on. Stop dawdling.*

"It'd help if you told me where we're going."

"The staff did that?" Rien eyed the new passageway. "Where does it lead?"

"Haven't a clue." Zelle stepped into the tunnel entrance, shivering as a breeze lifted the hair from her head. The tunnel itself was pitch dark, but a source of light at the bottom told her they didn't have far to walk before they reached their destination. Wherever *that* was. "Does Grandma know this place is here?"

No, she doesn't.

Having suspected as much, Zelle began to walk, with Rien at her back, until they came to the source of light. A single lantern hung from the wall at the end of the narrow passage, where it opened into a small cave.

Inside the cave lay a stone pedestal that came up to Zelle's shoulder, and on top of the pedestal lay a book.

Rien sucked in a breath, his gaze fixated on the book. Even from a distance, the crimson of its binding drew the eye, and patterns on its surface resembled twisting vines.

"Rien!" She reached for his sleeve, but he was already striding past her, his hand outstretched towards the pedestal.

Before he touched the book, the cave gave a tremor, the floor lurching beneath Zelle's feet. She braced herself against the staff with one hand, beckoning to Rien with the other. "Don't touch that—"

The ground gave way. Or rather, it simply disappeared, leaving Zelle's body abruptly in free fall. Air rushed past, buffeting her on every side. There was no wall to grab, no way to slow herself down.

Zelle tumbled into oblivion.

31

Rien stared at the spot where Zelle had been standing. One moment she'd been shouting a warning to him, the next... well, his eyes didn't want to believe it, but he was positive he'd seen the floor open up, drawing Zelle in before he could move an inch to help her.

All because he'd been distracted by the book.

His gaze snapped back to the pedestal, to which the book had been bound by thick ropes. No, not ropes but thorny vines, which appeared to grow from the cover of the book itself.

A red-bound book with thorns. He'd had the image in his head from the start, and yet its thorns put him in mind of another deity altogether. One who was no longer his to command.

His left hand reached out, almost of its own accord, exposing the scars creeping down his wrist and over the back of his hand to his fingertips. The echo of his godsmark glowed, white light spilling down the scars as the book drew him in. Intoxicating. Inevitable.

As his fingers brushed against the binding, a chill rushed over his skin, similar to how he'd felt when he'd touched the rock in the Sentinels' cave. The hole in his chest where his deity had been throbbed in response, and with a sickening jolt, he recalled the way Zelle had been drawn into the floor. There were no traces of her left, nor of the staff. She'd gone.

"Who are you?" Then, louder: "What did you do to Zelle?"

I did nothing, human.

That voice. It couldn't be—

"Astiva?"

Hardly. I am Zierne, and you are going to release me from these chains.

"Zierne," he echoed. "I know that name. You're... you're another of the sons of Gaiva. How can you be in here?"

How indeed.

Zierne had no Relics, none that anyone was aware of. Nothing in his family's records had ever mentioned one of Astiva's siblings having been in Zeuten the whole time. It was hardly more improbable than a lesser deity imitating a human form, but this Relic had remained hidden in the mountain, buried by the settlers for a thousand years. Hidden by the magic shrouding the Range.

No answers were forthcoming, and instinct brought him to a halt. In losing Zelle, he'd also lost the staff, and he had no magical defences of his own if the Relic turned on him. How did he know that setting it free from its chains would work out in his favour? For that matter, who had bound it to begin with?

Rien faced the book, his hand brushing against the cover. The surface hummed with power, while the voice spoke in his head once more: *Break these chains and I will be free, Arien Astera.*

"You know who I am?" Most Relics could read a person without speaking a word to them, he knew, but he wouldn't expect one that had been isolated for so long to know his name.

I know you lost your Relic. I know you owe your survival to another deity. And I know you are dying.

His throat went dry. "Can you help me with that? Will you?"

He barely remembered the ritual he'd been through as a child when he'd first claimed the power of Astiva, but he only recalled feeling confidence, not doubt or dread. This time, though, he wasn't picking up a Relic that had been in his family for a thousand years. This Zierne was an unknown. A sibling of Astiva's, yes, but one whose Relics hadn't been wielded by a human for centuries, if at all.

He and Astiva had entered a partnership of equals. Zierne, by contrast, already knew his weaknesses, since the book had read him and not the other way around. He'd always believed humanity could bend Relics to their will, but everything he'd witnessed in recent days had shaken his trust in that notion. Zelle's warnings. The mountain's seemingly unpredictable powers. And the Power that looked like a child, who left countless humans dead in his path.

Are you going to agree to help me? asked Zierne.

"Only if you agree to my terms." He knew he wasn't

being wise in challenging an unknown deity, but if he entered a partnership only to find himself ensnared in more foolish bargains, then he might have been better off letting Daimos kill him after all.

You wish for me to erase the bargains you made with that other Power and to replace what you lost?

"Yes," he replied. "I'd also prefer it if you didn't harm Zelle or my other allies either."

He wouldn't normally have considered the possibility, but given what he'd seen Orzen do to people, it was better to be secure in the knowledge that his new Relic wouldn't cause any unnecessary damage.

Very well. We have a deal. Now, break my chains and I will break yours.

Rien reached out with both hands, lifting the book off its pedestal. The vines didn't give way, not at first, but he remembered the words from his original ritual and found himself murmuring them.

"I am the son of Volcan Astera. I pledge myself to you—"

The vines loosened, instead wrapping around Rien's arms. He hissed in pain as the sharp thorns pierced the skin through his sleeves and then recoiled when the vines crept up to his neck.

"Stop!" he hissed. "I am Astiva's—"

My brother is not me.

The vines latched onto the medallion around his neck, snapping it free of its string and smothering its surface. A cracking sound reverberated through his bones as the medallion shattered before his eyes, crumbling into noth-ingness.

For a terrifying instant, he thought the thorns would

dig deeper until they'd skewered his whole body. Then the vines loosened, the pain faded, and as he held up the book in front of his face, crimson markings covered the knuckles of both his hands.

I am yours to command, Arien Astera.

―――――

Brightness filled Zelle's vision, while an odd weightlessness washed over her. She no longer felt like she was falling. She simply floated, as if in a pool of still water.

"Hello?" she called uncertainly. "Is anyone out there?"

Zelle Carnelian.

She hadn't truly expected an answer, and the booming response might have made her jump out of her skin if she'd been standing. As it was, she felt more like she was hovering in the fog conjured up by the rock in the Sentinels' cave—but this wasn't a vision, was it?

"Who are you?"

That would be telling.

"You're one of the deities, aren't you?" Only the Powers themselves were this reluctant to answer questions, but where *was* she? She'd fallen through the floor of the cave, but no signs of the book or the pedestal remained within sight. Nor Rien either. His attention had been on the book—and the brief glimpse she'd had brought back the memory of his odd mutters about a red-bound book with thorns.

That was when she realised the staff was still in her hands. She'd never brought a solid object into a vision before, but if she'd genuinely fallen through the floor of that cave, where was she? Zelle looked down, but nothing but bright emptiness surrounded her and the staff.

Addressing the knotted wood, she asked, "Are you the same deity? All of you—the staff, the rock, and whatever this is?" With her free hand, she gave a vague gesture at the emptiness in which she floated.

In a manner of speaking.

She turned that over in her mind. "That means yes. You're…"

Surely not Gaiva. Her family had always believed the staff contained a fragment of Gaiva's power, but it made no sense for part of Her to be this deep inside the mountain too. Gaiva was the goddess of creation and life and had always been depicted as being close to nature, not buried in the darkness.

You are correct.

She ought to have known the deity would be able to read her thoughts, too, like the rock in the Sentinels' cave. Their power came from the same source, after all. "Who are you, then?"

My name was forgotten long ago.

"You…" She looked from the staff to the emptiness and back again. "Are you the nameless god? The Shaper?"

How was that possible? Nobody even knew the name of the third Great Power, and even the claim that She was female was guesswork, since nobody ever depicted Her in their artwork. The stories did say that the Shaper had raised the land from the ocean and carved out the mountains of the Range, though… and this was rumoured to be the last region in which the Shaper's magic still resided.

You should have known who I am, given where you are.

If Zelle had been able to sink into a chair, she would

have done so at once. "You can't be serious. The Shaper doesn't *have* any Relics."

I am no Relic. The voice was an echoing boom in her head, and she clutched her ears, her heart in her throat.

"All right, you aren't a Relic," she said. "What should I call you, then?"

Whatever you prefer, Zelle Carnelian. I was separated from this world a long time ago, as were the other two Great Powers, but their given names remained amongst mortals.

"Gaiva and Invicten," she said. "No Relics of theirs have survived in this realm either."

The Shaper, though, bore no resemblance to any of the other deities. No surprise, given that She was one of the original three Great Powers, and unique.

Yes, I am. There was a touch of self-satisfaction to Her voice. Of *course* the voice she'd heard in the Sentinels' cave had been the same as the staff.

"Have you ever spoken to any of the Sentinels?"

Through the staff, yes. This situation, however, is unlike any a Sentinel has faced before.

"Is that why…" She trailed off. "It *was* you who spoke to me in the Sentinels' cave, wasn't it?"

Who else would it have been?

"You told me to—to close the doors," she said. "Grandma said that wasn't the Sentinels' job, but I'm hardly qualified. I'm not—"

Please cease your lament. It's tiresome.

She glared at the staff's wooden surface, since glaring at the empty air didn't have the same effect. "You might as well have asked me to grow gills and go to live in the ocean. Some things are impossible."

So is everything around you. Open your mind a little.

"You're a *god*," she said. "I'm human. Aurel would be much better at this than me."

The Reader has her talents. This is not one of them.

Arguing with a deity, especially one of the three Great Powers, was probably not a wise idea, but she could hardly believe the nameless *Shaper* was asking her, of all people, to stop Her fellow deities from escaping into this realm. From childhood, she'd known wielding magic at all would be as unattainable to her as flying among the birds. She'd been pushed into a box at so young an age that she hadn't noticed it had become a cage.

Now she was being offered a way out, oughtn't she take it?

She blinked hard. "Look, I have to get back into the cave. I left my friend behind, and he's prone to acting rashly. Also, there's a group of assassins and a furious deity waiting to kill us outside."

Ah, yes, him. Orzen was never my favourite of Gaiva's descendants. It's the human in him, I think.

"It's not *funny*," she said. "He killed countless people. He also survived being stabbed to death several times, so if you'd like to offer me a helping hand, it'd be appreciated. Fighting a war with a Power is a little outside of my experience."

You do not need to fight a war to rid the world of Orzen. However, the longer he stays in your realm, the more likely it is that his fellow deities will get the same idea.

"You mean they'll take on a human form?" she asked. "How did he even manage to achieve it himself?"

A ritual conducted by a human brought him into this realm, summoning him from his Relic. Suffice to say, as long as he keeps opening doorways between realms, the wider the crack between the two worlds will grow. And the more humans become aware of that breach, the more likely it is that they will learn how to summon deities to join Orzen.

"We both want to put a stop to that, then," she agreed. "You're not in the Powers' realm, though. We're somewhere in the mountain, right? How did you even get here?"

I was imprisoned here.

"By whom? The original settlers?" Curiosity stirred despite the urgency of their situation. How could anyone overcome a deity as potent as the Shaper? The Shaper had been the original creator of the world, according to the stories, although it was Gaiva who'd imbued it with life.

The other Great Powers, who believed Gaiva's descendants should have total control over magic in this realm. Regardless, I had the presence of mind to put a little of myself into the staff, which I managed to coax into your ancestors' hands when they came here countless years after my imprisonment.

Finally, some real answers. "What about that Relic that Rien and I found? Did my ancestors bring it here?"

Yes, they did. He never would have found it without me.

Smugness permeated the Shaper's tone. Zelle could hardly believe such power had lurked beneath her feet the whole time. Not just hers but all the Sentinels. The original settlers must have started the rumours of the lost Relic themselves, but the Shaper's magic had ensured that nobody had ever found it until now. Until it was needed.

"He'd have found it faster if he hadn't lost his memories. How did that come about?"

I took his memories myself.

Her heart missed a beat. "*You* erased his memories?"

He cursed our names, so I sent a construct to frighten him first, but yes.

"Why make him forget?" She knew better than to believe the Shaper had been attempting to do him an act of kindness, but Her actions might have saved his life.

I would have preferred his country's war not to disturb me here.

"Wasn't it inevitable?" asked Zelle. "Rien's family knew about the Relics hidden in the mountains. They probably weren't the only ones too."

Inevitable, perhaps, but unlike Gaiva's descendants, I gain little amusement from playing games with humans.

"That's what the gods think this is?" asked Zelle. "Are human lives a game?"

You humans have treated ours as such since the first Relics were created. The Powers were not made to serve mortals any more than mortals were made to serve us. Now you humans must fix the damage one of your number has done.

"You mean... Daimos." Rien's family's killer. "He's the one who found the Relic that enabled him to summon Orzen into this world. Right?"

Correct.

"And as long as Orzen maintains that form, he can't be maimed," she said. "He can also move between realms at will. It's not possible to close every door he creates, is it?"

Unlikely.

"Then how can I destroy him?"

No deity can be permanently destroyed. The only way to be rid of Orzen is to bind him into a new Relic.

"Bind him?" she asked. "Like the way the original Relics were created?"

Humans had created the first Relics, back in the days

when the deities had walked among them, but she'd never heard of anyone in the modern day attempting a similar spell. Yet that Relic they'd found in the cave had been sealed by the Shaper's power. If it was possible to trap Orzen in a similar vessel, then the Shaper might be able to help her do the same for him.

Precisely that, but your friend is in need of your help. Ask the Sanctum.

"Wait—" Zelle's sentence cut off in a gasp as she began to fall once again. She expected to land in the cave, but instead, she kept falling until the whiteness gave way to the face of a sheer cliff. Icy air struck her face, and the truth hit her like the buffeting wind: she really was falling off the mountain.

How she'd even ended up on the outside of the cave was a mystery but not one she was inclined to probe while falling to her death.

"Bloody Powers!" she yelled, scrabbling at the side of the nearest cliff. It was impossible to get a handhold while gripping the staff at the same time, but within a few moments, sharp branches caught her, knocking the breath from her lungs.

Zelle came to an unpleasant halt amidst the upper branches of a tree and lay there, sprawled and gasping for breath.

Movement nearby made her lift her head. She'd fallen off the side of the path where the Changers had confronted her and Rien—and now she had no way to reach him.

32

Evita yelled, tumbling over in the air as the cliffside rushed past—until Chirp's claw shot out and snagged the back of her cloak, slowing her fall. Wings beating, he lifted her up the cliffside and brought her to a shaky halt on a lower point of the path.

Evita slumped down in relief. The dragonet chirped in her ear, a warning sound, and her head jerked up. She glimpsed movement farther up the path, but the Changers were no longer cloaked in that odd cloud of shimmering magic. Instead, their forces had scattered, and she didn't see any signs of the deity, either. Or Rien and Zelle.

The ground felt unsteady as she rose to her feet, but Chirp remained at her side.

"Did you see where they went?" she whispered. "Rien and Zelle? That creature was chasing them…"

"Hey!" shouted a bedraggled-looking Vekka. "What kind of creature is that?"

The dragonet squeaked. Oh no. They couldn't see Evita, but her companion was all too visible. She placed herself in front of Chirp while the other Changers came to see what Vekka was pointing at, then she flipped her hood back, prompting several shouts.

"It's her!" said an equally dishevelled Izaura. "The traitor!"

"I'm not a traitor," Evita told them. "The Sentinels aren't the enemy. That boy was the one who murdered Master Amery. It sounds like he's killed a lot of you too."

A murmur passed among their group, but Vekka narrowed his eyes. "What's that weird lizard, then? Some kind of pet?"

"Chirp is my companion," she answered. "Your boss won't reward you if you find the Relics he's looking for, you know."

"Bullshit," came Vekka's response. "Tell you what, I bet he'll be happy with us if we finish you off."

As he advanced on her, she groped for an arrow and found none. She had no weapons, and even Chirp couldn't fight off all of them at once.

Before Vekka could reach for his own weapon, however, the ground gave a heave beneath their feet. The mountain itself shifted, as though some great beast stirred beneath the surface.

That doesn't sound good, thought Evita.

———

Rien staggered back, hands still stinging from the thorns, gripping the book tightly in both hands. Both knuckles were marked with swirling lines, which must be his new godsmark. It would never replace the hollow ache in his chest where Astiva used to be, but it was a start.

He had a Relic. Now he had to use it to get rid of Orzen—once he'd found Zelle, that was. No traces of her remained, however, and if he went back into the main tunnel and activated the mechanism to open the exit, he'd find himself nose to nose with the Changers and their leader again.

Then again, his new Relic ought to be more than a match for them, and there was no telling whereabouts Zelle might have ended up. He needed to be outside, fighting alongside his allies.

Rien carried the book under one arm as he left the cave and returned to the dimly lit tunnel leading uphill to the passageway. Wielding a book and not a staff would take some getting used to, and so would placing his faith in a new deity. He hoped that Zierne was ready to leap straight into a battle with a fellow Power, but Orzen was ranked lower than Zierne, a child of Gaiva Herself.

On swift steps, he returned to the passageway and sought out the hidden lever Zelle had used to open the exit. The cliff slid open, revealing the mountain path. Orzen had disappeared, as had the Changers, but Rien hadn't taken two steps before the path began to tremble underfoot.

"Hey, it's him!" shouted a voice. "Arien Astera."

A heavyset Changer barrelled uphill towards him, followed by several others.

"Zierne." Rien held up the book, a rush of energy flooding his veins. "Take them down."

Vines extended from the book in his hands towards the oncoming assassins, wrapping around their ankles and pulling them off their feet. The heavyset boy went down with a yelp when the thorns dug into his legs, and his female companion followed suit. Rien walked downhill, the vines tossing each of the Changers aside, but he hardly had a moment to enjoy the sense of victory. Where was Orzen? Would he think Rien a worthy opponent now he had another deity at his command?

A sharp yelp came from nearby when his thorns struck an unseen enemy, whose hood fell back to reveal a tangle of dark hair and a shocked face. Evita.

"Not her," he told the deity, but the vines grabbed at her ankles again, attempting to drag her to the ground. "Stop that."

Evita's eyes widened, but before he could voice an apology, she flew upwards into the air as if some great eagle had grabbed her from above. Not an eagle—a dragon. The small dragon he'd seen in the forest gripped the back of her cloak in its claws, and Evita's legs dangled over the mountain path as it carried her out of reach of the vines.

"What—" He turned in her direction, only for the thorny vines to lash upwards in an attempt to drag her out of the air. "Stop that. I told you to leave her alone."

He'd never had to reprimand Astiva in such a way, but all other thoughts fled his mind when another doorway opened in the air and Orzen stepped out, a grin plastered on his face.

"Arien Astera," said Orzen. "Will you fight me this time? Or will you run?"

Finally. Anticipation flooded him, and he took a step towards his opponent, gripping the Relic in both hands. The thorns returned to the book, ready to seek a new target.

The boy smiled down at him. "Found yourself a new toy, did you?"

The mountain gave another alarming lurch beneath his feet. Orzen wasn't causing the earthquake but neither were the Changers. Fog rolled in, obscuring Rien's vision. From Orzen's direction, a blast of icy air struck him like a blow, sending him staggering back down the path. His hand automatically jumped to where his staff should be, but of course, it wasn't there.

And neither was the book.

The mist cleared as the boy held up the red-bound book in front of his face. "Relics can be taken, you know. Or had you forgotten?"

The new marks on Rien's hands tingled. "Give that back."

He couldn't survive losing another Power, that he knew, but he refused to run. If he was to die, then he'd face death the way the other Asteras had. Without fear.

"Too stubborn for your own good," Orzen said. "You had the chance to escape, you know."

"Be quiet," Rien told him. "And give the Relic to me."

The boy regarded him with a mocking smile. "Why do you think I would?"

"Because Zierne serves me." Rien's heart hammered, but his voice was steady. "And Zierne's brother's Relics were stolen by the person who summoned you to this realm."

He willed the thorns to move and strike Orzen, but the vines had withdrawn back into the book's cover, and the Relic was out of his reach. *Not again. Powers, not again.*

"I might have offered you the chance to prove your worth to stand at my side," said Orzen. "Your family intrigues me, and I regretted that Daimos insisted that all of you needed to die. Yet I have my orders, and besides, you have caused me too much trouble to allow you to escape alive."

"Daimos isn't here." A sudden weariness tugged at him, and those days without his memories seemed a welcome relief. "You don't actually enjoy this, do you? Following Daimos's orders, that is. Wouldn't you rather act according to your own desires?"

"Daimos brought me into this realm." The boy's mouth twisted. "And I desire to kill you as much as he does."

Images filled Rien's mind, goading him with the vision of Orzen slaughtering him. Once Rien was dead, Orzen would turn his attention to the Sentinels, and Zeuten, like Aestin, would fall.

He couldn't let that happen.

Rien looked deep into those icy-blue eyes. "It's your last chance to give me the book. Someone buried it in the mountains for a reason. It's not the only thing they buried either."

As if to underline his point, the mountain trembled again, shaking the ground beneath both him and Orzen. The marks on his hands tingled, and a shiver travelled up his spine. *Zierne.* The Relic might not be in his hands, but their newly forged connection remained.

He focused on that certainty, and the anger deep within his soul, and clenched his marked fists. "Zierne and I would very much like a word with your master."

The book burst apart in a shattering of thorns. The boy actually screamed, a high-pitched noise as far from human as day from night. The book tumbled from his grip, but when Rien reached out to catch it, it wasn't a book he caught in his hand.

Instead, his fingers closed around the end of a crimson staff.

Orzen hissed, crimson streaming from his own hands —before he disappeared through a doorway that vanished in a blink. Rien began to curse, cutting himself off before he voiced the names of the Powers aloud. The staff's familiar weight in his hand unbalanced him almost as much as the trembling path. Why had the Relic taken that form? Had it been following his unconscious thoughts? Zierne and Astiva were siblings, so it made sense that their magic would be similar, but he hadn't anticipated the uncanny blend of familiarity and the unknown. Still, Zierne's presence filled the gap Astiva's absence had left behind, and that was enough for him.

Rien lowered the staff when a reptilian form descended onto the path, dropping a hooded figure in front of him.

"Hey!" Evita said indignantly. "You tried to stab me."

"Sorry," Rien said to her. "I'm adjusting to this new Relic. Where's—"

Evita let out a startled sound as someone fell past the cliff, tumbling head over heels through the air. "Where'd she come from?"

Rien stared over the edge. "Zelle!"

33

Z elle lay in a nest of branches, unable to believe the mountain had tossed her aside and left her with no way to get back up to her allies. One would think the Shaper would have better aim, or at least would be a little more careful with the person She had entrusted with getting rid of Orzen.

With the staff in one hand, climbing up the cliff would be difficult, and her legs were already cramping from her position on the branches. She shuffled into an upright position, holding her breath when the branches swayed, and tried to squash the sinking feeling that the Powers had forsaken her once again.

Then a dark shape detached itself from the cliff, heading right for her.

"Powers above." She raised the staff, but in another instant, she recognised the terrified face barrelling towards her. *"Evita?"*

She couldn't put an exact name to the dragon-like

beast which held the back of Evita's shimmering cloak, but she'd seen it before.

Evita reached out both hands. "I'll help you. Don't look down."

The squeak in her voice suggested she was talking to herself more than Zelle, but she was too startled not extend her free hand towards the former assassin. The Changer hardly looked strong enough to lift her, but that creature was somehow supporting her with its claws. In one beat of its wings, it carried both of them up the cliff face towards solid ground. Zelle gripped Evita's hand in her own, her heart lurching against her rib cage, but they were airborne for only a few moments before they touched down on steady ground.

It was then that she saw her second surprise in as many moments. Rien stood nearby, a crimson staff in his own hand. Relief flooded her at the sight of him, and his eyes widened when he saw her land in front of Evita.

"Zelle? You're all right."

"Just about." She glanced at Evita, who was trembling so badly that Zelle was a little concerned she might fall over the edge again. "Are you?"

"Yes—I don't like heights," Evita squeaked. "Ah, this is my companion. I named him Chirp. He's a dragonet, I think…"

The path lurched sideways, and Zelle braced her hand on the staff for balance. "Where're the other Changers?"

"They ran." For some reason, she was looking at Rien —or specifically, the staff in his hand. "The boy—I stabbed him in the back with a spelled arrow, but he didn't die. I don't think he can be killed."

"Except by another Power, perhaps," Rien murmured,

eyes on the staff in his hand. Whereabouts had he found it? He wasn't carrying the thorn-covered book she'd seen in the cave, but new markings had appeared on the back of his hands, glowing the same crimson as the staff.

She'd have to ask for the details later, because the tremors underfoot continued as though the Shaper was expressing Her displeasure at Orzen's violation. Yet the Shaper couldn't act against him directly. That was Zelle's job.

"No," she said to Rien. "That is—perhaps another Power can kill him but not us. I need to get to the Sanctum."

A shadow fell overhead, and fog swept across the path, forming elongated monstrous shapes. Wraiths. Had Orzen decided against returning to finish the fight in person and sent his constructs to fight in his place?

The mountain gave another tremor, and Zelle braced herself against the staff for balance. Rien did likewise, while Evita was forced to cling to the dragonet's side to keep from being knocked off the cliff.

"Damn you, nameless Shaper," Zelle said through gritted teeth. "I thought you needed my help. I won't be able to stop Orzen if you knock us all off the mountain."

The wraiths descended in a dark cloud, and Zelle raised the staff to repel them. More joined them, the cloud thickening, as if Orzen was drawing on every shred of power he possessed.

Does that mean he's killing people right this instant, to fuel his attacks? Nausea twisted inside her, but she didn't see any signs of the deity. Just a never-ending cloud of wraiths. How was she supposed to get to the Sanctum with Orzen mounting a full-on assault?

Rien swore under his breath. "What's that up there?"

Zelle lifted her head, spotting a dark haze moving down the mountainside. At first, she thought another avalanche was imminent, but the tide surging towards the wraiths moved more like countless pairs of feet running downhill.

Gremlins. Small constructs, but there were so many of them, and the mass of darkness grew as cracks opened in the rocks and more constructs emerged to join the crowd. Small, ragged, six-inch-long humanoids flitted out like moths and swarmed the wraiths, shrieking and cackling.

"What in the name of all Powers?" She gripped her staff, her gaze on the wraiths, who'd vanished under a thick layer of flailing limbs and sharp claws. The mountain was throwing everything it had at the wraiths, each heave belching forth more clawing humanoid shapes—gremlins, rattler-imps, and other creatures she had no name for, streaming out of the cracks in the mountainside like rainwater from a leaky roof.

"Where are they coming from?" Rien backed up to her side, his new staff held in a defensive position.

"It's the Power that lives in the mountains." Zelle pushed an imp off her leg. "Trying to fight off Orzen—but they can't kill him."

"Neither can we," Evita piped up from where she'd hidden underneath the dragonet's wing to avoid being knocked off the cliff by the tide of constructs. "He can't be killed by a regular weapon, can he? Even a spelled arrow didn't inflict any damage."

No deity can be permanently destroyed... The nameless Shaper had told her to bind Orzen's power into a new Relic, but She hadn't given her more specific instructions on how to achieve it. Besides, Zelle was fairly certain he was hiding behind one of his doorways.

Zelle turned to Rien. "I might be able to get rid of Orzen. Where is he?"

"He disappeared through a doorway." Rien struck a gremlin that tried to bite him with the side of his new staff, knocking it off the edge of the cliff. "When you say you know how to get rid of him, do you mean permanently?"

"As permanently as possible," she said. "By binding him into a new Relic."

"Binding him?" Rien echoed. "Like the first Relics?"

"Yes, but he's—look, you know how he's summoning those wraiths, right? He's killing people. I don't know who, but—"

Evita spoke up from under the dragonet's wing. "The Changers. He must be sacrificing them."

How delightful, commented the staff.

"I'll stop him," Rien said. "He won't be able to resist showing himself in front of me."

"There's no winning in a one-to-one fight, Rien," Zelle argued. "If you wound him, he'll take more lives to recover his strength."

"I'll go," Evita offered. "I can hide from sight, sneak up on him—give you all the time you need."

"You?" Zelle asked.

The former assassin lifted her chin. "Yes. I spent weeks with the Changers, remember? I don't want to watch them die."

It seemed unlikely that she could get the better of Orzen, but she'd managed to sneak up on him and stab him once already. Who knew, maybe the assassin would be able to take him off guard again. Zelle had one job to do, and she couldn't afford to distract herself with thoughts of who else might perish in the crucial minutes it would take to gain the information she needed. After all, the only permanent way to stop Orzen from sacrificing more lives was to bind him to a Relic.

"Go on, then," Zelle said. "Please—try not to get yourself killed."

Evita gave a wry smile. "I'll try not to."

The dragonet lifted her into the air once more, while Zelle and Rien were left on the path with the constructs and the wraiths. There seemed no end to either, as if both sides were pouring everything they had into the fight. She glimpsed Evita and the dragonet flying away... and another cloud of wraiths descending over the valley. Approaching Tavine—and the Reader's house.

They were Orzen's next sacrifices.

34

Evita dangled from Chirp's claws. At this point, she was so used to the terror that the flight felt almost relaxing compared to the precariousness of standing on a mountain that seemed intent on throwing her off. She would have questioned the wisdom of leaving Zelle and Rien alone up there, but she was more focused on keeping her balance. And not looking down. Especially the last part.

As for distracting Orzen without getting killed herself... she'd figure out that part later.

The dragonet swooped down and landed on a section of the path that was mercifully free of constructs or wraiths. There, she glimpsed several Changers huddled behind the various boulders scattered here and there. There was no sign of Orzen, but even away from the ongoing struggle between the swarm of odd creatures and the beasts the deity had conjured, the path continued to tremble underfoot.

Evita cleared her throat and approached the Changers. "Where's your boss?"

"Be quiet," Vekka hissed at her from where he crouched behind a boulder. "Do you want him to kill you next?"

"No, I want to distract him."

"You want *what*?" Izaura gasped. "You're mad."

"Maybe." She had no weapons, no magic, nothing to offer in this fight between humans and gods except for her talent for saying exactly the wrong thing at any given time.

Chirp grabbed her sleeve in his mouth, tugging her to face the right. That was when she saw the cloud descending over the valley, heading towards the village.

Orzen's next target would be Zelle's family.

Evita turned back to face the Changers' hiding places. "You've seen for yourself that he doesn't care if you live or die. If you want to stop him, then come with me and help the Reader. Otherwise, you can stay here and die."

"Some choice," said Vekka. "I'd rather eat dirt, thanks."

Evita ignored him, her gaze travelling over the others. "You still have the chance to help the Sentinels."

Ruben came out from behind a rock. "I'm with her. She's right—that creature doesn't care if we live or die."

"Neither does he." Izaura pointed uphill at Rien, who stood next to Zelle as they continued to fight their way past Orzen's forces.

Evita recalled all too clearly how Rien's thorns had come close to yanking her to her death, but from his reaction, he hadn't intended to strike her as well as the others. Besides, Orzen had done far worse.

"He and Zelle think you're working with the enemy—

with good reason," Evita told them. "Zelle is the Sentinel's granddaughter. The Sentinels are allies to the Crown *and* the Changers, so if you want to survive to see another morning, then I'd suggest you drop your grudge. And if anyone wants to help me stall the deity until Zelle can find a way to bind him, then you're welcome to come with me."

"Bind him?" Vekka asked. "That's not possible."

"It is." Evita didn't look back to see if any of them listened to her. The Reader's house was protected, but the other villagers wouldn't be so lucky, and the cloud of darkness drew closer by the moment.

She nodded to the dragonet. Understanding her unspoken command, Chirp seized the back of her coat and lifted her into the air. Without looking back to see if the Changers were following her, Evita faced the swarm of darkness from behind and let out a shrieking noise in an imitation of a mountain eagle.

The darkness turned on her, and within it, Orzen stood on the air as if it was solid ground.

"Do you have no value for your life?" he asked of Evita.

"No. Yes." Her bravado was rapidly fleeing in the face of the ice-cold monstrosities the deity had conjured. "I know what you're looking for. You won't find it in the village."

"Do you now?" He took a gliding step forwards, and Evita heard the dragonet give a faint whimper. She hoped that if Orzen took her life, the dragonet would be able to fly to safety.

"You're looking for the lost Relics," she improvised. "There's more than one, and I know where the others are hidden."

———

Zelle dislodged an imp that had tried to cling to her leg and spoke to the staff. "Orzen's going to the village. I won't let those monstrosities attack innocent people."

Then you'd better bind him first.

"You didn't even tell me *how* I'm supposed to bind him."

I told you what to do, didn't I?

"You might have sent me directly to the Sanctum instead of throwing me off the mountain." Powers above, Evita had better not get herself killed in her pursuit of Orzen, and Aurel and Grandma had better stay put in the Reader's house. "Rien, I'm going to the Sanctum."

"I'll come with you." He backed up to the cliffside, but she shook her head. It would take several hours for them to reach the Sanctum on foot, and the villagers didn't have that kind of time. Yet unlike Evita, Rien didn't have a dragonet to help him fly back down from the mountain path.

They needed to trust that the former aspiring assassin would be able to distract Orzen for long enough that Zelle was able to get what she needed.

Zelle ran the short distance to the partly open passageway, swatting constructs aside with the staff as she did so. Once the two of them were inside, she slammed the rock wall with her palm, and the opening sealed behind them. The opening in the wall leading to the cave where Rien had found his new Relic was still there, and Zelle hurried in that direction.

"I might have already been halfway to the Sanctum if

you hadn't thrown me off the mountain, you know," she muttered to the staff.

My focus was on my attackers, not on you.

"I think you just like making excuses."

Inside the cave, the pedestal lay bare, its book now in Rien's hands, but Zelle didn't stop walking until she reached the spot where she'd vanished before. This time she was almost prepared when the ground opened to swallow her.

An instant later, her feet touched down on hard stone, the Sanctum's ever-burning lanterns illuminating the area around her. Specifically, the pedestal upon which lay the book that contained a list of every text inside the Sanctum. Had the Shaper's hand been guiding her every time she'd been here? Not just Zelle but every Sentinel who'd come before her.

Even after everything she'd seen that day, the sight of the book's pages expanding to fill her vision remained as dizzying as it'd been the first time she'd peered up at the pedestal as a curious child. Words filled the pages, showing her a catalogue of everything in the Sanctum. She didn't have time to read through the entire list, so she asked the Sanctum and the staff alike: "Can you show me a book which contains a spell to bind a deity who walks in this realm into a Relic?"

Words began to form on the page, with no hesitation whatsoever. What had Aurel said earlier? *The closer your wishes align with the deity, the better your control.* Zelle and the nameless Shaper wanted the same thing. They both wanted to be rid of Orzen, and he'd been bound to a Relic once already, before Daimos had set him free. It wouldn't be easy to do the same again, but the nameless Shaper was

EMMA L. ADAMS

trusting her with the information, knowing the same magic must have been responsible for Her imprisonment.

A sense of pride and responsibility grew within Zelle, unlike anything she'd ever felt before. After all, she didn't need magic of her own to find the book she needed. The Sentinels were keepers of knowledge, first and foremost, and Zelle knew the titles of the Sanctum inside and out. Once she had the right spell, the Shaper would do the rest. *I hope.*

As she watched, the words on the page formed a specific title that would give Zelle the information she needed, which she memorised. Stepping away from the pedestal, she hurried past rows of dusty shelves until she found the right section. No gremlins barred her path. They must all be outside, driving off the wraiths. After a quick search, she tracked down the correct leather-bound book and opened its yellowing pages to search for the binding spell. To her annoyance, the book was written in the older form of the language that the settlers had spoken, so most of the chapter headings were incomprehensible to her.

She flicked through the pages and paused on an illustration that looked promising: a drawing of a bird and then an arrow pointing towards what appeared to be a rock. The bird must be a deity, and the rock... a Relic. What were the requirements, though? She'd heard of deities being sealed in stone or parchment or glass, but if there were any other specific rules, she didn't know.

With the book tucked under her arm, she turned away from the shelves. "Ah—Shaper? How do I get back to where I came from without having to walk?"

She could have sworn the staff sighed at her. *This way.*

35

Rien took a startled step backwards when Zelle came crashing through the ceiling of the cave whose floor she'd fallen through not a minute beforehand. "How did you do that?"

"The Shaper. Can you read that?" She thrust the pages of an ancient book under his nose. "It's a spell to bind a deity, but I can only read about a third of it."

"I can... if I had the resources, I might be able to translate some of it, but there's no time."

Not with Orzen on the move. If Evita hadn't been able to stall him, then they might already be too late to stop him from reaching the village. Unless the mountain was able to move Zelle to his location, but it was beyond him to figure out how it worked.

"No," said Zelle. "There isn't. We'll have to improvise, then."

They left the cave behind and returned to the passageway, where Zelle found the lever that opened the exit. Outside, the number of wraiths had noticeably decreased, and the remaining ones appeared to be heading downhill, pursued by a flurry of constructs. And wherever they were going, their master wouldn't be far behind.

Zelle sucked in a breath. "They're not going towards the village anymore."

Had Evita successfully distracted them, or had something else caught Orzen's attention? Rien moved downhill, fuelled by a new boost of energy from his new Relic, while Zelle hurried to keep up, her gaze on the swirling cloud of darkness over the treetops. It was definitely moving, though, towards the mountain path farther downhill from them.

Then the truth hit him. "Orzen's at the Sentinels' cave."

―――――

Evita led Orzen back to the mountains, dangling from the dragonet's claws and hoping that she wasn't leading herself into a trap. The deity walked on the air, the clouds swirling around him, until they left the forest behind and hovered above the path once more. Evita scanned the path, more to check on her allies than anything else, but Orzen followed her gaze with interest.

"The Relic is hidden inside that cave," he said suddenly. "I knew it."

"Wait, no." *Was* it in the cave? The last thing she needed was to genuinely give the deity an advantage, but it was the logical assumption to make, considering that rock was a Relic if she'd ever seen one. "No, it isn't."

He glanced at her, his gaze assessing. "Had a change of heart, have you?"

"No." Her heart thudded in her ears. "No, you can't get into the cave. It's protected."

"*You* got into the cave," he said. "Didn't you?"

Gaiva's tits. "I can't pick up the Relic. It'll make my skin melt off."

A smile curled his lip. "Good."

What have I done?

Orzen beckoned to her with one hand. "Come on. Or else I'll take your skin off myself and find someone else to fetch it for me."

"Wait." She glanced up at the dragonet in alarm—and Chirp's claws released her, sending her plummeting towards the trees below.

Evita tumbled downwards, branches reaching up to scrape at her hands and face, and the dragonet plunged into the trees behind her. Chirp let out a squeak before lifting her into the air again, Evita dangling precariously from his claws.

"What was that for?" she hissed at him. "He's not going to stop there. We were supposed to stall him."

The dragonet chirped again, a noise that possibly meant he didn't want to watch Orzen kill her—except if he was no longer pursuing her, then he'd go after her allies instead.

"Stop," she commanded. "We have to go back."

Chirp rose into the air, high enough that Evita could see the cloud of darkness spilling like ink over the mountain. The constructs had left Rien and Zelle's location, instead surging downhill—and the surviving Changers stood right in their path.

The cloaked figures scattered in all directions as the dark tide descended on them, drawing Orzen's attention.

He hovered above the forest near where Evita had fallen, his gaze now on the fleeing Changers. Evita was the one who'd convinced them to leave their hiding place, but it'd only been a matter of time before Orzen had hunted them down anyway.

Then a squat figure came hurrying downhill, and the creatures flew in all directions as if pushed by an unseen force. Evita stared at Zelle, who held the staff in one hand and carried a book tucked underneath her arm. Rien followed close behind her, his new staff in his hand, and Evita stiffened at a warning chirp from the dragonet.

Orzen had ignored Zelle and Rien outright and landed on the flattened area in front of the cave entrance. The swarm of indistinct creatures must have entirely shaken off the army of smaller beasts that had seemingly emerged from within the mountain itself, and when he pointed at Evita, they surged towards her.

The dragonet flew the pair of them higher, but Zelle had already spotted him. She raised the staff into the air, and a dazzling flash of blue light engulfed the monstrous beasts, scattering them before any could reach Evita. At her prompting, the dragonet flew her closer to Zelle and Rien, who continued to descend towards the Sentinels' cave.

"You managed to stall him, then." Zelle addressed the dragonet, not Evita; her cloak still hid her from sight, though she'd given up all pretence at stealth.

"I told him there was another Relic inside the cave. Sorry."

Surprise flickered in her eyes. "Not a terrible idea. He still can't get in."

"Don't speak too soon," Rien murmured, his eyes on

the path ahead. "Speaking of Relics, we still need one. To bind him."

"Right." A Relic. Of the three, Evita knew the least about Relics, magic, and the deities. She also had the least to lose. "Anything else you need?"

"It'd help if we had someone who can read old languages," Zelle said.

Evita gave a disbelieving laugh. "I can't even read."

A strangled cry came from below, where Orzen had grabbed one of the fleeing Changers by the throat. His monstrous fog-creatures closed in, and blood sprayed the path where he stood.

Her hands curled into fists. *I can't stop him. I...*

As Rien and Zelle overtook her, Evita fumbled in her pockets for anything she might use as a weapon, but she found nothing but the token she'd picked up during her trial, so long ago. The smooth silvery stone fit into her palm, but while it might be pretty, it had no practical use.

Or did it?

Orzen walked out to meet Zelle and Rien, his eyes glittering with malice. "You should have stayed hidden inside your caves, both of you."

———

Zelle approached Orzen outside the Sentinels' cave, still hardly believing that Evita had managed to divert his attention without getting killed in the process. The cave was a logical guess at where one might hide a Relic, after all, considering a piece of the Shaper's power lay inside the rock. Now she knew its true nature, she refused to let Orzen get anywhere near it.

She held up the staff, its blue light suffusing her palm. "Get away from there."

The boy's contemptuous glare flickered over her from head to toe. "This mountain of yours has quite the array of defences. Who created those constructs?"

"You wouldn't believe me if I told you." Her heart raced, but a heady rush of confidence seized her at the notion that he'd never guess the nameless Shaper was now her ally. She was beginning to understand why Aestin's Invokers had such a reputation of arrogance, born of a lifetime of wielding the strength of the Great Powers.

For Zelle, it was a new feeling, but caution warned her not to push too far. She wasn't about to throw away a lifetime of well-deserved wariness for a brief moment of glory. Besides, outright power wouldn't kill Orzen. He didn't know whose wrath he'd incurred, but the Shaper remained limited in several crucial ways. That was why She needed Zelle's help.

"Do enlighten me," said Orzen. "Why do you carry the Sentinel's staff when you have no gift of your own?"

"Why did you run away from her?" Zelle countered. "Oh, right... she turned two of the other deities against you."

Anger flickered in Orzen's eyes a moment before his gaze went to Rien. "That one seems intent on sharing in his brother's fate."

"You killed his family," Zelle said. "What do you expect?"

Orzen took a step in Rien's direction, the flickering shape of a staff appearing in his hands. It wasn't real, she knew, but the crimson thorns gleamed in an imitation of Rien's own Relic.

Rien gave him a hard stare. "That's enough."

Thorn-covered vines lashed outward from Rien's staff, and Orzen held up his own staff to block them from reaching him.

"Are you sure you want *that*—" he indicated the new staff in Rien's hand—"and not *this*?" He held up his own crimson staff, which trailed thorny vines in Rien's direction.

A mixture of emotions flickered over Rien's face— sadness, longing, resignation, and more that Zelle couldn't name—before he shook his head. "That is not the Relic of Astiva, and Zierne is my ally now."

Rien's vines pushed past Orzen's, wrapping around his opponent like ropes. The deity bared his teeth, but the vines squeezed tighter, crimson streaming from where the thorns bit deep.

Now was Zelle's chance.

"Hold him there!" she called to Rien. "Don't let go of him, no matter what he says."

Rien's face contorted in anger as the vines tightened against the struggling deity. "If you keep struggling, you'll bleed out, Orzen—and you can't kill anyone like this."

The boy made a choked noise. Despite Zelle's anger, a spasm of cold fear struck when she realised that he was laughing.

"I am a god," he snarled at both of them. "Arien Astera, your power is gone. Zelle Carnelian, you're not even a Sentinel."

"Wrong on both counts," Zelle told him, reaching

under her arm for the book. For all the good it did, given that she couldn't *read* the blasted thing.

Brightness spread behind the form of the deity. A doorway—which, when it opened, would allow Orzen to evade them once more.

"Stop." With the book in her other hand, Zelle held the staff out so that it pointed towards the open doorway. "I close this doorway, on behalf of the nameless Shaper."

She didn't know if the declaration would work, but the boy's eyes widened in shock.

"What?" Orzen bellowed. "Not *that* one. It's not possible."

"It is." A breeze rose behind Zelle, and the end of the staff began to glow faintly blue. The wood grew cold to touch, and light pierced the air, arcing from the staff to the doorway. The outline of whiteness blurred—and then vanished.

To her bemusement, the boy released another laugh, this one tinged with a hint of desperation. "If you trap me in this realm, then I'll bring ruin to your world."

"Be quiet." Rien gave a firm tug on his staff, and the thorny vines squeezed tighter, yanking the boy's arms behind his back. "You need blood to maintain a human form. I'm not averse to draining every drop from you if I need to."

"Then I will return to my Relic and lay waste to your pathetic country."

"Wait," Zelle warned Rien. "We can't let him return to his Relic—we have to bind him to a new one instead."

The god's original Relic must be across the ocean, in Aestin. In order to bind him, she needed another, but

Relics could be made of anything, and every part of this mountain was imbued with magic.

Orzen gave a high-pitched laugh. "You can try, mortals, but you will fail."

Something small flew over Rien's shoulder and hit the boy square in the face. Bewildered, he watched the silver-coloured, rounded stone tumble onto the path. Zelle glimpsed Evita and the dragonet hiding out of sight, and she flashed them a brief nod of gratitude before she picked up the stone. That would do nicely.

Zelle removed the book from under her arm and flipped it open, placing it upon the ground while she scanned the words of the binding spell.

"You're nothing!" the boy shrieked. "You can't serve the Shaper. The Shaper is long gone!"

"Stop talking," Rien commanded.

As for Zelle, she extended the staff towards the boy while keeping a close grip on the rounded stone in her other hand. The page wavered beneath her, the words half familiar and half not.

"Can't I just speak the words in my own language?" she whispered to the Shaper.

"You can," Rien answered, grunting as the deity strained to escape the thorny vines. "The people who created those spells did exactly that."

Zelle gripped the stone in one hand and focused her attention upon the page. "I bind you..."

The bluish light around the staff grew brighter. Did it matter if she matched the exact words written on the page? Someone needed to create the spell to begin with, and if it was anything like using a Relic, then intention and will mattered more than the precise phrasing.

Powers above. Maybe she knew more about magic than she'd thought.

"I bind you, Orzen!" she shouted. "I bind you to this Relic."

A rush of power roared through Zelle's veins, and she gasped aloud, unprepared for the sudden wild surge of energy that gripped her. Then cold air blasted outwards from the staff in waves, flattening the treetops, pushing the remaining wraiths out of existence.

Rien swayed, holding onto the cliff with his free hand to avoid being caught up in the gale. The boy remained upright, the vines loosening their grip, but in their place, blue light encased him. The stone in her hand glowed, as bright as the staff, as she repeated the words—"I bind you, Orzen."

Orzen's body collapsed in on itself, leaving nothing behind but a scattering of thorns on the path. He was gone.

Zelle lowered her hand. The silvery stone's glow faded a little, but it was cold to the touch in a way it hadn't been before. Orzen's new Relic belonged to nobody, and as far as Zelle intended, it would stay that way.

The rush of energy faded at once, to be replaced with a flood of exhaustion. Despite that, she found herself grinning at Rien. Tiredness lined his face, too, but he smiled faintly at her. It was the first time she'd seen him smile.

"We did it," she croaked.

Then Zelle fell forwards, her legs giving out. Her vision grew fuzzy around the edges before fading to blackness.

36

R ien paced outside the Reader's house. He'd been doing that a lot over the last day, since their defeat of Orzen, and since he and Evita had brought Zelle back to Tavine. The assassin didn't seem to know what to do with herself, but she'd remained in the Reader's house and nobody had got rid of her yet. At some point, he expected Grandma Carnelian to throw her out—and him, too, come to that—but like him, she'd been more focused on Zelle.

Glimpsing movement out of the corner of his eye, he turned back to see Zelle's sister walking out of the house.

"I thought you'd be with her," Aurel commented.

"Is she awake yet?" asked Rien.

"No, she isn't," Aurel replied. "What did you expect? She's not a Sentinel. I don't know why the staff let her use its power to bind a deity, but it shouldn't have."

"I wouldn't say that to her face," he said. "She was pretty comfortable wielding the staff for someone who isn't a Sentinel."

A flush spread across Aurel's face. "I wasn't trying to downplay what she did, but coming that close to one of the three Great Powers? She was lucky she didn't die."

I know, he thought. It made a kind of sense for it to be the Shaper, whose magic had created the Range to begin with, but he never would have believed the nameless Power would ever help a human. She had been banished from this world so long ago... no, imprisoned. He'd heard as much from Zelle during the brief moments she'd woken up, but there hadn't been many of them.

Trying to ignore the nervous twinge at the thought, he entered the Reader's house and climbed the stairs. Inside the guest room on the left, Zelle lay in bed, not having moved since he last saw her. No change. He couldn't easily forget the image of her glowing like a beacon, wielding the staff like she was born to it. She hadn't been, and yet he'd seen the evidence with his own eyes.

"Is she going to survive?" Aurel asked from behind him, having followed him upstairs. "You're the expert."

"One of the three original Great Powers joined forces with her," Rien pointed out. "Her body probably needs to adjust."

He'd had nosebleeds for weeks when he'd first claimed Astiva's Relic, and he'd carried the bloody handkerchiefs with pride. Rien shoved the memory away as it brought a fresh wave of grief along with it. Thanks to Zelle's state, he'd had few opportunities to dwell on his own loss, but it would take a long time for him to stop reaching for his staff and expecting to feel Astiva's presence on the other side.

"Would the staff help?" Aurel suggested. "Perhaps the Shaper can wake her up."

"Worth a try." Rien found his gaze drawn to the round, smooth stone sitting on the bedside table. It'd been Zelle's grandmother's idea to leave it next to her instead of risking the stone being lost amid the endless piles of junk in the house, but keeping the Relic that contained the essence of Orzen close to Zelle's sleeping body bothered him considerably.

Footsteps shook the stairs, and a moment later, Grandma Carnelian appeared in the doorway behind him. "Move aside."

He did so, more out of surprise than anything. He was still adjusting to the Zeutenians' abrupt manner and tendency to say what they thought without couching it in polite language. Or maybe that was just Zelle's family. In any case, he moved to the side of the bed while Grandma Carnelian pressed the staff into Zelle's hand.

Blue light shone from the staff's end, and a similar glow suffused Zelle's entire body, glowing beneath her skin. Rien recoiled, automatically reaching for his own staff—before the glow faded and Zelle's eyes flickered open.

"By all Powers, Zelle!" Aurel said from behind her grandmother. "What in the name of—"

"I wouldn't say *any* of their names." Zelle ran a hand over her forehead. "Ow."

Rien studied her in concern. "Are you all right?"

"I think so." She rubbed her forehead. "What happened?"

"You didn't lose your memory, did you?" he asked, before it occurred to him that was a foolish question. Yet he still had a perfect recollection of how overwhelming it felt to truly connect with a Relic for the first time.

379

Zelle grimaced. "I don't envy you Invokers. My head feels like it's going to split in two."

Rien studied her, concerned. It didn't appear that the staff had done any permanent damage, but if any Power could permanently change a person, it was the nameless Shaper.

"Other than that, you're fine?" asked Aurel.

"I feel normal." Zelle pulled herself into a sitting position in bed. "I think. Compared to how I felt on the mountain. That..." She trailed off, as if struggling to find the words.

"You'll remain the same unless you tap into the Shaper's magic again," said the Sentinel. "With the staff."

"But—it's yours," said Zelle. "Isn't it?"

Grandma Carnelian eyed Rien. "I understand why your family saw the need to split your power between several Relics. We, on the other hand, have only the one, and at the moment, Zelle needs it rather more than I do."

"Don't push yourself too hard," Rien told Zelle. "It's not always a smooth procedure to receive the blessing of a deity."

"It doesn't feel much like a blessing. Was it like this when you were first bound to Astiva?" He froze inwardly, and Zelle faltered as though realising what she'd said. "Wait. It's fine if you don't want to talk about it."

"Don't worry," he said, though he didn't want to talk about Astiva one bit. "I don't know if it's comparable, to be truthful. You and the staff talked to one another before you ever joined forces with the Shaper. I've never had that direct a connection to my deity before."

As far as he knew, it wasn't possible, even for an

Invoker, to regularly talk directly to their deity and receive a verbal response. Not after the initial joining, such as when he'd spoken to part of Zierne in the cave.

Zelle looked at Grandma. "The staff has always talked to you, though, right?"

"Constantly."

A smile tilted her lips upwards, and something stirred inside his chest in response. "That's fine, then."

———

Evita jumped out of her seat when she heard footsteps on the landing above her head. She hadn't seen much of the Reader, and her grandmother had hardly seemed to notice Evita's presence in the house. Rien too. They'd all been on edge while Zelle had been unconscious, but judging by the voices she'd heard from upstairs, it sounded as if she'd finally awoken from her sleep.

Evita, then, needed a new plan. She'd done her best to make herself useful by doing any chores that arose, but she was part guest, part... not exactly a prisoner anymore but not invited either. She'd happily have rented a room above the local tavern if she'd had any coin to speak of, but she had nothing of value except for the cloak, and she was reluctant to part with it after the number of times it'd saved her life.

As for the Changers? Evita hadn't seen a single one of them since her departure from the mountains. She didn't even know how many of them had survived, though her intervention might have helped spare at least some of them. Regardless, she had no desire to join their ranks again. Her revenge on Orzen, such as it was, had come to an end when Zelle had bound him into the token she'd saved from her first trial. The deity was gone, and while he'd haunt Evita's nightmares for a long while, she reconciled herself with the knowledge that she'd done something far more satisfying than simply *killing* a deity: she'd tricked him.

Going back to normality after this was an impossibility. No, as soon as she found employment, she'd be able to save money and go on a real adventure, preferably one that involved fewer heights and a little less mortal peril. Maybe the dragonet would come with her. She'd seen Chirp a few times, wandering around the forest near the Reader's house, and he seemed as attached to her as ever.

As the footsteps drew nearer, Evita swiftly grabbed a broom and began to sweep the floor, busying herself as Aurel entered the living room with her grandmother close behind her.

The elderly Sentinel eyed Evita. "You're still here? What are you doing?"

"I swept the floors," Evita told her. "And I cleared the spiders out from behind the cabinet."

"Is there a reason you're obsessively cleaning my house?" asked Aurel. "Where are those assassins of yours?"

"The survivors will have returned to the base by now," she said. "There's no need to worry that they'll come back. Their leaders are dead, and they've lost their new boss too."

"It's Rien who has more cause to worry about them," said Aurel. "Though I suppose the Crown Prince will clear up the matter."

"The Crown Prince?" she echoed. "Is *he* coming here?"

The notion of meeting the Crown Prince seemed as unreal as meeting the deities, and rather less impressive.

"When he learns we were at the centre of the action, I imagine he will," Aurel said. "He'll want to thank those of us who were responsible for protecting Zeuten."

"Don't count on it," said Grandma Carnelian. "He never leaves the capital. Anyway, you haven't said why you're still here, Evinne."

"It's Evita," she said. "I'm not going with the Changers, but he... Orzen burned my village to ashes. I have nothing left, no money or anything. I need to find employment."

"There's plenty to do here." Aurel studied the broom in her hand. "If Zelle's staying here for the time being, she's going to start lecturing me about needing a servant."

"Didn't you dismiss your last one?" asked Grandma Carnelian. "And the one before?"

"Yes, but this one's quiet," Aurel commented. "I pay well, by the way."

Evita didn't know what to say to that. "Did you just offer me a job?"

"I suppose I did," said Aurel. "You'll have to sleep downstairs, mind. Unless Grandma decides to go home."

"As if I'd miss any of this," the Sentinel scoffed. "Besides, Zelle has my staff."

It'd be an improvement on sleeping in a cave, if nothing else. "Thank you."

———

While Zelle's grandmother and sister went downstairs, Zelle herself changed into fresh clothes and did her best to ignore the shaky feeling the staff had left in her hands.

She hadn't dreamt much while she'd been unconscious, but now her memories of the battle were starting to come back. The rush of energy she'd felt when she'd wielded the staff seemed a distant sensation now, while the sight of the stone on the bedside table reminded her of another task that lay ahead of her.

She'd need to get rid of Orzen's Relic.

As she was walking downstairs, she heard Rien saying, "So you don't have a comprehensive list of the Relics that the settlers brought to the mountains? You didn't know a child of Gaiva might be there?"

"No," said Aurel. "If the settlers ever wrote anything down, then their records were lost a long time ago. Aren't the other Relics belonging to Gaiva's children in Aestin?"

"Yes," said Rien. "Aside from Astiva, Venzei's Relic is in the hands of the Martzel family, and Lauvet serves the Trevains... the last time I checked, at any rate." A touch of bleakness entered his tone, as though he was speculating on what might have happened in his home country during his absence. "Mevicen's Relic was confiscated by the Emperor following the Daimos family's betrayal."

Daimos's family had their Relics taken too. Perhaps that was why he'd felt justified in doing the same to Rien.

"That leaves one—Zierne," Rien went on. "And his was the only Relic I saw in that cave."

Zelle entered the room, seeing that Rien sat on an armchair next to Aurel and her grandmother. She was surprised to see Evita sitting with them as well.

Aurel's gaze went to the stone in Zelle's hand. "Are you going to get rid of that?"

"We have to ensure nobody frees Orzen from his

imprisonment," Zelle said. "If it's likely that anyone will try."

"The Shaper's magic isn't the only kind that can undo bindings," Grandma told her. "If his original summoner found his new Relic, he would be able to summon him back."

"Would the Sanctum be able to keep the Relic contained, do you think?"

"I don't see why not."

Zelle nodded. "I'll take the Relic up there, then."

"You're still recovering," Aurel protested. "You just woke up, and now you want to climb a mountain?"

Zelle had never seen her sister express concern for her so sincerely. It was heartening, if a little odd. "I've been asleep for long enough that people are bound to be talking. I don't think we should delay any longer."

"I'll go with you, then," Rien offered.

Aurel nodded and sprang to her feet. "I'll give Evita a tour of the property."

"Why?" asked Zelle. "Isn't she going back to join the Changers?"

"No," said Evita. "I'm the Reader's new servant."

"Seriously?" Zelle swivelled to face her sister then turned back to the former assassin. "It's your choice, but you've seen the state of the place, haven't you?"

"I can handle it," said Evita.

No doubt it was preferable to being an assassin. The Changers, if any survived, had some serious rebuilding to do, and she didn't blame Evita for not wanting to go back.

Evita might not last long in her new position, given her sister's temperament, but Zelle wasn't about to complain about a touch of cleanliness returning to the

Reader's house, especially if she was going to be staying here for the time being.

———

Zelle and Rien climbed the mountain path in companionable silence for a while. She carried the staff, while Orzen's Relic was firmly secured in her pocket. Despite her lingering tiredness, Zelle didn't mind getting away from the house, where the others would no doubt be waiting to bombard her with questions about the Shaper and her other recent experiences as soon as she returned. Or force her to go back to bed. Her limbs were sore, true, but she chewed on a piece of baked bread she'd taken from Aurel's supplies as they walked, which restored some of her energy.

When Zelle opened the first passageway in the cliff-side, she noticed that the new tunnel that had led to Rien's new Relic had closed up, leaving nothing but unmarked wall behind.

As they continued to walk through the passageway, she asked Rien, "Have you worked out what kind of magic Zierne gifted you with?"

Rien remained silent for so long, she thought he wasn't going to answer. Or he'd suffered temporary memory loss again. She knew he must be struggling to adjust in his own way. He'd never had time to process the return of his memories before they'd faced Orzen, and he was a long way from returning home.

"I don't know," he finally said. "The staff feels the same as Astiva did but… different."

He raised his left hand, showing the spidery lines

spreading across his knuckles like ink. Identical marks covered his right hand, though she knew that Astiva's mark had only covered the left. As she watched, the lines thickened, becoming vines dotted with sharp thorns.

Her eyes followed the movement. "You're controlling that?"

He nodded. "I used to be able to charm birds to fly to me, that sort of thing, but I haven't tried it yet. Zierne might be Astiva's brother, but the deities are as individual as humans."

"And just as unpredictable," she agreed. "Their wishes don't always align with our own either."

Rien said nothing to that, but Zelle knew he'd had to adjust his former view of the Powers in the last few days. As had they all.

"What do you plan to do, then?" he asked. "With the staff?"

"Whatever I have to." The staff already felt as comfortable in her hand as a well-worn coat, despite her knowledge that it wasn't truly hers. "I'm not sure Aurel will handle this well over time. She was always the one with the gift."

"She might surprise you," Rien remarked. "My brother and I argued all the time, but we would have laid down our lives for one another."

The regret in his tone brought a pang to Zelle's chest. "We'll see. Anyway, I only have the magic on a provisional basis, so I'm treating it like a loan."

She still didn't *quite* understand why the Shaper had chosen her, apart from a lack of any better options, but she wasn't about to question the will of one of the Great

Powers. Not when her very survival depended on their alliance. Daimos was still out there, after all.

They reached the end of the passageway, quicker than she'd anticipated. Hand extending to find the lever, she opened the cave entrance and walked out onto the path leading up to the outpost. No clouds marred the sky, yet the tower's crooked form appeared different to her eyes than it had during her previous visit.

Rien gave her a curious look. "What is it?"

A wry smile came to her mouth. "This all feels like too big a responsibility for a simple shop owner."

"A shop owner?" He returned her smile with one of his own. "I can think of another word."

"Don't say 'hero'," she scolded, but her tone was more teasing than angry. "I walked into this entirely by accident. I'm certainly not a magician... an Invoker."

If Zelle had ever had occasion to wonder what might happen if Aestin's magicians set their sights on Zeuten's hidden Relics, she would have expected an Invoker to be the first, not one of the Powers themselves. She'd never had cause to think of the Powers as individuals with goals of their own, let alone aspirations of returning to the world.

Then again, it sounded as though Aestin's Invokers were as oblivious as anyone else.

Zelle climbed the short distance to the tower and opened the door. On the inside, the downstairs room appeared exactly the same as she'd left it, but she habitually checked the corners for rattler-imps before she headed for the stairs for the upper level.

At the top, she unlocked the various bolts sealing the door closed, though she suspected the defences were mostly for show. If the wielder of the nameless Shaper wanted to get somewhere urgently, as she had the previous day, the mountain would take her there in a heartbeat. Still, going through the ordinary motions made her feel more at ease, and when the door opened, she breathed a sigh of relief to see the corridor as unchanged as ever.

This time, she left the clawed instrument where it was. Whatever she ran into on the other side, the staff would more than suffice.

Upon opening the second door, she peered into the corridor and shook her head. "I expected a gremlin infestation, to be truthful."

"I imagine the Shaper is recovering from the battle." Rien stepped up behind her. "Try not to fall through the floor this time."

She gave him an eye roll. "I expect the Shaper will be calmer now there's no longer another deity trying to attack the mountains."

"Is the Shaper... everywhere, then?" He gestured at the arched doorway, the shelves, and the stone walls.

"Yes," she said. "Kind of, anyway. I can only communicate directly with Her through the staff and in the Sentinels' cave, but the Shaper's magic permeates the entire mountain. The Great Power is imprisoned inside the Range itself."

Rien inhaled sharply. "I never would have thought such a thing was possible."

"Neither would I, believe me." She reached into her pocket and pulled out Orzen's Relic. "I need to find a secure place for this where nobody can find him, human or otherwise."

"I doubt that will be a concern," said Rien. "Daimos might have Orzen's original Relic, but he's an ocean away, and I don't see him coming back here to save an ally he no longer needs."

No. Daimos had the aid of Astiva now, and from the grim look that entered Rien's eyes, he hadn't given up on the idea of avenging his family and his deity at the same time.

Zelle approached the small room containing the book listing all the titles in the Sanctum then paused and consulted the staff instead. "Can you show me a secure place to hide this?"

Yes, said the staff. *Walk towards the wall.*

"You promise you won't throw me through the floor this time?" She turned to the left and faced the bare stone, extending the staff. As it touched the stone, the wall slid open to reveal a narrow passage leading into darkness.

"Was that there before?" Rien asked.

"I'm guessing 'no'." Zelle approached the passage opening, unable to see anything but pitch-blackness on the other side. "What now?"

Throw the stone.

She tossed the gleaming stone through the opening, and it tumbled downwards, vanishing into the dark. The passage slid closed, and an instant later, the wall had appeared as unmarked as ever.

"I didn't have to come all the way up here, did I?" she asked the staff. "You could have opened the passageway anywhere in the mountains."

I thought it would do you good to get some exercise after spending all that time in bed.

"You!" She shook her head. "Honestly. I suppose that's a deserved reminder of what I'm dealing with."

She'd barely scratched the surface of uncovering the mountain's magic, but while she'd have quite liked a break from the upheavals of the past few days, the staff in her hand was enough of a reminder that the deities weren't finished with her yet.

"Good riddance." Rien turned his back on the spot where Orzen's Relic had disappeared. "That's one deity taken care of, then."

One... but how many more will follow? Zelle wondered.

Still, she had the nameless deity on her side—provisionally, at least. She might not entirely trust the Shaper's motives, but it was in Her interests to keep Zelle alive.

Aloud, she said, "Yes, but I don't need to have magic to know the Great Powers are just getting started."

———

Far above, two deities looked down through a window separating the two realms, watching as the two cloaked figures made their way down the mountain. The deities' birdlike forms bore the markings of their torture at Orzen's hands, their wings missing feathers, their bodies raked with scars.

"That's the last time I trust a human," growled Kyren, her raven form shuffling close to the window. "I understand why our predecessors stopped intervening in human warfare."

"They never stopped," Xeale corrected her, his dove-grey feathers matted with blood. "Not until they were forced to, at any rate. Besides, if we'd stood behind Orzen to the last, we might have met the same fate."

"I can't believe Orzen fell at the hands of two mere children," Kyren remarked.

"I'm not surprised," replied Xeale. "The Astera boy has a new Power on his side. To think *that* one survived…"

Kyren peered through the window, her gaze moving from the male figure to the female one at his side, and to the staff in her hand. "What about the girl and *her* new Power?"

"The nameless Shaper." Xeale shook his head, scattering droplets of blood. "I knew the Sentinels had power, but who could have expected the lost deity to awaken?"

"Is it true, then?" Kyren asked. "Nobody *saw* the nameless Shaper, did they?"

"She has always been there," said Xeale. "It wasn't Mother's magic inside that staff. I saw it with my own eyes."

"It might have been a trick," said Kyren. "Like that Sentinel's. She's forgotten all about us now, I'm sure."

"Without a word of thanks for helping her," Xeale agreed. "No… that was no trick. The nameless Shaper has been among the humans all along."

"The traitor," Kyren hissed under her breath. "To think that we helped a servant of *Hers*…"

"She didn't know," Xeale said, with certainty. "None of them knew what lay in those mountains. And now that girl is working with Her… knowingly."

Kyren gave a dark chuckle. "A human and a Great Power. I wonder who will win in that struggle?"

There would be no contest, of course, but the aftermath would be the most entertainment the deities had seen in countless centuries.

And so they peered through the window and watched the humans scuttle over the surface of the mountain like ants. Most of them were utterly unaware of the beings that lay on the other side of the doors between worlds, but it wouldn't be long before they realised how mistaken they were. Orzen had only been the beginning, after all.

The deities could hardly wait to watch it all unfold.

ABOUT THE AUTHOR

Emma spent her childhood creating imaginary worlds to compensate for a disappointingly average reality, so it was probably inevitable that she ended up writing fantasy novels. She has a BA in English Literature with Creative Writing from Lancaster University, where she spent three years exploring the Lake District and penning strange fantastical adventures.

Now, Emma lives in the middle of England and is the international bestselling author of over 30 novels including the Changeling Chronicles and the Order of the Elements series. When she's not immersed in her own fictional universes, Emma can be found with her head in a book or wandering around the world in search of adventure.

Find out more about Emma's books at
www.emmaladams.com.

9 781915 250018